PRAISE FOR M...

THE SUGARHOUSE BLUES

"An extremely satisfying read."

—*Fresh Fiction*

"This is a well-written, smooth novel, ideal for a summer read, more depth than a beach read but with all of the fun!"

—*Novelgossip*

"I honestly felt like I wanted to move to Hidden Falls by the end of this novel!"

—*The Blonde Bookworm*

THE LAST CHANCE MATINEE

"The combination of a quirky small-town setting, a family mystery, a gentle romance, and three estranged sisters is catnip for women's fiction fans."

—*Booklist*

"A good read, with a nice blend of mystery, family drama, and romance. Readers will look forward to the next installment."

—*Library Journal*

"Mariah Stewart has blown me away with her new series featuring the Hudson sisters. . . . *The Last Chance Matinee* is a multifaceted story of family and what happens when you put three sisters together to bring their father's dream to reality."

—*Lovey Dovey Books*

"You know those books that are just easy to read? The kind where you want to know what happens next and want to sneak off to read just a few pages more? This was one of those books for me."

—*I Wish I Lived in a Library*

"A heartwarming read, full of surprising secrets, humor, and lessons about what it means to be a family."

—*That Book Lady Blog*

THE CHESAPEAKE DIARIES SERIES

"Rich with local history, familiar characters (practical, fierce, and often clairvoyant centenarian Ruby is a standout), and the slow-paced, down-home flavor of the bay, Stewart's latest is certain to please fans and add a few new ones."

—*Library Journal*

"The town and townspeople of St. Dennis, Maryland, come vividly to life under Stewart's skillful hands. The pace is gentle, but the emotions are complex."

—*RT Book Reviews*

"If a book is by Mariah Stewart, it has a subliminal message of 'wonderful' stamped on every page."

—*Reader to Reader Reviews*

"The characters seem like they could be a neighbor or friend or even a coworker, and it is because of that and Mariah Stewart's writing that I keep returning again and again to this series."

—*Heroes and Heartbreakers*

"Every book in this series is a gem."

—*The Best Reviews*

A DIFFERENT LIGHT

"Warm, compassionate, and fulfilling. Great reading."

—*RT Book Reviews*

"This is an absolutely delicious book to curl up with . . . scrumptious . . . delightful."

—*Philadelphia Inquirer*

MOON DANCE

"Enchanting . . . a story filled with surprises!"

—*Philadelphia Inquirer*

"An enjoyable tale . . . packed with emotion."

—*Literary Times*

"Stewart hits a home run out of the ballpark . . . a delightful contemporary romance."

—*The Romance Reader*

WONDERFUL YOU

"*Wonderful You* is delightful—romance, laughter, suspense! Totally charming and enchanting."

—*Philadelphia Inquirer*

"Vastly entertaining . . . you can't help but be caught up in all the sorrows, joys, and passion of this unforgettable family."

—*RT Book Reviews*

DEVLIN'S LIGHT

"A magnificent story of mystery, love, and an enchanting town. Splendid!"

—*Bell, Book and Candle*

"With her special brand of rich emotional content and compelling drama, Mariah Stewart is certain to delight readers everywhere."

—*RT Book Reviews*

ALSO BY MARIAH STEWART

The Hudson Sisters Series
The Goodbye Café
The Sugarhouse Blues
The Last Chance Matinee

The Chesapeake Diaries Series
Dune Drive
The Chesapeake Bride
Driftwood Point
That Chesapeake Summer

●◆●

Voices Carry
Brown-Eyed Girl
Priceless
Moon Dance
Wonderful You
Devlin's Light
Carolina Mist
A Different Light
Moments in Time

MARIAH STEWART

THE SUGARHOUSE BLUES

POCKET BOOKS

New York   London   Toronto   Sydney   New Delhi

Pocket Books
An Imprint of Simon & Schuster, Inc.
1230 Avenue of the Americas
New York, NY 10020

This book is a work of fiction. Any references to historical events, real people, or real places are used fictitiously. Other names, characters, places, and events are products of the author's imagination, and any resemblance to actual events or places or persons, living or dead, is entirely coincidental.

First Pocket Books paperback edition March 2019

POCKET and colophon are registered trademarks of Simon & Schuster, Inc.

For information about special discounts for bulk purchases, please contact Simon & Schuster Special Sales at 1-866-506-1949 or business@simonandschuster.com.

The Simon & Schuster Speakers Bureau can bring authors to your live event. For more information or to book an event, contact the Simon & Schuster Speakers Bureau at 1-866-248-3049 or visit our website at www.simonspeakers.com.

Manufactured in the United States of America

10 9 8 7 6 5 4 3 2 1

ISBN 978-1-9821-1346-9
ISBN 978-1-5011-4496-7 (ebook)

For David and Rebecca Jones,
with love and all best wishes for your own
happy-ever-after

ACKNOWLEDGMENTS

So many people to thank as I finish up this thirty-ninth (fortieth?) book! First and always, I must sing the praises of the absolute best editor on the planet. No one knows how to pull the best from me the way Lauren McKenna does, and I am so grateful for the opportunity to work with her. She is beyond gifted, and I am forever in her debt. And so many people at Gallery Books who work so hard to make every book look (and sound!) their very best: everyone in the art department, production, marketing, sales, audio. Your efforts are more appreciated than you know.

Many thanks to Judith Worrell for giving me the opportunity to support the fund-raising efforts of Laurel House, a comprehensive domestic violence agency that provides supportive and preventive services throughout Montgomery County, Pennsylvania. By virtue of her winning bid for the chance to have a character in this book named for her, she is now the proud owner of *The Goodbye Café*. Judy, I hope you like to cook!

Many thanks to those friends whose love and encouragement keep me sane, especially the Writers Who Lunch bunch: Terri, Carolyn, Gwen, Martha, Kate, Gail, and Helen. Very special thanks to Jo Ellen Zelt Grossman, friend since (gulp) kindergarten, and whose mother, Bea, was a woman I loved and admired. Jo, see if you can find the shout-out to your mother (yes, I know I was her favorite!).

Not the least of my gratitude to my family: my husband, Bill, who feeds me when deadlines get too close and puts up with my blank stares into space and muttering lines of dialogue that make no sense to anyone but me; my beautiful girls, Kate and Rebecca; my wonderful sons-in-law, Michael and David; and my adorable grandloves, Cole, Jack, and Robb.

THE
SUGARHOUSE
BLUES

CHAPTER ONE

Desdemona Hudson stood in the lobby of the old Art Deco theater in Hidden Falls, Pennsylvania, and raised her eyes to the water-damaged domed ceiling. Flares of color—red, gold, green—shot out overhead in geometric patterns from the elaborate crystal chandelier that hung from the center of a large plaster medallion.

"I'm sure the roofers had insurance. I remember seeing a certificate with the contract." Des couldn't take her eyes off the disaster. "Damn it. We finally got our new roof, and the first big wind to come along takes some of it."

Joe Domanski, the contractor who'd been hired to oversee the renovation of the Sugarhouse Theater, stood with his hands on his hips, a look of resignation on his suntanned face.

"This isn't their fault, Des, and this wasn't just a 'big wind.' This was a massive storm with hurricane-strength winds, a hundred-year storm. It's what you'd call an act of God, and I don't know of any insurance policy that doesn't exclude those."

"You called the roofers?"

"Called them before I called you. They should be here within the hour to check out the damage and make some temporary repairs in case we get more rain before they can replace the missing shingles."

Des nodded slowly. There was nothing she could say to Joe that he wasn't thinking himself.

How much was this going to cost? How long will this delay the renovations?

She was pretty sure the roof itself could be repaired, and maybe Joe could talk the roofers into replacing those missing shingles for free as sort of a goodwill gesture. The real problem was going to be restoring the intricate and decorative painting on the damaged ceiling.

A shard of plaster drifted downward, stuck in her auburn curls, and dangled over her forehead. She swatted it away and frowned at the patches of color that had scattered onto the floor.

"Crap," she muttered. She wiped sweat from her forehead with a tissue she'd pulled out of her bag. The air inside the theater was stifling.

"I'll do what I can," Joe told her.

"Just . . ." Des sighed. "Get me the estimate and let me know how long it will take to fix it."

She whistled, and a white flash darted out from the audience seats and ran up the aisle. "Time to go, Buttons," she said to the mixed-breed stray she'd rescued and taken in, pulling a pink leash from her jacket pocket. Des leaned over and snapped it onto the little dog's matching collar.

"Aren't you going to stay until the roofers get here?"

Des shook her head. "Cara should be on her way down here soon. She'd have come if she'd been back from her run when you called. Just have the roofers replace whatever flew off and let Cara take it from there. The actual building repairs are her department. I came because the money is my problem. Getting it fixed is Cara's. Paying for it is mine."

"Des, I . . ." Joe began, but she waved away whatever comment he was about to make.

Really, there was nothing more to say.

It wasn't Joe's fault that an early summer storm had blown through the Pocono Mountains over the weekend and sent several shingles flying onto the library's parking lot next door. While Des didn't hold Joe personally responsible, the last thing she needed was one more problem to strain their already tight renovation budget. She walked through the lobby and out the front door into the unseasonal heat, Buttons hustling to keep up. It was barely ten in the morning, and already the rising temperature and the humidity made for an uncomfortable walk.

It would still be spring at her home back in Cross Creek, Montana. The trees behind her log house would be budding, and the bulbs she'd planted last September would be in bloom. Here, peonies were nearing the end of their cycle, and local strawberries were piled high in green cardboard containers in the roadside markets that were springing up along country roads. In the Montana mountains, winter could be reluctant to leave. Here in the mountains of Pennsylvania, summer was already knocking on the door.

She slowed her pace as she walked by trees that had already leafed out, letting Buttons dawdle and sniff and paw at whatever caught her fancy. Cara drove by and stopped long enough to get the rundown from Des before taking off for the theater.

Des took her phone from her pocket to check messages. Usually, by this time in the week, she'd have heard from her friend Fran, who ran the dog rescue shelter Des funded back in Cross Creek. Still no messages. Des typed a quick *Everything okay there?* before tucking away the phone. Even though there were many miles between Des and Cross Creek, she kept her finger on the pulse of the shelter that was so near to her heart. She wanted to know what was going on with new dogs, animals that had been adopted, any staff that had been hired in her absence, and chatty Fran was always good for the information.

It was tough to be away from her home and her work for so long, especially after she'd established that shelter, funded it, and personally worked to rehabilitate the neediest of the abused. Every dog she'd worked with had taken a little bit of Des with them when she sent them off to their forever home. It had been several years since she'd decided that rescuing dogs was her calling in life, and she'd invested a lot of herself in making that happen.

And yet here she was, a couple of thousand miles

away, deep into the renovation of a ninety-year-old theater in a town she'd never heard of while someone else ran her shelter and worked with her dogs.

What was wrong with this picture?

Then again, back in Cross Creek, she hadn't kept any of the dogs she'd loved, because she'd loved them all. Here in Hidden Falls, she'd been able to keep Buttons, who'd quickly found her way into the hearts of everyone in the Hudson family.

Still, a day didn't pass when Des didn't wonder which place was really her home.

Gee, thanks, Dad.

Dad was the late Franklin—Fritz—Hudson, Hollywood agent and father to Des and her sister, Allie, via their mother, Honora—Nora—Hudson, the actress, who'd died four years earlier. Unbeknownst to them until recently, he'd also been father to Cara, whose mother, Susa, may or may not have been Fritz's legal wife. Things were a bit fuzzy where his marriages were concerned. Had he divorced Nora before marrying Susa? The paper trail was spotty, and Fritz's best friend and attorney, Pete Wheeler, hadn't been able to shed any light on the situation when it came time to sort out the legalities. After Fritz died, it had fallen to Pete to introduce Des, Allie, and Cara to each other, and to break the news to all three daughters about their father's dual families. Once the shock had begun to subside, Pete'd dropped the other shoe: To inherit Fritz's estate, the three women had to live together in their father's family home in Hidden Falls, Pennsylvania, until they completed the restoration of the family's boarded-up, run-down theater. If any one of the three refused or left before the restoration was complete, the entire estate would be donated to a charity of Pete's choice. Since Fritz's daughters each had her own reason for needing the money, they'd agreed to the absurd terms.

But it turned out that Fritz had kept other secrets.

There was that little matter of Fritz's sister, Bonnie—known to everyone in Hidden Falls as Barney—who'd been living in the Hudson family home. While Fritz'd never told his daughters about her, Barney had known all about them and the terms of her late brother's will, and was waiting for them with open arms when they arrived. It had been impossible not to love Barney, and they'd all taken to her immediately. Barney was not only smart, she was wise, loving, and had a heart of gold. She'd cheerfully filled in her nieces on the family history their father had neglected to share. Des knew her life was so much richer for having Barney in it.

And the more Des got to know Cara, the more she cared about this half sister who was down-to-earth and fun, and had been blessed with common sense, a logical mind, and an abundance of heart. She and Des even looked a little alike, both having the same curly auburn hair and heart-shaped face. Together they'd studied the family portraits displayed in Barney's front hall, trying to figure out which ancestor they resembled.

Cara was easy to get along with, certainly more so than Allie, who was the oldest of the three, and the tallest. She was slim, and her blond hair was long and straight. She had cheekbones that a model would envy, and features that guaranteed that more often than not, she'd be the most beautiful woman in the room. Allie had an innate sense of style that Des admittedly lacked. And while as a child Des had been the star of her own TV show, *Des Does It All*, she'd always felt invisible when Allie was around.

It had been years since Des and Allie had lived beneath the same roof, and Des still wasn't sure this was going to turn out to be a good thing. It was a source of pain to Des that the big sister she'd adored as a child had barely been in contact for over half Des's lifetime. Des knew the distance between them was Allie's way of never letting Des forget her resentment over the fact that long ago, Des had been chosen for the television role that Allie had desperately wanted. Ironically, Des had only auditioned because their mother had forced her—she'd never wanted to act, had never wanted the spotlight to shine on her. The crazy thing was that Des was a natural. The other side of the crazy coin was that Allie had no talent whatsoever, and for that, she'd blamed and never forgiven Des.

With the death of their mother, even the occasional contact the sisters once had fell by the wayside. Des had tried a number of times to bring Allie back into her life, but nothing had worked. She was hoping that during the time they spent together in Hidden Falls, she and Allie could work out their problems and become real sisters again, the way they'd been before envy and resentment had become more important than the bonds of sisterhood. At least, that was Des's plan.

When Des reached the edge of the vast front lawn of the spacious Victorian house that occupied one entire side of the first block of Hudson Street, she let Buttons off the leash. The little dog loved to dash to the porch and bark while she danced around the front door until someone opened it to let her in. Today Des's steps were slower than usual, and she could feel Barney's eyes on her as she approached the porch.

"That bad?" Barney held the door until Des stepped inside.

In her seventies, Barney had declared herself too old to wear shorts, so on days when the temperature soared, she donned a cotton knit dress that reached her knees and was really little more than a long T-shirt. With her blunt-cut blond hair and her trim, youthful figure, Barney could carry off the look at any age.

"Cara's down there now waiting for the roofers. Until we get their report, we won't know how extensive the damage is. I have no idea what those repairs are going to cost. But oh, Barney, some of that beautiful hand painting is ruined, and that beautiful peacock-blue ceiling has patches missing."

Des followed Barney into the sitting room, where the older woman had obviously been reading. A book lay open, facedown on the sofa, and a cup of tea cooled on the coffee table.

"Where's Allie?" Des asked.

"She came down earlier and made breakfast and

took it back up with her, as she's been doing every day about this time since Nikki left. I do sympathize. If Nikki were my daughter, I'd want her to be with me, not on the other side of the country with her father. But that's the arrangement Allie and her ex agreed to. Of course, at the time, your sister had no idea she'd end up here. It's hard to blame her for being unhappy."

"Unhappy and unpleasant are two different things." Des leaned against the doorjamb. "At her best, Allie falls just a notch above Elphaba."

"Who?"

"The Wicked Witch of the West. You know, from *Wicked*? The play? The wicked witch from *The Wizard of Oz*?" Des grinned. "You know, the one who said, '*I'll get you, my pretty . . .*'"

"'*And your little dog, too.*'" Allie finished the quote from the front hall. "What's going on over at the theater?"

"Nothing that a flock of flying monkeys couldn't fix." Des quickly filled Allie in on the water damage at the theater. "Once Cara gets back, we're going to have to figure out what our next step is going to be."

"If she's down at the theater with Joe, maybe she'll make it back by dinner. Maybe." Allie leaned on the jamb across from her sister.

"You're just jealous because Joe has a thing for Cara and not you." Des wondered if perhaps there wasn't a bit of truth in that. Cara had barely arrived in Hidden Falls before she'd caught Joe's eye, and all three Hudson sisters had agreed that the tall, buff blond contractor was not only good-looking, but a genuinely nice guy. Des herself had wondered what it would be like to have a guy like Joe crazy about her.

"Oh, please. Like I'd be interested in Joe." Allie rolled her eyes. "He's so not my type."

Des laughed. "Joe Domanski's every woman's type. Every woman with a pulse and an active libido. The man is hot by anyone's standards."

Allie pretended not to hear as she headed for the stairs. "Give me a shout when Cara gets back."

Des watched her sister climb the steps to the second floor, then turned to Barney and said, "I'm going to get something to drink, then I'm going into the office. I should call our insurance people about the mess at the theater. Feel free to join us when we finally get everyone together."

"I'll be in after I finish this chapter." Barney held up her book. "I'm itching to see if Maude gets away from the kidnappers. Buttons can stay here with me. She really has no head for business."

The dog stared up at Barney, wagging her tail expectantly.

"Oh, all right." Barney patted the sofa cushion next to where she sat. "Come on."

The dog hopped, rolled onto her back, and gave Barney her *rub my tummy* face.

Des sighed. "I'm wondering if any of us have a head for business. This is not as easy as we thought it would be."

"By 'this' you mean restoring the Sugarhouse?"

Des nodded.

"If it were easy, my brother would have completed the renovations before he died." Barney resumed reading, one hand absently rubbing the dog's tummy.

Des had just walked into the kitchen when Cara came in through the back door and hung up her car keys on their designated hook.

"So how'd it go? The roofers show up?"

Cara nodded. "They went up onto the roof and found several shingles that needed to be replaced. They also checked the plywood underneath. It's wet, but that can easily be replaced as well, which the roofers are going to do, no charge. But the damage to the ceiling looks pretty bad. Joe's going to have scaffolding erected inside the lobby. The roofers said they'd take care of that. They'll bring in as much scaffold as they have, but they said they don't have nearly enough to go all the way to the ceiling. They did agree to beg, borrow, steal, or rent whatever else is needed to reach the top so we can inspect the ceiling. We won't know more until that's been done."

"I guess it's time to call our insurance agent. I'm happy to hear the roofers are willing to step up to replace the shingles and the wood sheathing—which they definitely should do—but I don't know who's going to pay for the damage to the ceiling, the roofer's insurance company or ours, but we need to put in a report."

Cara pulled the elastic from her long auburn hair, a few shades lighter than Des's and only a little less curly. "Let me grab a drink and I'll come in and we'll check the coverage on the policy."

"Bring Allie, would you? I think we need to pow-wow."

Des crossed the wide hall and went into the office that had served several generations of Hudsons. She found it a little intimidating to think of those who'd sat at the large oak desk before her. Even the chair was imposing—a high-backed black leather chair that had first been used by Reynolds E. Hudson, Des's great-grandfather, then the second Reynolds Hudson, her grandfather, then finally by Barney when she took over as president of the bank that had been run by Hudsons for years. They were all bigger than life to her, even Barney.

Especially Barney, who'd been the president for more than twenty years after Fritz flew the family coop with Nora and took off for the West Coast to help make his beloved a star.

It had been expected that Fritz would follow in the footsteps of previous generations, but when that didn't happen, Barney had walked into the board of directors meeting and reminded everyone that Fritz wasn't Reynolds's only child, and she was better suited to run the bank since she was smarter and more focused than her brother had ever been. Once the ancient, all-male board gave in, they discovered she was everything she'd claimed to be. Barney was still revered in Hidden Falls for the many ways she'd helped the town hang on through rough times. Under her watchful eye, businesses had sprung up, new houses were built, and some older homes changed hands. She was proud of the fact that not one loan she'd granted had ever gone into default.

It was hard for someone like Des, who hadn't even taken a course in bookkeeping, to feel worthy of following in such footsteps. Yet here she sat, in the big black chair behind the fabled desk, files in front of her, ready to discuss the theater's financial state with her sisters. When it had come time to divvy up the areas of responsibility pertaining to the theater's restoration, Des had been selected as the one who'd hold the purse strings by virtue of the fact that she'd wisely invested the money she'd made as a child actress.

"Not much of a résumé," she muttered as she opened the file in front of her, marked RECEIPTS, and searched for the original estimate from the roofing company, Sennett and Masters. She reread their initial report, then the contract, searching for language that might throw responsibility for the leak back on them. But Joe had been right. The "acts of God" clause was right there in the fine print.

While she waited for her sisters, Des opened her laptop and pulled up the theater's bank account. For a long moment, she stared at the diminishing balance, then picked up a pen and began to tap it on the desktop in agitation. She'd tried so hard to budget carefully, but every system had had to be replaced and some new ones added. The building now had air-conditioning and Wi-Fi, two things that had been unheard of when the theater was built and were expensive to retrofit. Most of the big-ticket system replacements had been completed, but there was not a dime to spare.

And there were still hefty expenses to come. The carpets needed to be replaced and the chairs and marquee required repairs. The exterior needed painting and the ticket office had to be restored. The lights and the screen as well as the curtains in the staging area all had to be replaced and the stage needed refinishing, too.

And now they needed to fix the ceiling and all that meticulous detailed painting would have to be restored.

Des blew out a long breath. Sooner or later, they were going to run out of money. She prayed it wouldn't be sooner.

She rested her arms on the desk and looked around the handsome room with its stone fireplace, tall windows, and dark wainscoting, and wondered what financial crises other Hudsons had dealt with while sitting in this same chair. The first Reynolds, the one who'd built the theater, had seen the town through the Depression. Her grandfather, whom she thought of as Reynolds two, had managed to guide Hidden Falls through World War II, and Barney had navigated the town through several economic downturns. Des imagined both Reynoldses standing alongside the fireplace, their arms folded over their chests, tapping their feet, standing in judgment, waiting to see if she was up to the challenge and worthy to call herself a Hudson.

"Okay, gang's all here," Allie announced as she and Cara came into the room. "What's the big deal?"

"Take a seat." Des pointed to two of four dark green leather side chairs that flanked the desk and she brought them up to date about the damage and the question of whose insurance was going to pay for the repairs.

"I'm sure we have the kind of policy that covers wind damage. I remember looking it over when we received it." Cara went to the cabinet and pulled out the appropriate file. "It would be under 'Covered Perils.'" She scanned page after page. "Here it is." She paused to read the section. "Basically it says that if water damage is caused by wind, the resulting damage is covered."

"I'll call our agent right now." Des reached for the file and searched for the agent's number.

"It's the roofer's fault," Allie said. "Their insurance should cover it."

"The insurance companies can fight it out. I don't really care who pays for it, as long as it gets done." Des punched the number into her phone. "The bigger problem is going to be finding someone who can actually repair the decorative ceiling."

"Cara, the ceiling is part of the building, and since you're in charge of renovations, that's your job," Allie told her.

"I'm responsible for any repairs to the actual plaster. All the pretty painted details are yours, since you're in charge of décor. And from where I was standing, a lot of those pretty little details are toast."

Allie's phone buzzed to alert her to an incoming text, and she opened it immediately. After reading the message, she looked up at Cara and said, "Sorry. Nikki is filling me in on her summer plans."

"Isn't she coming here?" Des put her hand over the phone while she was on hold.

"I'm just getting the agenda. She's having her two weeks with Clint's parents in Chicago, which is fine. They'll spoil her rotten and buy her a bunch of summer clothes, so I'm good with that. Now I'm waiting to see what else her father has planned for her. I want her to spend the rest of the summer here, with me." She looked up from her phone. "Us, I mean. I want her to spend the summer with us."

"You know we all want her here," Cara assured her.

"For as long as we can have her," Des added. She knew how much her sister loved and missed her daughter, who was fourteen and the absolute love of her life. Allie might be many things—snarky and sarcastic came readily to mind—but no one could deny she was a terrific mother. Nikki was living proof that at Allie's core, there must be a very deep layer of goodness.

"Oh, don't worry. I will fight for as much time as I can get," Allie assured them. "Clint has her all year long. I'm entitled to having her for the summer."

"Definitely. She should be with us," Des said.

"I know you guys love her. I'm grateful for that. Really, I am. And I know she loves and misses you as well." Allie's lips curved into a half smile, her face visibly softening. "Maybe not as much as she loves and misses me, but still . . ."

Des laughed and tossed a piece of paper at her sister's head. "You're such a bitch, Allie."

"True. But you love me anyway. And in my own sweet fashion, I love you all, too." Her gaze shifted to Des. "I think."

"What's going on in here?" Barney stood in the doorway.

"You're just in time." Allie twisted in her chair to face her aunt. "We were just about to join hands and sing a couple of verses of 'Kumbaya.'"

"Oh good. A song from my generation. Shall I begin?" Barney grabbed a chair and pulled it next to Cara's.

Des smiled and said, "I think the moment's passed."

"So what did I miss?"

"Not a whole lot . . . yes, hello?" Des's attention reverted to her phone call. "I was on hold for Heather Martin?"

"I think we should all go look at the damage." Allie lowered her voice.

Cara nodded. "I agree, if for no other reason than we'll all know what we're dealing with. Any one of us could be called upon to speak with the insurance people or prospective artists." She paused. "Though where we're going to find artists who are qualified to work on historic buildings—not to mention the detailed painting itself—I have no idea."

"Althea College." Barney spoke up.

"What?" Allie and Cara both turned to her.

"Althea College. They have a wonderful Fine Arts Department. At one time, they offered a major in art conservation. Perhaps they still do, or at the very least, someone in the department might know of someone who could work with you."

"That's perfect, Barney." Des hung up the phone. "Heather, our agent, said she could meet with us anytime. We just have to call."

"I'll call the college." Allie rose.

"And I'll get with Joe to see about finding a plasterer." Cara folded the policy and returned it to the file drawer.

"The ceiling isn't our only problem." Des motioned her sister to sit back down. "I've gone over the numbers. The amount of money we have left might, if we stretch to the absolute limits, cover the remaining big expenses. Beyond that, we're going to be in trouble. We have to figure out how to come up with the funds to keep the place running while the renovations are being completed. Electric, water, heat, air-conditioning—those bills have to be paid while the work is ongoing. The work crews can't work in the dark, and from what Barney tells us, it gets really hot and humid here in the summer. I don't see the money for the monthly expenses in the remaining funds."

"Dad left us a million dollars," Allie reminded her.

"He underestimated." Des tapped her pen on the desktop again. "It isn't enough."

The room fell silent.

"Hey, we have a theater. Let's put on a show." Allie turned to Barney. "Isn't that what Mickey Rooney always said in those old movies you watch all the time?"

"*Babes in Arms*, I believe, was the only film where

that line—or something akin to it—was actually uttered." Barney, a fan of movies from the 1930s through the '50s, spoke with some authority.

"Don't knock it, Allie," Des said. "It may come to that."

"I was kidding." Allie rolled her eyes.

"I'm not. The theater is going to have to pay for itself. We're not going to have the money to run the place."

"Excuse me, but nowhere in Dad's will did it say we had to run it, Des," Allie reminded her. "It only said we had to renovate it."

"We may not be able to complete the renovations if we don't find a way for the building to make money, that's the point," Des explained. "That's what I'm trying to tell you. There are monthly expenses to be paid— electric, to keep the lights on and the air-conditioning running, unless we want the contractors to all die of heat stroke while working in the dark this summer."

"If I may make one other suggestion." Barney spoke up. "I'm on the board of trustees at Althea. The college was founded by Reynolds Hudson, who, as you all know, gave so much to the community during the Depression. Founders Day is next weekend. Why don't we all put in an appearance at the cocktail party? Who knows, once word goes out among the faculty, perhaps someone might step up with some ideas?"

"I'm in." Des didn't hesitate.

"Me, too," Cara said.

"Allie? You in?" Des waited for her sister to respond.

"Yes, I'm in."

"Wonderful." Barney rose. "Cara, let me know after you've spoken with Joe, and I'll call for tickets."

"And, Allie, see if you can get names of people in the Art Department we can hopefully schmooze next week at the gala." Des watched her sister rise.

"Aye-aye, Captain." Allie saluted as she walked past Barney and through the doorway.

Two days later, lured by the afternoon sun that spread across the backyard and highlighted Barney's flower bed, Des wandered outside, her notebook in hand and Buttons by her side. The garden was beautiful, with a few late tulips and peonies—red, white, pink, burgundy, and even yellow—interwoven with hydrangeas that were still leafing out and roses that had yet to bloom. Des pulled one of the Adirondack chairs from the patio into the sunlight to go over her list of things to do that could bring cash into the theater. But the combination of warm sun and the fragrance of the peonies made her drowsy, so she closed her eyes and rested her head on the back of the chair. She'd have fallen asleep if Cara hadn't accidentally slammed the back door on her way out of the house.

"Sorry." Cara pulled another chair from the patio to join Des in the sun. She wore dark glasses, khaki shorts almost identical to the ones Des wore, and a white tee. "Were you napping?"

"I shouldn't be, but I came close." Des sat up and gave her head a little shake. "What are you up to?"

"Just looking for a bit of sun myself." Cara situated the chair so she was facing Des, then placed her book on the armrest while she patted Buttons. "It's so peaceful here, and quiet, even though we're just a little more than a block from the center of town."

"My house in Cross Creek was right at the edge of town. It's pretty private and quiet there, too. After I'd lived in L.A. for so long, Cross Creek seemed like the wilderness." Des thought about her log home on three and a half acres. She'd bought it on a whim after visiting friends who'd settled there, and she'd never looked back.

"Do you miss it?"

"Sometimes. On the one hand, yeah—my own house. I can walk around all day dressed in nothing more than a towel and there's no one to tell me to get dressed."

"I heard a 'but' in there somewhere," Cara said.

"But on the other hand, I like having people around. I like having someone to watch TV with. It's nice to have someone to talk things over with." Des squinted when she turned to look at Cara, whose hair was curling over her ears in the same manner as Des's. "How 'bout you? Do you miss your house?"

"Sort of, but you know, I didn't really have a place that was just mine the way you do. Drew and I lived in an apartment while we were saving for a house. I moved out of there and into my mother's house after I found out about Drew and Amber. Nothing says time to move on like having your husband file for divorce so he can marry one of your best friends. *Former* best friends." Cara stretched her legs out in front of her. "It was a relief to be out of the apartment, but at the same time it made me a little sad to be living in the house without my mom. It was a small place, but it was one hundred percent Susa. There's no place I miss her more than in that house. She'd refinished a lot of the furniture and made some of the rag rugs, so her stamp was definitely everywhere. In that respect, it really wasn't mine. But do I miss it? Yeah, sometimes."

"I'm surprised Dad didn't try to make her move to a big place so he could furnish it with a bunch of expensive new stuff."

Cara laughed. "Oh, he tried a couple of times to get her to let him build her something big and grand along the beach, but Susa wouldn't budge from that little place. She'd bought it on her own and painted every inch of it herself before she met him. She had no interest in anything she hadn't had some part in creating. She loved finding old pieces of furniture and making them beautiful. It gave her pleasure, so after a while, Dad stopped trying to make her into someone she wasn't. Money meant very little to her. It just wasn't important."

"I know we've talked about this before, but it still strikes me as funny that he'd picked two women who were such opposites. Your mom so down-home and independent, mine so high maintenance and worldly and spoiled. It's almost as if there were two sides to him." Buttons reappeared and jumped onto Des's lap.

"I think a lot of people have two sides," Cara said. "We both answered the same question in basically the same way. Do we miss our homes, our solitude? And we both responded yes and no. That's like having two sides, right?"

"In a way, yes." Des's phone buzzed. She apologized to Cara for the interruption, took the call, and chatted for a few minutes with Fran about goings-on at the Cross Creek shelter.

"I apologize," Des told Cara after she'd finished the call. "That was the director of the shelter back in Montana bringing me up to date."

"I thought you were the director."

"Nah. I don't want to be responsible for the day-to-day operations. Of course, I want to know what's going on, but I'm happy someone else deals with it. I just want to work with the dogs. That's the part I enjoy. Fran's a good administrator, so I leave it all to her."

"I don't blame you. Running anything can be a pain. I'm so lucky to have someone who's taking care of my yoga studio in Devlin's Light while I'm here." Cara opened her water bottle and took a sip. "So what's new out there in the wilderness?"

Des laughed good-naturedly. "Three new dogs came in over the past week. Fran's working with the owner of the new hardware store to do a meet and greet with the dogs to try to find them new homes. Let's see . . . Oh, my book club changed their meeting night from Tuesday to Thursday. And Kent—I dated him a couple of times—has moved on to the new library assistant."

"Maybe there's a book club in Hidden Falls. Or maybe we could start one."

"Yeah, I do miss my book club."

"But not Kent?"

Des made a face. "The library assistant is welcome to him."

"So what's the notebook for?" Cara pointed to the pad that had slipped to the ground.

"I started to make a list of ways to bring in some cash for the theater. Nothing that's going to bring in a heap of money. It'll be more like a little trickle, but if we can pay even one bill every month, like just the electric bill, even that would be helpful."

"What's on the list?" Cara said.

"Well, for starters, I've been thinking about those old movie posters we found in the office. I'm trying to determine how we can make the most money off them. I did some research, and there is a market for reproductions as well as originals. The important movies like *Gone with the Wind* and *The Philadelphia Story*—you know, the classics, and Oscar winners—can bring in a nice amount. I'm just not sure if we'd make out better selling reproductions on eBay or offering the originals to a dealer."

"Once the original is gone, it's gone. But if we can keep making copies . . ." Cara thought aloud. "Then again, we could make copies of the originals before we sell them to a dealer. Get top dollar for the original and still have copies to sell directly."

Des nodded. "Though there's something about having those original posters." She sighed. "Maybe a good way would be to test the waters by sending one or two originals to an auction that specializes in movie memorabilia, see what kind of money we can bring in."

"I remember talking about having movie nights, maybe showing one of the old films that we found in the cabinet. We don't have to have all the renovations completed to do that. Of course, we'd need a projector," Cara pointed out. "I doubt the old one still works."

"I'll take a look at the projector while we're there this afternoon."

"A screen would be nice, too. The one we have is ripped on one side."

"Maybe we can tape it?" Des made a face. "More likely we'll have to replace it."

"So what else is on the list?"

"We'd talked before about doing a book of photos from the early days of the theater, and Barney said she wanted to work on that. Remember the pictures she showed us of our great-grandparents all dressed to kill standing in the lobby, holding a martini in one hand and shaking someone's hand with the other?" Des stretched out one arm and held an imaginary glass. "Barney's got a list of people she thinks might have some old photos. She's been calling them to see who has what and what we can borrow."

Cara smiled. "I love the story those photos tell about the people who lived in Hidden Falls back then. The ones who'd lost their jobs during the Depression but still got all dressed up to go watch a movie or see a play or hear a concert, all for free on a Sunday night." Cara's voice had gone soft. "He must have been quite a guy, that first Reynolds. All he did for this town. And can you imagine anyone today treating their employees the way he did?"

"It's hard to imagine. But his coal mines had made him a fortune, he didn't have to answer to a board of directors, and there were no shareholders. He made the decisions, and good or bad, he stood by them, so Barney says."

"She said his son—her dad—was the same."

"Makes you wonder about our father, doesn't it? Looks to me like Barney got all the strength and conviction in their generation."

"Dad had his strengths and convictions. They just didn't follow convention. He was convinced enough about your mother's talent that he left his family and moved across the country to help her chase her dream. He loved her enough to do that. And she did become a movie star."

"For a while. Until she drank herself out of one role after another."

"That was on her, Des, not him."

"Maybe he drove her to it. Maybe she knew about—" Des stopped, then blew out a long breath. "I didn't mean to imply that his relationship with your mother made her drink. I honestly don't think she knew about that, and frankly, I doubt if she'd have cared. Mom drank because she wanted to. And besides, the drinking came long before Dad met Susa."

"There's no point in speculating. We'll never know what caused him to fall in love with my mom."

"And it really doesn't matter, I guess. He's gone and they're both gone—Nora and Susa—so they're all together in the afterlife." Des grinned. "Wonder how that's going for the three of them."

"Yeah, it probably wasn't the happiest of reunions," Cara mused. "Then again, maybe the slights and hurts of this life don't follow us from one side of the veil to the other."

"You believe there's a veil that separates one world from the other?"

Cara shrugged. "I honestly don't know. When my mother was dying, she said something about how what happened next was all a big secret, and she was finally going to find out what it was. She didn't fear death at all."

"It would be nice to have that kind of faith." Buttons curled up in Des's lap and went to sleep.

Cara looked up at Des. "Maybe that's what it was, a kind of faith. Susa was open to all of life's experiences. She always said you had to open each new door and walk through to see what was on the other side. I think she saw death as just another door to be opened."

"She must have been a very spiritual person."

"She was. Not so much in a traditional religious sense, but in her own way she definitely was spiritual."

"I can't imagine what it would have been like to have someone like that for a mother. Mine was materialistic and totally of this world and out for herself."

"So we're full circle back to the opposites thing. I guess that says a lot about our dad. He had to have seen the contrasts. It makes me think there must have been something in him that was attracted to both, the spiritual and the worldly."

Cara's car pulled up the driveway, Allie behind the wheel. She parked in front of the carriage house and got out, a tote bag in her arms.

"Where've you been?" Des asked her.

"Oh, I just ran a few errands. Thanks again, Cara, for letting me use your car."

"You're welcome. Anytime." Cara nudged a chair with her foot. "Sit with us."

"I just want to run inside for a moment." Allie started toward the back steps. "Anyone want anything from inside?"

"No, thanks," they both replied.

Five minutes later, Allie was back. She grabbed a chair and pulled it into the garden, then sat and stretched her legs out.

Cara reached her hand toward the nearest peony and touched the petals with her fingertips. "If I ever got married again, I'd want an armload of these. The scents and the colors are heavenly." She paused, then made a face. "Oh, but not the white ones."

"Why not the white ones? White peonies would make a beautiful wedding bouquet," Des noted.

"Wait, is someone getting married?" Allie leaned forward.

"No one's getting married."

"Then why are we talking about wedding flowers?" Allie turned to Cara. "Good lord, don't tell me you and Joe are already talking about—"

"No, no. I just mentioned that if—if—I were ever

to marry again, I'd want peonies in my bouquet. Just not white ones."

"What's wrong with white peonies? They'd be perfect," Allie said.

Cara sighed. "The mother of my ex's new wife worked in my best friend's bakery. Every morning when I stopped in for a muffin on my way to the studio, this girl's mother would start talking about their wedding plans, as if I were dying to know."

"How insensitive. Way to rub it in."

"I know, right? So one day she was talking about how her daughter wanted white peonies and the florist told her she couldn't get them and the mother asked me if I knew where she could locate some."

"Wait, this woman asked you where her daughter could get flowers for the daughter's wedding to your ex?" Allie's eyes widened. "Her daughter who was sleeping with your ex before he was your ex?"

Cara nodded.

"That's incredibly bitchy. Just flat-out mean. Even I wouldn't do something that rude."

"And we know how high that bar is set." Des snickered.

"Ordinarily, I'd have a retort for that, but right now, I'm all out of snark."

"Allie, your snark well has never run dry."

"Well, it did today, Des. I used it all up on Clint." Allie grinned. "But it was snark well spent, believe me. He's agreed to let Nikki fly directly here from Chicago after her visit with his parents and stay until the week before school starts."

"Well done." Cara clapped.

Des nodded approvingly. "Snark well spent indeed."

"I was brilliant, if I do say so myself." Allie beamed. "I told him I'd go back to the judge and show how Clint has violated the original custody agreement. He countered that I had approved it, but I told him I'd maintain that he'd given me no choice since he was the one who moved and enrolled Nikki in a new school without consulting me."

"Well, as long as we have her company for the entire summer, I don't care what tactics you used. But I am proud of you, taking the logical approach instead of resorting to name-calling and hysterics," Des told her.

"New territory for me. But it worked."

"Must have caught Clint off guard."

"It did, and that made my day. Now all I have to do is survive the anxiety over the fact that his elderly parents will be taking Nikki to the Chicago airport and whether or not they get her onto the right plane."

"I'm sure she'll be fine, Allie. You don't need to angst over every little thing."

"Until it's your child, Des," Allie shot back.

"Nikki's very smart and very resourceful," Cara reminded them. "She'll get herself onto the right plane. I have total confidence in her."

"Good point. Thank you for that." Allie rested her elbows on the arms of the chair. "Anyway—here's something totally random I've been thinking about. Don't you think the kitchen could use a little update in décor? It's almost depressing."

"It does appear a bit . . . tired." Cara took a more diplomatic route. "Maybe a little paint."

Allie rolled her eyes. "Please. White walls with ivy stenciled all the way to the ceiling? How 1990s is that? The cabinets are just shabby chic enough to be cool—they do have that authentic vibe, especially the ones with the glass doors—but that yellow linoleum floor has seen its day come and go."

"So what would you suggest? We update here while we're redoing the theater?" Des took a drink from her bottle of water. "Personally, I have enough on my plate right now. Besides, it's not our kitchen. It's not our house. It's Barney's. We're here because she's letting us stay."

"Well, maybe we should talk to her about that. It would be nice for her to have something fresh and pretty to work in since she does like to do most of the cooking," Allie said. "It might help her to move on a little."

"What do you mean, move on?" Cara asked.

"Hasn't it occurred to either of you that it looks as if little or nothing has been done in this house in, like, thirty-five or forty years? Since Barney's fiancé died and Dad left?"

Des and Cara fell silent for a very long moment. Then Des said, "Yeah. It's as if after Gil died, her life just stopped. Except for her job, that is."

"Not that she'd ever forget either her lost love or her brother. But seriously, wouldn't a little change-up be nice for her?"

"I think you'd have to ask her, Al," Des replied.

"But I agree that a change might be a good thing. Maybe if we could get her to change her surroundings a little, we could help her to move on in other ways."

"Well, there she is." Cara nodded in the direction of the driveway. "No time like the present."

The three women watched their aunt's car disappear into the garage. Barney emerged, closed the garage doors, and walked toward the house. She was almost to the patio when she noticed her nieces sitting in the sun near her flower garden.

"Well, don't you three look relaxed." At the sound of her voice, Buttons jumped off Des's lap and ran to Barney, who knelt down to make the appropriate amount of fuss over the dog.

"Want to join us?" Des stood. "I'll help you bring your lounge over."

Allie turned in her seat. "Because we know you can't sit in a wooden Adirondack chair like the rest of us."

Barney laughed out loud. "Why would I sit on a wooden chair when I have this lovely lounge with its comfy cushion?"

Together Barney and Des moved the lounge to the lawn. Barney repositioned the back, then sat and slipped off her shoes. "It's another warm one, girls," she said as she shrugged out of her jacket.

Buttons stared longingly at the lounge until Barney patted the cushion next to her, and the dog happily jumped up.

"How was the luncheon?" Cara asked.

"It was lovely, thank you, and I think we raised a few more dollars for the scholarship fund at the high school." Barney looked from one face to the next. "What's up?"

Des shrugged. "Nothing, really. Just enjoying an early summer day in the garden and waiting for Joe to let Cara know when all the scaffolding is up."

"I got a text from him a while ago. A few more sections are going up this afternoon. He'll let me know when the rest is in place. Shouldn't be long now."

"Let me know as soon as you do. The insurance agent wanted to stop in and take a look," Des reminded her. "She said all she needed was a fifteen-minute heads-up and she could meet us there whenever."

"You'll know when I know," Cara assured her.

"So what were you talking about before I joined you?"

"Oh. We were talking about an idea for your house," Des said, a note of caution in her voice.

"What sort of idea?" Barney paused. "And it's not my house. It's our house. Someday it will pass to the three of you. You're entitled to whatever your father would have been entitled to if he'd died of old age."

"He was sixty-eight," Allie reminded her. "He was old."

"You hush, child. Sixty's the new forty. I thought everyone knew that. So what was your idea about the house, Des?"

"Actually, it was Allie's . . ."

"I was just thinking it would be nice if we worked

with you to freshen up the kitchen a bit." Allie softened the message.

Barney surprised them by agreeing. "Well, it's been a while since anything was done here. I think I had the walls painted and the ivy stenciled back in . . ." She paused to think for a moment as she tucked her blond hair behind her ears. "Let's see, it was the year that I . . . oh, Lord, could it really have been that long? Nineteen ninety-one? Where the devil did the time go?"

"I could help you paint, if there was a color you liked," Allie offered. "I painted all the rooms in my house in L.A. I'm pretty good at it."

"I'm sure you are and I'd be delighted to hand the project off to you. I guess I'll have to get to the hardware store and pick up some paint brochures for inspiration."

"I see hours of HGTV in your future, Barney," Des teased.

"As if I don't watch enough TV already," Barney replied.

"I don't think those morning game shows spend much time on decorating trends."

"Oh, you." Barney swatted playfully at Cara. "Now you've got me thinking. What would you do if you were me?"

"I'd freshen up the white paint," Allie said without hesitation, "and cover up the ivy. Assuming you don't want to replace the cabinets—and there's no reason to, they're in great shape—I'd go with light gray doors on the top and a darker gray on the bottom. Maybe replace the counters with a white granite or quartz that has shades of gray and maybe something else in it."

"That was all off the top of your head?" Des asked.

Allie nodded. "Gray is very popular right now, and both shades—the dark and the light—would pick up the gray in the fireplace. The stones also have a bit of gold and some taupe shades. The mantel is lovely and the stone is in great shape. Do you ever use the fireplace?"

"We used to a lot in winter when we were kids. Mrs. Allen, the housekeeper, would come over early to light a fire before she started making breakfast so that when we came down into the kitchen, the room would be cozy and warm. Didn't matter how cold it might have been outside, or how loudly the wind might be blowing, how deep the snow, it was always warm in the kitchen." The apparent pleasure of those memories brought a smile to Barney's face.

"If we're still around next winter, maybe we could use the fireplace in there. Like when you were younger," Des ventured.

"I agree. Except for the one in the sitting room, I haven't used the fireplaces in forever. I don't know why I stopped." Barney paused and seemed to reflect. "I guess I didn't want to bother only for myself. I should probably call a chimney sweep in to make sure they're okay to use."

"Well, we're all here now, and we'd love to have those fires burning again. Though maybe not until the weather cools off." Des smiled at the thought of having that first cup of morning coffee in a cozy room on a cold morning. "Maybe we could put a chair or two in front of the kitchen fireplace."

"That's assuming we're all still here come the cool weather," Allie broke in. "Once the theater's done, we can leave. I know I for one am outta here on the first plane."

Des caught the crestfallen expression on Barney's face. "I don't know," she said hastily. "Who knows how long it's going to take? And besides, even if it's finished, who's to say we wouldn't come back for Christmas? I'd come back, if Barney wanted me to."

"Nothing would make me happier than to have you all here with me for Christmas, regardless of the state of the theater. And the icing on the cake would be to have Nikki here as well."

Allie appeared to think that over. "I don't know if Clint would agree to that."

"Oh, just convince him it would be romantic to take his girlfriend to London or Paris for the holidays," Cara suggested. Her phone pinged and she dipped a hand into her pocket to retrieve it and read the incoming text.

"That could very possibly work." Allie nodded slowly, then stopped. "But we're getting ahead of ourselves—it's not even June."

"Joe just texted to let me know that the roofers put more scaffolding up and he and Ben were going to climb what's there to get a better look at the ceiling."

"Ben Haldeman is there?" Allie's eyes narrowed. "Why?"

Cara shrugged. "I guess he saw Joe's truck out front and stopped to see what was going on."

"Why isn't he patrolling the streets, keeping Hidden Falls safe from marauders?" Allie grumbled. "Isn't that his job as chief of police?"

CHAPTER TWO

Heather Martin was true to her word. Fifteen minutes after Des's call, Heather was in the lobby with Joe and waiting when the Hudson crew arrived.

Barney introduced her nieces, then Cara hung back to chat with Joe while Heather, Barney, Allie, and Des walked farther into the theater where the scaffolding reached two-thirds of the way to the ceiling.

Des went straight to the point, asking, "So is this covered or not?"

"The water damage caused by the wind, yes, but I'd like to see the coverage for the roofer, and I'd like one of our adjusters to go up and check the extent of the damage," Heather replied, her eyes still on the ceiling. "It's really a shame. That ceiling is just magnificent."

"It was." Des grimaced.

"It will be again," Heather assured her. "It's why you have insurance. To make you whole again."

"Is that Ben up there?" Barney followed Allie's gaze. "Benjamin Haldeman," she called, "you know what you're doing up there?"

"Yes, ma'am," Ben called back.

Out of the corner of her eye, Des watched Allie, who stood with her hands on her hips watching the man who began to descend carefully.

Heather glanced around the lobby. "I'm so glad you all are doing something with the theater. It's a Hidden Falls treasure, and everyone I know is tickled pink that we're going to have the theater back again. Of course, the young folks don't have firsthand recollections of it, but I remember coming to plays here in the summer when I was just a little girl."

"Well, maybe you'll get to do that again someday," Des told her.

Barney watched Ben drop to the floor from one of the lower rails. "Moonlighting as the roofing inspector now, Chief?"

"Just curious. I figured as long as the scaffold was already in place, I might as well climb up and take a look. I might never get another chance to see that chandelier up close. Sure is hot up there, though." Ben wiped the sweat from his face with the end of his T-shirt.

"Heat rises. Or hadn't you heard?" Allie stared.

He turned to her. "Well, Miss Personality. I'm surprised you left home to venture out on a hot day like this. Aren't you afraid your makeup will melt?"

"I'm not wearing makeup."

"You should. You could use some color."

"And you should be out chasing felons."

"I will be in about"—Ben looked at his watch—"fifty-five minutes."

"You should leave now. It'll take you at least that long to get prettied up for patrolling the mean streets of Hidden Falls."

"Gotta keep my town safe," he said, nodding in agreement, "from evil-deed doers and bitchery in all forms."

Ben raised two fingers to his lips and whistled. Seconds later, a black-and-white dog raced from the direction of the stairs that led to the basement and crossed the lobby in a flash to sit at Ben's feet.

"Good girl." Ben leaned forward to rub behind the dog's ear. He took a small treat from his pocket and gave it to the dog, who wagged her tail in response.

"Have you settled on a name for her yet, Ben?" Des asked.

"She answers to Girl, so maybe that was her name."

"Girl? That's it?" Allie raised an eyebrow. "You really named your female dog Girl? That's the best you can do?"

"What's wrong with Girl?"

"Your lack of imagination is stunning, though not totally unexpected."

"Yeah, well, what would you have named her?"

"Something more original than Girl."

"Come up with something better and I'll consider it." Ben dismissed Allie by turning away and addressing the others. "Good to see you, ladies." He called to

Joe, who was still off to the side with Cara. "See you around. Thanks for letting me check out the ceiling. I'd like to go back once you get enough scaffold to go all the way up."

"Anytime." Joe waved.

Des tapped Allie on the arm. "Why do you bait that man the way you do?"

"I don't know. Something about him just brings out the best in me, I guess."

"You mean the worst."

"No. I mean the best." Allie grinned. "He just tweaks that little old sarcastic streak of mine and I can't seem to hold back."

Des muttered something under her breath about not realizing that streak ever needed to be tweaked.

"Obviously I can't evaluate the damage to the painted portions of the ceiling," Heather was saying as she and Barney walked toward the door. "I can have a property adjuster over here as soon as I can shake someone free to take a look. But I'm afraid this storm has really overloaded our Claims Department. We're going to be backed up for weeks." She looked upward. "At the very least, I'm going to need photos of the damage to the ceiling."

"Seth took a whole bunch this morning. He couldn't get as close as he wanted to, but he used a telephoto lens and I know he got some shots that were pretty detailed," Joe said. "He went home to run some hard copies off his computer. I'll be happy to drop them off at your office."

"That would be very helpful." Heather smiled. "I

can send those to our home office and see if anyone there knows an artist we could contact. Thanks, Joe."

"And we'll let you know if we find someone who looks promising." Barney opened the door that led into the vestibule.

"Well, you have your work cut out for you," Des told Allie.

Allie nodded, the sarcasm now tucked away. "I'll start making calls as soon as we get back to the house."

"I'll see you there. I want to run upstairs to the projection room and check something out." Des turned and headed for the steps leading to the second level.

Once upstairs, she went into the projection room and opened the closet door. There were several shelves of metal film canisters. She opened one, then another. Most were empty, but a few contained rolled-up film. She glanced at the old projector. How to determine if it still worked without risking ruining a film?

Des heard voices down below, then one drawing closer.

Seth MacLeod appeared in the doorway. He was tall, had a totally shaved head, and was dressed in a pair of worn jeans and a faded red T-shirt that had Born to Ride emblazoned over the Harley-Davidson logo and did little to hide his broad chest. Deep brown eyes set off by long dark lashes drew her gaze to his ruggedly handsome face. Tattoos covered both well-toned arms, and in his hand he carried a brown envelope. "Joe said he thought I'd find you up here. I thought you'd like to see the pictures of the ceiling I took this morning."

"I would. Thanks."

Des went back to the projection stand, the man close behind. She returned the metal canisters to the closet to clear a space on the table for the photos, then held her hand out.

Seth opened the envelope and handed her a few of the prints.

"Oh crap." Des's face fell. "It's even worse than I thought."

"There are very few things that can't be fixed. This"—Seth picked up a close-up shot of one of the fleurs-de-lis—"can be fixed."

"God, I hope you're right."

"I am." Seth pointed at the projector. "So what are you doing with this little number? Planning on a little showing later?"

"Don't I wish we were at that point. And don't I wish I knew if this baby still worked. There are still a few reels of film around. I'd love to be able to see if any of them were any good. I don't know how to work the projector, though, and I'd be afraid I'd ruin the films, if they aren't already ruined."

"Why would the films be ruined? Haven't they been stored away?"

Des nodded.

"So maybe they're still good."

Seth stepped behind her, then reached around her to turn the projector toward him. He was so close

Des could feel his breath on the side of her face. For a moment, she froze, remembering another small room, another time when she'd been trapped between arms stronger than hers. She tried to pull herself away from that long-ago memory, and reminded herself that this was Seth—not *him*. Not someone intent on hurting her.

"This still might work," Seth was saying. "Mind if I take it home and tinker with it?"

Words stuck in her throat.

"Des?" His voice was soft, concerned.

He's not a threat. He's a friend. He would never hurt me.

"Des?" he repeated, one gentle hand touching her back. "You okay?"

"I'm good. Sorry. I just . . . yes, I'm fine." She cleared her throat. His hand had moved to her shoulder, and she instinctively relaxed into its warmth.

"So what were you thinking about doing with the films?"

She turned around and leaned back against the table.

"Maybe charging to show them. Or sell them. Anything to make a little money to keep the bills paid."

"Good thinking. In the meantime, I'll see if I can do something with that." He nodded in the direction of the projector, though his eyes were still locked with hers.

"All right." She tried to look away, but he held her gaze.

"So." His eyes darted from her face back to the photos that he'd left on the table. "I'll drop these off at Heather's office on my way back home. You want a copy? I'd be happy to run off an extra set."

"Yes, I'd like that, thanks. I'm sure they'll come in handy if we . . ." Des smiled before correcting herself. "When we find an artist."

"That's the spirit." Seth looked as if he was about to say something more, but after a moment, merely said, "I'll get you those photos."

"Great. Thanks so much." The spell was broken, so she walked with him to the top of the steps. "See you later."

"You will," he said without turning around.

She watched him descend the steps and cross the lobby, where he stopped to say something to Joe and Cara before he left. Des went back into the projector room to turn off the lights, thinking how grateful she was to have a friend like easygoing Seth, who was always encouraging and upbeat, who always looked for the good in everyone and every situation and always put people at ease. That's what real friends do. They make you feel good about yourself and help you when you need it.

Must be why he was elected mayor of Hidden Falls three times.

When Des had rescued the three dogs—Buttons, Ripley, and Girl—a few months ago from the theater, where they'd been making their home, she quickly needed to find foster families for them if not adoptive ones. She and Barney had been in agreement about keeping Buttons, the smallest of the three, but she needed good homes for the two black-and-white border collies. When she appeared before the town council to inquire about zoning regulations regarding a potential rescue shelter, and mentioned she was looking for homes for the strays she'd found, Seth had not hesitated to offer to take one of the dogs. He'd immediately seemed to understand how important it was to her that the dogs not be taken to a nearby shelter, where their fates would be uncertain.

It brought a smile to Des's face to remember how he'd all but bullied Ben into taking the other dog.

In the past, Des's relationships with men had mostly consisted of dates she wished she hadn't gone on. She couldn't deny they mostly ended because she always sensed something lacking. Even though she'd never managed to give that something a name, she knew whatever it was, it had never been there for her, but she suspected it was close to the truth to say it might have something to do with trust.

She told herself she'd know when she found it, but until she did, she wasn't going to settle for anything less. She'd heard too many cautionary tales about what happens when you compromise on what you really want. For heaven's sake, look at her sisters! Both of them were divorced.

What had they compromised on for the sake of love?

A question for another time, Des thought as she joined Joe and Cara near the front door. For now, it was enough to know such compromises were not in her future. Love was complicated and messy and demanding, but friendship was simple and straightforward and easy, and it lasted. That's what she had with Seth, and that was all she wanted.

"Girls, you picked one heck of a day to start working on the kitchen." Barney stood in the doorway, her face flushed from the heat. "It's hot as blazes in here."

Des grabbed a stack of dinner plates from an open cupboard and set them on the floor in front of the fireplace. The table and the counters were already piled high with the contents of the cabinets.

"Hot as blazes, all right. But the taskmaster"— Des nodded in Allie's direction—"decreed that today would be the day, so here we are."

"No time like the present." Allie stood in the middle of the room, a box of paintbrushes and supplies in her arms. "No point in putting it off, especially since we don't know when work can be started in the theater. Might as well use the time while we have it." She set the box on the window seat. "Barney, I have all the paint you asked for. I love that soft, warm white for the walls." She gazed around the room. "It's going to be fabulous."

"I can't wait to see it. How long do you think it'll take?" Barney asked.

"Maybe a week, if we all work steadily and don't get too distracted," Allie told her.

"Well, I'm ready." Barney rolled up the sleeves of her light blue shirt. "Where do I start?"

"We start by cleaning the cupboards and the shelves. Next, we'll take the doors off, wash those down, and let them dry. After that, we wash the woodwork. Who's doing the upper cabinets?" Allie asked.

"I am." Barney raised her hand.

"I have the lower ones," Cara said.

"Woodwork," Des announced.

"And I have the walls. If anyone wants to trade, speak up now." Allie's gaze went from one face to the next. No one offered. "Okay, good. We're set." She turned toward the box of supplies, then stopped. "Oh, if you need help getting the cabinet doors off, let me know. And once they've been washed down and dried, use the paint sprayer instead of a brush. The paint will go on faster and more evenly. Any questions?"

Cara shook her head. "Nope."

"Good. Des, I'll help you wash the woodwork and paint it as well. It takes the longest, and I can help you once the walls are finished."

"Shouldn't you paint the woodwork first, and then the walls?" Des asked.

"Everyone has their own theory on this. Mine is that you paint the walls first, then tape over and around the woodwork so if you're a little sloppy, the paint goes onto the tape. Once you're done, the tape comes off." Allie hastened to add, "Not that we're aiming for sloppy here."

"Got it." Cara nodded. "Wait, is there a screwdriver? I need to take the hinges off the doors."

"Yup." Allie pointed to the box of supplies.

"Wow, you really are all over this project, aren't you?" Cara went through the contents of the box and found the screwdriver, then proceeded to remove the upper cabinet doors with help from Barney.

"Once we finish washing the woodwork, I can give you a hand with the walls, Allie," Des offered.

Allie was looking up at the ceiling. "I'm wondering if I shouldn't paint that first."

They all stopped what they were doing to look up.

"I don't know. Won't that be a colossal pain to do?" Barney asked. "And it really doesn't look bad. I mean, it's not dirty or anything."

"I don't know. I feel like we're not doing the entire job." Allie frowned.

"We definitely will need a ladder for that," Cara said. "If you're just going to the top of the wall, you can do that with a roller, maybe stand on a chair to do that upper part near the ceiling. But I think you need a ladder."

"One thing I do not have," Barney said.

"We can get one from Joe." Cara pulled her phone from her pocket and speed-dialed. Within less than a half hour, Joe had delivered and set up a ladder for Allie.

"Want some help?" he said after he'd looked over the scope of their work.

"I think we're good, but thanks." Allie didn't wait for anyone else to respond.

"If you need me, you know where to find me." Joe gave Cara's shoulder a squeeze before heading out the back door to his truck.

"Nice to have a handy guy on call," Barney noted.

"Nice to have any guy on call," Des agreed.

"Depends on the guy." Allie turned on her iPhone and hit her favorite playlist, which contained mostly upbeat numbers favored by Nikki. "Music to work by, ladies. Feel free to sing along."

And they did sing along, to Taylor Swift, Lady Gaga, Pink, Katy Perry.

"I don't know any of those singers," Barney announced. "Except for the Swift girl. Did you know she's from right down around Reading?"

By late afternoon, the cabinet doors had all been washed and stood upright in front of the fireplace and along a wall to dry. The ceiling and one wall had been painted, all the woodwork had been washed and had dried, and three doors had been painted.

"It has to be about a hundred degrees in here." Allie pulled her hair into as high a ponytail as it would go.

"A hundred and twenty, easy." Des leaned against the counter.

Barney put down the paint sprayer. "Girls, stop what you're doing, we're wrapping it up for today. You've got thirty minutes to clean up. We're going out for dinner."

"That sounded like the closing whistle to me," Des said. "Don't have to tell me twice." She put down her paintbrush.

"Hey, you can't leave that there," Allie pointed out. "Clean off the brush." She pointed to the sink. "This paint cleans up with water."

"Okay, make it forty minutes," Barney said. "Allowing for cleanup here first."

"I'm done and headed for the shower," Cara announced before taking off for the back steps.

"I'm right behind you." Allie finished washing her brush, then laid it on newspaper they'd used to cover the kitchen table. She turned off the music, then wandered out of the kitchen checking her phone for messages.

"Go on, Barney. I'll finish up here," Des told her.

"You sure?"

"Yup. I'll just be a minute more."

The kitchen had gone from a chatty space filled with music and singing to silence. Des finished cleaning the brushes and rinsed out the sprayer, checked to make sure the paint cans were tightly covered, then followed the others upstairs for a quick shower.

It had taken more than Barney's previously decreed forty minutes, but soon enough, all four Hudson women were assembled in the front hall, cleaner and cooler and dressed casually and comfortably. Barney wore another of her cute T-shirt dresses—this one ocean blue to match her eyes—and both Des and Cara had put on khaki shorts and striped T-shirts and had to work to keep their curls under control. Allie wore a black tank and white shorts, and her hair looked perfect. Des couldn't help but comment as they walked out the front door.

"Al, you know I'd kill for your hair, right?" she said.

"Note to self: Sleep with one eye open." Allie

tossed that long sheaf of hair over one shoulder as Barney locked the door behind them and headed down the front steps to the walk. "Wait, why aren't we driving?" Allie remained on the top step.

"We're only going two blocks, Allie." Barney kept walking without turning around. "By the time I got Lucille started up and backed out of the garage, we could be there."

Allie groaned and muttered something about sweating to death, then followed the others.

"Besides," Barney continued, "Lucille's air-conditioning has been acting up lately. I keep meaning to take her into the shop to have it fixed, but I keep forgetting."

"Where's there a Cadillac dealer around here?" Des fell into step behind Barney and next to Cara.

Barney was obviously appalled. "I wouldn't take Lucille to a dealer. Why, those young folks they have working on cars today only know how to do what the computers tell them to do. They wouldn't know what to do with a fine vintage automobile like Lucille. Took her into the dealer for an oil change about ten years ago and they put in the wrong kind. She wheezed like an asthmatic. Had to have her engine drained. She hasn't seen the inside of a dealer's garage since."

"Well, where do you take her?" Des asked.

"Billy Jurczak, over on Constitution Avenue. That man understands the needs of a 1968 Cadillac DeVille. Knows his way around a V-8 engine." Barney looked over her shoulder to Des. "No one touches Lucille except Billy."

Des and Cara exchanged an amused glance. Their aunt's Cadillac convertible—complete with red leather interior—was Barney's pride and joy. They'd heard the story several times how the car had been a gift from Barney's father to her mother, how her mother had adored the car and drove it with a lead foot until her dementia became pronounced. It had fallen to Barney to hide the keys, "finding" them only to take her mother to the doctor or for a ride through the countryside on days when she was up to it. Everyone in Hidden Falls knew Lucille; she'd become sort of a celebrity in town.

"Barney, I keep meaning to ask you: Who lives in that house across the street from our driveway?" Des turned to point behind them to the Tudor that sat behind a tall row of evergreens. "I never see anyone around."

Barney turned to look. "Oh, that's the old Brookes place. Mrs. Brookes passed away last year, Mr. Brookes died years ago. Fifteen maybe? Anyway, it's been a while. They were both buried in Maryland, where they were from originally. All the services were there. Mrs. Brookes kept up the house as long as she could, bless her heart. She was a lovely woman."

"Who lives there now?" Des asked.

"No one. I think the children—Thomas, Emily, and Stephen—jointly inherited the property, but last I heard Emily's living in London with her family,

Stephen died in Vietnam, and Thomas . . . he joined the army after his brother was killed. Career officer, retired now, I'm sure. I haven't seen him in years."

She resumed walking.

"So the house is just sitting there?" Des was the last to catch up with the others.

"Until someone comes along to empty it, or sell it, I suppose it will."

"You must have known the family well. They lived right there. You were neighbors." For some reason, Des wasn't finished with the Brookeses.

"Of course I knew them well. Thomas and Gil were the same age and good friends, Emily was in my grade, and Stephen and your father were classmates. He and Fritz and Pete were inseparable for years. I checked in with Mrs. Brookes frequently over the years. She and my mother played cards together."

"Were you and Emily good friends?"

Barney didn't respond immediately. Finally, she said simply, "For a time."

They'd reached the corner of Main and Hudson, where the light was still green.

"Hurry up, and we'll make it before the light turns red," Barney told them. "I'm hoping it's not too late for us to get a good table at the Goodbye."

The Goodbye Café, so called because it had the reputation of being the place where you'd take your significant other to give them the news that they'd lost their significance, was one of only two restaurants in Hidden Falls—the other was the Hudson Diner—and the only one that understood what "farm to table" and "locally sourced" meant. The real name of the restaurant was the Green Brier Café, but only visitors to the town referred to it as such. The owner, Judy Worrell, was amused by its nickname, and even she referred to it as the Goodbye.

Tonight Judy was at the door greeting guests.

"Hello, girls. Barney, you're looking well." Judy smiled as they entered. "Four for dinner?"

"Yes," Barney told her. "We've come for a delicious meal in air-conditioned comfort. It's nice and cool in here, so we're halfway to our goal."

"Everything here is delicious, as you well know." Judy handed Barney four menus and flagged down a waitress. "Table for four. Enjoy, ladies. Barney, I'll need to talk to you before you leave."

"Oh? What's up?" Barney paused midstep.

"Some complications with Fourth of July. We'll talk after you've eaten."

Barney nodded and followed their waitress to their table.

"What happens on Fourth of July?" Des asked as they seated themselves.

"The usual hoopla that small towns all do. Parade complete with marching bands in the morning followed by games for kids at the park. Home barbecues. Fireworks at night. It's the same every year. Probably the same everywhere else, too." Barney began to read the menu.

"That's July Fourth in Devlin's Light exactly. I always loved those days." Cara pulled her chair closer to the table to permit a waiter to pass behind her.

"Same back in Cross Creek," Des told them. "So very traditional and fun. Classic USA." Des turned to Allie. "I don't remember much hoopla when we were growing up, but how 'bout in L.A. these days? Parades? Fireworks?"

Allie shrugged. "I suppose. I'm guessing there were parades. I might have seen one on TV one time."

"Are you telling us you never went to a Fourth of July parade?" Barney looked horrified.

"That's what I said, yes." Allie didn't raise her eyes from the menu.

"You never took Nikki to a parade?"

Allie shrugged. "What can I say? Clint hated that sort of thing, so we never went."

"So Nikki never took part in a parade or . . ."

"Unless she went with a friend sometime. Maybe she did. I don't remember." Allie focused her attention on the menu. "The Cobb salad with grilled chicken looks decent."

"I think I'll go with that, too." Vegetarian Cara added, "Without the chicken."

"Well, Nikki's going to get the full treatment this year." Barney put her menu down. "Maybe there's even a place for her in the parade, you never know."

"I'm sure she'll be thrilled to death to hear it." Allie finally looked up. "Everyone ready to order?"

True to her word, Judy showed up at the table as soon as everyone finished their meals.

"So how was everything?" She stood behind Barney and surveyed the table.

"Great," everyone agreed.

Judy pulled a chair from a nearby table and sat between Barney and Des. "So here's where we are for the Fourth. You know how Dan Hunter usually drives his classic Model-T Ford at the front of the parade?"

Barney nodded. "Been doing that for years. His father drove that car before him. I can't remember when that old car wasn't out there leading the parade."

"Well, it won't be this year. Maybe never again. Something's wrong with the engine—it needs some part or other—and Dan hasn't been able to find a replacement. So unless he's able to find that part, and someone with the know-how to replace it, we're without a classic car to start off the parade." Judy stared meaningfully at Barney.

"You want Lucille."

Judy nodded. "We do. The committee chair called an emergency meeting last night. Ross Whalen—"

"Cranky old coot," Barney muttered.

"Yeah, he is. Anyway, he offered to drive if . . ."

Barney's eyes grew wide, her brows reaching almost to her hairline. "Ross Whalen is not touching Lucille. No one drives her but me. No one." She paused. "Maybe one of my girls here, eventually, but Whalen? Nope."

"The mayor said you'd say that. He suggested you drive." Judy leaned back in her chair as the waitress cleared the dinner plates from the table.

"Bless Seth for having my back." Barney smiled.

"So what do you say? I know you like sitting there on the corner in your folding chair, watching the parade go by while you drink your iced coffee, but . . ."

"Oh, of course I'll drive Lucille in the parade. And afterward, you can buy me an iced coffee."

"Thank you. I'll make good on the coffee, and I'll let the others know you're in." Judy stood.

When Judy was out of earshot, Allie asked, "So what's the big deal about driving the car in the parade?"

"It's an honor to lead the parade, one that's always belonged to the Hunters, as they owned the oldest car in town," Barney explained. "I guess that makes Lucille the second oldest." She frowned. "The Petersons have a 1940 Dodge, but I don't know if it still runs. And it's not a convertible. Gotta have a convertible at the head of the parade."

"Why?" Des asked.

"So you can see the dignitaries in the back seat, of course." Barney stood. "Ready, girls?"

Barney paid at the register while the girls filed out onto the pavement. On the walk home, they peered into store windows, waved to the passing cars, and debated what qualified one for dignitary status in Hidden Falls.

They'd reached the sidewalk in front of the family home when a large black-and-white dog streaked across the lawn, then turned and headed directly for them.

"Ripley!" Des braced as the dog launched himself at her. "Down, boy. Get down." She looked up as Seth jogged toward them. "So much for all those hours we spent training him over the past few months."

"Down, Ripley," Seth reprimanded his dog. "Sorry, Des."

"He's all right. He's just happy to see me." Des pushed the dog off her. "Sit, bud. Sit."

The dog sat and looked up at her expectedly.

"He thinks you're going to give him a hamburger," Allie said. "Like the way you did to coax him out of the theater."

"Ah, the old burger lure. Works every time." Des recalled the day she lured the three dogs from the hole in the side of the exterior theater wall.

"Seth, I appreciate you speaking up for me at the meeting last night." Barney crossed her arms over her chest. "To think I'd ever let that fool Whalen behind the wheel of my car is ludicrous."

"We all knew that would never happen," Seth said. "You will do it, though, right? You'll lead the parade this year?"

"Of course. It will be an honor and a pleasure." Barney's eyes narrowed. "But I get to pick who rides in the back seat."

Seth laughed. "I told them you'd say that, too. You just do your thing, Ms. Hudson. The rest of us will fall in line."

"You're a good boy, Seth MacLeod." Barney patted him on the arm and headed for the house. "You keep working on putting some manners on that dog of yours, hear?"

"Yes, ma'am." He nodded.

"I have a few phone calls to make." Cara followed

Barney on the sidewalk that led to the front porch. "See you around."

"So do I. See you, Seth." Allie fell in step with Cara.

Des turned to Seth. "So where are you off to? Aren't you a ways from your place?"

"I was just trying to get my boy here out for some exercise."

"Good for all dogs, but yeah, border collies like to run." She glanced down at Ripley, who'd plopped at Seth's feet. "Do you want some water for him? He looks winded."

"I'm sure he'd appreciate it. Thanks."

As soon as Des and Seth turned toward the house, the dog took off up the path.

"I guess he remembers Buttons lives here."

"He always pulls on his leash when we pass by," Seth admitted. "I'm not sure whether it's Buttons he's looking for or you."

"Well, I was his first human friend here in Hidden Falls," Des reminded him. "A little hamburger goes a long way for a starving dog."

"I sometimes think about what might have happened to them if you hadn't come along when you did."

"Someone else would have noticed them going in and out of the wall eventually. And the bartender at the Frog was feeding them when they came around."

"True, but they'd have still been homeless. You got them to come out, got them to the vet, and bullied your friends until they agreed to adopt them."

"If I recall correctly, you stepped right up to take

Ripley, and if anyone was bullied, it was Ben when you twisted his arm into taking the female."

"Do you believe he still hasn't given that dog a proper name?"

"Yeah, I think we're going to have to shame him into doing something about that." Des grinned. "Even Allie was giving him a hard time about his lack of imagination."

"Allie seems to give Ben a hard time about everything."

"She enjoys it. Sometimes I think my sister isn't happy if she isn't giving someone a bad day."

Ripley reached the front porch, then sniffed around the door, wagging his tale.

"I'll go in and get some water for him and see if Buttons wants to come out and play. Have a seat." Des opened the front door and disappeared inside.

When she returned, water bowl in her hands and two bottles of beer under her arm, an excited small white dog dashed past her to greet her friends, canine and human. Des placed the water bowl on the porch, but Ripley raced past it and Seth, who'd seated himself on the steps, to chase Buttons across the front lawn.

Des handed Seth a beer and stood on the step to watch the dogs play for a moment.

"Thanks." He twisted off the cap and took a drink.

"The pups look like they're having fun." She sat next to Seth and watched Buttons pursue Ripley up the driveway toward the carriage house.

"Yeah, they're good friends. There's no telling where they'd been or what they'd gone through together. They do have a bond."

The two dogs raced around the side of the house and across the lawn.

"So did you have time to take a closer look at that projector?" she asked.

"I did. It's a Super Simplex XL. I'm pretty sure the body is from the 1930s or forties, but it appears to have been modified at some point, probably in the fifties or sixties. I'm guessing that's when the Xenon lamp illumination was added."

She stared at him, drop-jawed. "How did you find out all that so fast?"

Seth grinned. "Magellan Express, my favorite search engine."

"Do you think the projector still works?"

"Right now, it would not. There's a piece broken off from the shutter feed, and I'm not sure if it can be replaced."

"What's a shutter feed?"

"See if you can picture this. The film is on two reels, one near the bottom of the projector, one at the top." He held his hands at six and twelve o'clock. "It's fed from the bottom reel through the gate and the image is projected onto the lens, and the shutter feed moves the film onto the upper reel."

"What if you can't replace the feed?"

"There are a bunch of projectors of this vintage on eBay. We can replace it if we have to, but it would be way cooler to have the original to use in the theater."

"Why didn't I think of eBay?" she said.

"I didn't at first, either. But there are a few of this model for sale. If you want, I'll try to call around, see what I can find out about prices, conditions, that sort of thing."

"I don't want to impose on you." Her shoulder brushed against his upper arm, and she felt a sudden little zing where he touched her. She leaned away to rest her back against one of the porch pillars. She'd grown so comfortable in his company over time that the little bit of electricity caught her off guard.

"It's no imposition. I'm kind of intrigued by how it works. I'd like to learn more about how it's put together. Besides, it's interesting to see how projectors evolved along with the films."

"If you're sure you don't mind . . ." She opened her bottle and took a sip, wondering if he'd felt that . . . whatever it had been. There was no way she was going to put a name to it.

"I'm positive. Besides, I like being involved in this project. The theater was the heart of this town once. I think it can be again." He fell silent. "Being there this afternoon brought back memories. I remember once when I was about six or seven, they opened the theater for the Halloween parade. It had been pouring rain for days and didn't look as if it was going to let up. The town council was going to cancel the parade, but someone—in retrospect, it must have been Barney—suggested that the parade take place inside the Sugarhouse. We all dressed up in our costumes and paraded through the lobby, down the aisle, and up onto the stage. They gave prizes for the best costumes."

"Did you win?"

Seth laughed. "In my white sheet? Hardly. But we had a great time that night. Ben and Joe were ghosts, too, and the three of us ran back and forth across the stage yelling *boo* until someone corralled us and sent us back down the steps."

"I would have thought a performance like that would have earned a prize."

He shook his head. "There's no accounting for taste. I think first prize went to Cinderella, and the runners-up were a couple of pirates and a kid in a bear costume whose father was principal of the high school." He smiled at the memory.

"You three have been friends for that long?"

"Since kindergarten." He smiled. "Small towns are like that, Des. You grow up knowing everyone. You stay long enough, you become part of it."

"I don't think I even remember the names of the kids I went to kindergarten with."

"Did you change schools after kindergarten? Go to a different elementary school?"

"I didn't have friends from school. We were homeschooled after about second or third grade. I don't remember much before that."

"Your mother homeschooled you?"

Des burst out laughing. "My mother? Oh God, no. She'd have died first. No, no, we had a tutor." She paused. "You know I used to be on a TV show when I was young, right?"

"There was talk about Barney's nieces doing some acting. I'm pretty sure my sister watched your show for a few years." He added almost apologetically, "I never was one to sit and watch television much. I spent most of my time outside."

"No need to apologize. It was pretty much a girly show, though I wish we'd taken a different direction with it." She rolled her eyes. "Not that anyone ever asked me."

"You sound like you didn't like it much."

"I hated it. I never wanted to do it. It was my mother's idea." Des shook her head slowly. "I did everything I could to get out of it. That show took my childhood and ruined my relationship with my sister."

"You seem to get along okay now."

"Some of the time. But there's always this undertone of resentment. Allie has never forgiven me for getting that role. She wanted it, I didn't, I got it. That's the short version."

"Maybe someday I'll get to hear the whole story."

"Maybe someday you will." She tried to think of a polite way to change the subject.

Seth must have picked up on that, because he asked, "Do you miss the shelter you ran in Montana?"

"I do, but someone else actually runs it. Mostly I worked with the problem dogs."

"What constitutes a 'problem dog'? You don't mean vicious dogs?"

"No, no. Dogs that are poorly socialized, or have been abused and are fearful. Dogs with trust issues.

Dogs that are downright mean are something else. There are people who work with dogs like that, but you really have to be specially trained to do that sort of work. I did the easy stuff. Some dogs take longer than others to learn to trust."

"I guess dogs aren't so different from people. Some folks take longer to trust, too." He took another sip of beer. "You have such a calming way about you, you're so easy to be around. I suspect dogs sense that as much as people do, and just naturally trust you."

"Thanks, Seth."

"So have you thought about starting a shelter here? We get strays in town sometimes, and there have been cases where people have dumped unwanted animals up in the hills. When they get picked up, they're taken to the SPCA or to that shelter outside of Clarks Summit. No telling what happens to them from there."

"I do miss it. If I had a place to house the dogs, if I had a network here . . ." She shrugged. "I admit I looked at the carriage house as a possible space, but it's not a good idea."

"Sounds like a good idea to me, if that's what you want to do."

"For one thing, it's too close to the house. Dogs can get a little rowdy if something sets them off at night. I doubt Barney or the neighbors would appreciate a bunch of animals howling in the wee hours." She took another sip from the bottle, then set it on the step next to her. "Besides, I think it's too small to take in more than a few animals, and judging from my last appearance before your town council, I'd never get a full-sized operation past zoning."

"You have a friend on the council, you know that, right?" Obviously Seth meant himself.

"I do, and I appreciate it. But that's only one vote. And there's maybe the most important reason: I think Cara wants to open a yoga studio, and it looks like she has her eye on the carriage house."

"And what Cara wants trumps what you want because . . . ?"

"Because she's the most likely to stay when work at the theater is finished."

A long moment passed before Seth asked, "So is there someone waiting for you back in Montana?"

"Only the people who run the shelter, and my book club."

"I'll bet there are plenty of people here in Hidden Falls who'd join a book club if you started one."

"Cara and I talked about that. But I don't know if I want to get involved with anything and then leave. Dogs or people."

He seemed to think that over as he started to peel back the label from the bottle.

"When you go back to Montana, will you take Buttons?"

"I couldn't take her from Barney. She loves that dog, and the dog adores her. Whenever I go, Buttons will stay here."

"When do you think that will be?"

Des shrugged. "I have no idea now. We were pretty much on track to get the basic renovation completed, but the mess with the ceiling is going to set us back a bit."

"If I can help in any way, let me know. In the meantime, I'll get that extra set of prints to you."

Seth stood and whistled for his dog. Both animals stopped their play, then trotted to him. Buttons sat at Des's feet, panting.

"Tell Barney I said good night. Thanks for the beer." He hooked the leash onto the back of his dog's harness. "I'll see you, Des."

"Night, Seth." Des stood and watched him walk away. "Seth," she called to him.

At the sound of her voice, he turned back.

"I'm glad we're friends," she told him.

"Me, too."

She leaned on the porch rail, her gaze following him until he and Ripley disappeared around the corner.

A moment later, the door opened behind her.

"Was Seth here all this time?" Cara asked.

"Yeah. Rip looked thirsty, so I gave him some water, and Seth and I just talked for a while."

Cara bent down and picked up the empty bottle Seth had left on the step. "Clever dog, drinking out of a bottle."

"Seth was thirsty, too."

"I could go for a beer myself. Be right back." Cara turned toward the door. "Want another?"

"There aren't any more. Sorry. I took the last two. I'll replace them tomorrow."

"You mustn't have looked in the right place. I put a

six-pack in there myself last night when Joe was here, and we each had one. If you and Seth had one each, there should be two left." Cara went into the house but returned in minutes. "You're right, they're gone. Maybe Allie or Barney drank them. It's no big deal."

Cara sat next to Des on the step. "Seth's a super-nice guy."

"He really is. I was just telling him how glad I was that we're friends."

"You actually said that to him? 'I'm glad we're friends'?"

Des nodded. "Yeah, why wouldn't I?"

"Because it's pretty obvious that he likes you."

"I like him, too."

"Are you totally oblivious?"

Des stared blankly at her sister.

"Des, I think he'd like to be more than friends with you."

"No, he said he was glad we were friends, too."

It was Cara's turn to stare.

"Really, we're just friends and we like it that way."

"You mean you like it that way."

Des sighed and leaned over the railing and watched a small bird disappear into one of the box-woods below the porch. "He's not my type."

"What does that mean?"

"He's this big, tattooed giant who rides a motor-cycle and smokes cigars as long as my arm. We are exact opposites. I've never even been on a motorcycle and I hate the smell of cigars."

"So he's not your type because he represents a certain element of danger?"

Des ignored her. "And that's just what's on the surface. He's lived here all his life, he belongs here and he knows it. He's had the same friends since kindergarten."

"And those are negatives because . . . ?"

"He's used to a different kind of life. He's been involved in Hidden Falls forever. He's this big social guy, and I'm a . . ."

"You're a what?"

"I'm a loner. I didn't have friends from school because Allie and I always had a tutor. I lived most of my childhood on-stage, pretending to be someone I wasn't, and when I wasn't working, I'd lose myself in the pages of a book." Des took a deep breath. "I don't think Seth has ever had to wonder about who he was. I think he's always known."

"I would think that would be a good thing, Des. A guy who knows who he is, where he belongs, who values his friendships."

"I've never really belonged anywhere. I don't know what that would even feel like." Des had no idea where the words and the feelings came from, or how she found the nerve to express them, but she knew as she spoke that every word was true.

"But after your show was over, you went on to college, right? You must have made a place for yourself there."

"I roomed by myself because I didn't know how to act around other kids my age. I always felt like a stranger everywhere I went. I moved to Montana because the only friend I ever had—one of my 'sisters' on the show—lived there and I figured at least I'd know someone. But she has her own life, her husband and her kids." Her voice trailed off for a moment. "Seth, he's Mr. Popularity. People in Hidden Falls like him so much they elected him mayor, what, three times? I watched him at the last town council meeting. The room was packed and people were yelling and he just calmed them down and got everyone back to the agenda. I would have panicked and run out of the room. Seth'd be at home wherever he finds himself, and I don't know that I'm at home anywhere."

"You seem comfortable enough here with us."

"It's different. You're family."

Cara laughed. "We weren't until very recently."

"Barney could make anyone feel at home. And you . . . you're easy to be around. And I've always known how Allie is. No surprise there." She blew out a breath. "And Seth—he's the nicest guy I ever met, but he's fully entrenched here. He belongs here, and I won't be staying." She shook her head again. "Besides, he's just not my type."

"So if a guy who likes you enough to adopt a dog he didn't think he wanted isn't your type, who is?"

"Oh, you know, someone who's . . . well, maybe a little more sophisticated. More, I don't know, academic, maybe. I've always liked that buttoned-down look. Less . . . inked up. Not that that's a bad thing. It just isn't my thing. Doesn't mean he isn't a nice guy, or that he isn't right for someone else."

"I see." Her hand on the doorknob, Cara paused. "You can't always judge a person by their appearance, you know that, right?"

"I'm not judging."

"Really? Because it sounds to me that you are."

"I'm not. Seth is great, but we're too different."

"If you aren't judging, then you're making excuses. Either way, you lose out."

Before Des could protest, Cara had slipped inside and closed the door behind her.

CHAPTER THREE

Allie'd retreated to her room, citing a raging headache that was beginning to lead to a foul mood. After working in the hot kitchen all day, inhaling paint fumes, and using muscles that had been dormant for a while, she wanted to be alone with her phone—her lifeline to her daughter—and the bottle of vodka she'd picked up the day before.

She locked her bedroom door and went into the bathroom, where she opened the bottle and poured some of the clear liquid into the glass. She wished she'd had the presence of mind to have filled the glass with some of Barney's excellent lemonade before she left the kitchen, but there was no way she was going back down there now. Cara and Barney would probably be sitting around that table for the next two hours, talking and laughing, maybe playing a few hands of cards or a few rounds of Clue or Monopoly. Allie wrinkled her nose at the thought. The last thing she wanted to do right then was to try to match wits with her sisters and her aunt.

She pulled the comfy wing chair close enough to the window to see the woods behind the house, then took her phone from her pocket to reread the text conversation she'd had earlier with Nikki, who'd had a great shopping day with her grandmother Lee. They'd spent the entire day together, having lunch at a fancy place and shopping until they both nearly dropped. Allie was grateful that Clint's parents doted on Nikki, and that Nikki enjoyed spending time with them. But that her aging grandparents would be the ones taking her to the airport to fly to Scranton still gave Allie pause. So many things could happen to a girl traveling alone. There'd been so much in the news lately about human trafficking that if she thought about it too much, Allie'd go into a panic.

Allie took another sip and stared out the window, wondering what kind of grandmother Nora would have been, then laughed. Nora had been an absolute bust as a mother. Surely she'd have ignored Nikki as much as she'd ignored Allie once she'd realized Allie had no acting ability.

At least, that's what everyone said.

"Too bad," she'd heard a producer tell Nora. "That older girl of yours is a knockout, but she can't act her way out of a paper bag. The younger one's got all the talent, and she's cute enough. It's a shame you couldn't have combined them into one, Nora. You'd have had yourself a superstar."

But in Des, Nora did have a star. Des's TV show ran

for seven freaking years, from the time she was nine until she turned sixteen. At Nora's insistence, they'd given Allie the recurring part of one of the neighborhood girls, so she didn't have to be in every episode, and she rarely had more than one or two lines. She'd never understood why she was given so much ambition and so little talent, while her sister, who was in such demand, professed to hate the roles she had to play.

"Not funny, universe," Allie whispered. "Not funny at all."

Allie couldn't remember a time when she hadn't resented her younger sister for being a star, but even she had to admit that it wasn't as if Des'd asked to be blessed with so much talent. But that she had had been a bitter pill for Allie to swallow, made even more bitter by the fact that their mother sometimes seemed to forget she had two daughters.

That wasn't Des's fault, either.

For years, Allie'd believed that Des protested too much, that she was just saying she hated the show because it got her more attention from Nora. It was only since Allie and Des had been together in Hidden Falls that Allie began to consider that maybe Des hadn't been lying. Maybe she really hadn't wanted to do the show, that she did it only because Nora made her do it, that she hated all the attention. If Des'd really enjoyed the spotlight, would she have retreated to that tiny Montana village to rescue dogs, living so quiet a life that Allie would bet that most of the people in Cross Creek didn't know Des was a former child phenomenon? Wouldn't she have stayed in L.A., auditioned for roles she'd undoubtedly have gotten, and continued to be a star?

And yet that underlying sense of resentment lingered. There were times Allie regretted feeling the way she did, but it was so deeply ingrained in her she couldn't let it go. It was a part of her relationship with her sister, and all wrapped up with her relationship with their mother, and Allie couldn't seem to untangle it, couldn't even seem to talk about it. She'd tried, when she went to therapy right after she and Clint separated, but the therapist had told her she needed to face her sister and talk out their childhood issues, and Allie hadn't gone back.

Back when she was a child, her father had been her hero. He was the one who always took her side, the one who'd take her on a trip whenever Des's show was nominated for some award. Nora would crow about how talented her younger daughter was to the point where apparently even Fritz couldn't take it.

"Pack a bag, sugar," he'd tell Allie. "We're going on an adventure."

And they'd go to some fun place, just the two of them. Of course, those trips were fewer and further apart as she grew older and Fritz seemed to spend more and more time away from home. It was only recently that Allie discovered the reason for his long absences. He'd fallen in love with another woman, had another daughter. He'd betrayed not only Nora, but Allie and Des as well.

Yet as hard as Allie tried, she just couldn't conjure up the resentment for Cara that she felt her half sister deserved. Of course, their father's choices weren't Cara's fault any more than they were Allie's or Des's, but still, Allie hadn't expected to like Cara as much as she did. Cara was one of the most balanced people Allie had ever known. Even when Allie turned her bitch ray on Cara, it had seemed to miss its mark, and Cara laughed it off. But for Allie, the most startling thing about Cara was that she was willing to keep a secret even when it was obvious she didn't want to.

Like the morning Cara'd found Allie passed out in her bed after having had a few too many drinks the night before. Cara'd been *this close* to calling 911 when Allie finally came around. She'd made Cara promise not to tell anyone. It'd been very obvious to Allie that Cara had been genuinely worried about her, but she'd given a reluctant promise. She'd made it clear that she wouldn't hesitate to call an ambulance if it happened again, though, and Allie had no doubt Cara would be true to her word.

Allie resolved to be a little more careful, a little more conscious of how much she was drinking. The last thing she wanted was to have to explain herself to her sisters and her aunt. They'd never understand.

Several times she'd considered asking Cara to join her for a nightcap, though. God knew the woman had reason to tie one on. That jerk of an ex-husband had really done a number on her. Allie hoped Cara understood that she was much better off without him. He clearly didn't deserve her. She'd find someone better.

Actually, Cara had already found someone better. Allie didn't know Joe Domanski all that well, but it was clear that he was ten times the man stupid cheating Drew was. Joe'd never cheat on Cara, Allie just knew it.

Allie drank a silent toast to Cara. And another to Joe. And a third to Cara and Joe.

She checked her messages again, hoping to hear from Nikki, but there was no update on the shopping expedition. She pulled the blanket up to her chin, drained the glass, and closed her eyes.

"Des, do you have a minute?" Cara stood in Des's doorway, her hands behind her back.

"Sure." Des closed the book she'd been reading and gestured for Cara to come in. "What's up?"

Cara sat on the edge of the bed, clearly struggling to get the words out.

"Okay, spill it," Des told her.

"Ah, well." Cara cleared her throat.

"Cara, what's wrong?" Des sat next to her. It wasn't like Cara to be evasive. "Is everything okay? Are you okay?"

"I'm fine, it's just that . . ." Cara blew out an anxious breath. "I don't know how to say this, Des . . ."

"Then just say it."

"I think Dad was fooling around with someone other than your mother."

"Cara, that's been established. It's why you're here."

"No, I mean before my mother. Before Dad and your mom were even married, I mean before they left for California, *right* before they left, Dad was involved with another woman."

"What? No. That was the time they really were in love. Things may have fallen apart later, but back then, they were solid."

"Maybe not so solid as you think." Cara held up a box she'd hidden behind her back. "I found this upstairs in the carriage house, hidden in one of the window seat cushions. I've gone around and around with myself, trying to decide whether or not to share this with you."

She opened the box and handed Des an envelope.

Des removed a packet of papers from the envelope and looked up at Cara, who said, "Go on. Read the first letter."

A puzzled look on her face, Des unfolded the single sheet of paper and read it aloud:

J. ~

It's really hard for me to write this letter. I don't know how else to say it, so I'll just say that I'm leaving for California on Tuesday morning with Nora. I know you will hate me now and that is the worst thing about this. I know you will think I lied to you, but every word was true. You are the best girl I ever knew. I'm sorry I can't stay and be with you.

F.

"I don't understand . . ." Des whispered.

"Read the other one," Cara said.

Des unfolded the second sheet of paper and read:

F. ~

I'm sending back your letter. I don't ever want to see you or hear from you again. Not that I would anyway, since you're leaving Hidden Falls with her. You're just a liar and a cheat and I will always hate you for what you've done to me. I never should have believed you when you said you and she were just friends. It was just another lie, like "You're the only girl for me." I should have listened to my sister.

J.

"Who is J?" Des asked after she'd read the letters several more times.

"I have no clue. Maybe Barney knows."

"How long have you had these?" Des held up the letters.

"A month or so," Cara admitted. "I wasn't sure how to tell you, or when, but I couldn't keep it from you any longer."

Des nodded. She'd have done the same thing if she'd been Cara. She'd have sat on the truth for as long as she could, but eventually, she'd share what she'd discovered.

"What else is in the box?"

"Gil Wheeler's obituary from several local papers."

"So we need to talk to Barney." Des folded the letters and returned them to the envelope. "I'm assuming you don't want these back?"

Cara shook her head. "You should have them."

"Did you tell Allie?"

"No. I wanted to share them with you first." She handed Des the box. "You might as well keep it all together the way I found it."

Des stood and opened the door. "Thanks," she said, hoping Cara would understand she needed a few minutes alone.

"Des, I'm sorry." Cara gave Des a quick hug before leaving, closing the door behind her.

Des sat back on the bed and reread both letters.

So, Dad, you scoundrel, you had another girl—a girl you claimed to care for more than you cared for Mom—even as you and Mom were getting ready to run off to the West Coast together? Are you kidding me?

The truth burned at Des like a hot poker. She'd understood that over the years, her parents had grown apart, but in her heart she'd believed that back in their early days together, they had been deeply in love.

And now here, in Fritz's own words, was proof that he'd lied to Nora, cheated on her, right from the very beginning.

Who was J? Des wondered. Had she gotten over him and fallen for someone else, married and lived happily ever after? Was she still in Hidden Falls? Was she someone Des passed on the street?

There was only one way to find out.

Barney looked as if she were about to fan herself with the sheaf of papers in her hand. "Oh my."

"You know who she is?" Des sat on the stool in front of the sofa in the sitting room where Barney'd been reading.

"Well, as I've told you, your father was quite the ladies' man. There wasn't a girl in Hidden Falls he didn't date at some point. I'm sure there was someone whose name began with J. Probably more than a few someones."

Des watched Barney tap her fingers on the arm of the love seat. "Jane Stevens, Joan Walsh, Joanne Whitney, Jill Nathan. That's four right there and that's just off the top of my head. Oh, and Jenny Nathan, Jill's sister. JoBeth Watson." Barney sighed. "At one time or another, Fritz probably went out with every one of them, and others besides."

"But this is someone he would have been seeing at the same time he was seeing Nora." Des pointed out the obvious. "Like, even as he was planning on leaving for California with Nora."

Barney nodded. "I get that. But if he was seeing someone else, he never shared that with me."

"Don't you think it's strange that Dad chose to keep these letters when he could so easily have destroyed them? I mean, he was leaving town, turning his back on Hidden Falls and J, whoever she might have been. Why bother to keep the letters if only to hide them?"

"I have no idea, but J must have been important to him. Not important enough to break up with Nora and stay in Hidden Falls, but important enough that he chose to hold on to what may have been his last contact with her." Barney paused. "Of course, we have no way of knowing if in fact this was the last contact with her. For all we knew . . ."

"I thought of that, too. He could have been seeing her while he was married to Mom and Susa."

"That brother of mine." Barney shook her head slowly.

"There were copies of newspaper clippings about Gil's death in with the letters." Gil Wheeler, the love of Barney's life, the man she would have married, had fallen from the rocks above the falls, ending Barney's dream of happily ever after. What might her aunt's life have been like had he not died that day?

"May I see them?"

"Of course." Des handed over the box and watched Barney's face as she opened it and removed the faded news clippings.

"Funny, but there must have been at least a dozen news articles about Gil and his death and the police investigation, but I don't think I read any of them. I just couldn't bear to see any of it. I suppose I thought if I read about it in the newspaper, it meant it was really true." Barney studied one article, then a second. "Then again, I recall so little of that time after he died. It had been such a shock." She smiled wryly. "Sometimes I still feel blindsided by his loss."

When she finished reading, she refolded each

clipping carefully, then tucked them back into the box. She closed it softly and handed it to Des.

"Oh, I thought you might want to keep them."

"Honey, I don't need a bunch of old newspaper stories to remind me what happened to Gil." She patted her chest. "I know the story by heart. There's not a day that goes by that I don't think about it."

Des bit her tongue. She'd almost said aloud what she'd been thinking. Did anyone really know what happened that day, other than Fritz and Pete, who'd been with Gil at the falls? Of the three, only Pete was still alive. Des sensed there'd been more to the story than what the newspapers had reported: that Gil had been sitting too close to the edge of the rock, that he'd misjudged how close when he stood up, lost his footing, and fell. It seemed odd to her that someone who'd surely spent a lot of time at the falls over the years wouldn't have had a better sense of where he was. After all, he'd grown up across the street from the Hudsons and had known Barney all his life. Maybe it was the fact that her father hadn't given a statement, or that he'd left Hidden Falls within days of Gil's death, not even staying long enough to comfort his sister, that had made Des wonder if there wasn't more to the story.

"When did Cara find these?" Barney asked.

"She said about a month ago. She's been keeping this to herself because she didn't know how we'd feel about Dad being involved with someone else back then. The story we always believed was that Dad and Mom were so crazy in love they left Hidden Falls to seek their fortune in Hollywood together. And then there's this." Des held up the letters. "This doesn't fit the narrative we've been told, what we've always believed about our parents. Honestly, I don't know how I feel about Dad after finding out that he was cheating on my mother, even back then."

"That was very sweet of Cara to want to protect your feelings, to preserve your memories."

"It was. But she did the right thing." Des shook her head. "He really was a stinker, wasn't he?"

"You can do better than stinker, honey," Barney told her.

"I'm doing my best not to be crude. I wish I knew who this J woman was." Des tapped her fingers on the lid of the box. "You're sure no one stands out from that time?"

Barney shook her head.

"Would you tell me if you knew?"

"Of course." Barney thought for a moment, then asked, "Does it really matter who she was?"

Des shrugged. "In a way, no. But I guess knowing might help it make more sense to me. Was she an incredible beauty? A brilliant wit? What about her made her 'the best girl' he ever knew?"

"Not to be cavalier, but maybe she really wasn't all that special to him. Remember, your father was a playboy. It wouldn't surprise me if he'd used that line on more than one girl. Not to paint an unsavory picture of your father, but he really did like the girls, Des."

"I guess without knowing who J was, we'll never

know for sure. And I keep going back to the fact that he kept the letters." Des paused to reflect. "Maybe he hid them so he could reread them whenever he came home."

"Does Allie know?"

"No. I wanted to talk to you first, to see if you knew anything about this before I told Allie."

"I would tell you if I knew, Des."

"I know. I appreciate that. I wish I could say it doesn't bother me, but it does. Theirs was supposed to be this great love affair. I guess for Dad exclusivity wasn't necessarily implied." Leaving the box on the floor next to the stool, Des rose. "I think I'll take Buttons for a walk."

She'd thought to keep moving until the burning in her chest subsided, but even after walking the entire perimeter of Hidden Falls, Des still ached. She paused at the entrance to the park, then followed the path to one of the benches. After tying the dog's leash to the back of the bench, she sat, shoulders slumped, with her head resting against the wooden back.

She'd forgiven her father's "marriage" to Cara's mother—in whatever form that had taken—because she'd understood the marriage between her parents had fizzled out before Fritz met Susa. At least, that was the story she told herself. She'd forgiven her father wanting to marry Susa because it was obvious he'd loved her deeply.

That secretly he'd been fooling around with an-other girl before he'd left Hidden Falls—back when the fairy tale was supposed to have been true—hadn't been part of the legend.

Fritz's declaration, *"You are the best girl I ever knew. I'm sorry I can't stay and be with you,"* wasn't part of her parents' love story.

Nor was J's response: *"I never should have believed you when you said you and she were just friends. It was just another lie, like 'You're the only girl for me.'"*

How long had J carried a torch for the man who'd claimed he'd cared but left her anyway for someone else? Someone he'd said was "just a friend." Des couldn't help but feel sorry for J.

The mysterious J was right about one thing: Fritz was a liar and a cheat.

"Hey, is everything all right?" The deep voice seemed to come out of nowhere. Des raised her head just as Seth and Ripley were approaching the bench.

"Is this seat taken?"

Des forced a smile. "It's all yours."

Seth sat next to Des, who was unhooking Buttons so the dogs could romp.

"I was asking if you're okay."

"Sure." She tried to nod convincingly. "Why?"

"You looked so sad when I was coming up the path. A million-miles-away kind of sad."

"Oh. Well, yeah. Maybe I am." She wasn't even able to convince herself.

"Anything I can do?"

Des shook her head. "Nothing anyone can do at

this point, I guess. I just wish . . ." She let out an exasperated breath.

"You wish what?" He sat leaning forward, his arms on his thighs, his hands clasped between his knees, his eyes on her.

"I wish my father was alive." She watched Buttons follow Ripley across the grass.

"Oh, hey, I understand. I mean, him dying without you having the chance to say good-bye, not being able to tell him how much he meant to you . . ."

"That isn't it." She laughed ruefully. "That's the furthest thing from my mind right now."

Des told him about the letters, about the woman who'd only identified herself as J, who'd had something going on with Fritz at the same time he was getting ready to leave town with Nora.

When Seth opened his mouth to speak, Des jumped on him. "And don't say something like 'Boys will be boys,' okay? Because that doesn't ever excuse anything as far as I'm concerned."

"I was only going to say I'm sorry. I can see how upset you are. I'm just trying to understand why."

"Why am I upset? Are you kidding me?" Des stood, her eyes still on him. "My parents had a lousy marriage by the time it was over, but back in the beginning, back when they left Hidden Falls together, they were supposed to have had this great love for each other. That was supposed to have been real. Now I don't know what to think."

Seth reached out and took her hand, gently easing her back to the seat.

"Look, I didn't know your parents, and God knows I'm no one to give anyone advice where anyone's family's concerned. And don't take this the wrong way, but that all—whatever was going on—was between them. It had nothing to do with you back then. And it has nothing to do with you now."

She stared at him blankly.

"What I mean is, that was something that happened long before you were born, right? If your parents married and then they had you and your sister, and you were a family and you were happy, what difference does any of the rest of it make?"

"That's just it. They weren't happy. He may have wanted Allie and me, but she never did. I knew that before I was ten years old. So there was no happy family. We were four people who lived under the same roof—sometimes—who pretended to be happy. My mother pretended to be a good and loving mother when there were cameras around, but otherwise, she barely gave us the time of day. My father spent as much time away as he could." She forced a wry smile. "You can ask Cara about that period of his life, since she apparently knows more about it than I do."

"If you know all that, then why are you so upset to find out he had another girlfriend when he was dating your mother?" Seth asked.

"Because that was when the fairy tale was supposed to be real." Her eyes welled with tears, and she forced a patience she didn't feel. "The only time it was true. If that wasn't true, then none of the rest of it makes sense to me. Why did they leave Hidden Falls together? Why did they even bother to get married?"

"Maybe because they'd convinced themselves and each other that the fairy tale *was* real." He put his arm around her, his hand warm and strong on her skin. "Maybe for them, at that time, for a while, it was."

"If it had been, he wouldn't have been messing around with someone else behind her back."

"Why beat yourself up looking for answers you'll probably never find? Why does it matter so much?"

"Wouldn't it bother you to find out that your father wasn't who you thought he was?"

"Oh, I know exactly who my father was. I've always known. No mystery there."

Something in the tone of his voice caused Des to bite back the retort she'd planned.

"Everyone thought Donald MacLeod was such a great man. The doctor who made house calls in the middle of the night. The one who'd never turn you away if you couldn't pay for his services."

"Your dad made house calls?"

"He did. Of course, many of those visits were to his mistress, but it was a great cover for him. And sometimes the women who couldn't pay him in cash paid him in other ways, if you get my drift." An embarrassed cloud seemed to pass over his face before he continued. "My dad was said to have been a great mayor, too. All for the common good and all that." He sucked in a breath, let it out slowly. "But he was a tyrant at home. Terrorized my mother and my sister, and me, too, until I grew up." He stared into space for a moment. "Was your father a tyrant, Des?"

"No."

"Did he try to make you be something you weren't?"

"No, my mother did that. He could have stopped her, though. At least he could have tried."

"Do you know for certain he didn't?"

"No."

"Look, no one ever really knows how things are between two people. What goes on between them."

"True."

"So would that be so much of a stretch that he could have been lying to this J woman? Maybe it didn't mean all that much to him. So maybe it shouldn't mean all that much to you."

"To quote *Game of Thrones*, you know nothing, Seth MacLeod." She unwrapped Buttons's leash and snapped her fingers. The dog stopped her play, then ran to Des, who hooked the leash to her harness.

As she walked away, Des heard him mutter something that sounded like, "Not the first time I've stuck my foot in it. Probably won't be the last."

Des walked swiftly, her annoyance with Seth fueling her stride, the dog struggling to keep up. When they reached the corner, she paused to catch her breath and waited until the traffic signal turned green before breaking into a jog. She rounded the corner onto Hudson Street, then slowed her pace so Buttons could catch up. Once they reached the house, she unsnapped the dog's collar so Buttons could run to the door. Des took her time, her mind a jumble of emotions.

"What's up with you?" Cara called from the porch as Des drew closer. "You look like you lost your best friend."

Des nodded. "I think I just might have."

She took the chair next to Cara's and repeated the conversation with Seth.

"Can you believe he actually took Dad's side in this?"

"You must have skipped that part." Cara kept rocking.

"I just told you . . ."

"You told me that Seth said whatever happened between your parents was between them and had nothing to do with you, then or now. What part of that is wrong?"

"It's all wrong. It isn't the point at all."

"Then what's the point?" Cara stopped rocking.

"The point is that all my life I believed in something that wasn't real."

"It could have been real. Seth might be right, you don't know." Cara leaned forward. "How did you leave it with him?"

"Badly. I was annoyed and stormed off." Des toed off her sneakers. She looked up at Cara. "Go on, say it."

"I think he thought he was helping you to put things into perspective."

"I'm sure he did."

"Why did you tell him about the letters?"

"Other than you, and occasionally Allie, he's the

only friend I have in Hidden Falls. We spent a lot of time together when I was helping him teach Ripley some manners back when he first took the dog. Seth's always been easy to talk to; he listens. And I guess I needed to talk it out with someone I thought was neutral."

"Des, Seth is far from neutral where you're concerned."

Des sighed deeply. "I shouldn't have pounced on him like that."

"Probably not," Cara agreed.

"Since the night I met him back in March, he's been nothing but kind to me." She covered her face with her hands and groaned. "I owe him an apology."

"That's up to you."

"Everything he said about Dad and Mom and this woman was right."

"So what do you plan on doing about it?"

"Eat crow, offer an apology, and hope he accepts it." Des stood and picked up her sneakers. "Because it would really suck if we couldn't still be friends."

CHAPTER FOUR

Des stood outside Cara's bedroom door, her hand raised to knock, when she heard Allie's door open.

"Powwow in Cara's room?" Allie asked.

"Just wanted to see if she was going to watch TV downstairs tonight," Des replied. She wasn't about to go over the whole Dad-Mom-J thing with Allie, at least not then. She was still a little unsettled, and there was no way to predict how Allie would react.

That conversation could wait for another day. After a second full day of painting, Des wanted something mindless. She wanted escape. She wanted TV and popcorn and maybe enough wine to keep her negative thoughts at bay for a while.

"What's on tonight?" Allie leaned against her own doorjamb just as Cara opened her door.

Des shrugged and said, "No idea. Cara? Any idea what's on TV tonight?"

"No, but I'm up for a movie." Cara stood in the

open doorway, her gaze meeting Des's, an unanswered question hanging between them.

"I'll pass." Allie disappeared into her room and closed the door.

"Des, about the letters," Cara whispered as they went toward the stairwell.

"I'm fine, but I don't feel like talking about it, so let it go, okay?"

"Oh. Of course. But if you want to—"

"I know where to find you. Thanks. Really." Des descended the steps before Cara. She heard music coming from Barney's sitting room. "Let's see what Barney's watching. Hope it's a comedy. I could use a good laugh."

It wasn't a comedy, but season two of *Outlander* qualified as escapism, so Des and Cara were all in.

"Hold up. I'll make popcorn."

"None for me," Barney told her. "I'm having wine."

"Even better." Cara sat on a low hassock. "Count me in."

"Why can't you have popcorn with wine?" Des asked.

"Ruins the ambience. When *Outlander* is over, we can put on something less intense. We can have popcorn then." Barney gestured for Des to sit, but Des headed for the hall.

"Popcorn goes perfectly with intensity. I'll be right back."

Ten minutes later, Des returned, three wineglasses in one hand and a bowl of popcorn in the other. They watched in silence as Jamie Fraser, the hero of the saga, appeared near dead after the battle of Culloden, and was bracing for his execution only to be saved at the last minute, while in the 1940s, the love of his life, Claire, gave birth to their child.

"Would you time-travel if you had the chance?" Des asked when the show—and the weeping— ended.

"I would," Barney replied enthusiastically. "I'd love to experience life in other time periods. As long as I could come back to the present for things like medical care."

"Not me. I'm happy in this century. I like things like air-conditioning, central heat, and indoor plumbing. How 'bout you?" Des turned to Cara.

"I would, as long as I could choose the period and what I wanted to see while I was there." Cara appeared to ponder the possibilities. "And yeah, I'd have to be able to come back whenever I wanted. So you could watch something unfolding—like the American Revolution—but come back before it got bloody or scary."

"So you'd want to observe but not participate," Des said.

"I'd participate until it got dangerous. Or bloody. Or scary."

"Wimp," Des teased.

"Totally," Cara readily agreed.

"I'll have some of that popcorn now." Barney held out her hand.

Cara held up the empty bowl. "We ate it all. I'll make more."

As she began to rise, Allie called from the hallway, "Cara, can I borrow your car? I want to go to the drugstore to pick up some nail polish."

"I have some you can borrow," Des told her.

"I feel like getting out for a few minutes, but thanks." Allie poked her head into the room and looked at Cara. "Would it be okay?"

"Sure. You know where the keys are."

"Why don't you walk? The drugstore is only a block and a half away," Des reminded her.

"I want to go to the one out on the highway, in the shopping center. They have a better selection."

Cara rose, the bowl in her hand. "I'll be back with popcorn in about ten minutes."

Allie followed Cara from the room, and Des could hear their voices without making out the words as her two sisters walked toward the back of the house.

"By the way," she said to Barney, "Heather Martin called me a while ago. She checked around and got the name and number of a guy who teaches at Althea College who's not only interested in local history, but also writes grant proposals for organizations that are looking for funding. His name's Greg Weller." She got up and sat opposite Barney to face her. "Heather said he's been working with the historical society in Carleton, which she said is about thirty miles from here."

When Barney nodded, Des continued. "He's the one who helped their symphony orchestra get funding and organized their efforts to have Carleton's first dwelling obtain historic designation. Maybe he'll have some thoughts about applying for grants for the theater. It would help big-time if we could get an influx of cash, however much it might be."

"Well, don't start spending it yet, kiddo. Grants take time. There's endless paperwork." Barney rolled her eyes. "Years ago, when we were thinking about buying the old Stockton mansion to use as our town hall, we applied for several grants."

"How'd that work out?"

Barney snorted. "The house sold before we could even get our paperwork together. It's time-consuming, so keep that in mind."

Des couldn't hide her disappointment. "I was hoping it worked more like applying for a loan."

"Not quite."

"I guess the grant person, Greg Weller, will tell me the same thing when he calls back. If he calls back."

"Well, the money hasn't run out yet, so don't be discouraged. And the ideas you have for raising funds are good ones, though none of them will bring in tons of cash. But I think you'll find you can count on people in the community becoming more interested in the theater and more willing to support it the more they hear about it. Publicity is a good thing, Des. Get people behind your project, and I think you'll find things will begin to fall into place. I've already got more than a dozen folks digging around in their attics for old photos."

"I hope you're right." Des picked up the wine bottle and poured a small amount into her glass. "Dad's will didn't stipulate what would happen if we weren't able to complete the renovations with the money he left for the project."

"Oh, in that case, I suppose you'll have to stay in Hidden Falls until you can afford to finish the job." Barney grinned. The thought of her nieces on an indefinite stay obviously made her happy, and Des said so.

"Of course it would make me happy." Barney drained her glass of the remaining wine. "I never realized I was lonely until the three of you showed up, and then I wasn't. You've made an enormous difference in my life." The grin had faded and she became serious. "As harebrained as my brother's idea was, making you three come live here, I have to say I'd plant a big kiss on his cheek to thank him if he were alive." Barney rose and put her hand out for Des's empty glass. "Best thing that's happened to me in years. I never had children, as you know, so having the three of you is a gift."

"So for you, Dad's will had an unintentional silver lining." Des pondered Barney's admission of loneliness. It reinforced her growing suspicion that by spending so much time in the past, Barney'd denied herself a future. How, Des wondered, do we help her move forward?

"Unintentional?" Barney scoffed. "There was nothing random about any of this. I think he knew exactly what he was doing, bringing you all to me the way he did."

"What are you saying, that you think Dad did all this because he thought you were lonely?"

"That was just a small part of it. The last time I saw him, I admitted the thought of living the rest of my life alone . . . well. That was beginning to weigh on me a bit. But he knew as well that you and Allie were, well, let's say estranged, and he knew that Cara was alone. I think he wanted us all to be a family, Des. The theater was just the vehicle. Something to think about, dear. Now this little girl should take her last walk of the night. Come on, Buttons. Let's take a stroll around the backyard."

Buttons hopped off the love seat and followed Barney out of the room, leaving Des alone to wonder if Barney might be on to something.

Barney's words reminded Des of that other Fritz, the one who'd been thoughtful and caring. The one who paid attention when you talked, who asked you what you thought or what you wanted. The one you always believed knew you. That Fritz wouldn't be so easily dismissed.

Then again, the Fritz who left Hidden Falls with Nora, leaving behind an apparently brokenhearted J, only served to reinforce what she'd long since come to believe. Love didn't last, and in the long run, wasn't worth the pain. Nothing in Des's personal experience had ever shown her differently.

Which was why she was adamant that she and Seth would never be more than good friends. She liked him way too much to ever fall in love with him and risk the type of heartbreak that always seemed to follow.

Allie sat in the parking lot, engine running, the lights off, and waited until the pickup made a wide U-turn and headed for the highway. She'd parked far enough away that the driver wasn't likely to have seen her, but she hadn't wanted to risk it, hadn't wanted to have to make excuses if she ran into him inside the store. Not that she was doing anything he hadn't done, and it certainly wasn't against the law for a woman well over twenty-one to walk into a state liquor store and make a purchase. But still, she'd have to speak to him, and that was the last thing she wanted to do.

Ben Haldeman just seemed to be everywhere these days.

She watched the taillights disappear onto the highway before getting out of the car. She walked across the lot and pulled hard to open the door, which she remembered from previous visits weighed a ton.

She knew exactly what she wanted and where to find it.

"Mrs. Monroe." The young clerk nodded to her as she passed the counter and she flashed her best smile in return as she headed toward the third aisle.

She selected one bottle, hesitated for a moment, then added a second before heading for the counter.

"I see you found what you were looking for." Kevin, the clerk, couldn't have been more than twenty-five and he never made eye contact for more than a second.

"I did. Thank you." Allie paid in cash, then with one more smile, left the store.

Once in the car, she was tempted to open one of the bottles, but she knew better than to take a drink and drive back to town. With her luck, that pesky chief of police would be the first person she passed, and he'd pull her over just for the hell of it. The fact that she'd witnessed him coming out of that same liquor store wouldn't matter to him.

She drove a little farther up the road to a bar, where she picked up a six-pack to replace the two bottles she'd taken earlier in the week. Pennsylvania's laws regarding where you could buy or sell wines and liquors as opposed to beer, in her opinion, were inconvenient and made no sense at all. If you wanted wine or hard liquor, you had to go to a state-owned store that was operated by the state's Liquor Control Board. But if you wanted more than a six-pack of beer—which you could buy in a bar—you had to go to a beer distributor. She had read in the *Scranton Times-Tribune* that the law, which had been established following the fall of Prohibition, had been changed to permit wine and beer sales in certain approved supermarkets beginning in 2017, but none of the local markets were on the list.

Once back at the house, she stuck the two bottles of vodka, still in their bags, into her carryall, which she'd selected because it was large enough to hold her purchases. Not that it was a crime to drink. She just didn't want to share—or explain. She just wanted to go back into the house and retreat to her room, where she could enjoy a cocktail or two in peace and forget about the things in her life that she couldn't change.

Like her divorce, or the fact that her ex had talked her into letting Nikki go to a private school conveniently located near his house. Which just happened to be most inconveniently located far enough from hers that Nikki ended up staying with her father during the week and with Allie on the weekends, an arrangement that had effectively flipped the custody agreement upside down.

Allie hadn't wanted the divorce from Clint. She'd always thought he was the only man for her and that she'd love him till death. Their marriage wasn't perfect, but whose was? It wasn't until after he'd asked for the divorce that she acknowledged all the things that had been wrong between them. Now, when she looked back at their marriage, she saw all the cracks that neither she nor Clint had tried to fill. The best thing to come from those fifteen years was their daughter. Nikki was the bright spot in Allie's life, the only person she'd give her life for without hesitation or regret.

The divorce had come with an unforeseen pitfall. Clint had given her his share of the equity in the house they'd shared—the house she'd found and decorated and loved—but the maintenance and taxes, combined with her half of Nikki's hefty tuition, stretched her assistant director's salary to the limit. With Nikki living with Clint almost all the time now, he'd stopped paying child support. And when the TV show she'd been working on was canceled,

Allie'd had to face the fact that she'd have to sell her home. She'd put it on the market shortly before she learned of her father's death and the strange terms of his will, but then took it off, as her potential inheritance allowed her to rent the house rather than sell it. Eventually, she'd be able to move closer to Nikki's school, which would mean Clint would have to honor the original custody agreement. Only the thought of having her daughter with her during the week—every week—kept Allie in Hidden Falls. She knew if she could stick it out until the theater renovation was completed, life would be good again.

That she was lonely as hell for her daughter, well, that was the price to pay for her temporary move to Hidden Falls. The long-run payoff would be worth it.

If she needed a little help getting from here to there, who could blame her?

She'd seen lights on in the sitting room and was pretty sure the others were still in there. She went into the house as quietly as she could and hung the key on its hook next to the back door. She opened the refrigerator and placed two bottles of beer behind the carton of orange juice. She thought about taking the other four to her room, but even on her worst night, Allie would put her foot down at drinking warm beer. She put the others on the second-to-the-last shelf in the back, where they easily could have been overlooked. She could hear the others watching television in the sitting room, so she poked her head through the open doorway to let Cara know her car had been returned safe and sound.

Des was on the floor on a large cushion, a sleeping Buttons on her lap, the dog's four legs in the air.

"You realize that dog is snoring." Allie couldn't resist pointing out the obvious.

Des nodded. "That's because she's comfy and happy and feels safe. If she could purr, she would."

"If you say so."

"Every dog should be this lucky. They all deserve a home like this. It's why rescue is so important."

"Thank you for the PSA. See you all in the morning."

"Hey, come watch a movie with us," Cara called after her.

"I'll pass," Allie said.

"Wait, let's see the nail polish." Cara held her hand out. "What color did you get?"

"Oh. I didn't find anything I really wanted. Just feeling picky tonight, I guess. Thanks for loaning me your car, though."

"You're always welcome to use it. You know that." Cara held the remote control in her hand. "You sure you don't want to join us? We just discovered Barney's never seen *The Princess Bride*. Hard to imagine, right?"

"Inconceivable!" Des quoted one of the more well-known lines from the movie.

"Not my favorite, but you all enjoy." Allie turned to leave the room.

"Are you okay?" Cara asked.

"Just a headache. I'm going to go up and lie down."

"Let me know if you need anything." Cara's eyes

shifted from Allie's face to the large bag, as if she suspected what was inside.

Allie sensed Cara knew there'd been no stop at the drugstore.

"I hope you feel better, dear." Barney's face showed some concern. "This is the third headache you've had in as many weeks. Are you sure you wouldn't like me to make an appointment for you with Dr. MacLeod?"

"No, no. That's not necessary. I've always been prone to headaches. It'll pass, but thanks." Allie walked to the kitchen with a sigh of relief. She needed ice and a glass. "Any lemonade left?" she called back to the sitting room.

"Should be some in the door," Cara replied.

Allie filled a large glass with ice, then poured in as much lemonade as she could without causing an overflow. She took a sip or two, then headed for the steps and began her climb up the winding stairwell.

"Dr. MacLeod?" Allie heard Des ask. "Any relation to Seth?"

"His sister," Barney replied.

There'd been more conversation, but Allie was too far up the steps to understand what was being said. Once inside her room, she locked the door and went into her bathroom for the glass she kept there. She scooped a few ice cubes into her glass, then poured in some of the lemonade. Back in her bedroom, she sat in the chair next to the window and removed the bottles from her bag. One she slipped under the chair, the other she opened. She raised the window sash and topped off the lemonade with the vodka, then set the bottle on the table next to her.

"One for now, one for later," she whispered before taking a long drink.

From the window, Allie could see the path that led through the woods to the falls.

"The hidden falls of Hidden Falls," she murmured.

She took a sip and thought about the falls into which Barney's fiancé had fallen and where he'd drowned years ago.

At least Barney and Gil had never had the pain of growing apart, of watching their relationship shrivel and die. They'd never argued over the kids or money or who spent too many hours at the office or worked on weekends. Or who they were texting in the middle of the night.

Allie heard Cara's bedroom door close, and moments later she heard Barney and Des chatting at the end of the hall, then the sound of floorboards squeaking, and two more doors closing. The house fell silent except for the occasional tap of the pipes and the whoosh of breeze through the trees.

Allie pulled the chair closer to the window, opened it a little wider to bring in more of the breeze, then poured herself another drink. She watched the leaves on the trees sashay from side to side as the wind picked up. When she finished the drink, she pulled the throw from the back of the chair, wrapped it around her, and fell into a deep sleep. She awoke the next morning, surprised to find the throw, the chair, and the window ledge soaked from the rain that had blown in through the open window. She stood unsteadily, her head pounding, wet clothes clinging to her body, her hair a long, pale, damp mess.

"Ugh." She grabbed her phone in one hand and held her aching head in the other and shuffled into the bathroom. She peeled off her wet things and, still holding her head with one hand, got into the shower hoping to melt off the chill and chase away the hangover.

After a day of rain, the temperature took a dive toward cool, so before heading off to the theater in the morning, Des slipped on a favorite sweater over black pants. Normally she'd wear a sweatshirt and jeans, or something equally casual, but this morning, she had a ten o'clock appointment with Greg Weller, and she wanted to show a little bit of polish. After all, the man was not only a professor at the local college, but one who might be able to help obtain some funding for the theater. She knew there was truth to the old adage you only get one chance to make a first impression, and she wanted to make a good one. She even swiped on mascara and lip gloss before leaving the house.

"My, don't we look spiffy this morning." Allie had stood back and assessed her sister's appearance. "Wherever you're going, it must be important. You're not wearing denim in any form. And I find the sight of you in something other than one of your tacky T-shirts curiously disturbing." She ran her hand up Des's arm. "I didn't know you even owned any cashmere." Allie glanced down at Des's feet. "And you're wearing real shoes. Oh, let me guess. Those ratty old tennis sneakers of yours finally fell apart."

"I'm wearing this sweater because all my T-shirts with tacky sayings on them are in the wash. And I'm saving my ratty sneakers for our next night out at the Bullfrog."

"Well, if you can't wear the latest in country chic to the only bar in town, where can you wear it? So where are you going?"

"I'm meeting someone at the theater to discuss the possibility of having him work with us to obtain a grant." Des paused with her hand on the back door. "Where are we with the Art Department from the college?"

"I'm waiting for Dr. Lindquist to call me back." Allie looked at her phone and scrolled through her calls. "Oh wait. She called last night." Allie frowned. "Where was I?" Then a shrug. "Whatever. I'll call her this morning."

Des walked to the theater, dodging puddles from last night's storm. As she crossed the street, she noticed a man standing in front of the building, looking up at the marquee, which was still covered with boards. He turned when she drew closer.

"Des Hudson?" he asked tentatively.

Des nodded.

"Greg Weller." He approached with his hand

extended to her and stepped out from under the marquee into the sunlight.

He was a half foot taller than Des, with straight light brown hair, dark brown eyes, a slender build, and a very straightforward gaze. He pinned Des with those dark eyes and seemed to look right through her.

Cute.

"It's good of you to come." She shook his hand and smiled at the directness of his gaze. He was boyishly good-looking and casually but well dressed in khaki slacks and a light tweed jacket over a collarless shirt.

"Are you kidding? I've been wanting to get inside this old place for the longest time. I've heard stories about the Sugarhouse for as long as I've been at Althea."

"How long has that been?"

"I went to undergrad and grad school there, so we're talking fifteen years."

Fifteen years would make him just about her age.

"Aren't you young to have a doctorate?"

"Nah. Actually, I was a late bloomer. Didn't decide to get a master's until it occurred to me that I wouldn't get anywhere without one. Then it seemed foolish not to go all the way with it. Once you decide that your future lies in academia, there's only one path to get ahead, and that's with a doctorate. But hey, we're not here to talk about me." His attention shifted from Des to the theater. "Can we go inside and take a look?"

"Of course." Des opened the main door.

"This door is incredible." Greg stood back and

studied the turquoise door, where the tragedy and comedy masks rendered in stained glass took up the top fifth of the door. "Wow. That . . . wow. That's so unexpected. That window is beautiful."

"I know. We were surprised to find it, too."

"Any idea who made it?"

Des shook her head. "None."

"I've never seen anything like it." Greg was still staring at the glass.

"Neither had we." She walked through into the unlit theater, found the wall switches, and turned on the overhead lights.

"I don't know where to look first." Greg turned a very slow 360 degrees. When he finished, he did it again, as mesmerized the second time as he'd been the first. "The painting here in the lobby . . ." He was at a loss for words as he gazed at the hand-painted vines entwined with climbing roses that trailed around the arched doorways.

"I had the same reaction. We all did." Des stood in the center of the wide lobby and watched as he tried to take it all in.

"The colors are still so vivid. Any idea who the artist might have been?"

"No clue. There might be a name with the original plans for the building, but we haven't located them." Des paused to reflect. "Actually, we haven't really looked."

"Do you know who built the theater?"

Des nodded. "My great-grandfather."

She gave him the short version of how the first

Reynolds Hudson had built the theater as a gift to the town and to the miners who'd made him rich working in his coal mines.

"Wow. That's quite a legacy. But I meant the architect."

"I'm sure we have that information. I'll look it up and get back to you."

"After you called, I thought I should do a little research on the theater. Your father popped up, of course. And you inherited the theater from him? It's been in your family since it was built?"

"Except for a brief period when it had been sold. My father bought it back." No sense in going into the whole story of how Fritz had lost interest, sold it, and then bought it back when the buyer ran out of money and threatened to level it. Or of how, when he knew he was dying, Fritz developed a sentimental attachment to it.

"I wonder if your father gave the buyer all the pertinent construction documents." Greg frowned. "You really should begin to look for those."

"Why would they be important?"

"Well, if we're going to write a grant proposal for funds intended to renovate the building, it would make our case stronger if we could name the architect, as well as the artist who painted all the decorative elements. Famous architects and artists always make a project more valuable to the agencies who offer grants. If you're lucky, it'll turn out to be someone well known."

"Because that would add value to the building," she said thoughtfully.

"Exactly. It makes it easier to get the attention of whichever foundation you're targeting, because they're going to want to be part of any restoration that has historic significance. There are only so many dollars to be given out, and there's much competition for them. So the more historically important buildings—or those with the most important components—will have a better chance to obtain those grants. For example, if it turned out those stained glass theater masks in the front door were created by Louis Tiffany, it would get the attention of a lot of folks."

"I see your point." She looked up at the ceiling. "And if we were able to determine that an artist of note did all the painting . . ."

"Right. And if the architect turns out to be someone well respected, you'd be more likely to get what you need." Greg directed his gaze toward the ceiling. "Could I go up and take a look?"

"Of course."

Des watched as Greg easily climbed to the top platform, which had been erected the previous evening. He was more athletic than he appeared, and she wondered what his arms might look like under that jacket.

"Have you been up here?" he called down to her.

"Uh-uh."

"Oh, then you should see how—"

"Uh, no. No thank you."

"Seriously?" He leaned over the side of the railing and looked down.

Des's stomach flipped just imagining what the view from there must look like.

"As a heart attack." She looked away. "Besides, the painting's pretty much the same up there as down here. Except for the damaged areas."

"Different perspective, but okay." He walked the length of the platform, checked out the areas where moisture had caused flaking, then climbed down as quickly as he'd ascended. "This place is fascinating. It would be a crime not to restore it."

He walked around the lobby, then pointed to the arched opening that led to the seats. "May I?"

"Of course." Des followed him through the doorway. "We haven't had the time to begin the renovations on the stage, but it's in the game plan."

"What do you need?" Greg walked toward the stage.

"We need new stage curtains, new lighting, a new screen. The stage itself could use refinishing, but I suppose it's not critical that the wood floor looks new. It looks shabby to me."

He walked around the orchestra pit and climbed the steps to the stage. "It looks well used, that's all. Unless you're planning on hand-sanding and refinishing it yourself, I'd leave that on the back burner until you're up and running."

"Good advice," was all she said, not wanting to point out that since her father's will hadn't required her to hang around until the theater was up and running, she probably wouldn't be in Hidden Falls by the time it was operational. The thought brought an unexpected feeling of hollowness to her stomach.

She showed him the balcony and the projection room, where he made no attempt to hide his interest in the tins containing film from an era gone by.

"I guess it's too much to hope the old projector's still around," he noted.

"It was here. A part was broken, so a friend took it home to see if he could figure out how to fix it."

From there, they went downstairs into the basement to see the office, and she shared with him the stack of original movie posters that had once been in the glass frames in the outer lobby and outside under the marquee.

"These are amazing." He flipped through them. "Just mind-blowing. Look at these. Some of my favorite classic films: *A Farewell to Arms. The Philadelphia Story.*" He paused for a moment at the third poster in the pile. "I don't know this one. *Walk of Fear.*" He glanced over at Des.

"My mother." She tapped the name that was printed in large letters at the top of the poster. "Honora Hudson. That was one of her biggest roles. Her favorite, actually."

Nora's last significant role, the last time any studio had put big money behind her since she'd missed so many rehearsals due to morning "headaches." It didn't take long for the director to figure out that her headaches were hangovers, but Des saw no reason to go into any of that with Greg.

"Let's go back up and take another look at the lobby," she suggested.

They left the office, leaving the posters rolled out on the desk, and headed toward the steps.

"I guess the first thing I should ask is, do you think there's a chance we could be successful in obtaining a grant?" Des turned off the balcony lights. "And if so, would you be willing to work with us?"

"I'd love to work with you. And I think you could get some grant money. I think the history alone would make the theater of interest to several foundations. Let me talk to some people and see what their thoughts might be. In the meantime, if I could get some photographs of the building, it would give me something to work on." His eyes raised skyward. "Pictures of the ceiling before the damage and after could be of use as well. We might use them to point out the urgency of obtaining funds."

"Well, we have some funds left in the account my dad left us, and we're hoping to have some insurance coverage. We think we're eventually going to need a grant, because there's a good chance we're going to run out of money before we finish. We were just about ready to start refurbishing the seats and replacing the carpets before the storm caused the damage."

"So you're looking for funds in the event you'll need them down the road."

"It wouldn't be a good idea to wait until we've run out of cash to start looking for a bailout."

"True enough. And of course, the process isn't a quick one. The paperwork alone will take time."

"Which brings us to the question of how much that time is going to cost us. What do you normally charge for a situation like this one?"

"I've never really had a situation like this one." He smiled. "And frankly, I'd consider it a privilege to work with you to put the Sugarhouse back into operation again."

"No, no, we don't expect you to not charge a fee. That wouldn't be right."

"Des, do you know what I do at Althea?"

"You're a history professor."

He nodded. "My focus is on American history. This year, I started teaching a class on the era when coal was king right here in the Appalachians. What you've told me about your family—your great-grandfather's commitment to his miners—is just the sort of material I like to include in my lectures. It makes the history real to know personal stories about the players. I'd like to learn more about your great-grandfather and the operation of his mines and his remarkable philanthropy for the course."

"I'd be happy to share whatever I know, but I think you should speak with my aunt. She knows much more than I do."

"I'd love to meet her." He glanced at his watch. "And I'd love to continue this conversation with you, but I'm going to have to get back to campus. They're having graduation rehearsal this afternoon, and I'd like to be there with my students."

"Of course. I appreciate the time you've spent with me. I'll walk you out." Des headed toward the front door, Greg walking alongside her.

"I can't believe this place has been boarded up for so long." He looked around as they walked. "You'll have to tell me the story of how it came into your hands. I know you said you inherited it from your father, but I sense there's more to the story than a simple inheritance."

They left the building, and Des turned to lock up.

"Hey, you're just the person I'm looking for," Allie called from the sidewalk.

"Come meet my sister," Des told Greg.

When they reached the sidewalk, Des turned to Allie. "Allie Monroe, this is Greg Weller. He's going to look into the possibility of getting a grant for the theater. Greg, my sister Allie."

"Great to meet you. Des just gave me a tour of this wonderful building of yours. You must be thrilled to be an owner of such a treasure."

"It's been a thrill a minute," Allie deadpanned.

Greg laughed. To Des he said, "I'll be in touch. I'd like to continue the conversation over dinner one night this week."

"Great. You have my number."

Greg turned to Allie. "Nice meeting you."

Allie and Des watched him walk the half block to his car.

"He's kinda hot, in a tweedy kind of way. Nice shoulders. Cute face. Great eyes. Nice . . . walk."

Allie nodded slowly. "And he wants to 'continue the conversation over dinner.'"

"To talk about the theater."

"Over dinner? Please." Allie leaned over and whispered in Des's ear, "I bet he thought you were kinda hot, too."

"Maybe. With any luck."

"Luck's got nothing to do with it. He had that look about him. Like he's really interested. You?"

Des recalled her words to Cara about Seth. "He's definitely my type."

Well, Greg did check all those boxes that Seth did not. He was certainly academic enough by anyone's standards, and she'd always liked that buttoned-down look. She felt a stab of disloyalty to the man she'd professed to be her friend. Then a second stab, this one of regret, as she remembered having walked off without even saying good-bye to him in the park.

"Is Joe here?" Allie was saying. "I thought he said he had some photos of the ceiling. I finally caught up with Dr. Lindquist from the college's Art Department, and she said she didn't have time right now to drive out, but if we had any photos she'd take a look at them and get back to us."

"Joe doesn't have photos, but I know who does. I'll take care of it."

Chapter Five

In the short time Des had been in the theater, the sun reappeared to dry up the dampness and raise the temperature dramatically, causing her to squint as she walked along the shoulder of the two-lane road. Headed toward Hidden Falls' farthest boundary, she chided herself with every step for not going home to change her clothes and grab her sunglasses before embarking on this trek, but she hadn't wanted to get sidetracked or talk herself out of making the trip. Besides, it gave her time to figure out exactly what she wanted to say. She'd never been one to trip over an apology when she knew she owed one, but at the same time, she hadn't often been in a situation where she felt she'd caused someone to feel . . .

What exactly did she think she'd caused Seth to feel?

She really wasn't sure. All she knew for certain

was that she'd done him, and possibly their friendship, harm, and for that alone she needed to make things right.

By the time she arrived at her destination, she was sweating from the long walk in the hot sun. She was relieved when she reached the end of a narrow dirt-and-gravel driveway and the mailbox confirmed she was in the right place. Ancient weeping willows lined the right side of the drive as she started up the lane to the old farmhouse that stood on the very edge of Hidden Falls.

The house itself exactly fit Des's image of a late-nineteenth-century farmhouse, with one tall roof peak in the center of the top floor, a wide porch that ran straight across the front, and shutters at each of the windows. Of course, her imaginary farmhouse was freshly painted, there were flowers in pots by the front door and on the steps, and the wicker furniture on the porch was arranged to serve as an outdoor living room. Roses grew around the porch and hollyhocks grew tall at both ends to frame it with color.

So not like the real farmhouse before her, where the paint was peeling, the porch sagged a little on one side, and there wasn't so much as a rocking chair to be seen. The shutters all needed new paint, and one hung slightly askew. Still, the bones were good, and with the right amount of paint, it could be lovely. Its saving grace came in the form of peonies planted side by side to surround the porch with color.

The front door opened, and Ripley flew out

to greet her. The dog was followed by Seth, who stopped on the top step and watched Des approach. His hands were in the pockets of his jeans, and even though his eyes were covered by dark glasses, she could feel him watching her walk down that long driveway. The dog raced around her in happy circles as if celebrating her arrival ("You're here! At my house!"), only stopping long enough for her to pat his head and tell him what a good boy he was for not jumping on her even though she could tell he desperately wanted to.

"I see you've been working with him," Des called out as she drew closer.

"Yeah, some." Seth came down the steps and slowly walked toward her. "I've been trying to remember everything you taught him. Taught us," he corrected himself.

"He's a smart dog. He's catching on."

"When it suits him."

"I think he's wondering where Buttons is," she said as the dog's circles grew smaller until he was sniffing wildly at her clothing.

They met up at the end of the brick walk that led from the bottom of the stairs to the edge of the drive.

"So what brings you all the way out here? On a hot afternoon? On foot?" He pointedly looked her over from head to toe. "Kinda warm for a sweater and long pants."

"It was cool when I got dressed, and at the time, I didn't know I'd be coming out here. I thought I'd pick up the copies of those photos you had for me."

"I could have dropped them off." She was unaccustomed to his slightly cool tone, and it made her just a little sad.

"I thought I'd save you the trouble."

"No trouble, but come on in. Your pictures are ready."

He gestured for her to go ahead of him, and she stepped around him to follow the path to the porch. At the bottom of the steps, he paused to whistle for Ripley, who'd taken off across the adjacent field. The dog raced back, dashed up the steps, and waited at the door for his master. Seth reached past Des to open the screened door.

She pushed open the inner wooden door and was greeted by a gush of cool air.

"Oh man, that feels good." She lifted her hair from the back of her neck and looked around for a window unit. As soon as she found it, she was going to stand in front of it and let the air blow on her until the sweat that ran down her chest under her sweater formed icicles.

"I heard we were in for a hot summer. I had to replace the heater, so I figured I might as well do the heating and cooling at the same time." Seth walked past her. "The photos are back here in the kitchen."

"Wait, you have central air?" She followed him, trying to catch up.

"Seemed to be the best solution. I hate those window things. They're noisy and inevitably turn the room they're in into an ice box. Then you walk out of that room and bam! The heat smacks you in the face." He started to go through a stack of papers on the kitchen table, then hesitated. "You've gotta be thirsty. What can I get you to drink?"

"Water. Water would be fine."

He poured her a glass from a fat round pitcher he took from the refrigerator and handed it to her. While his back was turned, she glanced around the large square room. The wallpaper, a badly faded yellow-and-green plaid, covered three walls above beadboard painted a darker shade of yellow. The old faux-brick linoleum floor was cracked in places, missing in a few others, and she could see what looked like hardwood underneath. The one overhead light was woefully inadequate for the size of the room. But the windows were large and faced the fields behind the farmhouse, letting in not only light but peaceful views. The porcelain farm sink, chipped here and there, stood on wooden legs and was flush into a corner. She was certain it was original. Wooden cabinets were painted the same faded yellow as the wallpaper.

Talk about a fixer-upper. The room was in total need of a redo, but there was something homey and comfortable about it that she liked.

"Not so fast," he cautioned her when she began to drink steadily. "You're going to throw up."

"And that would make this little visit even more awkward than it already is." She took one last sip, then sighed. "I know you could have dropped off the photos. But I owe you an apology, and that means I should come to you."

Seth leaned back against the wooden kitchen

table, his eyes no longer shielded by those dark shades that looked so menacing when they were outside, and he waited. His expression turned soft, his mouth set in not quite a smile.

"I'm sorry I acted like such a brat. I should have remembered that anything you said to me you were saying as a friend, but I realized that too late. I came here to apologize."

"Thank you. But maybe I did overstep the line a little. Said more than I should have."

"You said what you thought. Which you're entitled to do as my friend."

He nodded.

"And yes, now thank me for walking all the way out here in the sweltering heat to apologize."

"That, too."

"I really am sorry, Seth. Your friendship means a lot to me. I don't want to lose it."

"You never will, Des." He smiled, and she breathed a sigh of relief.

"Good." She smiled back at him, knowing their friendship was intact, then took another few sips of water.

"I appreciate the apology, but you didn't have to get dressed up for the occasion."

"Oh." She glanced down at her sweater and black pants, which now were dusty from the walk up the unpaved driveway. "I had a meeting at the theater and decided to come straight out here when I was finished."

"Aren't you dying in that . . ." He pointed to her sweater.

"I am, I'm not gonna lie."

"How 'bout I get you something a little lighter to put on? T-shirt, maybe."

"That'd be great, but I'm afraid one of your T-shirts would be down to about my ankles."

"Wait here. I think there's a . . . I'll be right back." He disappeared into the hall, and she heard his footsteps on the stairs and the creaking of floorboards overhead. A few moments later he returned, a blue polo shirt over his arm.

"Try this. It's clean. I couldn't find a pair of shorts, though." He handed her the shirt. "There's a powder room right back there." He pointed in the direction of the back door.

Des held it up. It was a woman's shirt, without doubt. She wondered whom it had belonged to, and why a man would offer another woman's shirt to—

Never mind. We're just friends. It doesn't matter who it belonged to, or why it's here. It's none of my business.

"Thanks. I'll be right back." She went into the bathroom and closed the door. The room itself was surprisingly well decorated. On one wall there was black wallpaper with white dots, and the other three walls were painted white. The fixtures were white, and an old mirror with a metal frame hung over the sink. The floor was black-and-white tile, the curtain at the lone window black and white checked. She suspected this was one of the first rooms to have gotten a makeover.

Des peeled off the sweater and sighed with pleasure as the cool air surrounded her. She stood almost motionless until goose bumps began to appear on her arms.

A black-and-white-striped washcloth and matching towel hung on a rack on the back of the door, and she used both before pulling the blue shirt over her head. The fact that it was two sizes too big and too long didn't matter. It was dry and it was cool, and she welcomed the change from the stifling cashmere.

"I feel like a new person," she announced as she came back into the kitchen, her sweater over her arm.

"Good." He frowned. "I thought maybe you and Amy were about the same size, but I guess not."

"It's fine, really." She heard herself ask, "Who's Amy?"

"My sister. Haven't you met her?"

Des shook her head. "Barney mentioned a Dr. MacLeod the other day."

"That would be Amy. She's the good MacLeod. The one my dad was proud of." The lines around his mouth seemed to deepen, and his eyes narrowed slightly. Someone who didn't know him might not have noticed.

"Because she followed in his footsteps and became a doctor, and you didn't, you think he wasn't proud of you? Even though you graduated from college with honors—oh, I already heard about that from Joe. He said you were the smartest of the three of you. Won all the math prizes at Althea." Des leaned back against the counter, a teasing smile on her face. "He said he was the best athlete, Ben had the best people skills—my sister would of course argue that—and you were the smartest."

"I did okay. And I'd challenge Joe Domanski to a shoot-out on the basketball court any day of the week. He just grew bigger earlier and faster than the rest of us. Made him a natural for football. He was fast, too."

"Joe also said that in high school you won the state science fair every year."

"We've digressed."

"All the same, I'm sorry your father had that attitude toward you. I know a lot of people who'd have been delighted to have a son like you."

"Thank you for saying that." They stood looking at each other for a moment, Des remembering the zip she'd felt when his bare skin had touched hers.

"Come on outside." Seth picked up his shades from the kitchen table where he'd tossed them and gestured toward the back door. On his way, he grabbed a baseball cap from a rack on the wall and pulled it onto his shaven head. "I want to show you something."

There were four outbuildings behind the house. One was clearly a barn, but it was anyone's guess what the others were used for.

"Here, walk around this way." He took her elbow and directed her around the side of a small, low building with windows close to the ground.

"Chickens?" she asked when she saw the fenced area behind the building.

"Yup."

They reached the edge of the fence and she looked through the wire to where twenty or so hens pecked at the grass. She was expecting all white chickens, but there were none. Seth's hens ranged from buff to black to speckled to red.

"You must get a mess of eggs every day from all those chickens."

"I supply a couple of restaurants."

"What's the overhead wire for?"

"It keeps the hawks out. And the owls. I had to reinforce it"—he reached overhead to show the double layer of chicken wire—"because an owl got into the henhouse one night and helped itself to a few of my chickens."

"How did it get in through the wire? And don't you close the door at night?"

"It ripped the wire next to the gate there and pulled the door right off with those big talons. I never heard of such a thing, but that's what it did. I went in the next morning and there was blood and feathers everywhere." He must have seen Des flinch. "Anyway, I doubled the amount of wire, top and sides, and got a new door, put a lock on it. Also put up a motion sensor." He pointed to the roof of the chicken house. "When there's movement around the perimeter or overhead, a light goes on and an alarm sounds in the house."

"Has the alarm ever gone off?"

Seth nodded. "I've chased off a few foxes and another owl." He took her arm again. "So the tour usually goes this way after the visit to the chicken coop."

He led her through knee-high weeds to the back of the barn, where a field had been plowed into neat rows as far as the woods at the back of the property. The ground was soft from the recent rain, so her shoes—a favorite pair of ballet flats—sank slightly with every step. She really wished she'd gone home to change.

"What are you growing?" She nodded in the direction of the field.

"A bit of everything." He pointed to a row of tall, thin, light green, wispy branches that stretched upward like bony arms. "Asparagus, which is seasonal, and the season has pretty much ended. That was here when I moved in, which is fortunate because it can take a few years to mature. Strawberries—the season is just starting to wind down now, but it was a good year. Mostly because I planted several varieties, early, midseason, and late."

He took her arm and steered her across the rows.

"Tomatoes—more varieties than I care to admit to. I got a little carried away when it came time to ordering plants and I didn't keep careful enough records of what I ordered. I'm hoping they all do well this year. There are several heirloom varieties there that have become very popular, so my restaurant friends are psyched at the prospect." He smiled. "Now, the next couple of rows are cucumbers, a couple of kinds of squashes, several varieties of beans. Pumpkins. Then over here . . ." He took her arm again. "I have greens. Kale was big for a few years, but collards are coming into their own along with Swiss chard, so I've eased off the kale a little and planted more of the others. Lettuces—five varieties here." He stopped as if admiring his work. "I have plans for an herb garden, but haven't gotten beyond the basics—dill, basil, parsley, rosemary. On Saturday I'm picking up a bunch of blueberry bushes. They should have been in the ground by now, but a guy I know wanted to get rid of his extra stock and gave me an incredible price on them. Don't know if they'll fruit well this year or not, but we'll see."

Seth looked back over the fields he'd shown her. "These're all mostly cash crops. I take a truckload of produce to a couple of restaurants in Clarks Summit and a few in Scranton twice a week right through till fall."

"You never mentioned any of this to me before. I thought your job was being the mayor of Hidden Falls."

"Well, I am, but that's not a paying position." He stood with his hands on his hips and looked out at his fields as if seeing them for the first time.

"Did you always want to be a farmer?" She was still somewhat astonished that he'd never told her about his farm, and she said so. "Why didn't you tell me?"

"It never came up."

"That's pretty lame, Seth. We spent a lot of time together working with your dog at Barney's."

"Well . . . a lot of people think farming's something people do when they can't do anything else."

"What people are they? Farming's tough. Anyone can see that."

He smiled that half smile again, the one she was beginning to like a little too much. "Then let's just say that most women aren't interested in a guy who makes his living farming rather than working in a more respectable profession."

"Farming is respectable. You mean a higher-paying profession."

He nodded. "Yeah, that's what I meant."

"If women are turning you down because you're a farmer, you're meeting the wrong kind of women."

"Maybe." He slipped an arm over her shoulder, and though she sensed there was more he wanted to say, he fell silent.

"Well, I think your farm is great," she said. "What made you buy this place?"

"When I came back from Afghanistan, I was in pretty bad shape." He gave her some space but kept his arm around her shoulder.

"You were wounded?"

"Shot in the leg, but that's a story mostly for another time. Suffice it to say I wanted to find a quiet place." He smiled wryly. "It doesn't get much quieter than right here. When I was a kid, I used to come out here and steal apples. Of course, eventually I got caught. The old guy who owned the place promised not to tell my folks as long as I worked off my crime."

This time, Seth's smile reached his eyes.

"He taught me a lot. Of course, he didn't care about the apples. He just needed a hand here and there. This was the place I thought about all the time I was away, all the time I was rehabbing my leg. We kept in touch while I was gone, even when I was in the hospital. While I was recuperating, I got a letter from his son telling me his father had had a stroke, that his dad wanted me to come visit when I got home. Well, I did that, and it turned out that my old friend needed more than a little help by then, since he couldn't do much on his own. I was still a bit shaky, but I took care of a couple of fields, kept up his brood of hens. After he passed away, I found out he'd left instructions that if the farm was to be sold, I should be given right of first refusal."

"Obviously you exercised that right." She thought for a minute. "Did his son mind? That you were so close to his father?"

"No. Jim—that's the son—is a lawyer in Scranton now. He told me many times he had no desire to farm, but he was glad I did. He offered me the farm at a price far lower than he might have gotten from someone else, said he figured I'd worked off the difference by helping his father over the years."

"That was really nice of him."

"It was." He gazed around at the fields surrounding them. "The thought of coming back here kept me motivated through some bad times. Once I knew I was needed here, I couldn't get out of that hospital fast enough." His steps led toward the apple orchard on the other side of the barn.

"Returning to the scene of the crime?" she teased.

"Something like that."

A waist-high fence enclosed a small area between

the barn and the first row of trees. As they drew nearer, she saw a dozen white headstones standing within the enclosure.

"Your friend is buried here?" Des asked.

Seth nodded. "Henry Paul Bisler and his wife, Nancy. That small stone marks their daughter, Ellen. The others are his parents, grandparents, a sister who died young."

She tried to think of an appropriate thing to say, but she couldn't come up with anything other than, "Well, I guess it's good that he's here."

"Henry was the nicest man I ever met. Oh, I know we say that about everyone, but Henry really was the nicest person I ever met. Spending time with him was a gift. His friendship was a gift." Seth swallowed what appeared to be a lump in his throat.

"So you wanted to be a farmer because of him?"

"I wanted to live on this farm because I wanted to be like him. He taught me to appreciate the changes in the seasons. Taught me about soil and how to be a good steward of the land. He taught me everything he knew about growing things." Seth paused before adding, "And he taught me more about being a man than my father ever did. He never struck his wife or his kids, and he never bullied or insulted them or treated them disrespectfully. I loved to spend time here because it was such a happy, peaceful place. I didn't have any plans to farm the way he did—he had all the fields in corn and soybeans—but I figured if I was going to spend my time growing things, I'd grow things that were interesting to me. I knew a few guys who were just getting into the restaurant business and were looking for reliable sources of organic produce, and they introduced me to a few others. I figured I could fill that need. I did okay last year, I'll do better this year. I think Henry would have approved."

Seth turned to Des somewhat sheepishly. "Sorry. More than you wanted to know, I'm sure."

"No, no. Henry sounds like someone I would've liked. I wish I'd known him."

"You would have liked him. He'd have liked you, too." He stuck his hands back into his pockets. "Want to see the rest of the place?"

"Sure."

The barn held an array of farm equipment, most Seth had bought with the property, other implements he'd purchased at auction, and a monster of a black motorcycle. The tractors and tillers were all mud splattered, but the bike was spotless. When Des commented on the fact, Seth grinned.

"Can't be seen riding a dirty bike. It would be a serious violation."

There were two other outbuildings, one of which had a long dog run attached to the front and a large fenced-in yard in the back.

"Henry used to raise hound dogs," Seth explained. "He'd keep the ones he was selling out here before they went to their new homes. His wife liked dogs well enough, but she liked them best outside. I keep telling Ripley if he doesn't mind his manners, he's going to be spending a night in the kennel there."

"You wouldn't."

"No, I wouldn't. He's an inside dog." Seth ran his knuckles lightly over the top of the dog's head. "But it's a pretty nice space, all things considered. Henry had the building heated so if he had litters in the winter, they'd be nice and warm, and the building's situated so the pen gets afternoon shade. It's spacious and clean, so it wasn't much of a hardship for the dogs and their pups."

He started to walk away, Des and the dog following.

"Like everything else around here, it needs to be painted. I will get to it, but it's tougher than I thought it would be to keep up with the crops and do everything the house needs."

"The house looks fine."

Seth raised an eyebrow.

"Okay, so maybe a little paint on the outside."

"And on the inside."

Des nodded. "Yeah, that, too. But you'll get it done. I was lucky that the place I bought in Cross Creek was totally done. All I had to do was move in."

"You were lucky. Fixing a place up while you're living in it is a pain in the tail."

"The powder room looks great," she said as they approached the house.

"I did that and a bathroom upstairs over last winter. I have a lot more spare time in winter. The year before that, I did two bedrooms. This winter, I'm planning on the kitchen. I was hoping to have it done before it was time to plant, but that time came and went. I had to leave a lot of things on hold. I just haven't been at this long enough to get my routine down pat."

"How long have you been here?"

"Just three years. The place needed some work before I could move in because it sat vacant for a while. I had enough saved up to take care of the mechanicals, but that was about it."

"I can sympathize. I'm dealing with a monster that's been vacant for a long, long time myself."

Seth led the tour in the direction of the fields on the other side of the farmhouse. Des could see wooden structures rising from the ground, but it wasn't until they drew closer that she realized what she was looking at.

"You're growing grapes." She looked up at Seth. "Rows and rows of grapes. I'm guessing you're not going into the jam business."

"And your guess would be correct. What you're looking at here is the beginning of Willow Lane Vineyards. And hopefully, eventually, Willow Lane Wines."

"I didn't know you could grow wine grapes in Pennsylvania."

He nodded. "Oh yeah. It's a multibillion-dollar business in the state. There are wine tours, wine festivals, you name it. Some of the vineyards are B and Bs, and some are wedding venues."

"Sorry. I grew up in California. I just wasn't aware that other states were as into it," she said sheepishly.

"Well, you're excused, since you're from California," he teased. "I guess when most people think of U.S. wines, they think first of California, then maybe New York. Pennsylvania's making strides in catching up."

They walked along the rows, Seth stopping here and there to secure an errant vine to the trellis.

"Why wine?"

"I hadn't set out to do this when I bought the farm. But I went on a vacation two years ago—my first real vacation since I was a kid, I think." Again, that half smile. "Anyway, I went to Germany and northern France, Austria. I saw all these beautiful vineyards and I started to think how cool it would be to grow grapes and maybe have my own winery. As if it's that simple." He rolled his eyes. "But when I got back home, I visited a few vineyards in the area, talked to the owners, got a feel for what was involved. Then of course I had to decide if I wanted to commit to something that would require so much of my time and attention, not to mention the financial invest-ment. But after thinking it over, I decided I wanted to give it a go. I had the land. I had the time. I just had to educate myself, which I did over that winter. Then last year, I built the trellises—"

"You built all those trellises?" Des's jaw dropped as she looked over the field, at the rows and rows of white trellis.

Seth nodded. "I built them in the barn over the winter, and in the spring, I put them in the ground."

"That must have been backbreaking."

"Yeah, it got tense after a while. But all that work prepared me for actually planting the vines."

"You did all this yourself?"

"With some help from Joe and Ben, yeah."

"What are you, Superman?"

He laughed. "No, just determined. I had a schedule and I was going to stick to it, come hell or high water."

"How many acres of vines do you have?"

"Right now, just the first three you see here. I will be putting in more this fall, but I haven't finished the trellises yet."

"Any chance you might consider something entirely revolutionary, like, oh, maybe buying the trellises already made?"

"If I could afford it, I would. But right now, I'm on a tight budget, since my income is mostly from the produce I sell to restaurants."

"How 'bout taking investors?"

"Joe and Ben have both offered to buy in, but I don't know . . ."

"I'd invest in your vineyard. Once the theater is finished and I get my inheritance, I'll happily invest in you."

"Ah, but once that happens, you'll be on your way back to Montana."

"Well, yes, but . . ." She hadn't been thinking about leaving when she'd made the offer. "I'd still want to invest in the vineyard. It'll give me an excuse to come back to Hidden Falls."

"Is that the only thing that would bring you back, Des?" he asked.

"Well, no, there's Barney. And the theater. I'd like to see that running again." She paused. Was that disappointment she read in his eyes? She hastened to add, "And of course, I'd want to see you. And Joe, and Ben . . . and, well, you, of course." Her voice trailed off as the moment began to feel more and more awkward.

"You'll always be welcome here, Des," he told her quietly. "Rip and I will always be happy to see you."

She tried to think of a response, but Seth snapped his fingers and that quickly, the subject changed.

"You came out for the photos. Let's go inside and I'll get those for you."

"Is there any way I could get a second set? Allie needs them for the Art Department at Althea."

"Sure."

Des had to hustle to keep up with Seth's long strides as they covered the ground between the fledgling vineyard and the house. She waited in the kitchen while Seth went upstairs to his office. She sat on one of the kitchen chairs—an old oak armless straight-back without arms or a cushion that wasn't a match for any of the other three. It took but a minute for Des to realize that none of the chairs matched, though they were roughly the same size and made from the same golden oak. It gave the room an even homier feeling, like the chairs had been found in an attic and brought down as they were needed.

"Here you go. Two sets." Seth came back into the kitchen and handed her two envelopes.

"Thanks, Seth. I appreciate it." She stood and took her sweater from the back of the chair where she'd earlier left it, and picked up her bag. "I need to be heading back. Everyone's probably wondering what happened to me."

"You're not going to make that trek again in this heat. I'll drive you."

"That's okay. I'm sure you have other things to do."

"Nothing more important. Besides, I can pick up a few things in town. Ready to go?" he asked, and the dog's ears perked up.

She glanced down at the shirt she'd borrowed. "Give me just a minute to change."

"Nah. Keep the shirt. Amy'll never miss it."

"I'll wash it and return it."

"That implies you'll be back."

"I'd like to come back. I'd like to see your plants start to grow and learn a little about farming."

"Crops. When you have a whole field, you call them crops."

"Right. Crops."

She tucked the envelopes into her bag, then left with Seth through the back door. Ripley raced between them as they walked to the blue pickup truck parked next to the barn. Seth opened the passenger door for her, and she hopped up.

"Sorry there's no seat belt," he told her. "This baby came off the assembly line before they were mandated."

The first thing Des noticed was the half-smoked cigar in the open ashtray. She manually lowered the window, hoping to get the smell out.

There were few things she hated more than the smell of cigars.

I bet Greg doesn't smoke cigars, she thought.

Seth walked around the cab, and when he opened

his door, the dog jumped in first, then started to climb over Des.

"He's used to riding shotgun," Seth told her.

"Oh, well . . ." She scooted over about a foot closer to Seth to give the dog his place at the window, which put her leg next to the gearshift.

"Could you put that window up about halfway?" Seth pointed to the window she'd just opened. "I don't want to take a chance of Rip lunging after a squirrel or falling out when I go around a corner."

"Sure." She reached around the dog to raise the window.

The truck started with a rumble and a little shimmy, but once it got moving, the engine settled down and the shimmy disappeared. Seth paused at the end of the driveway and looked both ways before pulling onto the road. When he shifted the gears, the heel of his hand hit Des's leg.

"Sorry," he said.

"It's okay. I'm in the way." She tried to swing her legs a bit to the right, but the dog was there.

Seth shifted into third, then fourth, his hand almost on her knee.

"Sorry," he said again. "I don't mean to . . ."

"No, it's okay. I'm in your way. I'd move, but Ripley's right here."

Every time his hand touched her leg, she felt that little jolt again.

Stop it, she silently instructed whatever was causing her to feel his touch so acutely.

She watched out the window as they passed another farm, then another, as they drove toward the
center of town. They passed the police station and
the Bullfrog Inn, the local watering hole on the left,
and the library and the Sugarhouse on the right.

"Shifting into third, giving you a heads-up." Seth
rounded the corner onto Hudson Street and she
swung her legs to the right. "And second," as he
pulled in front of the Hudsons' house.

"And first into neutral," she said.

"You drive stick?"

"Sure. Thanks for the ride. And the photos. Get
back, Ripley." She reached across the dog for the
door handle. "Oh, and thanks for the shirt. I will get
it back to you."

"You're welcome whenever. Bring Buttons next
time."

"I'll do that. And I will invest in Willow Lane
Vineyards, Seth. No matter where I am."

Seth nodded, holding on to Ripley's collar while
Des let herself out. She stood on the sidewalk until
he drove off.

Tossing her sweater over one shoulder, she
walked across the lawn to the front porch and went
inside. Voices drifted in through the open kitchen
windows from the backyard. She peered through the
window and saw Allie and Cara sitting on the patio
talking to Barney. Des went upstairs and peeled off
the dirty, hot black pants and pulled on a pair of
white shorts. She slipped into a pair of sandals and

grabbed the envelope from her bag, then went downstairs and outside to where her family sat chatting on the tree-shaded patio.

"There you are. I was getting ready to call Ben and ask him to put out an APB on you." Barney sat on a rocking chair with green-and-white-striped webbing that formed the seat and the back. Buttons sat under a nearby chair and wagged her tail, but didn't bother to get up.

Des related her walk to Seth's farm to pick up the photos.

"That's not your shirt." Leave it to Allie to notice.

"It belongs to Seth's sister."

"Why are you wearing it?" Allie continued to prod, a little gleam in her eyes.

"Because by the time I got out there, I was dying from the heat."

"So how'd he get you to take off your sweater?" Allie was still smirking.

"He took pity on me and gave me this shirt. I changed in the powder room." She leaned toward Allie and said with a smile, "Seth has central air."

"Oh my God, did he say go home at once and bring back your entire family to wait out this heat wave?" Allie clutched at Des's hand.

"No, he did not. But I must say, it was lovely." Des leaned her head back and closed her eyes. "Now I'm exhausted. But that little bit of breeze from the woods feels good."

"It's why we're out here. Honestly, if I thought for one minute that this week's weather portended the entire summer, I would seriously think about air-conditioning this place." Barney tilted her head to look up at the back of the house. "It's such a monster, though. I don't think it would be an easy or inexpensive job. I should ask Joe what he thinks."

"He'll be over after dinner," Cara said. "You can ask him to take a look around before we go out."

"Let me guess." Allie turned to gaze at her. "You're going to go to the movies in that new triplex ten miles down the road, then you're going to go out to the lake and make out like a couple of sixteen-year-olds. After which time you'll go back to his house and have hot monkey sex."

"Jealous?" Cara raised an eyebrow.

"Pfft." Allie pretended to dismiss the idea.

"I'm jealous," Des said.

"I would be, too, if Joe wasn't like a son to me," Barney added. "When I was younger, he was exactly the sort of guy I went for."

"Did Gil look like Joe?" Cara asked.

"He was built like him, but that's the only similarity," Barney replied.

"Well, that would make him pretty hot," Cara said. "Joe's pretty fine."

"Speaking of hot guys . . ." Allie turned to Des. "How 'bout that cutie you were showing around the theater this morning?"

"What cutie?" Barney and Cara both said at the same time.

"Greg Weller."

Allie turned to Cara and Barney. "He said he'd

like to continue their conversation over dinner. And he'd call her."

"Allie, you were eavesdropping?" Cara pretended to be shocked.

"He said it right in front of me." Allie looked over at Des and said, "He really is cute, and he seemed very nice, and he was definitely interested. And very much your type. Not mine, of course, but yours, certainly."

"Sophisticated?" Cara asked.

"From what I could tell, more so than not," Des replied. "But in a good way."

"Obviously academic," Cara said.

Des nodded. "Obviously."

"No ink?" Cara continued.

"None that I could see." As opposed to the sleeves that spread up Seth's forearms to his biceps. She'd taken a few peeks, but wasn't able to discern exactly what those images were supposed to be.

"Cigars?"

"Didn't get a whiff of one." Unlike the cab of Seth's car.

"Definitely, by definition, your type," Cara concluded. "And Allie says he's a cutie."

"He's very cute. Boyishly cute."

"There you go. A match made in heaven." Allie stood. "Or at the very least, in the Sugarhouse." She started toward the house. "I'm getting something to drink. Anyone?"

They all opted for ice water. Cara went inside with Allie to help carry everyone's drinks.

"So what else do we know about your cute professor?" Barney moved her chair farther into the shade.

"Other than the fact that he isn't my professor and that his name is Greg Weller?" Des thought for a second. "I guess all I really know is that he seems like a really nice person. And smart. He's interested in the history of the theater. Oh, and he asked me if I knew who the architect was who designed the building and who the artist was who did the decorative painting. Do you know?"

Barney shook her head. "There's probably something in one of the file cabinets in the office, though. My grandfather never threw out anything. You're welcome to look."

"Thanks."

"You're welcome." Barney fell silent, and for a moment, Des thought she might have dozed off. But then she asked, "What did Cara mean when she asked if your professor was 'inked'?"

"She meant did he have tattoos."

"And the reference to the cigar?"

Des shrugged. "I mentioned once that I don't like the smell of them."

"I see."

I have the feeling you do, Des thought.

Her heart sank just a bit. Obviously Barney'd connected the dots and figured out who Cara was comparing Greg to. She was well aware that Seth was a favorite of Barney's. Des felt just a little embarrassed at having been caught putting Seth in an unfavorable light.

"I'm going to go take a shower. I'm still dusty." Des rose and started toward the house.

"Appearances are deceiving sometimes, Des." Barney rested her head on the back of her chair, her eyes closed.

Des wanted to respond, but somehow the only retort that came to mind was the tired *I know that*. She couldn't bring herself to say the words.

Why start something when you're not going to be around to follow through? she thought as she climbed the stairs to the second floor. How uncomfortable might that be when she came back to visit Barney and ran into Seth?

Then again, if their relationship never went beyond friendship, she'd feel free to visit him at the farm without apology. She could take Buttons out to play with Ripley. She could watch him transform that run-down property into a beautiful oasis, and there was no doubt in her mind that he'd do exactly that. She could make that investment, and over the years watch his vineyard grow into a successful winery.

To Des's mind, the bottom line was that a friend could be kept in your life forever, in ways an ex-lover never could. One very good reason to rethink her offer to buy into Seth's vineyard.

One more reason, a little voice inside her whispered, reminding her that lately she'd been coming up with any number of reasons to keep Seth strictly in the friend zone. *Maybe*, the voice whispered, *it's time to figure out if they were reasons, or excuses.*

CHAPTER SIX

The kitchen makeover was almost complete. There was a bit more woodwork to paint, and Cara had decided the window seat should have new cushions to match the room's pretty new décor. The sisters had taken Barney to a fabric store to select something bright and pretty, and while there, got the name of a woman who could sew the cushions for them.

"The window seat is going to be the coziest place in the house," Des told Barney on the way home.

"I love that yellow, white, and light blue fabric. I think it's going to look smashing. I can't thank you girls enough for thinking of this project, especially since you have the theater to deal with." Barney was beaming. "I can't wait to get new pull shades on the windows. And maybe hang up some pictures on the walls. Something pretty, I'm thinking."

"Maybe some photos of the theater," Des suggested.

"Or maybe an old movie poster or two," Cara added.

"Which brings me to ask, Des, did you hear back from that dealer in Las Vegas you were going to contact?" Allie asked.

"Not yet. I'm wondering if he isn't maybe looking for a buyer before he makes an offer."

The thought had occurred to Des that the dealer she'd contacted might do just that. She didn't care either way, if in the end he made a big, fat offer. How many original posters could still be around for *Possessed*, with a young Clark Gable and Joan Crawford as the leads? Or the original *Frankenstein* with Boris Karloff, or *Dracula* with Bela Lugosi? Either old movie buffs or collectors of horror movie memorabilia would be interested in those.

"Honestly, I have to admit that when this whole thing started, I thought it sounded like something we could accomplish in six months, maybe a little more. I mean, we had a million dollars to spend, right?"

"Yeah, who'd have imagined the money would go so quickly?" Allie sighed.

"Or that we'd get reasonably close to the end, only to have the roof fall in on us." Des paused. "Well, more or less."

"Or that we'd be having to repair that glorious ceiling. Or we would be, if we could find someone qualified to do it." Cara's sigh echoed Allie's.

"How's that search for repair people going, Cara?" Des asked.

"Three steps forward, two steps back," Cara replied. "I called a dozen historic theaters and got a dozen different names of artisans who worked on them. I call these restoration specialists and I realize none of the other theaters have had the type of damage we've had. Damaged ceilings, yes. The type of decorative painting needing repair, no. Plus the fees they charge just to come and take a look are astronomical. I'm not giving up—I know we'll find the right people—but it's disheartening. Everyone I call seems to be out of our league."

"Maybe someone at the cocktail party this weekend will have some recommendations for us," Barney said. "At least, I'm hoping someone will."

"Right now, I'm going to be completely shallow and fess up that I'm thinking about that cocktail party because I honestly don't have a thing to wear. Joe and I are going out to dinner after, and I want to look really nice," Cara said as she turned into the driveway.

"I think you want to go beyond nice, Cara. I think maybe you want to wow." Allie waited until Barney got out of the front passenger side before climbing out of the back seat. "I say we put all this doom and gloom, *waaaa, we're running out of money and the ceiling's peeling off* stuff aside and go shopping. Online. All in favor—"

It was a unanimous "aye."

"I'll meet you all in our lovely, newly redecorated, almost completed kitchen." Allie took off for the back door, house key in hand.

❖

"I like that black one, but it doesn't come in my size." Allie pointed to the image of the short sleeveless dress on Cara's laptop, which was open on the kitchen table.

Des leaned over Allie's shoulder. "It's pretty. Simple but lovely. Oh, but it comes in mine."

"Figures," Allie muttered.

Cara turned the digital page. "Allie, maybe this one. It's more your style anyway, don't you think?"

Allie studied the screen. "Could be a contender. Go back to the main page where all the dresses are."

"I can't get used to this idea of buying clothes online." Barney had poured a cup of coffee and slipped onto the window seat. "In my day, we went into Clarks Summit or Scranton to shop for school clothes and dressy things. A trip into John Wanamaker's in Philly or Lord & Taylor in New York for special occasions. We'd never consider buying something we hadn't tried on to wear for an important event."

"The times they are a-changing," Cara sang. "So what are you going to wear to the cocktail party, Barney?"

"Oh, I'm sure I have something. I haven't really thought about it."

Cara looked up from the screen. "I guess it would help us to know how dressy these things really are."

"Yeah, a cocktail party out here in the boonies probably isn't the same as a cocktail party in L.A." Allie reached around Cara to move to the next page of dresses.

"Allie, are you assuming that we 'out here in the

boonies' don't know how to dress, or that we don't know how to throw a proper cocktail party?"

"Maybe a little of both." Allie grinned without embarrassment. "Not meant as an insult, Barney. Just that I don't think things around here are as formal. In L.A., people wear lots of glitz. How much glitz can we expect to see at Saturday's shindig at Althea College?"

"Oh, probably none, unless you're wearing it," Barney conceded. "Generally, we don't dress up to quite that extent, but don't let that stop you if you're in the mood to sparkle."

"I'm always in the mood to sparkle."

"Not lately, you haven't been." Des pointed to a blue sleeveless dress on the screen. "That would be terrific on you, Cara."

"What do you mean, lately I haven't?" Allie tapped Des on the arm.

"Just that you've been sort of sullen and cranky." Des shrugged. "Tough to sparkle when you're cranky."

"What are you talking about? I have not been cranky."

Allie's sigh was exasperation touched with annoyance.

"I have a lot on my mind, okay?" Her face slightly red, she turned her attention back to the screen. "Click on that teal number on the end there, please."

Cara clicked and the requested dress appeared.

"That might be too low cut for the college faculty," Cara said when Allie started to scroll through the available sizes.

"Am I the only one who thinks it whispers, 'Do me'?" Des asked.

"Really?" Allie looked up.

Des and Cara both nodded.

"Oh, well, then, forget that one. No one around here I'm interested in doing." Allie closed the screen and moved on to the next.

"The party isn't just for faculty," Barney said. "It's for alums, benefactors, former faculty. It's a fund-raiser, so they try to include as many people as they can."

"That one's too low, too." Des pointed to the hot pink dress on the current screen.

"I bet it wouldn't be too low with that emerald necklace Althea is wearing in the portrait in the front hall. With those beauties around your neck— cleavage? What cleavage?" Allie barely looked up from the page. "If we could find it, that is. I'd need shoes to go with this. Strappy sandals with four-inch heels."

"Your shoes can wait. Cara and I need to find something to wear, too. So buy the dress or don't, but stop monopolizing the computer."

"Even if we ever found that necklace, we'd end up fighting over it," Cara noted.

"No, Barney said finders, keepers, right, Barney?" Allie stepped away from the table.

"I did say that. God knows I've looked everyplace I could think of. My guess is that my mother put it in something, then took that something into the attic and put it into something else."

"Are you sure she didn't give it away, or maybe it

was stolen? Or maybe it's in an old purse or a hatbox or something?" Not for the first time, Des thought of all the places in the big house where such an item could be hidden.

"She really didn't see anyone once she developed dementia. She never wanted visitors, and by the time we'd hired someone to help with her, the necklace had already been missing for quite a while." Barney shook her head. "It's in this house, I'm certain of that. It's just a matter of finding where." A slow smile crossed her lips. "Which of course means that the house will have to stay in the family at least until the damned thing is found. If it's still missing after I pass along, well, you're all just going to have to keep looking." Still smiling, she took a sip of coffee. "I think I'll call Pete this week and have him put that in my will."

"Don't you think Uncle Pete has had enough of the Hudsons' goofy inheritance stipulations?" Allie asked.

"I like to think he's merely accustomed to our creativity."

"It just occurred to me that once you pass to the other side, you can ask your mother what she did with the necklace, then you can leave signs around the house," Cara suggested.

"But it would have to be a sign that all of us got at the same time so we all had the same opportunity to look for it."

"Leave it to Des to come up with rules for the hereafter." Allie searched her bag for her wallet, then opened it to look for a credit card.

"Maybe we should get a Ouija board, girls, and I could communicate with you that way." The thought seemed to amuse the normally sensible Barney.

"What a swell idea," Allie muttered.

"Are you buying this dress?" Cara asked, her finger poised to go to another page.

"Unless I find something better. I want to take one more look." Credit card in hand, Allie moved toward the screen, and Cara got up to give her room. "I should warn you girls, though—Nikki has a to-do list for this summer, and right there at number one: find the emerald necklace."

While Allie monopolized the computer, Des wandered out into the hall, where portraits of a dozen or more ancestors watched over the family home. Althea Brookes Hudson—Des's great-great-grandmother, who'd had a college named in her honor—was third from the right of the front door. She wore a dark green gown, chosen, no doubt, to set off the emeralds that were set in gold and draped around her neck.

"My father described those stones as big as a lumberjack's thumbnails." Barney came into the hall behind Des. "Not that I know what a lumberjack's thumbs look like, but that was probably an apt description. The necklace was appraised once, but I forget what the carat size was. I do remember the stones were all identical in carat, clarity, color, and cut. It was definitely a work of art." She smiled. "I often wondered what the parents of that Spanish prince thought when they found out he'd given that lovely piece—probably an heirloom—to a young American girl who was just passing through Seville with her parents."

"I bet he lied and said he had no idea what happened to it."

"All I know of the story is what I told you girls before. That Lydia—she was my great-grandmother—was eighteen, and apparently very lovely. While on a grand tour of Europe with her parents, a Spanish prince fell head over heels in love with her and proposed marriage. He gave Lydia the necklace, which her parents demanded she return because they thought for sure it was the first step toward seduction. Lydia told them she'd given it back, and they whisked her back home to Pennsylvania. A few years later, she met and married Jefferson Hudson, and shortly thereafter began to wear the necklace. They said it was the talk of Hidden Falls because she wore it every chance she got."

"If we found it, we could probably sell it and use the money for the theater," Des mused. "Assuming that you agreed."

"I said it would become the property of whoever found it, and I meant that. I've gotten along this far in my life without it. So if you find it, you can do whatever you want with it." Barney chuckled. "On the other hand, if Allie finds it—well, good luck talking her into selling it and using the proceeds for whatever the theater might need by then."

"Good point." Allie finding the necklace on her own was a sobering thought.

"Hey, Des, come here," Cara called from the kitchen. "We found the perfect dress for you for Saturday night."

"Go on, see what they've found. I'm sure you'll be lovely in whatever you wear." Barney started toward her sitting room. "Come on, Buttons. Let's go read for a while."

"What did you find?" Des asked as she went back into the kitchen.

"Just the most perfect LBD." Allie got up and offered the seat to Des. "For those of you who aren't up on your fashion shorthand, that means—"

"Right. Little black dress. Believe it or not, we do get *Vogue* in Montana." Des sat and stared at the dress on the screen.

"See, it's perfect, right? Classy, but just sexy enough to turn Greg's head." Allie crossed her arms over her chest, obviously pleased with herself.

Des nodded. "I like it. I'd definitely wear that."

"All you have to do is grab your credit card and click on that little bar, and she'll be on her way to you within twenty-four hours. Free shipping today and tomorrow," Allie said. "And you can upgrade the shipping so that it's here in twenty-four hours."

"How 'bout we put all our dresses into one order and express ship them? We can share the shipping costs that way. The free shipping deal doesn't apply to express orders, but I don't want to run the risk that the package doesn't arrive until sometime next week."

"Great idea, Des. Did you find something, Cara?"

"I'm going with the blue one we were looking at earlier. Why don't we put them all on your card, and Des and I can give you checks for our share."

"Perfect. Let's do it." Allie took over the ordering for all of them. "I'm going with black as well, but a different neckline."

Allie put in her credit card number and hit *buy now* before anyone could change her mind. Then she sent a text to Nikki showing her what they'd all bought.

"I told her about the cocktail party," Allie explained. "She wanted to know what everyone was wearing."

"She's definitely her mother's daughter," Des noted.

"We can take pictures on Saturday night to send to her," Cara offered, but Allie was already on her way out the door, texting as she walked. Cara turned in her chair to face Des, who was staring out the back window. "I'm kind of looking forward to this party, actually. We haven't done anything like this since we've been here. Do you think your professor friend will be there?"

When Des didn't respond, Cara repeated the question.

"What? Oh, I don't know." Des shrugged. "Maybe."

"All right." Cara turned off the laptop and closed the lid. "What's on your mind?"

"What if we can't find someone to restore the ceiling? Then what? Do they paint over all that beautiful art?"

"I certainly wouldn't approve of that. If there's no one who can restore it, I'd leave it as it is before I'd destroy the rest, but you're getting ahead of yourself. There has to be someone. We may have to dig for a while to find her or him, but someone is out there."

"Ever the optimist." Des smiled and went to the sink for a glass of water.

"You gotta believe, to quote that T-shirt you wore the other day." Cara dug in the fruit bowl for a grape and popped one into her mouth. "Want to know where the expression came from?"

"It's just an expression. Everyone says it. You see it everywhere. On mugs as well as shirts."

Cara nodded. "Maybe, but it didn't become a *thing* until it was used by a pitcher for the 1973 Mets."

Des raised an eyebrow.

"It's true. The Mets were in last place through the end of August that year. At a team meeting, someone from the front office came in to give them a pep talk. One of the pitchers, Tug McGraw, yelled, 'You gotta believe,' and it became a kind of mantra for the team. Long story short, the Mets came back to win their division and go all the way to the World Series against Oakland."

"Did they win?"

"No. Oakland won, four games to three. But would they have even gotten to the series if they hadn't all decided to believe in themselves and in their teammates?"

"Why do you even know that?"

Cara laughed. "My mom was a big Mets fan.

I even remember their theme song. Want to hear it? 'Meet the Mets. Meet the Mets. Step right up and—'"

"That's okay. I'll pass on the rest of it." Des finished the little bit of water left in her glass. "Some other time maybe."

"But you got the point, right? That we all have to believe we'll find the right person and the ceiling will be restored and we'll finish the rest of the work and the theater will be ready to go."

"Go where, Cara?" Des stood. "What happens then?"

"I've asked myself the same question. And I don't have the answer."

"Do you think about staying? Here, in Hidden Falls?"

"Sometimes. But then I think about my life in Devlin's Light. My friends. The house I grew up in. My yoga studio." Cara shrugged. "I don't know what I'd miss more, Devlin's Light or Hidden Falls."

"Or Joe."

"Or Joe. Right. I don't know where that's going. I keep asking myself, what if we fall totally in love— like, deeply in love, can't-live-without-each-other love—and he asks me to stay?"

"What would you do?"

"I have no idea. On the one hand, I think he's probably the best man on the face of the earth. I would be the luckiest woman ever if he asked me to stay here with him. But Devlin's Light is my hometown. I've lived there all my life. It's hard to think

about walking away. Even with that messy little matter of my ex and his new family."

"I understand."

"How 'bout you? Do you think about your home
in Montana?"

"Every day. Oh, not so much my house. I didn't
grow up there. I have no deep emotional ties, but I
do wonder sometimes if that's where I belong. But
I've committed to this, and I'll see it through."

"You could run a lot of shelters with the money
from Dad once we can settle the estate. I'm sure that
motivates you."

"Some. But that's not why I came here."

Cara raised an eyebrow.

"The truth is, I wanted to see if I could somehow
fix my relationship with Allie. I wanted to see if we
could put aside all the old resentments and hurt and
just be sisters." Des's eyes filled with tears. "That
was—still is—reason number one. Reason number
two? I wanted to get to know you. I wanted to see
if we could be, if not sisters, then friends at least.
I wanted to see if I could figure out how I'd missed
that my father had another family that he loved.
Another woman he loved more than he loved my
mother. Another daughter . . ."

"I think he loved all three of us equally, Des."

"Maybe. Now that I know you, and know something about your mother, I have to wonder if maybe
he loved you guys just a little more. He spent more
time with you, those last few years of his life. There
was a reason for that."

When Cara started to protest, Des stopped her.

"It's okay. He obviously found a peace with your mom that he never had with mine. It's not your fault and it's not mine. I'm not responsible for driving my father away. I am responsible for the fact that I never tried all that hard to be a part of his life after he and my mother separated. I was content to go my own way. A distance developed between us, and I did nothing to close it. I regret that now, but I can't change it."

"Why do you suppose you did that? Left that distance between you?"

"I'm not sure. Maybe I was blaming him for not sticking up for me when I said I didn't want to do that TV show that my mother was forcing me to do. I mentioned that to Seth, and he asked me if I knew for certain Fritz hadn't tried to talk to her about letting me off the hook." A tear from each eye ran down her cheeks in parallel lines. "And I had to admit, I don't know if he did. I just assumed that he hadn't. And all that time I'd had to ask him I'd wasted being angry with him. And now I'll never know." She looked up at Cara. "It never occurred to me to ask."

"Seth is one pretty smart cookie."

Des nodded. "Anyway, I can't change that any more than I can change how Allie feels about me, but I'm grateful for the opportunity to know you. I may never be able to completely mend the rift with Allie so that the past isn't between us anymore, but I know I have a sister in you."

"You do." Cara got up and put her arms around

Des. "I am now and always will be your sister. You'll never have to doubt that, Des."

Having a great time! Went shopping in downtown Chicago again today! Gramma loves to shop almost as much as you do! Woo-hoo! Just one more week and I'll be on my way to you guys for the entire rest of the summer! Can't wait! Luv u!

The exuberant text from Nikki raised Allie's spirits enormously. Knowing that her daughter would be with her soon was the best news Allie'd had since her daughter returned to California after having spent her spring break in Hidden Falls. Breathing a sigh of relief, Allie went into her bathroom and poured her second drink of the night and took it into her bedroom to relax and celebrate.

It had been almost an hour since she'd heard the others close their doors and thirty minutes since she'd heard Des turning off the shower in her room across the hall. The house lay quiet and still around her, and on a whim, she got up and opened her bedroom door. There was no sign of life from either Cara's or Des's rooms, and it appeared the only light in the house came from the night-light at the end of the hall. Grabbing her drink and the pack of cigarettes she'd picked up at the drugstore on her way back from the theater the day before, Allie tiptoed into the hall. She crept to the stairs, and keeping to one side to avoid the steps that creaked, she made it to the first floor.

The front door would be a challenge, but what was life without those little challenges?

She unlocked the door and, inch by inch, opened it. Leaving it slightly ajar, she padded onto the porch in bare feet and sat in the dark on one of the rocking chairs. Amused by the fact that she'd made it outside with such stealth, she lit a cigarette, tried not to cough, and put her legs up on the railing. She'd given up a short-lived smoking habit long ago, but every once in a while she bought a pack of a brand she didn't really like so she wouldn't want to smoke the whole thing. She knew it was disgusting and would kill her if she picked up the habit again, but tonight she wasn't thinking about any of that. Tonight she just wanted to sit in the night air and forget everything negative that had happened to her over the past few years. Her ever-present resentment of Des. The divorce from the man she'd loved with all her heart. The separation from Nikki. The death of her father. The realization that he'd been lying to them all for over thirty-five years. She wanted it all to just drift away with the smoke and disappear forever.

When she was in this mood, her mind always took her to the same place, that part of her brain that wondered how Fritz had kept his secret for so long.

Then again, who would suspect their parent of living a double life? It wasn't as if that was something you'd search online. What would you type into the search engine? *Franklin "Fritz" Hudson—double life?*

She could accept Cara as her sister, but she refused to think of Susa as her father's wife. There was no denying Allie felt a certain amount of curiosity about Susa, though. She was obviously the exact opposite of Allie's own mother, and that alone made her wonder what it would have been like to have a mother like the one Cara had described. A mother who was always interested in what you did. Who was positive and fun and who did so many things with you. Granted, some of those things included tie-dying T-shirts and learning how to knit and macramé, organic gardening, and making things like jam and pottery, none of which Allie'd ever had the slightest interest in, but still, Susa sounded like a fun person.

Allie wouldn't have admitted it, but sometimes she envied Cara and the life she'd had with her laid-back mother, who'd apparently brought out the best in their father.

She finished the cigarette and went down the steps to stub it out in the grass, taking care to make sure it was dead before placing it on the step. She'd remember to take it back inside and wrap it in a tissue before she tossed it into the trash.

The breeze picked up a little more. She sat in the rocker, her head back, her face up to the cooler air. Overhead the stars were blinking through the leaves on the trees, and all was incredibly quiet. She'd have one more cigarette, finish her drink, and take herself back up to bed. There were nights when she'd drink until she passed out, but this wouldn't be one of them. The sweet night air soothed her, the motion of the rocking chair relaxed her, and the text from her daughter had reassured her.

She lit the cigarette with an old lighter that had belonged to her mother, one of the few possessions of Nora's Allie had kept. It was blue enamel with a three-dimensional pink flower on the front. A clear crystal had once been set in the center of the flower, but the crystal was long gone. She flicked on the lighter and sat watching its flame for a moment or two, then lit the cigarette. She'd just about decided that she didn't really need to smoke, and started from the chair to put it out, when she realized a car had stopped in front of the house.

Allie froze momentarily as the car door opened and a man got out. He'd taken ten steps onto the front walk when she realized the car was a police cruiser. Which meant the man could only be one person.

Of course it would be him. It was always him.

Defiantly, she took a long drag from the cigarette, and suppressing the cough she could feel building in the back of her throat, leaned against the porch pillar and let the smoke curl slowly from her mouth.

"Evening, Sheriff," she whispered when he reached the bottom of the steps. She was well aware that his title was chief of police, but it had tickled her contrary nature to pretend to forget his position because it had always seemed to tweak him. Tonight he appeared not to have noticed.

"Ms. Monroe," Ben whispered in return.

"Nice night."

He nodded. "Uh-huh."

"So what brings you to Hudson Street at . . . oh,

one-thirty in the morning?" She took another drag off the cigarette because she suspected he disapproved, then turned her back and sat in the chair and began to rock gently.

"Just my normal patrol," he told her. "And it's two."

"So you stopped because I'm breaking some arcane law? Oh wait, let me guess. Illegal use of a rocking chair? Rocking over the speed limit? Or maybe it's DWR? Drinking while rocking? Or would that be reckless rocking? Rocking without a license?"

"Have you finished amusing yourself?"

"I'm not sure." She downed the rest of her drink. "Why are you here? Rocking jokes aside, I have to assume it's not against the law to drink one drink on one's own front porch at any time of the day or night. Am I right?"

Ben nodded. "Absolutely."

"So why are you here?"

"I saw the light from your cigarette, and I know Barney doesn't smoke, and I'd bet any amount of money that neither Des nor Cara smokes, so I wanted to rule out the possibility that someone was trying to set the house on fire."

"You said you figured Des and Cara didn't smoke. So you thought I did?"

Ben sighed. "Allie . . . there's no assuming anything where you're concerned."

"What's that supposed to mean?"

"It means you're unpredictable."

For some reason, Allie was inordinately pleased.

"Why, Sheriff, that's the nicest thing you've ever said to me. That was almost a compliment."

"Yeah, well, don't let it go to your head." He sat on the top step, his back against the railing post. "How's your daughter? She coming out sometime this summer?"

"She'll be here in a few days." Nice of him to remember Nikki, she'd give him that.

"That'll be good for you. Good for the rest of us, too."

"What's that supposed to mean?"

"You're always a lot nicer when she's around."

"Why, if I were a sensitive person, I'd think you meant to imply that I am otherwise not a nice person."

"Hey, if the shoe fits."

Did that particular shoe fit? Ben wasn't the only one to imply she wasn't always the nicest person to be around.

"I'm going to overlook that remark."

"Nice of you."

"See? Precisely my point. And Nikki isn't even here."

"Why are you like this?" For once, he didn't appear to be baiting her.

"Like what?"

"You know. Pretending to be a hard-ass about everything."

"Maybe I am a hard-ass."

"I don't think so. I don't think that's really you."

"Why would you care about the real me?"

"I didn't say I cared. I'm just curious."

"Well, see there? You just did the same thing you're accusing me of."

"Maybe we just bring out the worst in each other." Ben stood.

Allie recalled her recent conversation with Des. "Maybe that's the best of us."

"That would be sad, if that were the best either of us had to offer."

"What difference would it make to you?"

"I'm just trying to understand, that's all." He raised his hand and tipped an imaginary hat. "Glad you're confining your drinking to the comforts of home these days, Ms. Monroe. See you around."

Ben turned his back and went down the stairs, Allie watching every step he took.

"I will never understand that man," she muttered. "It's a shame that a guy as fine looking as Ben Haldeman is also one colossal jerk. Possibly the very biggest jerk I've ever met."

Ben made a K-turn in the middle of Hudson Street, then drove toward town. Allie waited until the lights from the cruiser disappeared before going down the steps to put out the cigarette she'd forgotten to smoke. It had burned down to the filter, its ash scattered in the grass. She picked up her empty glass and the remains of the first cigarette she'd smoked. She crept back into the house and relocked the door as quietly as she could, then tiptoed up to her room.

In the bathroom, she hesitated, the bottle in one hand and her glass in the other. She rinsed out the glass and returned it and the bottle to the shelf in the wall cupboard where she kept them behind the towels. Nikki would be there soon. Nothing else mattered.

Even sparring with Ben Haldeman couldn't take the shine off that.

"I don't know why you feel like you have to come with me," Allie grumbled as Des followed her out the front door. "I'm perfectly capable of meeting Dr. Lindquist on my own. And besides, I'm supposed to be in charge of the interior design and décor, right?"

"You are in charge of the interior design and the décor." Des closed the door behind them and followed Allie down the front steps. At nine fifty in the morning, the sun had risen above the pines that lined the driveway but left the sidewalk still in shade from the oak and maple trees, and the temperature was seasonably moderate. Not a cloud in the sky, she noticed. Perfect for a pleasant morning walk.

"Then tell me again why you think I can't do this alone today."

"I have no doubt you can have the necessary conversation with Dr. Lindquist. That's entirely your department. Absolutely." Des resolved to remain collected even as she could see her sister's temper rising. "My department, however, is the money, and I need to find out what we can expect to pay for an artist, if in fact there is one, and then figure out how to pay her or him."

Des caught up with Allie and tried to match her short stride to her sister's longer one.

"Short legs," Des muttered.

"What?"

"I'm trying to keep up with you on these short legs of mine, which are no match for your long ones."

"You know what they say about short people." Allie grinned but slowed her pace. She started to sing an old Randy Newman song. "'Short people got no reason, no reason—'"

"Yeah, I know. Something about them having no reason to live." The teasing she'd been subjected to was only one reason Des hated doing *Des Does It All*. She was the youngest, the smallest, and yes, the shortest person in the show, and resentment from other jealous cast members had made most days unpleasant. Back then, it had seemed everyone had a reason to dislike her.

"I remember that. Brandon . . . what was his name?" Allie's face scrunched slightly as she tried to recall.

"Whitman." It hurt Des to say his name out loud.

"Right. Brandon Whitman. He was a couple of years older than me. He used to sing that song every time you came on the set 'cause you were the shortest of the kids. I'd forgotten."

"He was five years older than me," Des said under her breath.

"Which made him two years older than me, right. Remember how he thought he was such hot stuff? Cute but a jerk. Most of the other girls on set didn't think so, though. I heard he scored with everyone." Allie laughed. "Did I ever tell you about the time he followed me and tried to kiss me during a break? Okay, so I flirted with him just a little for fun, but he knew better than to really mess with me. I'd have decked him."

"Yes, you told me." Des's jaw clenched tightly. She hated thinking about those days, but especially she hated thinking about Brandon Whitman.

And yeah, he'd figured out which of the Hudson girls to mess with, and which one to leave alone. Des had had nightmares for years about being trapped with him in a small, dark room where his groping hands were everywhere and his voice had taunted her when she began to cry. Thank God for therapy. She'd never told Allie—never told anyone except her therapist. It had been the worst experience of her life, and had been too humiliating and frightening to share.

"I heard he even hit on Cathy Jacobs," Allie went on. "Can you imagine hitting on your own TV mother?"

"Yeah, he was a real dog." Des tried to change the subject. "What time did you tell Dr. Lindquist you'd meet her?"

"Ten. So did he ever hit on you? Brandon?"

They reached the corner across from the theater.

"It's almost ten now. Oh hey, look, there are several cars out front. I'll bet she's there already." Des's mind snapped closed like a steel trap, and she stepped into the street to cross it without waiting for Allie to catch up.

"Dr. Lindquist?" Des approached the woman whose back was to her and who appeared to be studying the stained glass in the front door.

"Yes." The woman turned slowly, as if hesitant to take her eyes off the glass. She wore a red shirt tucked into khaki pants, Dansko sandals, and dark glasses. Her white hair was shoulder length and tucked behind her ears. "Are you Allie Monroe?"

"No, I'm her—"

"I'm Allie." Allie took two steps past Des and extended her hand to the visitor. "Thanks so much for coming, Dr. Lindquist. This is my sister Des Hudson."

"I'm happy to meet you both. And it's Teresa. Dr. Lindquist sounds so stuffy once I'm off campus." She gestured around at the theater's exterior. "I came a bit early to acquaint myself with your theater. The style is quite interesting. Art Deco, but with a little something almost Moorish in design." Teresa walked to the sidewalk and pointed up. "The design of the roof in particular. Do you know who the architect was?"

Allie glanced at Des, who replied, "We're in the process of researching that."

"Shall we step inside?" Allie gestured to the door that Teresa had been studying when they arrived.

"I've never seen stained glass like this. I don't suppose you know who the artist was." Teresa paused in front of the door.

"We're looking into that as well." Allie opened the door to usher the woman inside, glancing over her head to Des, who merely shrugged. They should have researched that important information before meeting with the head of the Art Department, and they both knew it.

"The interior is such a surprise," Teresa said as she walked into the lobby, taking a long look around before turning her gaze to the ceiling. "I wasn't expecting such grandeur. The fountain, the painting . . . one feels as if one's in a courtyard in some sunny place, don't you think? Even with the photos—which were excellent, by the way—the colors are startling. Glorious. But yes. Yes, you do need help." She walked to the edge of the scaffold and said, "Do you mind?"

Des and Allie shook their heads.

Teresa kicked off her sandals, dropped her bag, and began to climb.

"Oh man, I get this feeling in the pit of my stomach every time I see someone do that." Allie looked up for a moment, then down at the floor.

"Me, too. It's so far from here to there." Des watched the woman climb, her heart pounding. "I think just about everyone we know has been up there except for thee and me." Their fear of heights was one of the very few things she and Allie had in common.

Fifteen minutes later, Teresa climbed down and slipped back into her sandals.

"You need more than an artist to replace the missing painting." Teresa rubbed her hands on the back of her pants. "You need first to have the plaster repaired by someone who knows what he's doing. I don't mean your local guy who puts up drywall and occasionally repairs cracks in the walls of the old houses around here. I mean a master craftsman who understands the importance of careful historic restoration. It's indeed an art form all its own."

"Is there someone you could recommend?" Des asked.

"I strongly suggest you contact James Ebersol at the Balfour Group. They're one of the leading historical restoration companies on the East Coast. They have everyone on staff that you'd need, from their plaster artisans to their artists who specialize in period painting. They'll be able to analyze the paint colors and match them so closely no one will be able to tell the new from the original." She picked up her bag from the floor, opened it, and took out a card case. She handed Allie a business card and flashed a smile. "Give James a call and tell him I referred you."

"We were hoping you'd know someone local. A conservation student, perhaps, or a local artist." Des had a sinking feeling in her stomach it wasn't going to be that easy.

"Oh no, no, no. You need highly trained professionals for this. I know of no one in the area who's capable of re-creating the motifs on the ceiling, or properly repairing and preparing the plaster. You can't trust this restoration to amateurs."

"Any idea what a job like this would cost?"

Teresa looked back toward the ceiling. "It's hard to tell. I'm sure James'll send someone out to assess the repairs, and they'll give you an estimate. Of course, you get what you pay for." She took a few steps toward the front of the building. "Mind if I take a closer look at that stained glass in the door?"

A deflated Allie shrugged. "Be our guest."

"Thanks. Oh, and I don't suppose you know the artist who painted the ceiling."

Before Allie or Des could respond, Teresa added, "Let me guess. You're still researching that as well?"

Des nodded.

"Thanks for letting me take a look. I love your building. I hope you're able to properly restore it. It's certainly worth saving."

"I'll walk you out," Allie said.

"I know my way." Teresa waved without turning around and disappeared into the entry.

"Well, that went . . ." Des searched for a word.

"Yeah, didn't it, though?" Allie blew out an exasperated breath and turned over the card Teresa had given her. "Other than referring us to James at the Balfour Group—the name even sounds expensive—she wasn't very helpful."

"So what do you think?" Des followed Allie toward the exit.

"I think I'm going to hand off the name of this Balfour guy to Cara and have her call."

Des and Allie went straight to the office and found the door open and the lights on.

"Hi." Cara looked up from the papers she'd been reading. "Do you need your desk? I can—"

"No, stay. I'm going to be looking in the filing

cabinets." Des set her bag on one of the chairs and went to the first cabinet.

"What do you need?"

"I need to find the original building plans for the theater, for starters."

"There's a set of plans on the bottom shelf." Cara pointed to the bookcase. "Rolled up in that tube. Joe gave them to me a month or so ago." Cara moved her papers from the center of the desk so Des could roll out the blueprints.

"Where did Joe find them?" Des spread the sheets on the desk.

"In his mother's garage, of all places. His dad had done some work on the theater for the guy Dad sold it to. No one was looking for them after his dad died, so the plans just sat on his workbench."

"Ha. The name of the architectural firm is on here—Jones, Latham, and Mathews—but not the individual architect. The address is 14 Spruce Street, Scranton." Des looked up. "So that's one question answered. I guess you wouldn't happen to know where we'd find the name of the artist who made the stained glass."

"Sorry. Can't help you there."

It took about another hour before Des discovered the identity of the stained glass artisan.

"Colin Patrick McManus!" She all but shouted the name. "That's him! Colin Patrick McManus!"

"What? Really? You found him?" Allie dropped the file in her hand into the cabinet drawer. "How'd you find him?"

"The bill for two stained glass windows. 'Paid in full, to Colin Patrick McManus, the amount of ninety-two dollars for the design and crafting of two pieces of stained glass to be fitted into the uppermost section of the front door of the theater.' That must have seemed like a lot of money during the Depression." She looked up at Des. "It's signed by Reynolds Hudson and C. P. McManus. I can research him and see if he's done any other significant work."

"Two down, one to go." Des decided to take a break and make her weekly call to Fran, the director of the shelter back in Cross Creek, to touch base and see how they were faring without her. She went to her room to grab her phone from her bag, and found there were several missed calls but only one voicemail.

"Hi, Des. It's Greg. Greg Weller." She could hear him take a deep breath. "I know it's really late notice, but I was wondering if you might be free for dinner tonight. If not tonight, then maybe another night. Like tomorrow, maybe? I'd really like to see you. So. Yeah. If you get to listen to this sometime soon, maybe you could give me a call. Anytime. Really. Anytime. Just . . . call."

Des sat on the edge of the bed and listened to the message again. He certainly did sound interested. And more than a little tentative, which appealed to her, like he wasn't expecting her to jump just because he called and asked her out.

She debated within herself. To call or not to call? Des had often been accused of overthinking things. She tapped the return call icon and listened as the phone rang.

"I hope you like Asian fusion." Greg smiled at Des from across the console of his SUV.

"I like pretty much everything. I'm easy to please." Des settled back into the passenger seat, wishing he'd turn down the volume on the car radio just a bit. It was difficult to follow his naturally low voice when NPR was broadcasting an interview with Will Ferrell.

"Can't remember the last time I heard a woman say that." He smiled again, as if his little joke amused not only her but himself as well.

Though not amused, Des forced a smile, then wondered why she did.

"So where are we going?" She glanced out the window as the car turned off Main Street and onto the highway.

"I thought we'd go into High Bridge. That is, if it's okay with you?"

"It's fine. I've been meaning to go. That's where the college is." She glanced out the window at the passing scenery, the dense woods and endless hills.

"Right. Some connection to your family, right?"

"Althea Hudson was my great . . . I think great-great-grandmother."

Des shared what Barney'd told them about Althea and the emerald necklace.

"That's some tale. Not everyone can claim to have heirloom jewels gifted by royalty."

"I know. Our family is really a mixed bag. We— my sisters and I—always know we're in for a treat when our aunt starts to tell a family story."

"You've probably heard them all a hundred times before over the years, right?"

Des paused, wondering how much to tell him about her background.

"Yes, we've heard them all more than once." She couldn't have said why, but Des didn't feel comfortable relating the entire story to someone she really didn't know. Maybe when they knew each other better, assuming they got to know each other better. She felt more protective of her family's story than she'd realized, more defensive than she'd been when she'd discussed it with Seth. But then again, Seth was a friend of the family. He'd known Barney way longer than she had.

Thinking of Seth reminded her of the photos he'd given her.

"Before I forget, I have those photos you'd asked for. The ones taken inside the theater?"

"Oh great. Yes, they'll be helpful when we start to put together our grant proposal." Greg stopped at a red light. When the light changed, he made a right turn, then midway down the street turned into a small parking lot next to a group of storefronts.

"We're here?" Des looked around after he parked the car. "This is High Bridge?"

"It is."

Greg got out of the car and walked around to the passenger side, but Des had already opened the door. He held it while she climbed out.

"I hope you like Lotus," he was saying as he guided her to the sidewalk. In his other hand he carried a bottle of wine. "It's my favorite place."

"I'm sure I will."

He guided her into the restaurant with one hand on her back, a gesture she always found annoying. Strike one.

"It's a pretty room," she said, looking around at the pale gray walls accented with paintings of landscapes, flowering trees, and colorful gardens as they sat. The furniture was all black lacquer and the dishes stark white on polished wood tables.

The smiling host led them to a table and held Des's chair.

Greg followed her gaze to the artwork.

"They're all originals, I've been told. Artists who lived and worked in the area over the past hundred years or so. Improbable as it sounds, the owner—he's a friend of mine—said he bought the lot on a whim at a sale of one of those storage places. You hear stories about people buying the abandoned units and finding something of value inside, but never expect it to happen to someone you know."

"Oh, you mean like the stories of people buying an old painting for five dollars at a yard sale and finding the missing copy of the Declaration of Independence hidden in the frame?" Des grinned. "But good for your friend for having such good luck. I'm no connoisseur, but from here, anyway, most of those paintings look pretty decent."

"Speaking of painting, let's look at those photos."

"Oh. Right." Des grabbed her bag and searched inside for the envelope Seth had given her. "Here you go. Take a look, and see if they suit your purpose."

He took the prints out one by one. "These are excellent shots. Who's your photographer?"

"A friend."

"Is he a pro?"

"No. Just a friend."

"He did a great job." He finished going through the stack, then tucked them into the envelope and into his jacket pocket. "These will come in handy when we start to do our thing."

"Would you like me to open your wine, sir?" the server offered.

"Yes, thank you." Greg handed over the bottle of wine. Once it was opened, the waiter poured a glass for each of them, and menus were presented.

"Is Jason here tonight?" Greg asked.

"No, Dr. Weller. He left early, but I'll tell him you were here."

"Please tell him I'm sorry we missed him." Greg turned to Des, who was scanning the menu. "Anything strike your fancy?"

"A few dishes look intriguing."

"I can recommend the fried rainbow trout with mangoes, apples, and chili paste over noodles, topped with ginger sauce," he suggested. "It's one of my favorites."

"Hmmm, that does sound good, but I think I might try the prawns and squid stir-fry with the lime vinaigrette." She closed the menu. "With a side of sticky rice."

After they placed their orders, he asked about her life in Montana, and she showed him photos on her phone of her log cabin and told him about the shelter. She'd just started to explain how the shelter operated when their meals arrived.

"So that's what you do, then? You find strays and then find homes for them?"

"They come to us in a variety of ways. I'm speaking now of the shelter in Montana. We have strays that the sheriff brings us, and dogs whose owners can't care for them or no longer want them. We have problem pets and unwanted litters. We keep them at the shelter until we can find homes for them."

"And if you never find appropriate homes?"

"Then they stay with us at the shelter." Des felt a wave of melancholy, thinking of the dogs that remained in the shelter for far too long, those that were too old or had health issues or were just not cute enough to be adopted.

It must have shown on her face, because Greg said, "I think it's a really great thing that you do. I bet every dog you find a home for would thank you if they could."

"They do, in their own way." She pushed the rest of her seafood around her plate, no longer hungry. Every time she thought about the fate of all the dogs she couldn't save, she got sick to her stomach.

"Did you always want to rescue animals?" Greg was asking.

"When I was younger, I wanted to be a vet. I was going to save every sick animal that ever was," she admitted. It had been years since she'd thought about how she'd wanted to go to veterinary school before someone told her she'd have to operate on animals.

"What you're doing is important," he said, as if deciding it to be so. "You help heal the spirits of all those lost dogs, right? And make people happy at the same time."

"Thank you for understanding that." She put her fork down. "Not everyone gets that."

"What's to get?" He shrugged. "Seems simple enough to me."

She mentally erased that first strike.

He offered Des a little more wine, and she nodded. "Just a splash."

The waiter stopped to check on things, and assured that all was well, left them with the dessert menu.

"Oh, by the way," Des said, "we did find the name of the architectural firm that designed the building. It was Jones, Latham, and Mathews out of Scranton. And the artist who created the stained glass was Colin Patrick McManus. Dr. Lindquist had been most interested in the stained glass and we hadn't located him at the time."

"I'll see Teresa at a meeting in the morning. I'll mention that to her." He took out his phone and proceeded to write down the names she'd given him, pausing once to ask her to spell McManus.

"I'm sure we'll see her on Saturday at the cocktail party."

"Oh, you're coming to the party?"

"Barney goes every year, and she thought it would be a good idea for us to go with her, get to see the campus, meet some of the faculty, that sort of thing. She's on the board of trustees."

"That would make sense, to have a Hudson on the board." He finished his wine. "Are you up for dessert? The green tea ice cream is good, and the sesame balls are interesting. Sticky rice with red bean paste inside . . ."

"Thanks, but no. I'm good."

Greg signaled to the waiter. "Just the check, please."

On the way out of the restaurant, Des stopped for a quick look at the paintings. The landscapes in particular drew her eye, but she didn't want to be rude and lean over the diners at the tables. She made a mental note to come back. She really wanted a closer look.

"Your friend really was lucky," she told Greg on their way to the car. "Some of those paintings are wonderful. It looked like a few of them are signed, but I couldn't read the names. Has your friend re-searched any of the artists?"

"Good question. I'll ask him when I see him next time."

"He could have a gem or two there." They reached

the car, and Greg opened her door. Des slid in and fastened her seat belt while Greg made his way to the driver's side. "Something about the landscapes are familiar, but I can't say why."

"Then I'll definitely encourage him to try to identify the artists. I admit I've looked at a few of the signatures, but couldn't really make out the names."

"Same here."

"Say, would you like me to give you a driving tour of the campus while we're here?" Greg said. "Though you probably won't be able to see much since it's gotten dark."

"Good point. I'll wait till the weekend, but thank you."

He really is very attractive, she thought as the car headed back toward Hidden Falls. *And he's really very nice. I like that he's easy to be around, that he can keep a conversation going, that he picks up on things that I say and remembers them.*

But the conversation had been pretty much one-sided—all about her.

"So where was home for you?" she asked him. "Where did you grow up?"

"Upstate in a place you've never heard of."

"Try me."

"Millstone."

"You're right. I never heard of it."

"Small town—not as small as High Bridge or Hidden Falls, but small enough that you knew your neighbors and they knew you. The town doctor and the chief of police knew everyone by name, and you knew every kid in your entire school, or one of their siblings."

"Is your family still there?"

"Oh yeah. My dad's the head of the school board and my mom teaches first grade. My sister, Melissa, is the school nurse. She's married to her high school sweetheart and they have three really cool little kids."

"How'd you decide on Althea for college?"

"That was a no-brainer for me. They offered me a scholarship to play soccer, and they have an outstanding History Department. Always have."

"You got an athletic scholarship?" For some reason, this surprised her.

"Yeah." That boyish grin again. "My glory days. Seems like a long time ago." Greg laughed. "Well, it was a long time ago."

He slowed the car as they came into the center of Hidden Falls, where the posted speed limit was twenty-five miles per hour. He slowed again to make the turn onto Hudson Street and once more as he pulled into the driveway at number 725.

"Would you like to come in?" Des asked as he parked halfway up the drive.

"I have an early meeting, so I'll take a rain check. But I will walk you up." He got out and walked around the car to the passenger side and opened her door. "This was fun. I'm glad you called me back. I did apologize for calling so late, didn't I?"

"You did, but it's fine. I didn't mind."

They walked along the path to the front porch. He stopped at the foot of the steps and took her arm.

"Listen, since we're both going to be at the cocktail party on Saturday, how 'bout I give you a tour of the campus afterward? We could grab dinner or a movie or . . . or something."

"'Something' sounds just fine."

"Great. Want me to come get you and we can go together?"

Des hesitated. "I think my aunt wanted us all to go together. But I don't have to go home with them."

"Well, then, I guess I'll see you there."

She nodded, and as she did, he slipped a hand around the back of her head and kissed her on the mouth. She kissed him back and waited for bells to chime and a spark or two to fly.

No bells. No sparks.

First date, she told herself as she pulled away. Who hears bells on the first date?

"I'll see you on Saturday." Greg watched from the walk as she went up the steps to the door.

"See you then. And thanks for a nice evening."

She stood in the doorway and watched as he backed down the driveway and eased onto Hudson Street, then disappeared onto Main Street. She pushed open the door and went inside. She heard voices in the kitchen and paused, deliberating whether to join them. Her sisters would want to know about the evening. They would tease her and grill her about every detail, the way sisters do. Which would be a totally new experience for Des.

She smiled and headed toward the sound of the voices.

CHAPTER SEVEN

Des's instincts had been right on the money. Allie and Cara had grilled her good-naturedly for an hour after she got home, and she suspected they'd be ready for her again first thing in the morning. She rose extra early, got dressed, and crept down the steps. She brought her coffee into the office, where she resumed her search for something that would help them identify the artist who'd painted the theater's walls and ceiling. She'd carefully gone through half a dozen files when she heard a crunching sound near the office door.

"So not even a little zip when he kissed you good night?" Allie took a bite from the English muffin in her hand.

"It was a very short kiss. Hardly a kiss at all." Des glanced up to see both her sisters enter the room, Allie in shorts and a T-shirt, Cara in a long sleep shirt. "Gee, Allie, you're completely dressed and it isn't even noon."

"I have to run a few errands." Allie turned to Cara. "Could I borrow your car?"

"Sure. I'm not going anywhere today."

"Thanks." Allie smiled at Cara, then asked, "The first time you kissed Joe, what was it like?"

"Like picking up a live wire and being tossed across the room."

"That's chemistry." Allie wagged her eyebrows and took another bite of her muffin.

"And when was the last time you kissed anyone, chemistry or no?" Des folded her arms on the desktop.

"Oh God, what year is it?" Allie put her head back dramatically. "It's been so long I can't even remember. But"—she leveled her gaze at Des—"I know what chemistry feels like. Believe me, once you feel that zap, you don't forget it. And it's either there or it isn't. You can't make it happen."

Des rolled her eyes. "I can't believe I'm being schooled by two women who are divorced."

"The divorce wasn't my idea," Allie and Cara protested at the same time. They laughed and high-fived each other.

"All I'm saying is that chemistry is really important, and if it isn't there, the relationship is not going to work."

"There is no relationship yet, Allie. You're getting ahead of yourself. I had one dinner with Greg. Who knows what will develop?" Des raised her mug to her lips. "Just because that one short kiss didn't turn me into a puddle of mush doesn't mean it never will."

"Not gonna hold my breath," Allie said.

"It sounds like you like this guy," Cara noted.

Des sighed. "I do. He's interesting and he's just my type."

"Well, that's good. I hope it works out for you."

"So what is your type, Desdemona Hudson?" Allie asked.

"Ummm, I like cute more than handsome. Preppy. Smart."

"Ahhh, right." Allie nodded. "Khakis. Blue—or in a pinch, white—cotton button-down shirts rolled up to the elbow. Navy polos and Docksiders. Glasses optional."

"Yes. Those things. And I like someone who keeps me on my toes. Surprises me," Des added.

"So what about Greg surprises you?" Allie asked.

"That he had an athletic scholarship to go to Althea." Des started to take a sip of her coffee when the doorbell rang.

"I'll get it." Des went down the hall and looked through the glass in the door before opening it.

"Hey, Ben. What's up?" Des said as she glanced down at the big brown dog that was shaking all over but sitting next to Ben. "Oh, who's your friend?"

"No idea. Someone picked her up out past the lake this morning and brought her to the police station. She has a collar but no tags. I took her over to the vet, but Doc Trainor says she doesn't have a chip and he didn't recognize her. He did say that the pads of her feet looked worn, like she's run a long way or been out on her own for a while. So I'm bringing the dog to you."

"Here, girl. You don't have to be afraid of me." Des knelt and held out her hand, but the dog merely hung her head. "She's a chocolate Lab, and as a breed they're usually pretty friendly. But she seems awfully tentative."

"I thought so, too. Like she's not sure if you're going to help her or hurt her."

"You're a pretty girl," Des told the dog in her softest voice, but the dog kept her head down. "Aw, was someone mean to you, sweetie?"

"Well, well. Nothing like an early-morning visit from the local lawman to start your day with a smile." Allie stood in the doorway. "What's up, Sheriff? Showing off a new friend?"

"She's a stray, and Ben did the right thing by bringing her here," Des said over her shoulder as she continued to try to soothe the dog.

"And how's Girl today?" Allie leaned against the doorjamb, her coffee mug in hand.

"She's not Girl anymore. I finally found the right name for her." Ben made no attempt to hide the fact that he was staring at Allie's bare legs.

"Really? Do tell."

"She's Lulu now."

"Lulu," Allie repeated flatly, one eyebrow arching ever so slightly.

"Yeah. It's a great name. When I was growing

up, our neighbor had a black-and-white dog named Lulu."

"Ah, still a little short on originality, eh?"

Ben scowled. "I was honoring an old friend."

"Well, I guess that's understandable, since most of your friends are probably four-footed."

Ben's smile was slow and sure. "Hey, you always know where you stand with a dog."

Allie laughed before turning her back and shutting the door.

"Ben, don't pay any attention to her." Des looked up. Ben was standing with his hands on his hips, staring at the closed door. "Allie has that effect on a lot of people. Now, what to do with this little girl."

"Not so little. She weights forty-one pounds. But the vet did say she'd been spayed."

"She's underweight. She should be between fifty-five and seventy pounds." Des stood. "I'm going to have to find a place to keep her until we can find her a permanent home."

She bit her bottom lip, knowing she would have to find not only a foster home, but a permanent one as well. Tough to do without a network, and she really didn't want to approach Barney to take in another stray. While Buttons had worked out perfectly, asking to bring another dog, and a large one at that, into the house was probably pushing her luck.

"I guess it would be too much to ask you to keep her for a while?" Des was pretty sure she knew the answer before she even asked.

"Can't do it. My apartment is crowded enough

with the last homeless dog I was talked into taking." Ben hastened to add, "Not that I have any regrets. I really like my dog. She's good company. It's nice to have someone around, especially at night, even if that someone is a dog."

Des nodded. Ben had lost his wife and child to a drunk driver a few years earlier, the tragic accident being made even more horrible by the fact that the driver of the car that killed them was Joe Domanski's alcoholic father, who also died in the accident.

"Seth has lots of room out at his place. Maybe he could take her until I can figure out what to do with her," Des said, thinking out loud. "I'll text him."

Des sent a quick message to Seth, asking if he could take another dog temporarily, then waited hopefully for Seth's response. Des brought the dog water and a handful of Buttons's kibble to see if she was hungry. Normally a dog that had been on the run and was so obviously undernourished would be eager to drink and to eat, but this one's head remained down, as if afraid to go for it without permission, though her eyes were on the food in Des's hand.

"Here, it's okay, baby. This is for you." Des moved her hand closer to the dog, who finally looked up at Des with the saddest eyes she'd ever seen. "This girl was tormented. I bet some yahoo with a sick sense of humor put food out for her, then punished and bullied her for going after it. No wonder she's underweight."

"I'll never understand people." Ben nodded thoughtfully. "There's room in my jail for whoever mistreated her."

"It would be tough to prove legally, especially since we have no idea where she came from, but it's pretty obvious that this girl's been abused. She's still shaking." Des pushed the bowl of water closer but the dog still hesitated before lowering her head and drinking. "At least she's taking water. That's a good sign."

Ben waited until the dog finished, then tried to pet her, but she shied away.

Des's phone pinged, and she swiped the screen to read the message. "Seth said bring her out and we'll see if she gets along with Ripley." She looked over at Ben. "Is he the best or what?"

"Des, I think you could ask Seth to take fifty dogs, and he'd take them in just to please you."

Des ignored the obvious intent and replied, "Seth's a dog lover and he has lots of space, that's all."

"If you say so."

"Let me get my bag and a handful of treats . . . oh wait, I have no car. Cara is the only one of us who brought her wheels."

"I'll drive you out. Get your stuff and let's go. I'm covering for one of my patrol officers at ten, though, and it's already nine twenty, so we have to hustle."

"Be right back." Des went into the house, explained to Cara where she was going, and grabbed her bag and a handful of treats.

Between Des and Ben, they were able to coax the dog into the back seat of the car. Des sat with her, talking softly to her all the way to Seth's farm.

"I see Seth has one of his many manly toys out

this morning," Ben said when they pulled into the driveway at the farm. He pointed out the window. "That man loves that ride-on mower of his. I swear he cuts the grass every time it grows half an inch."

The mower turned back toward the drive, and as it drew near, Seth waved. Des waved back and got out of the car, taking a deep breath of air scented by freshly cut grass.

"Hey, guys." Seth drove the mower to the edge of the driveway, then cut the motor. He hopped off and peered into the back seat of Seth's car. "That's the new dog?"

Des nodded. "I'm not sure if she's afraid or stubborn, but she doesn't want to come out of the car." She turned back to the dog. "Come on, sweetie," Des cooed. "You're going to stay here for a little bit."

Seth whistled, and a moment later, Ripley dashed around the corner of the house.

"Oh look, there's Ripley," Des told the dog, who was refusing to budge. "He's going to be your new friend."

Tongue lolling out of the corner of his mouth, Ripley made a mad dash for Des, then stopped at the open car door when he picked up the scent of the Lab. His tail merrily wagging, he climbed halfway into the car to greet the newcomer. When the Lab turned her head away, he gently nudged her as if to say, "Hey, look at me! I'm a fun guy! Let's play!" Finally the Lab swung her head around and whined softly.

"She's scared and she doesn't know where she

is or what's happening," Seth observed. He stood behind Des and watched his dog attempt to lure the Lab out of the car. Finally, as if resigned to her unknown fate, the dog jumped out and stood at Des's side on the grass. Ripley did his best to make the dog play, running around her and barking, but she didn't budge.

"It's okay, girl. You can play," Des urged her. Looking up at Seth, she said, "She's probably weak and tired, and I know she's got to be hungry, but she seemed afraid to eat."

Seth watched the Lab for a moment. "I've got just the thing." He turned and jogged to the house.

Moments later he returned with a plastic container in his hands. He opened the lid and stood in front of the dog. "Chicken," he explained to Des and Ben.

"Good move, feeding Rip first," Des observed, "so the Lab knows it's okay to take it. I think you're a natural." She knelt next to the dog, who this time did not shrink away, though she did shake slightly with trepidation at Des's touch.

"Thanks. I learned everything I know from Ripley." Seth petted his dog on the head. "And from you."

"Well, glad this is working out for you," Ben said, "but I have to get back into town."

Des hesitated. The dog had accepted food and was beginning to let her guard down a little, but Des wasn't sure how the Lab would react if she left so soon.

"I'll take you back, Des, if you want to stay with her for a while," Seth offered.

"Are you sure? I know you must have other things to do."

"Nothing that can't wait," he assured her.

"Well, good. That's settled." Ben closed the car door that Des had left open. "Des, good luck. I hope you find a permanent home for her, but I think you need to have a plan in place if you're going to insist on strays being brought to you instead of taken to that shelter over in Churchill."

"I looked into that place." Des stood. "It's over-crowded, the staff is poorly trained, and if an animal is not claimed in the first month, it's euthanized. I would never take an animal there."

"Well, then, come up with an alternative. You can't keep expecting Seth to bail you out every time a stray wanders into Hidden Falls."

"I think I can speak for myself, but thanks, bro." Seth stepped up to the car.

"Just pointing out the obvious, my friend," Ben muttered. He closed the car door and started the engine.

"He's right, you know," Des said as they watched Ben back out of the driveway. "I need some sort of a plan. I can't keep looking to you every time a stray's picked up."

Seth stood with his arms crossed over his chest. "Why not?" he asked.

"Because . . . because it's a big responsibility. A big undertaking."

"Right now, it's just one extra dog." He nodded in the direction of the front lawn, where the Lab and

Ripley were playing a somewhat subdued game of doggy tag. "And she seems to be doing okay."

"She's better, but still a little unsure. See how she's hesitating before she follows Ripley? But you're right. Rip's doing what we can't do. He's reassuring her in ways we can't."

"He's a good dog," Seth said softly.

"I will never be able to thank you enough for taking him," she told him. "I honestly don't know what I would have done with the dogs if you hadn't taken him and bullied Ben into taking the female." She smiled. "He finally named her, by the way. Lulu."

"After the Hoffmans' Lulu, I'll bet. Ben's neighbors when we were growing up." Seth grinned. "Now, there was a dog. Lulu was a Chihuahua and Jack Russell mix. Nasty little pup. The feistiest thing on four legs."

"I had the impression from Ben that she was a sweet dog."

Seth scoffed. "She had a mean streak, and you never knew when she was going to turn on you."

The thought crossed Des's mind that perhaps Ben's early dealings with his neighbor's dog had prepared him to deal with Allie, but before she shared that with Seth, he took her arm.

"Let's see how the new girl does inside," Seth said as he turned them both toward the farmhouse. "We'll see if she's housebroken."

"You're willing to take the chance she isn't?"

"Sure. Only one way to know for certain. And if

you're going to try to find a home for her, that's one of the things you should know, right?"

"True. Still . . ."

"I'm not worried. Let's see how it goes." Seth whistled for Ripley, who stopped in the midst of play, then ran to his owner. After hesitating for almost a minute, the Lab followed.

"Good girl." Seth opened the front door and watched the dog cross the threshold with Ripley.

Once in the house, the Lab stayed at Des's side.

"Looks like you have a friend," Seth said.

Des had followed Seth into the living room, where he gestured for her to choose a seat. The room was a cheerful blend of the 1970s and the present. The furniture was a mixed bag of formal marble-topped side tables and a mishmash of lamps, and upholstered pieces that had hung around for a decade or two too long. A large gray-stone fireplace took up one entire corner, and over it hung a photo of what appeared to be the farm in better days, the house and the barn painted and tidy, the porch level, flower beds blooming, the fields high with corn, and the apple trees heavy with fruit.

The windows were open on two sides and a cool breeze eased in. Des sat on the green-and-white-plaid sofa, the Lab at her feet. Seth took one of the club chairs and turned it so it faced her.

"So now tell me," he said. "How are you going to find a home for our new friend?"

"I can contact the local newspaper and see if

they'd like to do a feature. You know, 'Pretty Lab retriever needs a good home, maybe yours.' It could help. I could also talk to Doc Trainor and see if I could put some flyers up in his office."

Seth nodded thoughtfully.

"What?" she asked.

"I was just thinking. Let's say the dog's owner saw the newspaper article and claimed her. Could you hand her over, suspecting she'd been abused?"

"I don't know how I could avoid giving her back if someone could prove she was theirs." Des bit her bottom lip. She didn't like the odds of that happening. "We could document her condition, the fact that she's so undernourished, but that could be explained by saying she'd been loose for a while."

"And the behavior she's exhibited? How is that explained?"

Des shook her head. "It would be their word against mine."

"But you are experienced with dog behavior, right?"

"In Montana, but that means nothing out here." Des sighed. She knew he was playing devil's advocate, but the points he raised were legitimate.

"The place you have in Montana keeps the dogs you can't find homes for, right?"

"Right," she said. "We don't turn any animals away."

"At some point, maybe you should set up a shelter like that here in Hidden Falls."

"It's not that simple. I can't establish a shelter

here, then abandon it when I move back to Montana."

"Then you've already decided not to stay?" Seth asked.

"I haven't decided anything. I'm just saying it's a big decision. I've been happy there. I've done good work there. I'm not sure I'm ready to walk away for good."

"Des, sooner or later, the theater is going to be finished. You're going to need to decide."

Des frowned. "Commit or let it go, and don't bother you anymore, is that what you mean?"

"Yes, except for the part about bothering me." He reached across the space that separated them and took one of her hands. "I'll never turn you away. But at some point, the dogs might suffer. They'll need attention beyond feeding and sheltering them. Rip and I do just fine. We might even do fine with her." Seth nodded in the direction of the Lab. "But I don't know how fine it would be if there were a dozen or more of them without some sort of advance plan. Right now, it's not a problem. Hidden Falls has never been overrun with strays. I do have some room here, so if you'd come out to work with them, between the two of us, we could make it happen."

"You already have so much responsibility here. I'd hate to add to that," she told him. "This morning you were the first person I thought of. Maybe I shouldn't have . . ."

"I want you to think of me first. Always, and for anything. I'm just saying, you need a plan. I'd be happy to work with you on one." He gave her hand a squeeze, then dropped it and stood. "For now, let's leave this pretty girl here with Rip, and I'll get you back to town."

"You're going to leave them here, unattended, in your house?" Des raised an eyebrow. "That's a little risky. You don't know if she's housebroken, or if she has anxiety issues and will eat your furniture. Seriously, Seth. That's a possibility."

Seth appeared to think that over. "I don't know what else to do with her."

"What about that pen you have out back? Couldn't she stay there for a little while?"

"Let's find out how she feels about confinement." Seth called his dog, and unbidden, the Lab followed Ripley through the house and out the back door to the pen his friend had built for his litters of hounds.

Seth unlocked the old pen and went inside, both dogs following.

"Ripley looks like he's going to stick with his new friend," Des said.

"I'll get them a bowl of water, and we'll see how they react once I leave."

The dogs didn't seem to mind the enclosure, settling down in the shade even as Seth and Des walked away.

"How long do you think before they start barking or howling?" Des wondered aloud.

"That's not something Rip would do. He'll wait for me to come back, and that should keep the Lab calm as well."

"I hope you're right." She glanced over her shoulder as they walked away.

"And even if they bark, who do you think they'll disturb out here? It's not as if I have neighbors who'd complain."

"Good point."

"Any guess how old she is?"

"Not much more than twelve to eighteen months would be my guess. She looks really young, but the vet could give you a better estimate."

Seth's pickup was in the driveway, and Des walked toward it. But after a few steps, she realized he was walking in a different direction. Puzzled, she watched him open the barn door. A moment later, she heard a roar, and a startled Des jumped just as the motorcycle emerged, sputtering and puffing like a feisty black dragon. Seth rode it to the back porch, where he let it idle, and got off.

"I'll be right back," he told Des as she walked toward him. "You're going to need a helmet."

He took the steps two at a time and disappeared inside the house. Des stopped five feet from the shiny black beast, which growled softly even at idle. She'd never been that close to a bike like that before, and it was a formidable sight. She walked around it, eyeing the machine as if she was unsure if it could bite.

"Here. Try this on." Seth came down the steps wearing a leather jacket and carrying two helmets and a second leather jacket. He handed a helmet to Des and she strapped it on. She was sure she'd have the worst helmet hair in the world, but there were worse things that could happen on a bike.

"And you need the jacket, because if we take a fall—which is unlikely—the road burn would be excruciating."

"You sound as if you have personal knowledge."

He nodded. "Something I don't want to repeat. You're in luck, though, because Amy left her jacket here over the weekend."

She slipped on the jacket, which was, like his sister's shirt, several sizes too large, but she zipped it and pulled the sleeves back far enough to free her hands.

"You ever been on a bike before?" he asked as he adjusted his helmet.

"Nope."

"Too much of a walk on the wild side for you?" He slid his shades onto his face, effectively covering the twinkle in his eyes.

"Just never had the opportunity."

"And you're how old?" There was no covering up the teasing grin.

"Thirty-five."

Still smiling, Seth got onto the bike. "You're going to get onto the seat behind me. Don't worry. You're not going to fall off, but you might feel a little more secure if you hold on to me."

She climbed onto the bike, slid her arms around his waist, and settled into the seat. She could feel her heart beating in her chest, but she wasn't sure if it was due to trying something new she'd never expected to do—never really wanted to do—or her proximity to Seth's hard-as-a-rock body.

He turned and looked over his shoulder. "Ready?"

Des nodded. *As I'll ever be.*

He put the bike in gear, and the low growl became a rumble as he eased the machine onto the driveway. At the end, he paused for the one car on the road that was headed toward town. Des expected Seth to take the left that would have them following the car into Hidden Falls, but he surprised her by turning right.

"Where are we going?" she asked.

"I thought we'd take the long way home. Hold on."

The bike took off and gradually built up speed. Des ducked her head behind Seth's shoulders to keep the wind from her face, but after a few minutes, she looked up to see the countryside flash by. It was like watching a slide show. Seth took the curves and dips in the road like a pro, and before she knew it, she was leaning her face against his shoulder to catch the air.

Up hills and past farms, fields green with emerging corn, ponds surrounded by ducks and geese, and fences where horses hung their heads over the top rails to see what the commotion was before dashing away as the bike passed by. She leaned into Seth's leather-covered back as they rounded the bends in the road, and she tried really hard—unsuccessfully—to ignore how solid and strong his body felt against hers.

She realized they'd approached Hudson Street from the opposite direction when they passed the house Barney had once identified as the house where her lost love, Gil Wheeler, had lived. Seth slowed the bike, then turned into Barney's driveway and drove straight up to the carriage house. He cut the engine, then turned around.

"So whatcha think of your first ride on a Harley?" His face was so close to hers she could feel his breath on her cheek. He removed his shades so they were eye to eye.

Des knew if a woman stared too long into those dark pools, she might be lost forever. A smart woman would look away.

It was a long moment before Des heeded her own advice.

"It was fun," she said truthfully. "I liked it. A little unsure at first, but it was fun."

She got off the bike and took off the helmet just as Cara and Barney came down the back steps.

"Whoa, check you out," Cara called to Des. "Black leather, cool helmet. I must say, that biker chick look is very becoming on you."

Des laughed and took off the jacket, handing it back to Seth, who appeared very amused.

"I'm sure I have massive helmet hair, and I doubt that's becoming, but thank you. I think."

"My, I haven't ridden one of these in years," Barney said as she joined them in the driveway.

"You used to ride a bike?" Des's eyes widened.

"Oh yes. Your father went through a stage where

he thought he was James Dean. It was very short-lived because Mother was horrified, but for those few months, we did have fun." Barney patted the handlebars. "Nothing quite as masculine and danger-ous as this little number, but enough that it set many a girl's heart on fire when Fritz drove it around town, I assure you."

"Just what Dad needed. Something else to attract girls." Des wondered if J was one of those girls who was lured by the sound of the engine and the little bit of danger it represented.

"I daresay it worked its magic on more than one of the locals."

"So, Barney. Want to hop on, take a spin around town?" Seth asked.

"Not today. I'm hardly dressed for an outing, but thank you." Barney gestured toward her low-heeled shoes and pretty shirtwaist dress. "I have a luncheon with friends. But another time, yes, I'd love to."

"You name the day and time, and I'll be here." Seth turned to Des. "I'll let you know how things work out with the new dog."

"I really appreciate you taking her in. I honestly don't know what I'd have done." Seth stowed the jacket Des had handed him in a covered bag behind the passenger seat and fastened the helmet over the area where she had been sitting. "Thank you again."

"I'd say anytime, but you might take me up on that." Seth grinned. "Just kidding. It's always okay. Barney, don't forget. Anytime goes for you as well. And Cara, you're welcome, too."

"I'd go on that thing. Definitely." Cara nodded.

"'That thing,'" he repeated as if wounded.

"Your lovely bike," Cara corrected herself, unwittingly digging the hole deeper.

"Cara, a Harley is not lovely." He held a hand over his heart.

"I should shut up." Cara laughed and turned toward the house. "See you around."

"Thanks again, Seth," Des said. "For everything."

"You're welcome." He put his glasses back on, covering the softness in his gaze as he looked at Des. He turned the engine on and put the bike into gear.

"I'll be in touch," she told him. "About the dog."

Seth nodded, and blew a kiss to Barney, causing her to shake her head and laugh out loud as she blew one back.

"My, my," Barney said as Seth turned onto Hudson Street and disappeared behind the trees. "That did take me back."

"You never told us Dad had a motorcycle." Des turned from the street as the sound of the bike faded.

"I'd pretty much forgotten about that time. It was one of those things that just wasn't done, you know." She took Des's arm as they walked toward the house. "Back in my day, guys who rode bikes were considered daring and dangerous, which I suppose was the attraction." Barney smiled. "Still is, I guess. That aura of danger can be very appealing."

They reached the bottom of the steps.

"Or it can be frightening, if you're not up to the challenge it might represent."

Barney's words rang in Des's ears for the rest of the day. The questions that grew from that one simple comment were ones Des wasn't sure she could answer.

Wasn't sure she wanted to answer.

Was she hiding behind the wall of friendship, using any excuse she could think of, to avoid a deeper relationship with Seth?

No risk, no reward? Was she honestly okay with that?

Was she more comfortable with a guy like Greg, because he seemed so much safer? Because deep inside, she knew she could never have those deeper feelings for him?

And if the answers were yes, and yes, what did that say about her? Why did the thought of a relationship with Seth, one that went beyond friendship, frighten her?

She knew why. What she didn't know was what, if anything, she wanted to do about it.

Des wandered into the office the following morning and found Cara at the desk, a sheet of paper in front of her, a pen in her hand, and a dark expression on her face.

"Why so glum?"

"I just got off the phone with James Ebersol at the Balfour Group." Cara glanced up at Des. "These numbers are horrifying."

Des walked around the desk and leaned over her sister's shoulder.

"Two hundred dollars an hour?" She picked up the sheet of paper where Cara had jotted down her notes. "Are you sure you heard him correctly?"

"Nothing wrong with my hearing, Des. These guys are priced way beyond anything we could ever pay. That two hundred starts when they leave the office. They fly from Columbus, Ohio—business class. If they stay over, for whatever reason, we pay to put them up plus their hourly rate."

"So they're making two hundred dollars an hour while they're sleeping? Who gets paid like that?"

"Apparently James Ebersol and crew. They usually travel as a party of two, by the way. Ebersol likes to personally inspect every potential project. And of course, he's accompanied by one of his artisan craftspeople. For the theater, he said he'd probably bring his ace plasterer."

"My brain is still stuck on two hundred dollars an hour. Is that hourly for each person?"

"I was in so much shock, I didn't ask. But it really doesn't matter, since we can't afford to pay that for one person. Oh, and the minimum they charge for their report is five thousand dollars. We are so screwed." Cara turned all the way around in the chair.

"Okay, so we need a plan B." Des sat on the corner of the desk.

"I'm working on one. Give me a little time to think this through. First I need to call Joe. He knows everyone."

❖

At two in the afternoon, at Cara's request, all three Hudson sisters met up with Joe in the theater lobby.

"So tell them what you told me." Cara nudged Joe. "When I asked you if you had to repair really old plaster, who would you call."

"Same guy I always call," Joe replied. "Giovanni Marini."

Cara gestured impatiently. "Tell them why."

"To start with, he's ancient—don't tell Barney I said that. He's in his seventies. He's been doing plaster jobs for more than sixty of those years. He told me once that starting on his eighth birthday, growing up in Italy, he studied with his grandfather, who was a master plasterer."

"And you think he can fix that?" Allie pointed to the ceiling.

"Yes, I think he could." Joe turned to Cara. "Didn't you say the recommendation from this outfit in Ohio was to hire some pretentious plaster person? An 'artiste'?"

"Yeah. We need a 'master at the art of plaster.' So I started thinking, who is this guy, this *artiste*. And where did he get his experience? I called Ebersol back and asked him, what makes your guy so good, so much better than anyone else? And he said, well, he trained in Italy with a master craftsman."

Cara looked from Allie to Des.

"Anyone here think that maybe Mr. Marini's

grandfather/master craftsman might be about as good as the Balfour Group's master craftsman?"

Joe scoffed. "Hands down, sight unseen, I'd put my money on Marini any day."

"Definitely worth a shot," Allie agreed.

"We should at least talk to him," Des said.

"We're going to." Cara took her phone from her pocket and checked the time. "In about two minutes."

In less than that, Giovanni Marini came into the theater whistling a tune that Des vaguely recognized as an old Frank Sinatra song. He was short, wiry, and dressed in a T-shirt and shorts that showed off his bowed legs. He cheerfully introduced himself, then wasted no time by pointing overhead.

"That's the patient?"

"That's the one." Joe stood next to the man, dwarfing him.

Without missing a beat, Giovanni climbed up the scaffold. He walked the highest plank as if he were walking to his car, nonchalant, taking his time, all the while staring straight overhead. From time to time, he touched the ceiling, running his hand over the damaged area. After twenty minutes or so, he made his way back down as casually as he'd gone up.

"Looks like the work of Jack O'Brien," he told Joe. "Jack and his brother were doing a lot of plasterwork when I first came here."

"How can you tell?" Des asked.

"A master plasterer's hand is like a signature. He uses a certain amount of pressure, mixes his plaster in his own way. I've repaired a lot of O'Brien's work over the years. I'm familiar with his mix."

Cara asked, "If we asked you to do the repairs up there, what would you do?"

"Assuming you want me to match the original, I'd take a chunk of plaster out, see what mix he used. Jack had three mixes he liked. One for walls, which he wouldn't have used here. The other two"—he shrugged—"could be either."

"How could you tell them apart?" Cara followed his gaze as he looked upward.

"Some have more plaster, some more or less water, depending on what he was looking for. Sometimes more gypsum, sometimes a little more lime, sometimes vice versa."

"What's the difference?" Des asked.

"A higher concentration of lime would take longer to set up. Gives you a different finish."

"Why one over the other?" Des persisted.

Giovanni shrugged. "Personal choice is the best answer I can give you. You get to know what a job calls for after you've done it long enough."

"So how would you go about repairing that mess up there?" Cara asked.

"Well, first you have to scrape off whatever is loose, then you decide what mix you want. You apply it, you smooth it off. You can use your hands or a trowel, whichever gets you what you want, however many layers you think you need."

"Now the big question, Mr. Marini. What would you charge to work on that ceiling?" Des'd almost been afraid to ask, but surely he couldn't be as much as Ebersol's plasterer.

Giovanni stared at the ceiling for a few moments. "Well, you know, it's domed there in the middle where some of the damage is. I'm going to need to bring in a carpenter to work on the other side of the ceiling, replace the lathe if it's wet." He turned to Joe. "You could probably do that for me, right, son? Check out the lathe?"

"The roofers already looked at it. It's dry up there now. The roof only leaked that one time, and we got right on it."

"Good, good." Giovanni nodded. "You won't be insulted if I check that myself, though."

"I'd be disappointed if you didn't." Joe smiled.

"So say we just have that one domed section, and that flat part over there on the right . . . maybe eighty-five an hour. That takes into consideration I'll be matching the plaster mix exactly to the original, of course."

"Eighty-five dollars an hour," Des repeated.

"Too much?" Giovanni asked.

"No, no, that would be fine." Des glanced at Cara and Allie. "What do you think?"

"I think we've found our artiste." Cara patted Giovanni on the back. "When can you start?"

They'd said good-bye to Giovanni, who promised to draw up a contract for the job over the weekend. Cara stayed behind to talk to Joe, and Allie and Des set out for the house.

"That was a brilliant move on Cara's part," Des said.

"Let's hope Giovanni turns out to be just as good as Mr. Plaster Artist from Ohio." Allie stubbed her toe on a section of raised sidewalk and yelped, stopping briefly to rub the sore spot before catching up with Des.

"I bet he is." Des felt pretty confident that Giovanni would be every bit that. "He's going to have to be, because he's all we can afford. We still need a painter, though." The plaster may be the cake, but the decorative painting was definitely the icing. "And I have no idea where we'll find one, if we're cutting out Ebersol and his people. Dr. Lindquist didn't have a second choice, did she?"

"No, but I have an idea about that."

"Which is?"

"I'm working on it, Des. Let's leave it at that."

As they approached their front walk, a car drove up and parked in the driveway of the house across the street. A tall man with thick white hair got out and disappeared behind the wall of pine trees that obscured the property.

"Didn't Barney say the woman who lived there died last year?" Des stopped halfway up the walk and turned around.

"She did." Allie watched for a moment, but the man didn't return to the car. "Maybe he's one of the kids."

"There's only one of them around, Barney said. The one son died, the daughter's in London, and the other son was in the army."

"That might be him, then."

"Or it could be someone set to rob the place," Des suggested.

"Not in broad daylight."

"Are you kidding? People get robbed in broad daylight all the time."

They mentioned to Barney when they went inside that the empty house across the street seemed to have a visitor.

"Oh." Barney looked up from her book. "It could be Thomas." She appeared to ponder the possibility before marking her page and closing the book. "Perhaps I should check."

"We'll go with you," Des said.

"No need." Barney rose from her chair and slipped into the sandals she'd kicked off.

"What if he's, you know, a burglar?" Allie hung over the back of the love seat. "It might not be safe."

"I'll take my trusty guard dog with me." She snapped her fingers and Buttons hopped off the stool, where she'd been curled up for a nap.

"Does she even weigh twenty pounds?" Allie asked.

"Closer to fifteen, last time she was at the vet." Barney headed out of the room, the dog at her heels. "I'll just get her leash and we'll go over and see what's what."

"At least take your cell phone so you can call for help."

"Of course. I have you both on speed dial." Barney's voice trailed down the hall.

"If you're not back in ten minutes, we're coming over," Des called to her.

"If, as I suspect, it's Thomas, make it twenty," Barney called back.

"How would we know?" Allie asked as the front door closed.

"We wait fifteen minutes, then we check it out."

"Agreed." Allie put her phone on the desk. "I'll watch the time. Fifteen minutes. Then we wander over just in case she needs backup. In the meantime, we can go through some files and see if we can get a lead on our painter."

They waited the full fifteen.

"I think we should just go and make sure there's nothing funny going on over there, Allie."

"All things considered, I think Barney is capable of taking care of herself. But it has been a while. It wouldn't hurt to just ring the doorbell." Allie closed the file she'd been looking through and stood. "I'm beginning to think we're never going to figure out who the theater's artist was."

"It's inconceivable there'd be no mention of him—or her—anywhere. We just haven't looked in the right place. There has to be something." Des was first to the front door, which she opened, then paused. "Think Cara wants to come along?"

"Her car's not here, so she's probably not back from the gift shop. She said something about picking up a birthday card for a friend of hers in Devlin's Light." Allie slid her sunglasses onto her face and caught up with Des, who put her hand out to slow Allie as a car passed them, apparently not having noticed the pedestrians. When they reached the arched front door of the house across the street, Allie hit the doorbell without hesitation.

"I don't hear anything, do you?" Des asked.

Allie cocked her head to the left as if listening. "No, I . . . wait, yes. I hear Buttons barking. If no one opens the door, we're going to—"

The door opened quietly, and a tall, thin man with a shock of thick white hair stood inside.

"May I help you?" he asked.

"We're Barney Hudson's nieces," Des replied. "We think she stopped over—"

"Yes, she's here." He opened the door wider. "Come in, come in. We were just out back."

He led them through the hall that went from front to back. "She's right out here. Bonnie," he called as he opened the back door—arched to match the front—"your nieces are here seeing to your safety."

"Are we that obvious?" Des felt color rise in her cheeks.

"I'm afraid so." He offered a hand first to Des, then to Allie. "Tom Brookes."

Des and Allie introduced themselves.

"Hello, girls." Barney stood at the end of a stone patio surrounded by a low randomly set stone wall. Twenty feet behind the patio, a carriage house matching the main house was almost completely covered with ivy. "Thank God you're here. You just saved me from . . . well, whatever heinous thing Thomas was about to do to me."

"I'm still debating whether to bore you to death with tales from my war experiences, or a slide show from my trip to Iceland last year," Tom deadpanned.

"You went to Iceland?" Des asked.

He nodded.

"What was it like?"

"Cold. And not quite as icy as it used to be. A lot of it's melting." He flashed an easy smile. "Your aunt and I were just catching up on old times. And between times since we last saw each other. Care for a beer?"

Des immediately declined, but Allie appeared to think about it for a moment before saying, "We're not staying, but thank you."

"You're welcome to stay," Tom assured them.

"I think we're okay here." Des leaned over to pet Buttons. Even the dog seemed relaxed in Tom's presence.

Allie smiled at Tom. "Nice to meet you. Will you be staying in Hidden Falls for a while?"

He nodded. "I should have come back to stay for a while last year after my mother passed away, but I'd already had plans for a couple of trips I'd been looking forward to. Emily, my sister, was going to come over and start to clean out the house, but her daughter was having a rough pregnancy and she was needed there. But I'm here now and hopefully will get the house in order in no time."

"You'll be selling it, then?" Des asked.

"I can't see any reason to hold on to it." He looked up at the ivy-covered back wall of the house, not near as impressive in size as the Hudson house, but stately in its own way. "Emily's not coming back to live, with her children and grandkids settled in London."

"And you're living where?" Des asked.

"Right now, I'm here." He smiled. "My wife and I raised our family in Boston. She's been gone for almost four years now, and our son and his wife wanted to buy our family home. I'd been thinking about selling it, but didn't have the heart to see it go out of the family. Charlie and Jeannie are happy there, and I'm happy to have passed it on to them. Win-win."

"So you're more or less homeless right now."

He laughed. "I guess you could put it that way."

"Well, welcome back to your old neighborhood," Des said. "If we can help you in any way when it comes time to haul things or whatever, just let us know. We're right across the street."

"Bonnie was just mentioning that she had a full house these days." He turned and smiled at her. "I'm glad for you. It's nice that Fritz's girls have come to keep you company for a while."

"Well, the stinker didn't leave them much of a choice, but that's another story." Barney smiled back.

"Knowing Fritz, I can only imagine." He raised an eyebrow. "I can't wait to hear it."

"You'll have to come over for dinner one night," Allie said. "The story's a killer."

"I'm looking forward to it."

The thought crossed Des's mind that there was still a bit of the story that Allie hadn't heard yet. For the first time in years, they were getting along—most of the time—and Des didn't want to bring up anything that could potentially lead to a disagreement. Since she didn't know how Allie would react, she thought the letters between Fritz and J were a topic best left for another time.

"I guess we'll be seeing you around." Allie turned toward the door. "We'll see you back at the house, Barney. Don't forget we have the cocktail party tonight."

"I'll be along shortly," Barney assured her.

"That nickname." He grimaced. "Definitely something that a younger brother would tag his big sister with. She's always been Bonnie to me." He looked over his shoulder at Barney. "I remember even as a boy thinking that a pretty girl deserved a pretty name."

Des thought his expression was in fact boyish, as if he was remembering that other time.

OMG, was Barney blushing? Des did a double take.

Tom took a few steps forward as if about to show Des and Allie out.

"We're good," Des told him. "We can let ourselves out."

"It's no bother." He escorted them to the front door. "I can't wait to see what you're doing in the theater. I have fond memories of that place. Bonnie was just starting to tell me what's going on."

"You'll have to stop in and see our progress." Allie was the first one out the door after Tom opened it.

"I will definitely do that. Nice to meet you both. I'll see you again, I'm sure."

Des followed Allie down the path to the driveway. Once on the other side of the pines, Des grabbed her sister's hand and said, "She was blushing, did you catch that?"

"When he said that about her name? Yeah, it was a cute moment. *He's* cute." Allie wiggled her eyebrows as they crossed the street. "There's a history there, trust me."

"Barney was in love with Gil. She said he was the love of her life, the only man she ever loved, yada yada."

"Yeah, well, I'd bet anything Tom's feelings for Barney—excuse me, Bonnie—weren't platonic back in the day."

"You think he had a thing for her?"

Allie nodded. "Unrequited, maybe, but yeah. I think he had a big-time crush on her. I bet he still does."

"Could be. Remember, Barney said Tom and Gil were good friends. Maybe Tom didn't want to upset his friendship with Gil, so he kept quiet and just let Gil have the girl."

"Especially if he knew how Barney felt about Gil, I could see a guy putting his own feelings aside."

They reached the front porch, where Allie dropped dramatically into a rocking chair and Des sat on the porch railing.

"It's sort of romantic, don't you think?" Allie picked at her nail polish.

"It could be. She can't—she shouldn't—spend the rest of her life mourning Gil. Maybe Tom is the ticket to getting her to go forward with her life in a more meaningful way than merely updating the kitchen."

"That would be a kick, right? Barney in love? Can you imagine?"

"I don't know if it needs to go that far."

"Why not? Tom's a nice-looking man, he seems interesting and smart, and definitely interested in Barney." Allie smiled. "I do like a good second chance at a love story."

"You're getting way ahead of yourself. He's just here to clean out his family's house and get it sold."

"Right. So he says. Plans can change."

CHAPTER EIGHT

"I think I should sit in the front seat," Allie said as Barney backed Lucille out of the garage. "My dress is shorter and tighter than either of yours."

"Your choice, not ours," Des replied.

"I didn't plan it. I'm just tall and my legs are really long," Allie said.

The car stopped next to them and Barney rolled down the window.

"Hop in, girls. We're running late."

"We've been ready," Cara reminded her. "We had to wait for you."

"It isn't every day you get to catch up with an old friend you haven't seen in . . . oh, I don't even know how long it's been." Barney watched Cara and Des slip into the back seat. "We think it may have been since Gil's funeral."

Allie got into the front seat and closed the door,

smoothing the skirt of her dress over her thighs, then turned to her aunt.

"Barney, you look hot, if I may say so."

"You may." Barney smiled as she turned onto Hudson Street.

"You do look good in white," Des added. "It complements your blond hair, and you're starting to get a bit of a tan."

"The tan is from all the time I've been spending in the garden, but these days, the blond is from a bottle. I'm not ashamed to admit it."

"Why would you be? Nothing wrong with some chemical enhancements, I say." Allie lifted her hair to flow over one shoulder.

"Not that you've had to resort to such things," Des said. "Your hair has always been that beautiful shade of blond."

"Mine was like that back in the day," Barney noted. "Almost the same shade as Allie's." She glanced in the rearview mirror. "You all look lovely. I'm proud to introduce you as mine."

"Thanks, Barney," Cara began. "We—"

"Hold on." Barney hit the gas, and Cara's thought was lost in the wake of Lucille's V-8 engine as the car took off for the highway.

Des put her head back and stifled a laugh. They never quite knew what to expect once Barney got behind the wheel of her beloved Cadillac. She pushed back a few curls that had found their way onto her forehead, grateful Barney hadn't decided to put the top down. Her hair was tough enough to manage without all the wind damage she knew from experience would ensue.

It was a perfect early evening in June. The air was fragrant with the scent of roses as they drove through the tall stone entrance to the college and past several well-kept native limestone buildings backlit by the sun that had begun to set. The road through the campus was lined with maples in full leaf that shaded the walks. At the entrance to the main building, tall black iron urns overflowed with ivy and geraniums. The campus was quiet, most students having left at the end of the semester, and the summer classes not having yet begun. Barney parked Lucille in a—what else?—no parking spot. She hung her trustee tag on the rearview mirror and got out of the car. She beckoned her nieces to follow her down a cobbled path that led to a wide green, then gestured to the statue of the woman for whom the college had been named.

"There she is, girls. Your great-great-grandmother."

Des, Allie, and Cara stopped in their tracks and followed Barney's pointed finger. The statue stood eight feet tall and depicted a woman in a long, flowing dress wearing a wide-brimmed hat, holding something in her outstretched right hand.

"My, she was tall," Cara quipped.

"All the better to keep an eye on the students' doings, my dear," Barney replied.

"Why is she dressed like a pioneer?" Des frowned. "And what is she holding in her hand?"

"She's supposed to represent the pioneer spirit

that beckoned our ancestors to the Allegheny moun-
tain range." Even Barney looked amused. "She's
holding a lump of coal, representing the rocks that
funded this esteemed center of learning here in the
wilds of the Poconos."

"Think she ever actually saw a piece of coal?"
Allie walked toward the statue. "And I doubt she ever
wore anything like that daughter-of-the-prairie smock
she's got on. Hardly the thing one might wear with
emeralds."

"Oh, that's the artistic interpretation by the sculp-
tor." Barney laughed. "She wouldn't have been caught
dead wearing something like that, I'm sure, and the
story was she never wore a hat because she liked to
show off that gorgeous hair of hers." She elbowed
Allie. "So like our own."

"Which building is the party in, Barney?" Des
looked around, ever conscious of the fact that the
blond gene had missed her completely.

"Hudson Hall, right behind us. Shall we?"

Barney herded her nieces into the building and
up a short flight of steps to a lobby where several others were gathered.

"We sign in, we get our name tags, we head for
the champagne," Barney whispered from one corner
of her mouth as they walked toward a long table.

"Ms. Hudson, so nice to see you again." A gray-
haired woman wearing a tidy white blouse buttoned
to the neck and a gray skirt several inches too long
greeted the group. She oozed efficiency and order.
"And these must be the nieces."

"Margaret, nice to see you as well. Meet Allie, Des, and Cara. My brother Franklin's daughters." Barney made the first of many introductions she'd make that night.

Des stepped forward to shake the woman's hand.

"Margaret is Dr. Post's right hand," Barney explained, "and has been for many years."

"Dr. Post being the president of the college." Des recalled the school's hierarchy as Barney had explained on their way to High Bridge.

Des pinned on the name tag Barney handed her and looked around the lobby. Artwork of varying degrees of proficiency hung upon the walls, and a flag of the United States stood between that of the commonwealth and the college banner in front of a pair of double glass doors. Another set of doors opened to a room on the right from which Des could hear violins playing just below the sound of lively chatter.

"This way, girls." Barney led the way toward the music. "Let's see who we can see, who we can corner to chat up the theater project. You never know when a casual conversation might lead to something beneficial."

Over the course of the next forty minutes, Des was convinced Barney introduced them to every faculty member, board member, and donor in attendance. She wandered over to the enticing table of food and was looking over a tray of pastry-wrapped hors d'oeuvres when she felt a light hand on her shoulder.

"Des."

She turned and smiled when she met Seth's eyes. "What are you doing here?" she asked.

"Alum." He shrugged. "I'm just another loyal son of Althea, what can I say?"

"You clean up really good," she said with a grin.

He did. In dark slacks and a light gray shirt, he'd pushed the sleeves of his navy linen sport jacket almost to his elbow, showing off the tattoo that wound its way from his wrist toward his shoulder. His dark shades hung from the V made at the neckline of his shirt, and he looked better than just good. He looked hot. He looked adorable. Manly and adorable at the same time. Just looking at him made her smile.

"Thanks. So do you." He glanced at her from the corner of his eyes. "Not that you usually look like you need cleaning up. What I mean is, you always look good."

"Thanks." She laughed. "I appreciate that."

"Glad we got that straightened out." He rolled his eyes and looked slightly chagrined.

"I meant to call you today," she said. "How's the new girl?"

"Still shadowing Ripley, but he doesn't seem to mind. She's doing okay."

"No problems, then?"

"Nope. None at all."

Des stared at him for a long moment. "You're going to keep her, aren't you?"

He shrugged. "It's just one more dog, and Rip seems to like some canine company. Besides, she's a good dog, a sweet dog. I feel terrible about what must have happened to her. She's skittish and that bothers me. She needs to know that every human isn't going to hurt her or abuse her in some manner."

"You need to be careful. You're starting to sound an awful lot like someone who rescues," she said, teasing him. "Have you named her yet?"

"I'm working on it." He leaned back, as if taking her in, and smiled. Des felt her pulse race under its warmth. "I'm open to suggestions."

"She's a pretty girl, so it should be something pretty." *Gah. Did I really just say something that lame? What is wrong with me?*

Seth didn't seem to notice.

Allie joined them, champagne in hand.

"So, Seth. I hear you bailed out my little sister again. Better watch out, she'll have you running a kennel before too long."

Seth shrugged. "There are worse things that could happen."

It appeared Allie was about to say something else, but her attention seemed to be drawn to the doorway. Des turned to look as Cara, Joe, and Ben walked toward them.

"Can I go anywhere without the local law showing up?" Allie grumbled.

"You flatter yourself, princess. I'm just here for the festivities." Ben toasted her and glanced at Des. "Looking good, Des."

"Thank you, Ben. You're looking pretty sharp yourself." Des returned the toast. There was no denying that dark-haired Ben was a stud in a light blue shirt and a seersucker suit.

Allie rolled her eyes. "By festivities, you mean free wine and free food?"

"If you say so." Ben's expression was unreadable, but Des thought there might have been a glimmer of a smile in his eyes.

"What is it with those two?" she muttered to Seth, who laughed softly. Movement across the room caught her eye, and she tapped Cara on the arm. "There's Dr. Lindquist. You want to tell her about your conversation with her friend at the Balfour Group, or do you want me to?"

Teresa Lindquist was dressed in a long, flowing yellow dress, her hair in a tight bun, tortoiseshell glasses on the top of her head. She appeared to be scanning the room, and when she saw Des and Allie, she started toward them.

"I'll talk to her." Cara took a few steps forward.

"Please, allow me." Allie put out a hand to hold Cara back. "I've got this." She turned and walked to meet the woman in the middle of the room.

They watched as Allie and the head of the college Art Department greeted each other, and for several moments, their conversation appeared to be cordial. Minutes later, however, Des could tell by the way Allie's back suddenly straightened and her hands rested on her hips that something was not right. Dr. Lindquist's expression changed from friendly to haughty.

"Oh, God, Allie, what are you doing?" Des bit her

bottom lip, then grimaced as Allie turned her back on Teresa Lindquist and flagged down a nearby waiter to trade her empty glass for a full one. She charged back to where Des and the others stood with fire in her eyes. Des was not blind to the fact that Ben was watching intently as Allie drew near, taking her in from head to toe.

Inwardly Des groaned. *No, Ben. Do not go there. Don't even think about it. Anyone but Allie.* She wondered how to let Ben know that would not be a good idea.

"I take it that didn't go well," Cara said.

Allie took first one sip of her champagne, then another, before responding.

"She thinks we are idiots," Allie growled.

"Why? What did you say to her?" Des could see Allie's eyes were still flashing lightning.

"She asked me if I called Ebersol, and I said my sister did but we found they were way out of our league, and beyond anything we could handle financially."

"All true." Des shrugged. "What did she say?"

"'How unfortunate for you,' was the first thing she said," Allie said before she threw back more champagne. "I said, not really, because we were able to find a master plasterer who was local, who had basically the same training as Ebersol's man—"

"Joe already filled Seth and me in on the situation, so let me guess," Ben interrupted. "She said there was no local guy who could possibly be as good as the guy she recommended, and if you use anyone less, the ceiling would be ruined and your project is doomed, you'll never get grant money, and you should have taken her advice."

"That's almost verbatim. How did you know?" Allie frowned.

"That's Dr. Lindquist. She's always been a tad on the snooty side," Joe replied.

"Yeah, I had her for art back when she was just Mrs. Lindquist. She was a pain back then, so it sounds as if nothing's changed." His eyes on Allie, Ben added, "She's one of those people who hates to be challenged, and just wants everything they say taken as gospel. I'm sorry she turned on you."

"Thanks," Allie muttered.

Des thought there had to have been something more to the conversation, because it had seemed to have gone on longer than what had been repeated, but Allie had turned away to sample several of the hors d'oeuvres. Des would catch her later back at the house and see if she could find out what else had been said.

"Des, hi."

Greg had approached her from her blind side. She had forgotten he'd said he'd be there.

"I'm sorry I'm late. I wasn't watching the time." He touched her arm, then pointed to her empty glass. "Can I get you a refill?"

"Ah, no, I'm fine. Thanks, Greg." She looked up at Seth and said, "Greg Weller teaches history here. He's going to try to help us get a grant to finish the renovations at the theater."

"That would be great." Seth offered his hand to Greg, who seemed to be studying Seth with some interest. "Seth MacLeod."

Des introduced the others, but Greg seemed more interested in Seth, who was standing comfortably next to Des.

"Your name's familiar," Greg said. "Have we met before?"

"It's possible," Seth replied. "I've been around."

Greg shrugged as if to dismiss him, then took Des's arm. "I wanted to introduce you to Sarah Stevens, one of my colleagues who has some thoughts about several grants we might want to go after. Do you have a minute to meet her?"

"Of course." Des glanced first at Seth, then at Cara. "Excuse me while I just go—"

"Go. It's a good opportunity." Seth stepped back to let her pass in front of him.

"Nice to meet you all." Greg steered Des toward the far side of the room.

She could feel Seth's eyes on her every step of the way.

"So how is the hunt for an artist going?" Greg asked as they strolled through the crowd.

Des explained what had transpired with the Balfour Group, then added, "But Allie says she has an idea she isn't ready to share. I hope it's a good one."

"Does Allie know an artist she could call on?"

"She did take a lot of art classes when we were younger, but I doubt she knows anyone of the caliber we need."

"Ah, there's Sarah." Greg guided Des to another side of the room, where a small group gathered. "Sarah, meet my friend Des Hudson." He introduced the others, then told them, "Des and her sisters are restoring the historic theater over in Hidden Falls, and are hoping to procure some grant money to help with the renovations. I stopped by this week, and trust me, the building's well worth preserving."

Sarah immediately began to inquire about the Sugarhouse. How old was the building? Who built it? Had it always been a theater? Des responded as best she could, grateful to have the answers to almost every question, all the while her eyes straying back to her sisters and Seth. Was it her imagination, or was Allie trading in another empty glass for a full one? How much champagne had she already put away?

Her attention drifted in and out of the conversation, and from time to time, she caught Seth's gaze. She felt awkward, as if she'd let him down somehow, and she knew it was because he was wondering what role Greg played in her life. How could she explain to him when she wasn't certain herself? Greg had seemed like such a good idea at the time. Now maybe not so much.

"Hey, I promised you a tour of the campus," Greg was saying. "How 'bout we head out while it's still light?"

She opened her mouth to answer, but at that moment, Dr. Post called everyone's attention to the front of the room. She stood upon a small stage surrounded by several others whom, after her opening remarks, she introduced as trustees and college administrators, including the director of finance and scholarships, who took the microphone to make an announcement.

"I'm pleased to tell you that our fund-raising goals for the coming year have been met, and well exceeded." The director was middle-aged and bald, and had what Des considered the caricature of a happy face: round eyes, small button nose, perpetual wide smile. "Our scholarship fund has increased, and thanks to many generous gifts, we will be able to offer more financial aid to more students than at any time in the past."

A scattering of enthusiastic applause from the gathered crowd followed.

"I'm especially pleased to announce the funding of two new scholarships that will completely cover the education of two exceptional students in the field of mathematics. I know there's been talk and speculation about it this week, so let me just say that the committee will be looking for students from the Pocono area who excel in math and who would be unable to attend college without this assistance. So if you know any kids who show great promise but who have no hope of affording a four-year education, please let us know. Those of you with contacts at the local high schools, spread the word that we're going to be taking applications for the Seth A. MacLeod scholarships beginning immediately. Mr. MacLeod is an alum, a former math major and athletic star here at Althea. Some of you might know him as the mayor of nearby Hidden Falls and our assistant basketball coach. He's with us here tonight, so please feel free to express your gratitude for his generosity."

He pointed in the crowd to Seth, who nodded modestly at the applause.

Dr. Post took the mic and reiterated the college's appreciation, then after a few remarks about the summer study abroad program, she thanked everyone for coming and herded her colleagues off the stage.

Des's mouth had been hanging open since the first mention of Seth's name. At one point, Greg had leaned over and said, "Say, isn't that your friend . . . ?"

She'd nodded, and Greg had made a sort of humph sound, then added, "He doesn't look like someone who would have much of an interest in math. Basketball, yeah, but math?" He shook his head.

"Why would you say that?" Frowning, Des took a step back.

Greg shrugged. "Just look at him. Does he look like the scholarly type?"

"Looks can be deceiving, Greg," Des said, even as she recalled her own comments to Cara about Seth, which had been so like the ones Greg had just made. Embarrassingly so. Her cheeks reddened at the memory. She recalled what Joe had told her about Seth. "He won the state science fair every year when he was in high school."

"He did?" Greg stared at Seth for a moment. "That's why his name sounded familiar. That guy beat me out two years running. Damn. I can't believe I still remember that."

The applause died down, and Greg took her arm again, a gesture that was beginning to annoy her, though she wasn't sure why. "Let me take you on that campus tour now."

As he directed her toward the exit, she looked back and caught Seth's eye. He winked, smiled somewhat uncertainly, and turned away. A hole began to slowly open in the pit of her stomach. She followed Greg through the door and out into a beautiful summer evening where the first stars were beginning to emerge from the darkening sky and the air was ripe with the fragrance of wild roses and early honeysuckle that grew everywhere. The atmosphere was pure romance, and she should have felt light, like the night and the breeze that blew across the pretty mountaintop campus.

But Greg's hand felt uncomfortably heavy on the small of her back, and she had the nagging feeling that something important was missing from the picture, something that was being left behind, the distance growing with every step she took.

Allie left the house shortly after dawn and walked along quiet Hudson Street to Main, where she crossed to the theater. She unlocked the front door and slipped inside, turning on each light she passed until she reached the lobby. She stood at the base of the scaffold and looked up.

All the way up.

Her stomach lurched, already uneasy from too

much champagne and a few vodka chasers when she arrived home from Althea the night before. She definitely could have used a few more hours of sleep, but once the idea had taken hold, it became an obsession. It had nudged her awake at the crack of dawn, and headache or no, she had to see it through.

Her heart began to beat a little faster and her hands shook. She swung her bag over her shoulder and paused, wondering if she should go barefoot or keep on the sneakers she'd put on. Deciding she could always kick off the sneakers if she needed to, she hoisted herself up onto the first rung, then climbed to the plank above.

Don't look down. Do. Not. Look. Down.

Allie climbed slowly, the bag swinging slightly as she cautiously grabbed one rung after another. Fear forced her into taking her time, her mantra repeating over and over inside her head: *You've got this. You can do this.*

Halfway up she almost lost her nerve. She stopped for a moment and took several deep breaths. She was sweating from every pore, the palms of her hands wet and slippery on the rails, making her insistence on forging ahead even less rational. But she couldn't stop. This was her chance to prove that she had something real to offer. This would be her turn to shine.

You've got this. You can do this.

"Yes. I can. I will." She wiped her sweaty palms on the back of her jeans.

It was a long way to the top, and it took more

time than she'd anticipated. But when finally she stood on the highest plank, she blew out a long breath, then looked straight up.

If the ceiling was stunning from the lobby floor, it was glorious up close. The colors were so vivid, the geometric pattern leading from the chandelier so intricate, it took her breath away. Whoever had designed this had been a true artist, and for a moment she was overcome by a sense of awe, of being humbled to be so close to something so magnificent. Of wondering what the hell she thought she was doing there.

She pushed away the little voice that poked at her and demanded to know why she ever thought she could be worthy of such a challenge.

Then she remembered where she was, and her hands began to shake again. She pushed every other thought from her mind, every bit of self-doubt and fear, and focused on the task she'd set for herself.

She wiped the sweat from her eyes with the front of her shirt, then opened her bag and took out the paring knife and one of the little plastic bags she'd taken from the kitchen. She held it under a spot where the peacock-blue paint of the ceiling was bubbled.

Hands still shaking, she patiently scraped as large a chip of the brilliant color as she could get without damaging the ceiling further before closing the bag. She repeated the process until she had scraps of each color in the overhead design and their variations of shade and depth—the red, the green, the gold, the cream, the brown that hadn't been apparent from the floor. Satisfied she had all that would be needed to match the colors, she dropped the bagged chips into her shoulder bag and took out one of several sheets of tracing paper and the soft lead pencil she'd taken from the desk.

Allie carefully placed the paper over an intact area of pattern and began to trace the intricate design. When she finished, she marked every detail as to its color, then held the completed design over the damaged section.

Once satisfied she had done her best to duplicate the original, she tucked the sketch into her bag, and with a clean sheet of paper, went on to trace the next section of pattern. Each time she completed an area, she placed the tracing over the missing piece until she was satisfied. Soon she had a template for every damaged inch of the ceiling.

She'd forgotten where she was, until she began her descent from the top of the scaffold, repeating over and over, *Don't look down*.

Once she reached the bottom plank, she jumped the rest of the way to the floor, and danced jubilantly.

I did it! I made it all the way to the top, and I didn't fall, and I didn't panic! I did it.

Proud of herself for having done what she wasn't sure she could ever do—something she wasn't sure she could do again—Allie turned off the lobby lights as she made her way to the exit. She held the bag close to her body, the precious bags of colors and her sketches her secret for now.

She returned to the house as quietly as she'd left it, then went into the kitchen for coffee. In spite of the slight hangover, she felt like a million dollars. She took her coffee out onto the back patio, sat in her favorite chair and closed her eyes, and mentally relived her triumphant morning.

"You're up way early this morning." Des stood in the doorway. "You sick?"

"No. Just woke up and decided to get up." Allie's eyes were still closed.

Des came out onto the porch, a bowl of cereal in her hands, and leaned over the railing. "I'm surprised you're not hungover."

Allie's eyes flew open. She turned and faced her sister. "What are you talking about?"

"It looked like you had your fair share of champagne last night."

"One, I don't remember asking you to keep track of how much I drank, and two, I don't know how you could know since you left before the party was even half over."

"Sorry. It just seemed to me you were belting them back, as they say." Des came down the steps and took the chair opposite her sister. "Perhaps I was wrong."

"Perhaps you were." Allie rested her head against the back of the chair and closed her eyes again. She was feeling pretty good about herself, and she wasn't going to give in to the familiar urge to spar with Des. Not today. "So how was your date with History Boy?"

"It was fine."

"That's the best you can do? Fine?" Allie craned her neck to look at Des.

"The campus is beautiful. I was happy for the opportunity to see it. The buildings are so nicely designed, and the landscaping they have there must cost a fortune to maintain. The athletic fields are top-notch, and they're building a new dorm."

Allie sat all the way up and opened her eyes. "Des, you sound like a tour guide."

"Well, you asked." Des turned her attention to her cereal bowl, giving it way more attention than it merited.

"I'm going out on a limb here, and I'm going to guess that Greg didn't exactly light your fire."

Des hesitated. "He's a nice guy. He really is. But he's not . . ."

Allie smiled. She was pretty sure she knew who Greg wasn't. "So did he kiss you good night?"

Des nodded.

"More than a peck?"

Another nod.

"And . . . ?"

"And nothing."

Allie grinned. "Didn't I tell you? Didn't I say the chemistry is either there or it isn't? And obviously, it's not."

"I feel bad. I know he likes me. I wanted to like him. But . . ." She held her hands out in front of her, palms up. "Actually, I do like him. Just not in that way."

"Chemistry—attraction—between two people is not a 'fake it till you make it' type thing. You don't consciously pick who's going to turn you on by the way they dress or the way they look. You might think you do, but either you feel it or you don't."

"This is one of those times when I have to admit you're right."

Allie smiled to herself. There was a good chance that before the day ended, Des would have another reason to pat her big sister on the back.

She stood and drained the now-cool coffee from her mug. "Did you notice if Cara was up yet?"

"She stayed at Joe's last night."

"Then I guess she won't care if I take her car this morning." Allie picked up her bag and walked toward the house.

"Where are you off to?"

"Just running an errand."

"By the way, what day is Nikki coming?" Des called after her.

"Wednesday." Allie's smile grew just thinking about a reunion with her daughter. Just one more thing to make her happy this morning.

She went inside, took the key for Cara's car off the hook, and rinsed her mug before going back out.

"I won't be long," Allie called to Des as she walked to the driveway.

It was a twenty-minute drive from Hudson Street to the shopping center that was Allie's destination. She parked outside the store, which had yet to open, and read email for twenty minutes until she saw the front door swing open.

"You're an early bird." The middle-aged man wore

a light blue shirt with a name tag that read HOWARD. "Something we can help you with?"

"Your sign says you can match any paint color." She'd noticed it in the window when she'd stopped on what had become her twice-weekly vodka run to the state liquor store four doors down.

He nodded. "Yes, ma'am, we can. That's our specialty. Sets us apart from every other paint store in the valley, even those big-box stores."

"Who's the best person on your staff when it comes to matching color?"

"You're looking at him."

"How 'bout very old paint from very old chips?"

"Depends on how much I have to work with." His smile told her he was up to a challenge. "Show me what you've got."

Allie followed him to the back counter and took the paint chips from her bag. Sliding them across the smooth wood, she said, "I need each of these duplicated as near perfectly as you can get."

An eyebrow raised, he studied first one, then another. "You're not giving me much to work with here."

"Sorry. It's the best I could do."

"Never let it be said I don't love a challenge." He rubbed the back of his neck for a moment, then reached for one of the bags.

"Let's see what we've got here." He gestured for her to wait while he disappeared into the back room. When he returned, he held what looked like a large cell phone. He held it up and asked, "You know what this is?"

"Yes, sir. It's a spectrophotometer."

He seemed pleased as he removed one of the blue paint chips from its container. "Know how it works?"

"On a very elemental level. I know that you put the chip inside, then flood it with light and the light gets reflected inside where the color is analyzed."

"Right. There's a filter in here that reflects out every color except the color of the sample, and converts that remaining color to an electronic signal that goes to the computer software in here"—he tapped the spectrophotometer—"and formulates the exact amount of pigment you need to make the match."

Allie smiled. "That was the short version, right?"

"More or less." He smiled back as he set the chip in place. He hummed as he worked, at one point asking Allie, "You know you can buy these for home use nowadays, right?"

"I do. But I've heard they're not as accurate as the professional models." She pointed to the one he was using.

"That's my understanding also." He saved something on the screen, then removed the chip and returned it to the bag he'd taken it from.

"You got a reading?" She craned her neck to see.

"Uh-huh. Let's see what else we got." He ran the second chip, then the third. By the time he'd gone through each of the chips, Allie was all but jumping up and down with excitement.

"You got them all." She was beaming, and had to restrain herself from throwing her arms around his neck and hugging him.

"I got something for each one. Let's do a printout and see how close we've come." He glanced across the counter. "How much of each were you looking for?"

Allie considered how many of the prototypes she was going to create before she actually tried her hand painting on the ceiling.

She held her hand up, showing the size of the containers she wanted.

"That much, eh?" he teased.

"If these work out the way I think they will—the way I hope they will—I'll be back for more."

"Deal. I'll mix them up for you."

"You wouldn't know where I might find an art supply store somewhere around here, would you?"

"There's a shop over in High Bridge on Main Street right off the campus by the college there. Althea College—know the place?"

"I do."

"Nice school. Sent my youngest boy there. Had an ROTC scholarship. He's over in Iraq now, paying back those four years the government paid for over here."

She paid for the little sample jars and thanked Howard profusely for the time he'd spent with her.

She was in such an upbeat mood, she turned the radio up full force, found an eighties station, and sang at the top of her lungs—something she rarely did—all the way into High Bridge.

Like the paint store, the art shop opened late on Sunday, so she walked around the small college town, which was so like every other small college town she'd ever seen. Handsome shops for gifts and books, an upscale food store and a discount market, a pricy boutique and a thrift shop whose windows overflowed with summer merchandise. She stopped for take-out coffee at a preppy coffee shop, and wandered across a leafy town square, imagining how excited Des would be—how amazed she'd be—when Allie showed her how the work on the ceiling could be done. Would be done.

She finished her coffee and went into the now-opened shop, purchasing the brushes and the paper she would need. Tucking the bag under her arm, Allie went back to the car and headed for Hidden Falls, her outlook as sunny as the day was shaping up to be.

She saw an opportunity to save the day, and she was taking it. It just might even help rejuvenate her relationship with Des.

"Desdemona, you just wait till you see what your big sister has up her sleeve."

Des sat on the edge of her bed, the box containing the letters between her father and the mysterious J in her hands. She'd put off showing Allie, but more and more, as she and Allie seemed to grow a little closer, she felt increasingly that she was holding something back that Allie had the right to know. She hadn't seen Allie since she'd brought back Cara's car that morning, but she was pretty sure she was in her room.

Des knocked on Allie's door, the box still in her hands.

Allie came to the door but held it open just a crack.

"What's up?" she asked.

"I need to talk to you about something."

"Now?" Allie frowned.

Des nodded.

"Can it wait?"

"Not really." Afraid of losing her nerve, Des pushed the door open all the way and went into Allie's room. She walked around the bed and sat on the wing chair near the window.

"Do make yourself comfortable." Allie stood at the side of the bed and pulled the light summer spread over the mattress. "What's in the box?"

Des opened it and took out the sheaf of letters. "Cara found these in the carriage house. Read this one first, then this one." She handed over the letter from J before the one their father had written.

Allie opened them, first one and then the other, her only reaction being one raised eyebrow. When she'd finished, she handed them back to Des.

"I can't say I'm surprised, Des. We already figured out Dad was a horndog of the first order."

To Des's eye, Allie seemed more distracted than upset over this revelation.

"Nice way to talk about your father, Allie."

"What would you call him? To hear even Barney tell it, he nailed everything that moved in this town."

"She never said that," Des protested.

"That's what she meant when she talked about what a ladies' man he was, how the girls in Hidden Falls lined up for him." Allie shrugged. "So what's the big deal with this J person? You act like it's news. Like it's something to be upset about."

"Doesn't it bother you that he was doing this even when he and Mom were just starting out? They hadn't even gotten married yet, they were getting ready to run off together, and here's evidence he had another girlfriend, one he claimed was 'the best girl he ever knew.' That doesn't bother you?"

"No, because I'm not surprised by anything he did. Now, if that's all . . ." She moved toward the end of the bed as if to dismiss Des.

"Allie, maybe Mom knew. Maybe that's why she was the way she was."

Allie's laugh was harsh and quick. "Des, Mom was the way she was because she was a self-centered narcissist who never did a damned thing that wasn't in her best interest. I wouldn't be surprised if she knew Dad was cheating on her but didn't care as long as he got her to Hollywood and helped her to become a star."

"How could you even say such a thing?"

"Oh please. Don't tell me that never occurred to you."

"No. That was the time they were supposed to be in love."

"'Supposed to be,'" Allie said sarcastically. "Maybe because it was getting Mom where she wanted to go."

"You think she didn't really love Dad, that she just used him?"

"Des, when did Mom ever show any compassion or caring for anyone, even Dad? She pushed you into something you didn't want, she pushed me aside. And eventually, I think she pushed Dad right into Cara's mother's arms. So if you're expecting me to mourn the death of this fairy tale, that they were in love and set off for Hollywood, two crazy kids chasing a dream with stars in their eyes, no thank you. Not buying it."

Allie glanced at the bed, then moved a bag that was on top of the spread, as if covering something up.

"What's that?" Des noticed a swatch of color under the bag.

"What's what?" Allie's eyes shifted to one side.

"That stuff under the bag." She rose from the chair and put her hand out to move the bag. Allie grabbed her wrist to stop her, but not before Des saw several sheets of paper half hidden by the spread and partially under the bag.

"What is that? It looks like the pattern from the ceiling in the theater."

"That's exactly what it is."

Allie's expression, just moments before one of annoyance, changed completely. She was almost beaming as she pointed to the chair and told Des to sit back down.

"I wasn't going to show you any of this until I had it down pat, but since you're here and you already saw it . . ." Allie's excitement was visible, and growing as she drew the stack of paper from its hiding place and held up one sheet.

"This is the design from the domed section of the ceiling, where the pattern just begins to arch." She held up a second sheet. "And this is the section of that sort of geometric ray that comes out from the center. And this one is—"

"Wait, Allie, where did these come from? Where did you get those sketches?"

"I made them. And they're not exactly sketches, they're actually tracings of the intact sections." Allie held up the rest of them, one by one.

"What do you mean, you made them? How did you make them?" Des reached out and a confident Allie handed the stack to her.

"I climbed up the scaffold and traced undamaged sections that corresponded with the areas that were damaged, so that I—"

Confused, she held up her hand. "Wait. Stop." Des wasn't sure she'd heard correctly. "You climbed to the top of the scaffold?"

An obviously proud Allie nodded. "I did."

"That has to be . . . oh my God, I don't even know how high that ceiling is." Des's palms began to sweat at the very thought of it. "How could you have . . . weren't you . . ."

Allie laughed. "I was scared out of my mind, I'm not gonna lie. It was about the highest I've ever been off the floor, but I kept telling myself, *Don't look down, don't look down.* And I made it. All the way to the top."

"What's the point? I don't get it. Why'd you do that?"

"I did it because I had to. It was the only way to get . . . look." Allie took the tracings back from Des and spread them out on the bed the way they might appear on the ceiling. "Most of the patterns are pretty much geometric in shape, right? So I figured if we had tracings, we could re-create them exactly."

"I'm sorry, I'm not following."

"I traced the patterns so I could paint them on the missing sections of the ceiling." She held up the bags of paint chips. "I took scrapings to a paint store and had the colors matched. See, here's the peacock blue from the dome, and here's the—"

"You have to be kidding. Are you delusional?"

"About what?" Allie looked up.

"You're not an artist, Allie. We need an artist—a real artist—and you are not one."

Allie stared at her sister, the color draining from her face. "I can do this, Des," she said quietly.

"No, you can't. This is a historic building we're dealing with. A real artist created that masterpiece on the ceiling and a real artist is going to repair it."

"Des, I studied art for years. I used to paint, I know how to—"

"No. You're an amateur. What's the most you ever painted? A few still lifes back in college? A mural on your daughter's bedroom wall? Allie, you could totally ruin that ceiling." She shook her head. "We'll find someone else."

Allie was still staring, her expression going darker, her eyes narrowing.

"Des, may I remind you that we don't have the money to hire someone who has the kind of credentials you're talking about?"

"Then we wait until we do. But we don't send an amateur to do a pro's job."

"Des, I honestly believe I can do as good a job as anyone else."

"Based on what?"

Allie exploded. "You know, we have a problem here, and I have the solution. I've thought it out carefully, I've worked out every little detail. I would think that you would be supportive and at the very least, you'd say, 'Allie, that's a great idea. Way to think out of the box.' Or at the very least, 'It wouldn't hurt to try.'" She took a deep breath. "But instead you come in here and tell me how incompetent I am, and how I don't have any talent and—"

"I didn't say any of those things."

"That's what you meant, though. That I don't have the talent or the ability. Just like I didn't have the talent or ability to have a bigger role on your stupid TV show."

"That wasn't my decision and you know it."

Allie continued as if she hadn't heard. "You could have taken my part, could have stood up for me, asked them to give me a bigger role, but you didn't. And you're not doing it now. I'm asking you to believe in me, to give me a chance to show you what I can do. What I know I can do. But you're so negative where I'm concerned and have been all my life."

"None of that's true!" Des protested.

"All of it's true."

"It isn't. I never felt like that about you."

"Then prove it. Support me on this. You're my sister, Des. You should have my back."

Something that had built up in Des for more than twenty years poured out in a rush. "Don't talk to me about having your back. When I needed you to have mine, you looked the other way."

"When did you ever need me, Des?"

"When Brandon . . . when Brandon . . ." The cold began in her chest, then spread throughout her body. She hardly realized she was crying.

"Brandon? Brandon Whitman? What's he got to do with anything?"

Tears rushed down Des's face, and in her panic, her throat began to close. "When he . . ." she managed to gasp out.

"When he what? What are you talking about?" Still obviously angry with Des for shooting down her plans for the ceiling, Allie stood with her hands on her hips. "Wait, let me guess. He tried to kiss you? He tried to kiss everyone. It was the big joke on the set. Everyone knew it." She threw up her hands and all but yelled, "What has that got to do with anything?"

When Des found her voice, she whispered through tears, "He tried to rape me."

Allie's mouth dropped open. She blinked as if she hadn't heard correctly. "He . . ."

"Tried to rape me. While the rest of you were talking about how cute he was, what a fun guy he was, he came into my dressing room and locked the door and tried to rape me."

"Des, you never said . . ." Allie's face was white with shock. "You didn't tell anyone?"

"I tried to tell you!" Des sobbed, her entire body shaking with rage.

"Des, if you had told me he'd tried to rape you . . ."

"I did try," she insisted.

"Did you say, '*He tried to rape me*'?"

"I didn't know what words to say, Allie. I was twelve years old and terrified. And everyone thought he was so cool. And what was I going to say? This guy who was the big draw for the show—my stage big brother—the guy they'd brought in to draw preteen girls to tune in every week to boost the ratings, the guy whose father was one of the biggest stars in the universe." She stood, shaking, her words uneven. "What was I supposed to do? Who would have believed me, even if I'd had the nerve to tell someone?"

"Oh, Des . . ." Allie's eyes began to fill with tears. "Oh, honey, I am so, so sorry."

"So don't talk to me about having your back, because when I needed you, you didn't have mine."

Slamming Allie's door behind her, Des rushed blindly across the hall and sought refuge in her own room from the nightmare she'd tried to wipe from her memory and deny for more than two decades.

CHAPTER NINE

Des stood with her back to her bedroom door and tried to will herself to stop shaking. Admitting out loud what had happened took her back to that day, to the confusion and the fear and the feeling of being frozen, unable to move, when Brandon's hands had held her wrists and pinned her body down. In retrospect, she could have screamed, she could have kicked, but as a twelve-year-old who'd no experience with people who meant her physical harm—especially someone she had liked and trusted—she'd gone mute. When the director's assistant had pounded on the door to let her know her presence was required ASAP, Brandon had flashed one of his friendliest smiles, placed a finger to his lips, and whispered "Shhhhh" before releasing her.

The next day on the set, Brandon acted as if nothing had happened. He'd been his normal, teasing self, but he'd smiled at Des as if daring her to tell, which of course she did not. And she'd never bothered to ask why her, because deep inside, she knew. He'd never have attempted such a thing with Allie, whose beauty was intimidating. Allie was assertive—never passive—and would have laughed at him before she'd screamed her head off. Even as young as Des was at the time, it hadn't taken much for her to figure out that she was the perfect target.

Des had gone on as if nothing had happened, but she made sure she was never alone with him again, and from that day on, never neglected to lock her dressing room door.

Now it was out in the open, at least between her and Allie. The words she'd swallowed for so long had been spoken. She'd told. And Allie had acted as Des had wanted her to react all those years ago, with the same shock and disbelief Des herself had felt. Yet she still felt the same sense of shame that had all but suffocated her back then, the feeling that somehow she'd been at fault, even though she knew she hadn't been.

Des went into the bathroom and splashed cold water on her face. She was no longer hyperventilating, but she still felt raw. Gutted.

She grabbed her phone from the nightstand, and without giving it a second thought, sent a text to Seth.

Are you busy?

Never too busy for you. What's up? Seth texted back.

Would you come get me?

Where are you?
Home.
On my way, he wrote.
On the bike, I hope.

"That sounds like Seth." Barney looked up from the travel magazine she was reading and glanced out the front window when the Harley pulled into the driveway.

"It's Seth. He's here to pick me up." Des grabbed her bag.

"Oh?"

"I'll be back later," Des told her before Barney could say anything else.

Seth stood next to the bike holding the black jacket Des'd worn last time in one hand and a helmet in the other.

He held the jacket out to Des. "My sister might start charging you rent."

"It'll be worth it." She smiled at him, and for the first time since her argument with Allie, her heart lifted.

She strapped on the helmet, slipped her arms into the sleeves, and met Seth's eyes. "Could we go?"

"Sure." Seth got onto the bike and waited while Des situated herself before asking, "Anyplace in particular?"

"No. Just drive."

He started the bike and headed for the road. Des wrapped her arms around him, the strength of his body giving her comfort, and she felt the tension leaving her back and her shoulders and her mind like vapors rising from the falls behind Barney's house.

Seth hit the gas and took off, headed for the back roads outside Hidden Falls. The road he chose had more than its share of curves and hills, and there were times when Des felt she was hanging on for dear life. But at the same time, she felt free, and for just a while, she forgot about angry words and tearful confessions. She closed her eyes and let the wind blow into her face, wishing it were that easy to blow away bad memories and hurtful accusations.

Seth slowed a little, and the roar of the engine became a purr.

"Ever been to Rose Hill?" he shouted.

"No. What's Rose Hill?"

He accelerated the bike again and took off in the direction of two church spires she could see in the distance. Ten minutes later, the friendly message WELCOME TO THE VILLAGE OF ROSE HILL greeted them as Seth coasted to the bottom of the hill where the main street stretched along three short blocks.

Seth looked over his shoulder and asked, "Hungry?"

"Sort of."

"There's a nice restaurant right down the road, but there's also a really good market. If you're up for a steak, I can guarantee the best you ever had. No one grills beef better than I do. Not bragging, just stating a simple fact." He stopped the bike at the curb and turned to look at her. "Your choice."

"You're on."

"You won't be sorry, I promise."

He parked and they walked three storefronts down to the market, where Seth bought one of the biggest steaks Des had ever seen and a couple of potatoes.

He stopped in front of the dairy counter. "To sour cream, or not to sour cream?"

"I pass."

"Me, too. I'm a purist when it comes to my potatoes. Unless, of course, they're in potato salad. Then all bets are off." He was doing his best to keep the conversation light for her sake, and she knew and appreciated his sensitivity. "Oh. Dessert."

He grabbed her by the hand. "They have a bakery section. Really good baklava. Excellent chocolate cake."

"I haven't had baklava in . . . I don't even remember the last time."

"Baklava it is." He ordered two, then changed the order to four. "Might as well pick up breakfast while I'm here."

"You eat baklava for breakfast?"

"Hey, it's honey, nuts, and a little bit of almost bread. So it's almost like toast with honey."

"Phyllo pastry is not almost bread." She laughed at the face he made.

"What else do we need?" He looked around the store.

"Nothing. We're done."

They neared the checkout counter, where he paused and said, "Not quite."

He grabbed a bunch of yellow roses from a display and handed them to Des without a word. She could feel her heart melt inside her chest, and she smiled.

He tucked the packages into the saddlebag and they set off for Hidden Falls.

The dogs were happy to see Seth, and happier still to see Des. She crooned and praised both Ripley and the Lab for having been good while Seth was gone. "No furniture chewed. No accidents," she said as she gazed into the living room. To Seth she said, "You're either very good at making your expectations known, or you've been very lucky in the dogs you took in."

"Maybe a bit of both." He smiled and went into the kitchen, where he fed both dogs. "Besides, they mostly sleep while I'm gone."

"What can I do to help?" Des asked.

"Glad you asked." Seth opened a cabinet door and pulled out a colander. "You remember where the garden is?"

Des nodded.

"While I get the grill going, you go on out and pick some green beans for dinner."

"Sure."

She found the beans growing on small bushes planted in very straight rows. Des pushed aside the leaves and began to pick, filling the colander as she moved between the rows. It was early evening, and the sun was sinking just enough to color the fields with a soft glow, and the air was heavy with the scent of clover. She felt the day's stress slip away, and she was grateful to be in that spot at that moment.

"I like your farm," Des told him when she walked back to the patio. The dogs were side by side, watching Seth handle the steak, lured by the scent of the meat. "It's beautiful and peaceful. Thank you for bringing me here."

Seth had opened a bottle of wine, which he was pouring into two stemmed glasses.

"Thanks. It suits me. It's always seemed like home to me, even when I was a kid." He passed one of the glasses to Des.

"It's a lot of work," she thought aloud as she looked at the fields beyond his barn and the orchard that lay to the left of his house.

"Keeps me busy." The steak was on a large round platter, and he lifted it with a long-handled fork to place it on the grill. "Makes me feel like I have a place on this planet." He looked up to the sky, where the very first stars were barely visible. "Everyone needs to have a purpose. Bringing back this farm, growing things, that's mine."

Des thought for a moment what her purpose might be. Until now, she'd contributed little more than rescuing lost dogs, and she said so.

"That's your way of making things better." He turned and smiled.

"Some people say they're only dogs."

"Some people are stupid," he said. "We're all creatures of the universe, Des. We're all in this together."

She smiled at his back, knowing he understood

her in a way every other guy she'd ever known had missed.

"You can put those flowers in a vase—there's one on the sideboard in the dining room—and put it on the table here. Then you can work on that wine while you wash off those beans. There's a pot on the stove if you wouldn't mind tossing them in."

"I don't mind at all."

Seth's giving her a task had pleased her. Yes, she was his guest, but by including her in the dinner prep, she felt he'd offered her a place there, and the thought warmed her. She liked feeling part of his world.

True to his word, the steak Seth served was the best she'd ever had. They ate out on the patio at the small round table under a maple tree and drank a second glass of wine. They finished up with the baklava, which was every bit as delicious as Seth had promised.

The sun had all but set, and Seth brought out two fat candles to the table and lit them with a long wooden match. A breeze picked up, making the flames sway slightly, and in their light, his tan skin seemed to almost glow. She liked looking at him, and she knew it was more than the wine.

"I bet it's really pretty across the fields when the fireflies come out."

"Come back in a few weeks and see for yourself. It hasn't been quite warm enough for them yet."

"I guess you never miss living in town."

"I like having space. I like being able to shoot tin

cans off my back fence if I feel like it without worrying about disturbing anyone or, God forbid, hitting anyone. I like being able to get up early and walk into the morning with a cup of coffee and my dogs to greet the day." He set his glass on the table. "I think everyone needs to know where they belong, then find that place and go there." His gaze pierced her and he asked, "Where do you belong, Des?"

"I'm not sure. I used to know. At least, I thought I knew."

"What changed your mind?" He leaned back in his seat, one arm over the back of his chair.

"Coming here. Finding family I didn't know I had. Cara, Barney. They mean the world to me. I don't want to ever not have them in my life."

"And Allie?"

"That's a little more complicated." She toyed with the stem of her glass. "Growing up, we had such a mixed-up life. I told you about my parents, and how my sister resented that I had this TV show and she didn't. The thing is, she always wanted to be the center of attention, and she couldn't understand why I didn't."

"I guess you got used to it after a while, though."

Des shook her head. "I didn't. You never knew who was your friend, and who was trying to use you for something. I had this one friend, she was one of my character's classmates on the show. I liked her a lot. We started eating lunch together every day on the set, and it was nice. I finally had a friend. I thought."

Seth raised a questioning eyebrow. "You thought?"

"Turned out her father had her recording our conversations. I never did find out why, but how creepy is that? Who cares what two thirteen-year-olds talk about?"

"Was he looking for gossip or something?"

"I don't know." Thinking about her old friend led to thinking about Brandon, and thinking about Brandon made her think about the fight with Allie.

"I hurt my sister," she told Seth. "I said some terrible things to Allie today. She was trying so hard, and I laid something very heavy on her conscience."

She could feel Seth's eyes on her, then felt his hand reach out for hers. He tugged on her hand, bringing her close, then he reached over and led her from her chair to his lap.

"Talk to me, Des." She rested her head against his shoulder, and he listened without interruption.

She told him everything, starting with Brandon and how Allie had sworn she hadn't known.

"Wait. Stop right there. Are you telling me this guy actually tried to rape you?"

She nodded.

"And you were how old?"

"I was twelve." She sat back and watched his face tighten from understanding friend to a man with fire in his eyes.

"He tried to rape a twelve-year-old." He repeated the words flatly. "Where is this guy now?"

"Last I saw, he was on a sitcom. That was about two years ago."

"He's a predator. He ought to be in jail, Des."

"If you're suggesting I blow the whistle on him

now—not gonna happen," she said, shaking her head. "It was hard enough to admit to my sister what had happened, harder still to repeat the story for a second time in the same day, telling you. There's no way I could tell a stranger about what he did to me. When you talk about it, it's real again."

"Des, it's always going to be real, whether you talk about it or not."

She shook her head again. "No."

"What if he's still doing it?"

She held up a hand. "Stop. Don't try to guilt me into doing something I know I'm not capable of doing right now. Maybe someday, but not today."

He nodded slowly. "All right. I get it. 'Maybe someday' is better than never."

"Why does it matter to you?"

"Because it matters to you. Because it was a terrible thing to happen to an innocent twelve-year-old, and because you've carried that burden alone for a very long time. Sometimes just letting someone else share it helps. Sometimes it takes more than that. Sometimes it seems you can't be free of it until you confront the person who hurt you. But it's up to you—always. No one can tell you how you should feel or what's best for you. You're a very smart woman. You'll do what's right, and what's right for you, I'm certain of it."

"You really are my best friend, Seth."

"I always will be." He pulled her close again. "But none of this explains how you think you hurt Allie. What's that all about?"

She told him about the plan Allie had come up with to repair the painting on the theater ceiling and how she'd crushed Allie's ego by all but mocking her.

"I told her she was delusional if she thought she was good enough. I told her she wasn't a real artist, and I had no right to say that."

"Does she have any artistic ability?"

"Maybe. I don't really know. And because I don't know, I should have kept my mouth shut. Worse, I shouldn't have made her feel so incompetent and foolish for thinking that her idea was a good one." She turned to face him full-on. "Especially since now that I think about it, it doesn't sound so stupid."

"Did you tell Allie that?"

"Not yet. I was so upset I had to get out of the house. That's when I sent you the text. I just wanted to run away." She paused. "Actually, I wanted to ride into the sunset on the back of your bike, the wind in my hair."

"Sorry, no helmetless riders allowed. But I am glad you thought of me."

"You were the only person I thought of."

"So did the ride through the countryside and the steak make you feel better?"

Des nodded. "The ride was great, but the steak was amazing. And I do feel better."

"See? That's why it's always good to talk things over with a friend."

"We are good friends, aren't we?"

"We are."

"I don't think that's enough anymore. For a while,

I thought that was all I wanted, but now . . ." She took his face in her hands and kissed him unexpectedly. She waited for him to kiss her back, but when he didn't, she opened her eyes to see him staring at her.

"Why didn't you kiss me back?" she asked.

"I'm still in shock. That was the last thing I expected you to do. All that BFF talk, I figured you really did just see me as a friend. Which really wasn't my first choice when it comes to you, but it seemed to be yours, and I've been trying to respect that."

"That might have been really dumb on my part."

"Want to try it again?"

In the light from the candle, she could see his mouth form a teasing half smile.

She kissed him again, and this time he kissed her back, slowly at first, as if savoring his first taste of her. His arms tightened around her, and his lips claimed hers as if they'd been his all along. He tasted like honey and red wine and smelled like fresh air and early summer, and when his tongue slipped into her mouth, she sighed. Suddenly everything seemed so clear to her, so right.

A moment later, she pulled back and said, "Did you feel that?"

"Ahhh—I'm not sure if you're asking me if we felt the same thing."

She laughed into his neck. "That zingy feeling. Didn't you feel it?"

"Girl, I get a zing every time I look at you. I've been wanting to kiss you since the night I first saw you in the Bullfrog." He tucked one of her errant curls behind her ear. "Though a simple thank-you for dinner would have been sufficient."

"The steak was delicious. Thank you."

"Forget I said anything. This was way better than thank you."

She shifted in his arms. "I remember that night at the Bullfrog. It was the first night we'd all gone out together. Barney drove us in Lucille and she parked illegally—as she so loves to do—so no one could scratch the car. Allie and Ben had the first of their many scuffles and I remember watching Cara dancing with Joe and thinking how perfect they looked together."

"You got that right. They do belong together. I hope Cara stays. I think it would really mess him up if she left."

"We never talk too much about leaving or staying when the theater's done. Not really. I think we're both torn." She thought for a moment. "Not Allie. She'd leave tomorrow. But Cara . . ."

"You said both. Both torn." He turned her chin gently toward him. "Are you?"

"In some ways. I've come to love it here. I love the town, and being here with my sisters and Barney has made it all so special I don't want to think about a time when we're not all here together."

"Let me know when you figure it out, would you?"

From the look in his eyes, she knew he was about to kiss her again when her phone buzzed.

She stood and dug her phone out of her jeans. It was Cara.

"What's up?" Des asked.

"Just wondering what's going on. Allie won't come out of her room and you disappeared in a flash of Harley black. Is everything okay?"

"Pretty much." She knew Cara was wondering, so she added, "I'm at Seth's. I'll be home in a while."

"Sorry. I wasn't trying to check up on you. I just got a little worried, since I'd heard some yelling between the two of you earlier."

"Yeah, well, about that . . ."

"You don't owe me any explanation, Des. I just wanted to make sure you're all right."

"I'm good, thank you."

"Good. Oh, and by the way, Nikki called. Her flight's been changed. She'll be in tomorrow morning instead of Wednesday."

"Why the change in plans?" Des asked.

"I don't know. I didn't talk to her."

"I'll be home soon," Des told her. "We just finished dinner."

"Oh. Nice. You went out to dinner with Seth?"

"No. We cooked in." Des glanced up as he was removing the dishes from the table. "It was great," she whispered.

"Can't wait to hear about it," Cara whispered back.

"Why are you whispering?" Des asked.

"Because you were." Cara laughed. "I'm hanging up now."

"See you in a while."

"Take your time. It sounds as if you're having a good time."

"I am." Des ended the call and slipped the phone back into her pocket. To Seth, she said, "Let me help clean up."

"I'm just going to put these things inside and give the dogs a few scraps."

He carried the plates and she grabbed the serving platter and followed him into the house.

"Everything okay at home?" The dogs sat at his feet, patiently awaiting a treat from the plate in his hand.

"Nikki's coming out a couple of days early."

"So I hear."

"How'd you know before I did?" she asked.

"She and my cousin's son, Mark, have been in touch since she was here on spring break. He called this morning to ask if he could bring her out and show her the farm while she's here."

"Nice. I knew she'd met some kids her own age, but I didn't know they'd kept in touch."

"Every day via social media, from what I understand. He's a good kid." He rinsed the plate and left it in the sink. "Let's get you back home."

They locked up and walked to the end of the driveway, where he'd left the bike. He got on and waited until she was behind him and holding on before starting the engine.

"Des," he said before he put the bike in gear. "That guy at Althea."

"Greg Weller."

"Right. Him. Do I need to worry about him?"

She rested her forehead against the back of his neck and smiled.

"Nah, you don't need to worry about anyone," she told him. "Besides, he's not my type."

Des had tapped on Allie's door when she got home, but there was no answer, and the door was locked. Whether Allie was ignoring her, or really was sleeping, Des couldn't be sure. It was after ten thirty in the evening, so it wouldn't be unusual for Allie to be in bed. She often turned in earlier than the others.

Had she fallen asleep still feeling wounded?

Recalling all she'd said to cause that wound, Des regretted her words.

Her reaction to Allie's carefully thought-out plan had been unnecessarily harsh, like slicing a piece of pie with a hatchet. She could have rejected her sister's idea with kinder words, should have been more gentle in her opinion of Allie's artistic ability. But she had never seen any sign that her sister had serious artistic inclinations. She'd assumed that for Allie, it was just another one of her whims.

That Allie had forced herself to climb to the top of the scaffold should have told Des this was more than a whim. They'd both had a fear of heights for as long as she could remember, though she had no recollection of why.

In retrospect, Allie's idea wasn't such a bad one, and the more Des thought about it, the more she thought it could have merit. Why wouldn't a tracing or a stencil, copied from the original, be just as good? Okay, maybe not just as good as the artist's original work, but it could still work, couldn't it? Especially if the colors were perfectly matched and one was viewing from thirty or forty feet below the dome?

She owed Allie an apology for her callous dismissal of a good idea—certainly one worth trying. If nothing else, it demonstrated Allie had put a lot of thought into a solution that Des herself hadn't sought.

She heard a sound from across the hall—a cough maybe?—so she got up and knocked on Allie's door. Allie definitely was up and about, but it wasn't until the third knock that she opened the door. The sisters stared at each other for a long moment.

"Des, I'm sorry. I didn't know. I swear to you, if I'd known—" Allie's voice was so low it was almost a whisper. "Dear God, if I'd known, I'd have killed him. I swear to you, I never would have let that slide. I'd have told the producer, I'd have called Dad, we'd have called the police . . ."

"I know, I know. I should have said something a long time ago. It was so hard to put it into words, Al. It was so hard to make myself focus on what happened." She paused. "But I'm glad I told you. I just wish I'd done it another way, and under different circumstances. I wish I'd confided in you, but I was so confused. Especially since Mom always fawned over him, calling him the son she never had." Des tried not to feel bitter. *Too late for that*, she reminded herself.

"Mom wanted his father to cast her in a movie, that's what that was about. I think she thought cozying up to the son would get his father's attention." Allie shook her head. "Like I said, Mom was only interested in Mom. I feel sorry for both of us that we never had better."

"I didn't understand it in those terms back then, but looking back, I think you're right. It's a terrible thing to say, but the really terrible part is that it's true."

"And I was of no help to you, and I should have been. I was three years older and I should have known better. I was so wrapped up in myself. So angry that I couldn't be you." Her thoughts seemed to trail off for a moment. "I'm so sorry you had to go through that alone. That I didn't see . . ." Allie swallowed hard. "You always seemed so unhappy back then. I should have tried to make things better for you."

"Don't be so hard on yourself. You were a kid, too. How could you have known? Besides, we both had good reason to be unhappy then. It isn't as if we'd had a happy home life."

"Our screwed-up family aside, the bottom line is you were right. I should have had your back. I was older and I knew Brandon's reputation for putting girls in situations they shouldn't have been in." She shook her head. "I should have been looking out for you on the set. You were right to call me out on it. You should have done it sooner."

"It's done. Maybe now that it's out in the open, I can start to move past it. Seth thinks maybe I should—" She stopped, not wanting to open up the *should she go public or not* debate for comment.

"You discussed it with Seth?"

"I did."

Allie nodded. "He's so into you, Des. I hope you can see it. He's a good man. Maybe even good enough to be worthy of you."

"He's an exceptional guy," Des agreed. "I don't know why it took me so long to see it."

Allie forced a smile. "Well, you know, he's really not quite buttoned-down enough for you."

Des groaned. "I can't believe I said those things about him. Who cares if he smokes cigars as long as he doesn't smoke them around me? And who cares about a little body ink? He's the best guy I ever knew." Des reached out for Allie's hand. "Anyway, I wanted you to know I don't blame you for what happened so long ago. And I don't hold it against you."

"That's very generous of you. Thank you." Allie looked slightly embarrassed. "Now, if you'll excuse me . . ."

"Not until I finish." Des stuck her foot in the door so Allie couldn't close it. "Look, what I said about your idea, about the ceiling . . ."

Allie held up a hand. "Don't. Just . . . don't. I don't want to talk about it."

"Al, I think—"

"I already know what you think. It's okay." Allie appeared beaten down in a way Des had never seen before.

"Allie, listen . . ."

"I did listen. And you were right. Thanks for stopping me from making a fool out of myself in front of everyone." She began to close the door, but not before adding, "It was a stupid idea."

"Allie, that isn't what I was going to say."

"It's what you already said. Case closed," Allie said without emotion. "Move past it. I have."

Well, obviously not, Des thought as she backed away. From the other side of the door, she heard the lock slide, and she knew Allie had said all she was going to say on the matter. But it wasn't a closed door as far as Des was concerned. The idea was too good to be put aside. There had to be a way to make Allie believe in herself again. It was just a matter of finding it.

CHAPTER TEN

Nikki Monroe blew into the old Victorian house with the force of a hurricane, hugging and kissing and talking at gale speed.

"It's a shame she's so lacking in personality," Des joked as Nikki flung herself onto Barney.

"So shy and awkward. Pity," Cara agreed.

"Aunt Des!" Nikki's arms were filled with a wiggling fluffy white mass of dog, but she tried to hug Des anyway.

"Nikki, we are beyond delighted that you're here." Des wrapped both arms around her niece and Buttons licked both their faces at the same time.

"Me, too! I'm so excited for this summer. I just couldn't wait until school was over. Of course, then I had to go visit with my grandparents, but that was fun because I got to shop with Gramma and go to the pool at their complex." The dog squirmed and Nikki put her on the floor.

It always fascinated Des that Nikki barely seemed to take a breath.

"They live in this place with other old—" She glanced apologetically at Barney. "Ah . . . senior people, like retired people? They have a beautiful pool, but there was hardly anyone in it while I was there, so I got to practice my strokes every day. One of Grampa's cousins died and they wanted to go back to Indiana for the funeral, so they let me come here a little early."

Nikki hugged the dog again. "Buttons, I've missed you, too." The dog resumed licking her face, and Nikki laughed. "See, Aunt Barney, she remembers me. She missed me."

"Of course she remembers you," Barney assured her.

Des watched Allie's eyes as Allie watched Nikki. As annoying as her sister could be at times, Des knew Allie would do anything for her daughter, that she loved her as purely and as deeply as she could ever love anyone. The resemblance between mother and daughter was so strong that when Des looked at Nikki, she could almost believe she was looking at Allie at fourteen. Nikki was slightly taller than Allie had been, but they shared the same long, straight blond hair, startling bright blue eyes, long legs, perfectly proportioned body, and angelic face. What set Nikki apart was the fact that she lacked the bitterness her mother had carried with her even as a young girl. Nikki's smiles could light up the room, and her positive energy flowed around her like a magic cloak.

She happily shared her sunshine with everyone who came into her orbit.

Des thought the boys at her school must think she's a goddess. And they'd be right.

"I can't wait to see what's happening at the theater. Tell me again about the ceiling. Is it fixed yet?" Nikki chatted on as she picked up her carry-on bag. "The airline couldn't find my big suitcase. The one with all my new stuff in it." She rolled her eyes. "They said they'd bring it out as soon as they located it. Probably sent it back to L.A. I want to put this stuff in my room. Can we have dinner early? I'm starving." She started up the steps, pausing only to plant a kiss on her mother's cheek before continuing toward the second floor. "They only had these little bags of pretzels on the plane, and ugh. Carbs. Aunt Cara, could you make granola for breakfast tomorrow?"

She disappeared at the top of the steps, still chatting happily, and the four adults she'd left in her wake laughed softly.

"Welcome back, Nik." Barney beamed. "Oh, how we've missed you."

Des realized Allie hadn't moved from her spot on the step.

"You okay?" she asked.

Allie nodded slowly. "She's . . . she's everything."

"Yes," Des agreed. "She certainly is."

In honor of their California girl, they had chicken and avocado quesadillas for dinner and a large pitcher of

Barney's lemonade, which Nikki had declared her favorite drink ever.

"Wow, the kitchen looks so beautiful! I love the new cushion on the window seat! But the ivy's gone. I kinda liked it. But the all white is so clean and pretty, and the cabinets look awesome. Courtney's mom watches HGTV all the time. She'd love this. And oh! I almost forgot to tell you!" Nikki had slapped her forehead, a touch of drama for emphasis. "I wrote this essay for English class about the theater? It was about how my great-great . . ." She paused and looked at Barney. "How many greats for the one who built the theater?"

"I believe for you it's three," Barney said.

"Well, how he owned all these coal mines and how he built the theater and how when the Depression came he showed movies and had plays there and let everyone in town come for free." Nikki flashed a pleased smile. "My teacher entered it in the county writing competition, and guess who won first prize? This girl." She pointed to herself with her thumb.

Amid the "Yay, Nikki" and the "Way to go, Nik," the doorbell rang.

"I'll get it!" Nikki jumped up and ran to the hall, Buttons in pursuit, before anyone else had a chance to budge.

"You'd think she was expecting someone," Allie commented. She'd joined them for dinner but had merely picked, her stomach still in a state of flux.

Nikki's happy chatter could be heard coming toward the kitchen, and a moment later, she walked in with Tom.

". . . so I'm here for the summer," Nikki was telling him. "I just got here today."

"So I heard." Tom could not contain a smile.

Nikki's joy had apparently rubbed off on him immediately.

"Sorry to interrupt your dinner," he said. "I just wanted to drop off something to Bonnie."

"We were just finishing up. Can we give you something cold to drink?" Barney got up. "What's that you're bringing me?"

"You mentioned you were still in the garden club, so I thought you might be interested in some of my mother's old files. She was the first recording secretary of the group, and she kept a lot of notes."

"Oh, I'm sure the club would love to have those."

Tom handed the file to Barney, while behind him, Nikki held up her hands, her fingers forming the shape of a heart, obviously implying that Tom and Barney had something romantic going.

Everyone tried with mixed success to ignore her.

"Let's go into the other room and see what's in here." Barney held the file in her left hand, and as she and Tom left the room, she made a lighthearted swat at Nikki's behind, murmuring, "You little minx" as she did so.

"Aunt Barney has a boyfriend?" a wide-eyed Nikki whispered as the pair left the room. "And he called her Bonnie. Why'd he do that?"

"He grew up in the house across the street, so

they've known each other for years. He thinks Bonnie suits her better than Barney," Allie explained. "He's been away for a long time, but he's here to clean out his parents' house so it can be sold."

"So he'll be around for a while?" Nikki asked.

"At least for the next month or two, I would guess."

"Sweet."

The doorbell rang again, and Nikki dashed back down the hall, Buttons chasing her, barking all the way.

"For a house that rarely sees visitors after six p.m., there seems to be a lot of activity tonight." Allie rose. "I wonder who that is."

They'd expected Nikki to return to the kitchen, but minutes passed as Cara and Allie cleared the table and Des rinsed off the dishes and stacked them in the dishwasher. When they heard Nikki coming back down the hall, they heard a second set of footsteps.

"Mom, look who's here." Nikki came into the room, a tall, dark-haired boy around her age at her side. "You remember Mark."

"Mark?" Allie frowned. She obviously had no recollection of Mark. Des could almost hear the questions swirling inside her sister's head: Who was he, and how did he know her daughter was there?

"Remember when I was here back in April we went to that gun club where they were playing bluegrass music? I met a bunch of kids and we got to hang out for a little bit?" Nikki was obviously trying to jog her mother's memory, but Allie's expression gave no indication she had any recollection of Nikki meeting a boy—or anyone else—that night.

"Oh, of course," Des said. "You're Seth's cousin's son, right?"

"Right. My mom's his cousin Roseanne," Mark said, grateful that someone remembered him and had spoken up to break the ice.

Nikki looked up at the handsome young man with obvious stars in her eyes.

Des caught the look on Allie's face.

Uh-oh.

Silence filled the room.

Cara jumped in to kill the awkward moment. "So do you live in Hidden Falls, Mark?"

"Yes. Over on Third Street. Across from the old church."

"Are you working this summer?" Des asked.

"I'm helping Uncle Seth out on his farm. He's not really my uncle, but we all call him that, so . . ." Mark shrugged.

"It's a beautiful farm. If you like being outdoors, you should have a good summer," Des said.

"Yes, ma'am."

"Let's get lemonade and go sit on the porch." Nikki had apparently been quiet long enough. She filled two glasses with ice, then poured in lemonade and handed one to Mark. "My aunt Barney makes the best. I'm going to drink it all summer. Let's go outside."

Mark nodded a sort of *see you* to the sisters, then followed Nikki.

"She didn't tell me about him." Allie's face was rigid. "I had no idea there was a guy . . ." She turned to Des and Cara. "Did you see the way he was looking at her?" Allie almost screeched. "Puppy dog eyes."

"Of course he looks at her that way. What teenage boy wouldn't fall all over her? She's gorgeous and fun and funny and smart and lively and—"

"I know my daughter's attributes, thank you." Allie sat on the window seat. "She's too young to have guys 'falling all over her.'"

"She's almost fifteen, Allie," Des pointed out.

"I am aware of her age, Des," Allie snapped. "And she's still only fourteen. How old do you think he was? Eighteen?"

"He's the same age as she is," Des told her.

"How would you know?"

"Seth told me last night."

"There's a story we still have yet to hear," Cara reminded her. "Where did you guys go? What's going on with you two?"

Before Des could respond, Allie said, "Could we keep this conversation on track, please? My daughter hasn't been here for four hours and some strange boy shows up looking for her? How does that happen?"

"Not by accident. Seth said they've been keeping up with each other on social media and that Mark knew Nikki would be coming today instead of Wednesday."

"Well, isn't that special. She could have mentioned it to me."

"It's not a big deal, Allie. He's a good kid, and—"

"How do you know he's a good kid? Because Seth said so?"

"Seth did say so, and I believe him. Allie, you act like the guy came in here with punk green hair, smoking a joint and grabbing her butt."

"Just because he didn't doesn't mean I trust him with my daughter."

"Then trust her just a little. Trust her judgment. Sooner or later, you're going to have to."

Des leaned on the back of the chair next to the window seat where Allie sat and touched her sister's hand.

Allie shook her head. "She's so young."

"She has to start to grow up sometime, Al. Be happy it's here, where you are, and now, when she's surrounded by people who would fall on the sword for her. You've given Nik all the tools. Trust her. You have no reason not to."

Allie looked at Des with sad eyes and sighed loudly. For a moment, Des was afraid she was going to begin to wail.

"I'm not ready for her to have a boyfriend."

"None of us are. But just be grateful the boy she seems to have her eye on is not that green-haired, pot-smoking, butt-grabbing—"

"Okay, okay, I get it." Allie wadded up a napkin and threw it in Des's direction.

To Allie's mind, Mark had stayed too long, and Nikki spent too much time on the front porch with him in the dark. She had gone out once under the guise of offering more lemonade, and while she was there, she turned on the porch lights. She debated whether to watch TV with Des and Cara—which would give her cover while she waited for Nikki to come inside. Or she could go upstairs and go to bed.

Like that was going to happen with her fourteen-year-old daughter out on the front porch with a boy.

Allie excused herself from the kitchen and went up the back steps to her room. She gathered up towels that had been left on the floor after she got out of the shower, and a glass that had fallen onto the floor from the nightstand. She folded the throw that belonged on the chair and changed the sheets. She disposed of several empty vodka bottles and opened both windows, hoping to dispel the stuffy, slightly rank odor that hung in the air. There was just enough cross-ventilation that the breeze swept the staleness aside.

She bundled up her trash and took it downstairs to the large can, then went back upstairs to wait for her daughter.

"Mom? You awake?" Nikki rapped softly on Allie's door not long after.

"Come on in."

"What are you doing in here by yourself? Everyone's downstairs binge-watching season one of *The Blacklist*."

"Just a little tired tonight, that's all."

Nikki took out her phone and sat on the bed next to her mother. "I have pictures to show you. Here's the spring dance Courtney and I went to."

She held up the screen. Nikki and Courtney stood with their arms around each other, in dresses of similar style though different colors.

"You texted me that one. I remember asking about the dress because I didn't recognize it." Allie forced a smile. "You mentioned that Courtney's mother took you both shopping for dresses." She watched Nikki's face for a sign that she knew that her best friend's mother and her father were an item, but she saw nothing there.

"Right. This one—" Nikki swiped the screen. "This is from our class trip to Sacramento to the capitol building."

Nikki had a seemingly endless stream of photos, and she showed Allie every one, sharing the highlights of her life since she'd returned to California after having spent spring break in Hidden Falls.

Nikki moved from the side of the bed to the chair, presumably to respond to a text. The toe of her foot hit the bag Allie had tucked away.

"Oh, sorry, Mom." Nikki bent down to grab the bag, but when she picked it up, it was sideways, and several of the tracings fell out. "Mom, what's this stuff?"

She held up Allie's tracings.

"So pretty." Nikki stared at them for a moment. "These look like the ceiling in the theater."

"They are, sort of." Allie reached for the bag but Nikki held on to it.

"Why do you have them?" Nikki took the rest of the tracings from the bag and looked them over.

"I had an idea about filling in the missing places

on the designs, but in retrospect, it wasn't a very good idea." She reached again for the bag but Nikki ignored her.

"Did you make these?"

"Not freehand, but yes, I traced them. Like I said, it was a half-baked idea."

"What was your idea?"

"Not a very good one. I scrapped it, so there's no point in talking about it. Nik, put everything back in the bag and I'll toss them. I meant to do that yesterday, but I forgot."

"Can I have them?"

Allie laughed. "Why would you want them?"

"Because they're pretty. I bet if these were painted like the ceiling, they'd look exactly like it."

"Doubtful. Give 'em the old heave-ho." Allie held out the wastepaper basket.

"No. You don't want them, they're mine now." Nikki yawned. "I'm going to bed. I just wanted to come in and tell you how much I missed you and how happy I am to be here with you and everyone."

"Everyone including Mark?"

"Sure. He's the coolest guy."

"What makes him cool?" Allie asked.

She seemed to ponder that for a moment. "He doesn't try to be cool. He's just himself. He's not pushy or mean or anything. He's just nice. We texted a lot when I was home. He has interesting ideas, and when we talk about things, he always asks me what I think. Courtney thinks he's—" She stopped and looked away.

"Courtney thinks he's what?"

"She thinks he's corny and geeky because he studies and he's crazy smart and 'cause he doesn't smoke . . . anything. She thinks that makes him uncool, but I think it's just the opposite. It's like he knows he doesn't have to be like everyone else. He's okay being who he is."

"What's Courtney doing this summer?"

Nikki half shrugged but didn't reply.

"Isn't she your best friend?"

"Not so much anymore." Nikki yawned again. "I'm going to bed, Mom. I'll see you in the morning."

"How 'bout I come and tuck you in?"

Nikki rolled her eyes. "I'm almost fifteen. I tuck myself in these days." She kissed her mother, and Allie hugged her long and hard before kissing the side of her face.

"Sweet dreams, baby."

"You, too, Mom. See you in the morning."

Nikki padded out of the room on bare feet. Allie heard the occasional squeak of a floorboard as her daughter made her way to her room down the hall and around the corner.

Allie picked up the one tracing that had fallen under the chair and placed it on the bedside table, wondering what was going on between Courtney and Nikki, who'd been best friends since before Nikki moved into Clint's house to be closer to the tony private school he'd enrolled her in before even checking with Allie. The girls would either make up or they wouldn't. Allie had never been all that fond of Courtney, though she'd never told her daughter, since she knew one of the golden rules of parenthood was to never express strong dislike for your child's friends. To Allie, Courtney had always seemed to lean a little too far into mean-girl territory. She'd heard Courtney talk about other girls when they weren't around. She'd once asked Nikki how she'd feel if she found out that Courtney said such things about her behind her back. Predictably, Nikki had been insulted.

"Mom, she's my best friend. She wouldn't talk about me."

"I bet those other girls think she's their friend, too."

"Mom. Stop."

Allie had dropped it, but she never did warm to the girl.

Well, not her problem. Nikki was three thousand miles from Courtney and Courtney's mother. Of course, Nik was only a few blocks away from a boy who had puppy eyes when he looked at her. Allie got into bed and turned off the light, not quite sure who—Courtney or Mark—posed the greater danger to her girl's heart.

The following afternoon, all five Hudson women sat in the kitchen, eating breakfast and enjoying the chatter. Times like this, when they were all together, made this house, these women, this place, feel like home.

"I need a job," Nikki announced. "All of my friends have summer jobs. I should pull my own weight."

"What kind of a job are you thinking about?" Des asked.

"I don't know. What's around here?"

"Well, I don't know about Hidden Falls in general, but I do know of someone who's writing a book who needs an assistant." Des winked at Barney.

"Aunt Des, that would be perfect for me." Nikki put down her spoon, her eyes shining. "I'm a really good writer."

"I believe the job your aunt Des has in mind would be more of a research position to start with, am I correct, Des?" Barney asked.

"You are."

"I can do that. I'm really good at looking stuff up." Nikki was definitely getting into the idea.

"Not so much looking stuff up but more like searching for source material," Barney said, amending her comment.

"OMG, even better! Like being a detective, right?" Nikki added confidently, "I've never lost at Clue."

"Well, those are certainly skills one would need." Barney's smile went all the way to her eyes.

"Where do I apply? Who's the writer?"

"Me," Barney told her. "I'm writing a book about the theater, and I need help locating photographs and putting together stories from people in town who were there when it opened. There aren't too many of those folks left, but I know who they are and where to find them."

"What would I have to do?" Nikki was all ears.

"You'd be interviewing them, asking them to share

their photos and their stories, their memories. I've tracked down a dozen or so of them but I know there are more. Think you're up to talking to a lot of old folks about old times? Even folks older than me?" Barney asked.

"Oh yes, I'd love that. Think of all the stories I could hear." Nikki looked off into space as if she were imagining exactly that. "But it doesn't sound like a full-time job."

"I think it could be as part-time or as full-time as you make it. You in?"

Nikki nodded. "I'm in. I promise I'll do a great job. When do I start, Aunt Barney?"

"Tomorrow, if you like. Today's your first day back, so we'll relax. But we'll put you to work first thing tomorrow. I'll show you some boxes of old photos I'd like you to go through and pull out any you think are connected to the theater. Then we'll try to identify some of the people in the photos, see if they're still around, and if so, ask if they'd like to talk about their memories."

"Piece of cake," Nikki said confidently. "Will I be paid for this?"

"I was thinking of this as more of an intern-type position, but we can negotiate."

Des had watched the exchange with amusement. Nikki's enthusiasm for everything she did was infectious.

"And when you're done helping Barney, you can come to the theater and catalog the old films and movie posters," Des suggested. "We're going to want to sell some of them."

"You already did get some bids on those posters for those old horror films from the dealer in Las Vegas," Cara reminded her.

"Not enough. I'm going to negotiate a steeper price. I could tell he was interested when I spoke with him on the phone this morning, but I think he was lowballing me to see if I had any idea what they're really worth. I turned him down, but he'll be back."

"What horror movies?" Nikki asked.

"*Frankenstein* and *Dracula*. The original ones," Des told her.

"OMG, really? Vampires are so hot now, right?" Nikki's eyes widened. "If you had the films, you could do a spooky movie night on Halloween."

"That's actually a good idea," Barney said.

"We might have the films. There are so many of those metal canisters around, I never did get to look at all of them," Des said.

"I will put that on my list of things to do." Nikki took out her phone and made a note. "I'm totally into this. The theater is part of my DNA, right? And besides, I like to act. I had a role in my eighth-grade play, remember, Mom?"

"I do, indeed." Allie looked up from her coffee. "Auntie Em in *The Wizard of Oz*."

"It really would have been nice if we'd been able to do some summer stage at the Sugarhouse this year, but with the scaffold up, there's no way we could risk the liability," Des said.

"Why's there a scaffold?" Nikki asked.

"Because someone is going to have to go up to the ceiling and make the repairs," Cara told her. "We do have someone who's going to start fixing the plaster next week, but we're still looking for an artist."

Nikki looked across the table to her mother.

"Didn't you show them?" Nikki asked.

"Nikki—" Allie tried to wave her off.

"My mom did the most amazing thing. She has these tracings of the ceiling patterns that she made so she could use them to complete the missing pieces of the designs." Nikki turned to her mother. "That's what you meant, right?"

"Nik, you haven't even seen the ceiling. You don't know how complicated it could be." Allie rose and went to the sink, turning her back on the others.

"I don't know that it's all that complicated after all," Des said. If she was ever going to give Allie the credit she deserved, it was now. "I saw the tracings Allie did. The idea is really out of the box, but I think it could work. It's definitely worth trying."

"Des, you don't have to—"

"Where are the tracings you made?" Des asked.

"I have them." Nikki jumped from her seat and flew up the back steps.

"You didn't tell us you were working on a solution," Cara said. "Why didn't you say something?"

"She did say something." Des spoke before Allie could make an excuse. "She said something to me, and I blew her off without thinking it through. I insulted her and I made her feel like it was a stupid idea because I was upset about something else. But it's the best chance we have right now, and Allie, I'm sorry I shot you down without even giving it fair consideration."

"It's okay, Des. I told you, it's not a big deal. I'm over it."

"Here, look at what Mom did." Nikki laid the tracings out on the table, then she took out her phone. "Look, this is a picture I took of the ceiling when I was here before." She enlarged the detailing as best she could, but it was distorted.

"We have better photos." Des took off for the office. When she returned to the kitchen, she had Seth's photos in her hand. "Seth took some close-up shots. Here's one of the missing sections, and here's one of an area that was not affected by the leak."

"Aunt Cara, see how much Mom's look like the photos?" Nikki hung over Cara's shoulder.

Cara picked up several of the tracings and compared them to the photos.

"You know, Des is right. This could work." Cara tossed the photos onto the table. "I say Allie should see what she can do."

"Mom's a really good artist," Nikki told them. "She painted a mural in my room when I was little. It was a forest, and she painted all the little animals in it, but they were sort of hidden among the leaves and the flowers so they were camouflaged. So if you looked at it from one direction, you could see the animals. If you looked at it from a different place in the room, they were hidden. It was the coolest thing in the world. I used to fall asleep pretending I was in that forest with all my little animal friends. It was the best. Here, look. I have a picture." She scrolled through the photos on her phone again.

"You have a picture of your old bedroom wall in your phone?" Allie asked, obviously touched.

"I do. I look at it sometimes when I feel homesick for my old house and my old room."

"Honey, you didn't tell me you felt homesick."

"It's just sometimes, Mom." Nikki smiled. "It's okay. My room at Dad's is more grown-up. Sometimes I just like to pretend I'm back with my animals."

Des suspected Allie wasn't the only one with a lump in her throat.

"Wow. You did that freehand?" Cara stared at the image on the screen, and Allie nodded.

"Then making some stencils and following a pattern should be easy peasy for you. When do you want to start?" Cara handed the tracings and the photos to Barney, who studied them carefully.

Barney handed the tracings back to Nikki, but her eyes kept returning to the photos. Her fingers tapped on the table.

"What are you thinking?" Des asked, having noticed Barney's continued scrutiny of the photos.

"There's something about the colors. I don't know what I'm missing." She threw up her hands and seemed to dismiss whatever thought she'd had.

After breakfast, everyone went their own way. En route from the kitchen to the front hall, Des passed the dining room but was derailed by the scent of peonies. She went into the room and leaned into the vase that stood in the center of the table, inhaling deeply. These were the flowers Cara'd picked a few days earlier.

"What are you doing in here?" Allie stood in the doorway.

Des turned so Allie could see the vase.

"Oh, we should bring them into the parlor instead of leaving them here in a room where no one ever goes and Barney refuses to use."

"It's because of the mural." Des pointed to the wall, where the artist husband of a distant aunt had painted a scene of the waterfall that gave the town its name. The same waterfall where Barney's fiancé had fallen to his death. "I don't blame Barney for not wanting to look at it every day. It certainly doesn't hold a pleasant memory."

Allie had pulled the vase close and buried her face in the flowers.

"Des, you're right. We'll take these into the parlor where we can all enjoy them."

"Allie—look at the mural." Des stood in front of it, her hands on her hips.

"Oh, I've seen it. As much as the subject matter haunts Barney, it's a great piece of art. It almost looks like the water is flowing over those rocks. But if it hadn't been done by a well-known artist of the day, she'd have had it painted over a long time ago." Allie lifted the vase. "Which means we'd be eating in the dining room once in a while instead of the kitchen all the time. Not that I mind, but—"

"Who was the artist again?" Where had she recently seen something similar?

"Oh. Alistair Cooper. He painted a lot of landscapes in the early thirties. He met our great-great-aunt Josephine at college and they fell in love, but her parents had higher sights for her than a penniless artist. The parents went on a trip, and when they came back, they found that Alistair had painted this mural on the dining room wall, and they recognized he had real talent and figured he had promise. So they let Great-Great-Aunt Jo marry the guy. At least, that's how I remember it. He went on to become pretty famous, though it took awhile. He had a reputation for his amazing colors, their saturation. It was one of the things that set his art apart—his signature, if you will. His work has become more desirable over the past twenty years or so. That mural is worth major bucks." She narrowed her eyes. "What are you thinking?"

Des turned on the overhead light, then drew closer to the mural. "That the blues in the sky remind me a lot of the blue on the ceiling at the Sugarhouse. That peacock shade? See, right here." Des pointed to the sky above the falls.

Allie put the vase down and stepped closer. "I do see." She spoke slowly as she studied the other colors in the mural. "The green in the trees . . . the gold sunlight. The red of the flowers down near the basin . . ."

"I'll be right back."

"Don't drop something like this on me, then leave. Where are you going?"

"I'm getting Seth's photos."

Des returned with the photos, a clear shot of the ceiling in one hand. She held the photo up to the wall. "Okay, let's make allowances for lighting, and for the fact that this is a photo. Still, I think the colors are awfully close."

"I guess you're thinking what I'm thinking."

"If you're thinking that Alistair Cooper painted the ceiling at the Sugarhouse, yeah."

"The theater was built in the 1920s. Cooper painted this in the early thirties. He'd have been out of college by then, maybe hanging around Hidden Falls because of Josephine."

"We should find out. There has to be some mention somewhere."

"We've been looking for the name of the theater artist for a couple of weeks and we haven't found anything," Des reminded her.

"Maybe the ceiling wasn't painted when the theater was built. Maybe the fancy painted décor came later."

They both fell quiet, thinking of the possibilities.

"Maybe we've been looking in the wrong place," Des suggested. "Maybe the name of the artist isn't in the original files because there was no artist working on the theater when it was built. Maybe it's in a later file, or maybe someone kept a journal. Josephine, maybe, or her mother."

Allie groaned. "If there are journals, you know where they'd be."

"In the attic. Where Barney's mother stashed everything she didn't want or wasn't using, but never,

ever tossed away. It's worth looking for. Think of how much more likely we are to get a grant if we can prove that the ceiling and the lobby were early works by Alistair Cooper."

"Not if I touch them up." Allie leaned against the back of one of the dining room chairs. "I could ruin the whole thing."

"No, you won't. Let's go ask Barney if she knows where any journals might be."

"Wait, you said the mural made you think of two things. The ceiling was one. What's the other?"

"Could we have that table there, near the back of the room?" Des asked the friendly waiter.

"Of course." He led the way and handed them each a menu when they were seated. "We're not quite set up for lunch yet since it's early, so take your time. I'll be back for your beverage order."

Allie's eyes were on the framed artwork that hung on the walls of Lotus.

"What did I tell you?" Des said.

"Let's take a little walk around. There's no one else here, so we won't be disturbing anyone."

They started at the closest landscape.

"Look at the signature." Des pointed to the lower-right corner.

"Forget the signature, look at the greens in that field. That's as much his signature as his name there in the corner. The quality of the color, the chroma, if you will."

"You really did study art in college, didn't you? Why didn't you pursue it?"

Allie sighed. "Because I was stupid. I married Clint and he convinced me I'd never make any money painting. We wanted to buy a house in a certain neighborhood and we both knew I'd make more money working in TV because I could play off my family's name, which I did for years."

"Damn. I'm sorry, Al. He really sold you short."

"I sold myself short. I could have stood up to him, or I could have gone back to painting after the house was paid off. I did neither. It's on me."

They moved around the room slowly, from frame to frame, lingering longer over some than others.

"What do those rocks remind you of?" Des asked.

"They're the same rocks as the ones in the dining room, the rocks that overlook the falls. Only these are in a woodland scene. Interesting how he used elements from one in the other." Allie bit her bottom lip. "I wonder which he did first."

When they returned to the table, Allie sat next to Des and said, "I counted eight definite Coopers. They're all dated between 1924 and 1936. There are three others that are in his style, but there's no signature on those."

"I noticed that. And there are those two others where we couldn't read the name, but it's definitely not Cooper's."

"Someone needs to have a chat with the owner. If he has no idea what he has hanging on his walls, as

Greg told you, he's grossly underinsured for fire and theft."

"I'll give Greg a call."

"She said reluctantly," Allie observed. "Have you heard from him since the weekend?"

Des shook her head. "Nope. There's not much point, honestly."

"So it's Seth or nothing?"

"Something like that."

"I turn my back for one minute, and my little sister runs off with a bald, tattooed giant on a Harley. What's wrong with this picture?"

Des laughed. "Actually, it's the right picture. Finally."

"How'd you get that so wrong?" Allie asked.

"I think I wanted someone who didn't make me feel threatened. I wanted safe, nothing dangerous."

"You mean physically?"

Des shook her head. "No. I mean emotionally."

The waiter arrived for their orders.

"I'm not as hungry as I thought. Could I please just have a cup of coffee?" Des said.

"Same for me." Allie handed over her menu.

"Two coffees," the waiter mumbled as he walked away.

"Seth does present a danger," Des admitted. "He's dangerous because deep inside I think I always knew I could care about him. But if we just stayed friends, he couldn't hurt me the way Clint hurt you and Drew hurt Cara." Des swallowed hard. "And the way Dad and Mom hurt each other. I liked him enough that I wanted to keep him in my life, and for a time, I thought the only way to do that was to just be friends with him."

"You really believed that?"

Des nodded. "I said, for a time."

"And that's changed because . . . ?"

"His heart, his goodness, his honesty—those are the things that matter. When someone is as good, and kind, and sweet, and as caring as he is, it's hard not to want more. And I realized I do want more."

"How much more, exactly, did you have along with your steak?"

Des laughed at the not-so-subtle innuendo. "I kissed him. And I made him kiss me back." She smiled at the memory. "I think he was in shock at first, but he adjusted quite nicely."

"Zing went the strings of your heart?"

"Totally. Like being tossed across the room by a hot wire, to paraphrase Cara."

"And this leaves Greg where?"

"Searching for someone else to date, I suppose. Look, he is a genuinely nice guy. But he's the one I should be just friends with."

"Does he know yet?"

"It's not a big deal, really. I only went out with him twice. It's not like there was anything between us except for a few anemic kisses."

"You knew that after the first time you went out with him, so why the second date?"

"I was hoping I was wrong, I guess. I thought

dating Greg was a good idea because I think I knew instinctively that I'd never fall in love with him."

"That's just plain mean."

"Agreed. But it's what was in my twisted little mind at the time."

"What untwisted it?"

"Seth," Des told her. "Seth just being Seth."

"Awww, that's so cute. And he made you dinner."

"You scoff, but it was a very romantic dinner, out under the trees, with candlelight, flowers on the table, wine, a gentle breeze blowing across the fields, starlight." She sighed, remembering. "Oh, and incredible baklava."

"Oh dear Lord, this is more serious than I imagined."

Des laughed. "Let's go home and tell Barney and Cara what we found here, and I'll give Greg a call so he can alert his friend that he has some valuable artwork on the walls of his little restaurant."

Des called Greg from the car and left a voicemail. When he called back twenty minutes later, she was already home and in the midst of telling Barney, Cara, and Nikki what she and Allie had discovered.

"I thought maybe we could do dinner again one night this week," Greg said.

"Actually, I'm kind of tied up right now. I just wanted you to tell your friend who owns the restaurant that some of those paintings are probably worth a lot of money. He needs to bring in a credible art appraiser."

"Wow. That would be amazing, wouldn't it, after

finding all those things in a storage shed? How crazy is that?"

"I know. But it does happen. The point is he needs to secure them and make sure he has them properly appraised and insured."

"I will tell him. Now, how 'bout this weekend? Are you free?"

"Um, no, I've got plans."

"Well, could I come over and chat with your aunt about the Hudsons and the coal mines? You know, for that class I was telling you about."

"That would be fine. I'll check with her and get back to you."

"Great. Thanks. I'll look forward to it."

"I have no idea where my great-grandmother's journals would be, if in fact she kept such things," Barney was saying when Des rejoined the conversation. "Unless they're in the attic."

"I volunteer to look," Nikki said. "I was going to search up there for the emerald necklace anyway. Finders, keepers, right, Aunt Barney?"

"That's the deal." Barney nodded.

"So we know for certain Cooper did this mural, and Allie and I saw some of his work today, and some of it was dated, so we can prove he was in the area from the 1920s through at least the midthirties. The colors in the mural are very distinctive, and they are really close in quality to the colors in the theater. I think we could make a case for him having done the work in the theater."

"I suppose it would help a great deal with grants

and obtaining historic designation for the Sugarhouse if we were to prove that Alistair Cooper did all the painting," Barney said.

"I'm sure it would. In the meantime, we have the plaster repair starting next week. I'd have liked to have gotten that done faster, but Giovanni had several other jobs lined up before ours and didn't feel he could bump them. Allie, you need to be ready to go to work once the plaster is dry."

"I didn't say I'd do it. I'm still not sure that I—"

"All in favor of Allie repainting the damaged parts of the ceiling, raise your hand." Des ignored her by counting the votes. "Let's see, that would be unanimous."

"It's not. I didn't vote," Allie protested.

"Doesn't matter. You'd have lost."

CHAPTER ELEVEN

Des had offered to help Cara water the backyard flower beds and the planters for Barney, who was off at a last-minute meeting for the Fourth of July parade. The hose was already connected and in a heap on the patio, so Des was surprised to find Cara standing in the yard, staring at the carriage house.

"You're looking awfully dreamy this morning," Des noted as she picked up the hose and began to work out the kinks.

"I do love that building," Cara sighed.

"Me, too. It's a shame it isn't being used for anything these days. It would be a great space for, oh, I don't know. Maybe a yoga studio?"

"Or a home for wayward pups?" Cara countered.

"It would never work. Too noisy. Plus the building's too close to the house."

Des turned on the water and began to spray the black iron urns where Barney had planted bright red geraniums and English ivy. "Besides, you've had your sights on that place almost since day one, and you're right. It would make a perfect yoga studio."

"How did you know?" Cara frowned.

Des tapped her temple. "Psychic. It's pretty obvious that out of the three of us, you're the one who's going to stick around after our work at the theater is completed."

"Am I that transparent?"

"Hey, if I had a stud like Joe following me around with his tongue hanging out, I'd have a change of plans, too."

"He is hot, isn't he." It wasn't really a question.

"Totally hot. And he's so totally into you."

"It's mutual."

"So have you talked about staying with him?"

Cara nodded. "But more like if I did stay, maybe I could do this, or maybe I'd do that. Just in general terms, you know?"

"That's how those conversations begin. Next thing you know, you'll be flashing a pretty ring and looking for a caterer."

"Whoa, slow down. There's been no talk of rings or caterers." Cara began to deadhead an early rosebush. "But there has been some talk about me helping fix up that fixer-upper of his. He has a darling Cape Cod a few blocks from here, but it's totally 1972 once you step inside. It's dingy and dark and needs all sorts of things to spiff it up. Once Joe heard we'd redone Barney's kitchen, he figured he and I could redo his."

"You up for another project?"

"It would be fun. It's so much smaller in scale than the theater, and I wouldn't have to worry about running out of money because I wouldn't be paying for it."

"So one might assume one could be living there at some point in the future. If one were so inclined."

"One might assume that. Of course, this one would still have to earn a living."

Des took the hose into the yard to water the beds, and Cara went inside. She emerged a moment later and held up a key as she headed to the carriage house. She unlocked the door and disappeared inside.

She's going to ask Barney if she can use the second-floor space, and she and Joe are going to live happily ever after in Hidden Falls, Des mused.

Des had just finished up when Lucille roared into the driveway. Barney left the car there and stormed toward the house.

"Barney, what's wrong?" Des walked to the end of the path.

"Those damned idiots. If they think for one minute that they're going to dictate who is riding in my car and who is not, well, I'm giving them something else to think about."

"What are you talking about?"

Barney plunked herself down in one of the chairs on the patio.

"I am talking about the fact that the committee—and who put that crew in charge? I'd like to know—was trying to tell me what my agenda is for the parade. I have lived in this town all my life, I have gone to more July Fourth parades than anyone in that half-assed group has, and I know for a fact that the lead car gets to choose who rides in the back seat. Dan Hunter always got to pick who was being honored that year, and by damn, if they want Lucille to lead the parade, I get to pick who I want."

"Do you know who you want to ride with you?" Des asked.

"Of course." Barney waved one hand. "And that person is going to be in my back seat early on Wednesday morning, or there will be no classic convertible at the head of the parade." She paused as if considering. "Strike that. The hell with 'em. Lucille and I will be there with bells on."

Barney had calmed down enough to agree to meet with Greg, and when the doorbell rang at seven, Des answered it.

"Hey, Greg. Come on in. My aunt is in the front parlor." Des showed him the way.

"Great. I'm happy for the opportunity to talk to you about your family," he said as he followed her the short walk from the door to the parlor.

Des reintroduced him to Barney, then said, "Barney, Nikki is still in the attic, but she's going to the park later with Mark and some friends. Allie is down at the theater and Cara left for a birthday dinner for Joe's mother. I wouldn't look for her to come back tonight."

"Thanks, Des." Barney smiled at Greg. "So hard to keep up with all my girls sometimes. Do come in and have a seat."

Greg stood aside to allow Des to precede him, but she shook her head. "I'm on my way out, but I'm sure Barney will keep you enthralled. She's the keeper of the family history and knows everything. Well, almost everything."

"Oh, you're not . . ." He looked confused.

"No, sorry. I do have plans, as I mentioned on the phone. But really, Barney's a much more interesting subject."

The sound of thunder coming up the driveway cut her off.

"There's my ride." Des kissed Barney on the top of the head and said, "I won't be late. The farmer rises early in the morning." With a little wave to Greg, Des left the house by the front door.

"Where to?" Des asked Seth, who'd remained seated on his bike.

"I thought you could maybe help me get a few things ready for Wednesday," he said as he handed her the leather jacket. "You know, like help organize."

"Organize what?" She put on the jacket, strapped on the helmet, and climbed aboard. "What happens on Wednesday?"

"The First Annual MacLeod Farm Fourth of July Bash."

"You're having a party on the Fourth?"

"Big cookout." He started the engine.

"How many people?"

"Depends on how many show up."

"Well, how many did you invite?"

Seth paused. "I dunno. What's the population of Hidden Falls?"

He turned the bike around and headed for Hudson Street. From there, he turned right and took off for the farm.

"So what exactly do we have to do?" Des asked after they'd pulled into the driveway in front of the farmhouse.

"I don't think I've ever had a party before," he confessed. "So I was hoping you could tell me what I should do."

"This is your first gig ever, and you invited half the town?" She hopped off the back of the bike. "I hope you're kidding about that."

"More like most of the town." He took off his helmet and held a hand out for hers.

"Great. Good planning, bucko." There was something sweet about a guy who invited everyone he knew to his home to celebrate a national holiday, while at the same time being totally without a clue. "Let's see if we can work up a game plan."

The dogs raced merrily around the front yard when Seth let them out. They watched them play for a few minutes, then he whistled to bring them back, telling Des, "I don't like leaving them outside if I'm not with them. Our new girl likes to chase cars."

"Does the new girl have a name yet?" Des followed Seth into the kitchen.

"Yeah, she's Belle now. Doesn't answer to it yet,

but hopefully she'll get used to it." He checked the dogs' water bowls and refilled them when he found them half empty. "There's no way to know what her first name was. Then again, new home, new life, new name."

"I totally agree." She pulled up a chair at the table and reached into her bag, searching for a pen. "We're going to need a pad of paper."

"There's a yellow legal pad on the desk in the front hall."

She went into the hall, retrieved the pad, and came back to the table. "Let's do this thing."

"What are we doing?" Seth took the chair opposite her.

"We're making lists."

"Lists," he said flatly. "I thought you were going to help me figure out what I'm doing."

"Exactly. And you do that by making lists. Work with me here, Seth." She slid her feet from her sandals and pulled one leg up under her. "We need to zero in on how many people. Realistically, who do you know for certain is coming, as opposed to people who said maybe, or who were noncommittal?"

He started to rattle off names as she wrote them down.

"Okay, so how many of those people would you feel comfortable calling and asking them to bring something?"

"Why would I do that?"

"Because you need help. You have a rough idea how many people you invited, but you don't know how many of them are coming. You can't possibly prepare for X number of guests when you don't know what X represents. So if you ask people to bring something, you'll know if they are coming, and you can tell them what you need." She picked a name on the list. "So you call this Jim Lister and you say, hey, are you coming over after the parade—"

"No, after the stuff at the park," he corrected her.

"What happens at the park?"

"Games and things for the kids."

"No games for adults?"

"That's why we're all coming back here. Baseball. Horseshoes. Maybe even touch football or rugby."

"Sounds like fun. So okay, you call and you say, could you bring a salad? Or could you bring some drinks? That sort of thing."

"I can do that." Seth took the pad and checked off most of the names. "I can call these people this week."

"Don't wait on it, though. You don't have all that much time."

"Got it."

Des stared at the list. "You really think all these people are coming?"

He nodded. "They said they would."

"So how 'bout we figure out what you should ask them to bring? You don't want fifty people bringing salad and no one bringing dessert."

"Makes sense."

"After you call everyone, you'll have a better idea of how many to expect, so you'll know how much stuff you need to buy. You think maybe, what, eighty people at the most?"

He snorted. "Maybe closer to double that."

"You are a crazy man," she muttered.

"Maybe, but we're going to have one hell of a good time."

She laughed and made a list of things he'd need, then together they figured out what he needed to buy and what he should ask others to contribute.

"Trust me, you'll be glad you asked for help. You could go bankrupt feeding all those people. Do you know anyone who belongs to one of those warehouse clubs? You know, where you can buy things in bulk?"

"My sister does, I think."

"Find out. I can go with you to shop, if you want."

"I'd really like that. Thank you." He leaned over and kissed her, a long, slow, sweet kiss that made her heart leap and her toes curl.

"Ahhh—you're welcome," she said when he pulled away.

He took her hand and tugged her to her feet. "It's almost sunset," he told her. "Let's walk out to the vineyard. You get a perfect view there, right where the sun drops below the hill and sparkles on the pond down near the woods."

It was another perfect night, and Des thought that walking hand in hand into the vineyard at dusk was the most romantic thing she'd ever done.

"The way the light plays off the trellises just takes my breath away. You're so lucky, you get to see this every night."

"Usually with a beer in hand instead of a beautiful woman, but yeah, not too shabby. And I'm happy to share the view with you anytime. It's my favorite time of the day, and the invitation for you to spend it here with me is an open one."

They stood at the edge of the rows where he'd planted his seedlings. She thought how wonderful it would be to watch those vines take hold and grow, to twine along the trellises, to see fat bunches of grapes ripen in the sun. She was filled with longing to see it happen.

He started to walk between the rows, holding her hand to take her along, pointing out the different varieties of grapes he'd planted, sharing his dream of one day turning the barn into a winery, making the MacLeod name a respected member of the Pennsylvania wine industry.

The thought that someone else might eventually walk these fields with him and share that dream suddenly made her overwhelmingly sad, and the feeling haunted her long after he took her back to Hudson Street.

"No emeralds, Nik?" Des sat at the desk in the office on Tuesday morning, paying the theater's utility bills.

"Not yet, but I will find them." Nikki danced into the office holding a long white Victorian-era gown up against her body. "How beautiful is this? I wonder who wore it. Do you think it could have been a wedding gown? Did they wear white wedding gowns long ago?" Without missing a beat, she said, "You know, if we ever did plays at the theater, we have a ton of clothes and things we could use as costumes. Of course, we'd have to do period stuff, like *Our Town*, but it would be so fun. I love to play dress-up."

"Barney said you were welcome to try on anything you found," Des reminded her.

"Oh, and I did. There are some beautiful, like, ball gowns. We had some really fancy ladies in our family, you know."

"So I gathered from the portraits in the front hall."

"Not just the ladies, either. There are fancy men's suits. And stuff that I don't even know how you would wear them. Underclothes and stuff. I have to go online and do a search."

"If nothing else, you're getting an education in fashion this summer."

"I like clothes and things, I'm not going to deny it, but there's more to life than pretty things, you know?" Nikki sat on one of the chairs in front of the desk, the white dress folded on her lap.

Des put down the pen, wondering where this was leading. "Do tell."

"Did you know there are people who don't even have clean water to drink or to take baths in or wash their clothes in? Can you imagine having to give your baby a bath in dirty water?" Nikki made a face. "Why should anyone have to live like that?"

"Excellent questions."

"You know those hurricanes that hit all those islands? Some people still don't have homes. They're living in tents." Nikki paused. "And other people—kids, even—are going there to help rebuild their houses and help dig new wells. I want to go, but Mom and Dad would never let me."

"Who do you know who's volunteering to do those things?"

"Well, Mark and his sister and a couple of the other kids in town. They're leaving next Sunday for two weeks with their church group." She sighed heavily.

Ah, so Mark has awakened Nikki's awareness of social injustice.

"I never thought about stuff like that before. I never paid attention." Nikki looked Des in the eye and said, "That makes me a really shallow person."

"No, sweetie. It makes you someone who's fourteen who's been sheltered from a lot of the world's problems. If you were truly shallow, you wouldn't be concerned about it now."

"Mark and his sister already knew. They went last summer to Haiti and helped build a house."

"That's very good of them. But you know, they live in a different environment than you."

"I think theirs makes more sense. I think how many pairs of shoes you own or what kind of car your parents drive are stupid things to talk about. I think the kids here are smarter than the kids back home, no matter what Courtney says."

"And what exactly does Courtney say?"

"She thinks that people who live in places like

this are just too dumb to move to someplace cool. That it's more important to live in places like L.A., where there's a lot happening. She said she wouldn't be caught dead in a place like Hidden Falls."

"And you said . . . ?"

"I told her about the bluegrass concert we went to at the gun club back in April." Nikki's smile was pure mischief.

Des laughed. "I'm sure she was so jealous."

"She was when I showed her the picture of Mark that I took that night, 'cause he's so hot." Nikki leaned closer to the desk. "You don't have to tell my mom that I think Mark is hot, okay?"

"Your secret is safe with me."

"Mark said you and his uncle Seth are like, together."

"Sort of together," Des corrected. "Or maybe it's more like thinking about being together."

"Mark said he's the best guy in the world and he wishes he was his father and not his uncle. Or cousin, whatever." Nikki leaned her elbows on the desk. "He said when his dad got mean and hit his mom, his uncle Seth went over there and picked his father up and put him in his car and told him to drive. Mark said all Seth said was, 'Drive.' That's pretty brave, right? Seth was in some sort of special forces thing in Afghanistan and got injured trying to save some of the guys in his group, so of course he would be brave. That would make him a hero, right?"

"It would, yes." Des could see Seth putting his own safety aside for the sake of someone else.

"Well, they gave him a medal for it, anyway. Mark saw it. He said it's the bomb."

"I bet it is."

"Anyway, I'm going to the party out at the farm on the Fourth. All of my friends are going because all their families know Seth. We're going to have the best time. I can't wait. We never did stuff like this on July Fourth back in L.A. Dad and Mom usually just wanted to relax 'cause it was a day off for them."

"Well, I predict you will in fact have the best time at the party. I know I'm planning on doing exactly that myself."

"I love that our whole family will be there. I like us doing stuff together." Nikki held up the white dress. "I think I'll take this back up to the attic. And maybe give some serious thought to how I'm going to search for things up there this summer. Not just the necklace. I want to find some family journals, if there are any up there, and Barney said somewhere there's a box of photos from the theater. I need a plan. We already started going through the pictures some people have given Barney. Everyone looks so festive and dressed up. This book about the theater is going to rock."

Nikki got up and left the room, still chatting as she went into the hall.

"Des!" she heard Cara call.

"In here," Des called back.

"Barney wants us outside," Cara told her, appearing in the doorway.

"What's up?"

Cara shrugged. "She didn't say. She just said, go get your sisters and bring them out here."

Des followed Cara into the hall, where they met Allie. The three women filed out the back door.

Barney had turned Lucille around so the car was parked partly on the driveway and partly on the grass, and the top was up.

"What's going on?" Des asked.

"I'm recruiting the three of you to give Lucille a bath. The parade is tomorrow, and she has to look her best."

"Barney, not that I mind, but you do know there are car washes, right? There's one out on the highway past the . . ." Allie's words seemed to die in her throat when Des nudged her and gestured toward Barney, the look on her face enough to frighten the dead.

"Will you think about what you just said? You're suggesting I trust Lucille to a bunch of strangers with those big fat brushes and all those harsh chemicals?"

"Sorry," Allie apologized. "I lost my head."

"I guess you did." Barney pointed to the grass next to the car. "One of you can man the hose, one can do the soap, bucket, sponge thing, and one of you can do the chrome. I don't care how you divvy up the work, but I would be ever so grateful to you if you'd take care of this for me." Barney rubbed her hands, her expression softening. "The arthritis in my hands was a gift from my mother. I hope the genetic gods have spared the three of you from this family curse."

"Hey, we're happy to do it, Barney. Right, girls?" Des picked up the hose.

"Totally. We love Lucille, and I agree, no commercial car wash for her." Cara went for the rags to polish the chrome.

"I'll man the sponges." Allie pointed to the bucket. "Des, spray some water in here and let's get started."

"Hey, me, too!" Nikki came flying out the back door. "I want to help wash Lucille, too. Mom, toss me a sponge."

"I thought you were hunting in the attic," Des said.

"I was, but this is more fun. The attic will be there later."

By the time they'd finished, it was hard to tell who'd had control of the hose. All four were soaking wet and had traces of foamy white soap in their hair and on their clothes. Lucille was sparkling, her chrome polished and gleaming. Her tires had been scrubbed and not a speck of dirt remained anywhere.

"You girls are fabulous, you know that?" A beaming, approving Barney examined their handiwork. "She looks as good as when Mother drove her off the lot. Actually, she looks better. I can't thank you enough."

"We were happy to do it. It was fun." Des grinned.

"I can't remember the last time I laughed like that." Cara's face was still stretched into a smile.

"I hate to admit it, but yeah, it was fun." Allie squeezed the last bit of soapy water from the sponge down Des's back. In retaliation, Des aimed the hose and hit Allie square in the middle with a long stream of cold water. The two chased each other around the yard until they realized that Cara was drying off, and Des felt compelled to turn the hose on her.

"Come inside when you're finished playing, children." Barney started toward the house, but not before Des aimed for the center of her back.

"Oh, you—" Barney burst into laughter. "I should have known better than to turn my back on you. Now I suppose I will have to change before I go out."

"Where are you going?" Des turned off the hose, then turned off the water at the hookup near the back steps.

"Tom and I are going to Rose Hill to see an old friend of ours." She looked over her shoulder as she went up the steps. "No need to wait up."

"Did Barney tell you who's riding in the car with her this morning?" Des joined Cara on the front steps. "What do you suppose is taking Allie so long?"

"She's getting pretty." Cara rolled her eyes. "It takes her so long because she has to work so hard at it."

"Tell me about it. I've always lived in the shadow of 'the pretty one.'"

The door opened and Allie came out onto the porch, looking cool and perfect. Where Des and Cara were similarly dressed in navy shorts and white T-shirts, Allie wore a short light blue cotton skirt and a sleeveless white blouse.

"No red, white, and navy blue for our girl." Des looked at Cara.

"I can't help it if you two lack imagination. Let's go." Allie took four steps down the path, then stopped. "Wait, where's Nikki? I thought she was out here with you."

"She left with Barney." Des fell in step with Cara.

"Is she in the parade, then? Riding in Lucille?" Allie said.

"Who knows? I'm sure Barney had a plan."

They reached the center of town and walked across the street. The parade was setting up at the library, next to the theater. There, at the very front of the line, Lucille sat at idle, Barney behind the wheel, Nikki beside her on the passenger seat, Buttons in her arms.

As they approached the car, Des said, "Why doesn't the visiting dignitary get to sit in the back seat?"

Nikki giggled. "I'm not the dignitary. I'm the honor guard. Me and Buttons."

"Then who's sitting in the back seat?" Allie looked around. "No one looks particularly dignified to me."

"Morning, guys." A leash in each hand, Seth walked his dogs along the sidewalk. He stopped at Lucille's driver's side and asked, "Where do you want us?"

"Wait, what?" Des stood on the opposite side of the car. "You're the guest of honor?"

"Well, me, Ripley, and Belle." He pointed to his two dogs. He touched her arm. "Ready for the big bash this afternoon?"

"I'm ready. Are you?"

"Sure. Nothing to it. I'm counting on you to play hostess."

"And my duties would be . . . what, exactly?"

"Greeting and smiling at the guests. And maybe flipping the occasional burger, hunting down more bags of chips, that sort of thing."

"Sort of like second in command."

"Right. It'll be fun."

"We'll check in with you later today on that," Barney said. "Now get in the back with the dogs and let's get this show rolling."

"Why the dogs, Barney?" Allie asked.

"I decided we should use this opportunity to focus on a good cause. This year, we're focusing on rescue dogs. Of which we have three. If Ben could get here on time, we'd have four." Barney scanned the crowd.

"See the signs Seth and Mark made?" Nikki held up two signs affixed to what looked like pickets from a fence. One read, DON'T SHOP—ADOPT! The other, ASK ME ABOUT MY RESCUE DOG. "So cool, right?"

"Very cool," Des agreed.

"Ben's here." He came up behind them, Lulu on a leash. "Where do you want her?"

"Right in the back there." Barney turned around in the seat as Seth climbed in with the two dogs. "Seth, can you handle three dogs by yourself?"

"Might be easier if I had someone else back here with me." One eyebrow raised, he looked at Des.

"I'm in." She got into the back seat and grabbed the Lab's leash. "Come over here, Belle. Sit with Auntie Des and be a good girl. Just hold your head up, yes, just like that. Let everyone see how pretty you are."

"That's it. We're off." To Cara and Allie, Barney said, "You two go on up ahead to the center of town and watch the parade."

Allie hesitated. "Nik, where will I meet up with you after the parade?"

"At the park," Barney told her.

"Which park? Where is it?"

"Just follow the crowd. Now go. We're going to be taking off in another minute or so, and you want to get the whole effect of the entire parade." Barney shooed them off.

"My mom's afraid someone's going to grab me and take off with me," Nikki said.

"Hmph. I'd like to see anyone get past these four guard dogs." Barney looked into the back seat. "Not to mention the guard mayor and your two aunts. Your mother needs to relax a little."

"I keep telling her that."

The parade was about to start, and from somewhere behind Lucille, Des heard the marching band tuning up.

"Is that the Hidden Falls High School band?" Des turned in her seat and craned her neck to see behind them.

"We have a regional high here," Seth replied. "We've never had enough kids to warrant our own high school. We do have an elementary and a middle school, but they're understandably small."

"I always wanted to play in a marching band," she told him. "But I was homeschooled, so no chance of that."

"What instrument would you have liked to have played?" Seth asked.

"Something big and loud, I think. Like maybe a tuba, or one of those really big drums."

"Might have been a challenge for you, carrying and playing one of those big guys at the same time."

"I'd have given it my best." She turned back around. "I hope they sound better than that once they start marching," she said.

"They will. I think they're just goofing off."

"The school I go to is really small." Nikki leaned over the front seat as the car began to move forward. "We don't have a band. You can take music lessons, and we have a choir, but that's about it."

"Do you play an instrument or sing with the group?" Des asked.

Something about the question gave Nikki pause. Finally, she said, "No," and turned back to the front.

"Did you want to?" Des tapped her on the shoulder. "Any particular instrument?"

"Sort of. I like the sound of the clarinet, so maybe that." She glanced back over her shoulder. "Like Kenny G, you know?"

"I think Kenny G plays the saxophone."

"Right. Something like that."

"So why didn't you?"

"It's not cool," she said so softly, Des wasn't certain she'd heard her.

"Not cool—is that what you said?"

Nikki nodded.

"Says who?" Des frowned.

Nikki shrugged. "Says everyone. All my friends."

"Hey, Nik? You do you, girl," Seth interjected. "If your friends think you're uncool for doing what you like to do, maybe you need other friends."

There was no further comment from the front seat.

Lucille floated down Main Street, people on either side applauding, waving their hands and flags of various sizes, and calling to Barney as the parade passed by. From time to time, Nikki held up Buttons to wave to the crowd, and each time, she was greeted with applause.

"Oh, there's Mark! Hey, Mark!" Nikki called when they reached the corner of Main and Lake Drive. "Mark, I love the signs you made!"

Because of his height, Mark stood head and shoulders over the group of teens he was with. "Hey, Nikki! Thank Uncle Seth! It was his idea," he called back. "Don't forget to look for me up at the field after the parade."

"I won't! See you there." She'd twisted around in the front as the car continued to roll. "Hi, Kayla!" Nikki waved to a girl standing next to Mark.

"Your dog is so cute!" the girl squealed.

Nikki made sure Buttons waved, then she held up one of the signs.

"Hey, Uncle Seth!" Mark called to him. "We're all coming out to your place later."

"So I heard. You been working on your pitching skills?" Seth leaned toward the side of the car.

"Yes, sir."

"In that case, I've got a spot for you on my team."

"I'll be ready."

"Kayla, you ready for the outfield?" Seth asked as the car slowed.

"Uncle Seth, I am so ready!" she called back.

"Is she Mark's sister?" Des asked.

"No, she's Amy's daughter. Mark's sister is Hayley, the girl in the red shirt." Seth pointed her out in the crowd. "You'll meet them all later this afternoon. They'll all be at the party. Along with most of their friends. I told Mark he could invite whoever he wanted."

"Did you count them in the final tally?" Des had tried to calculate how many people would actually show up, and she'd given up. "Did you remember to pick up all the paper plates and napkins?"

"No, but my sister did, and she and my cousin are bringing a ton of food, so don't worry. We'll be fine." Seth patted her knee to assure her.

"I have visions of people lined up for miles for burgers but we've run out. They're carrying pitchforks and chanting your name. I'm hiding out in the vineyard with the dogs, by the way."

"Not gonna happen. I have enough burgers to feed my old army platoon and then some." Belle sat on the seat between them, and Seth reached across her to tuck a wayward strand of hair behind Des's ear. "It's covered. We're good. Don't worry. It'll be fine. And what's the worst that could happen? People have to eat more brownies and cupcakes than hot dogs? People in Hidden Falls know how to cook for a crowd, my friend. This might be my first blowout bash, but it's not the first Fourth of July party to be held in this town."

She hoped he was right. While she herself had never hosted a huge party like the one Seth was having, she knew enough to know that food was always the linchpin. Hearing that his sister and their cousin were in on it gave her hope.

The car slowed to take the corner, and a group of kids on the corner stepped toward the car to get a closer look at the dogs. Barney stopped the car. A pretty blond girl around Nikki's age reached for Buttons, coming close enough to the car that the little dog licked her hand.

"I love your dog," she told Nikki.

"Thanks. We do, too."

"Ella, how's your grandmother doing?" Barney addressed the girl.

"She's feeling better this week, thanks, Miz Hudson."

"You tell her I was asking after her, please."

"I will."

Behind them, the band had stopped in the middle of town to play a medley of patriotic tunes, and Barney waited until they'd finished to resume her slow drive to the park. Once they arrived, the car emptied while the rest of the parade marchers joined the gathering crowd in the park.

Several people stopped Barney, wanting to know

more about rescue dogs, and Des noticed that every time, Barney took the opportunity to talk about the importance of having a rescue shelter in the area.

"No kill, of course," Des heard her say over and over. "There's no point in warehousing dogs if you're going to kill them," a blunt sentiment that made more than one person flinch. "I don't know what I'd do without our little Buttons." Barney took the dog from Nikki's hands. "She's the best companion, and I love her to death. I'm so glad my niece rescued her and brought her home. And you know, the police chief has a rescue dog. Mayor MacLeod has two."

"She's really talking it up," Des told Seth. "You'd think she was lobbying to open a shelter on her own in town."

"Nothing that woman does would surprise me," he replied.

"Me, either."

They wandered through the crowd, pausing for the benediction that was given by Reverend Hollister and the singing of the national anthem, after which the winning floats were announced.

"I didn't even see the floats." Des looked around. "Oh, over there."

Seth took her hand and they wandered over to the area where the small floats were parked. Representing the Boy Scouts and Girl Scouts, the DAR, the civic association, the local Elks lodge, and for the first time, the gun club, the floats were all decked out in red, white, and blue crepe paper. The same colored streamers were wrapped around the handle-bars of bicycles, tricycles, and strollers.

"This is just like the parades in Devlin's Light," Cara told them when they met up with her and Joe. Allie trailed behind them, scanning the crowd.

"It's the same everywhere," Joe said. "I spent one summer with my grandparents in New Jersey, and they had almost the identical groups on floats."

"It's an American tradition," Seth agreed. "Every kid wants to deck out their bike on the Fourth for the parade."

"Remember the year we made a float out of that big wagon of Ben's? Won third prize in the small-float category," Joe said.

"Yeah. Third out of three." Seth laughed and told Des, "Not much competition that year."

"And in retrospect, it was a poor excuse for a float," Joe recalled.

"We thought we could make my grandfather's dog pull the wagon," Seth said. "But he took off as soon as the band started to play, so the three of us had to take turns pulling it down the street."

Allie caught up with them. "Have you seen Nikki?"

"She was over by Lucille with Barney last time I saw her." Des pointed behind them, and Allie took off.

"She's going to make that child crazy," Des said.

"I think it would take more than an overprotective mother to do damage to that kid's ego," Seth said.

"You didn't have a crazy mother," Des told him.

"Does a crazy father count?"

Ben wandered up and took back his dog, and so many people stopped to talk to Seth that Des's head began to spin. It seemed as if everyone mentioned coming out to the farm later.

They wandered over to the playing fields and watched the sack races and the egg toss, games Des had never played.

"Oh look, there's Nikki and Mark." Cara pointed to the egg toss lineup.

"What are they supposed to be doing?" Des asked.

"There's definitely a huge hole in your education," Seth told her. "You are about to observe the classic American egg toss. You line up across from your partner. Every couple has an egg. When the whistle blows, the egg is tossed from one partner to the next. If you catch it unbroken, you each take a step back, and you toss it again. You keep tossing it back and forth until there's only one couple left."

"Is the egg hard-boiled?" Des asked.

Seth laughed. "No. The point is to catch the egg without breaking it."

"I get it. Look, Nikki caught the egg and it's not broken. Go, Nikki!" Des shouted, and Nikki gave her a thumbs-up.

Back and forth they threw the egg, until, on the fifth try, the egg broke in Nikki's hands.

"Oh yuck!" she yelled, and held up her dripping hands. All but falling over herself laughing, Nikki left the playing field with Mark.

"Here, Nik, here's a tissue." Cara dug one out from her bag.

Still laughing, Nikki wiped her hands. "That was so fun. Can we do it again?"

"Not until next year," Mark told her. "It's a one-and-done thing."

"I'll have to make sure I'm here for that."

"Hey, they're handing out ice cream. Wanna go over to the truck?" Mark asked her.

"Sure." Nikki and Mark took off.

"Well, they seem to be having a good time," Des commented as she watched them walk away. "I wonder where Allie is."

Cara pointed to the crowd off to the right, where Allie was moving in Nikki's direction.

They watched Allie stop her daughter and engage her in conversation for a little too long.

"What do you suppose that's about?" Cara asked.

"Probably grilling the kid on where she was and what she was doing." Des watched for another minute, then said, "I can't take it." She started off toward her sister and her niece.

"Des, she's not your kid," Cara reminded her.

"No, she isn't." Des watched as a moment later, Nikki and Mark continued on their way to the ice cream truck, while Allie remained in the same spot.

Des walked across the short field. "Al," she said as she approached, "is everything all right?"

"She's with Mark again." Allie's face said it all.

"There's nothing wrong with that." Des followed Allie's gaze to where Nikki and Mark joined another group of kids who'd been in the egg toss. "See, they're just going to hang out and have a good time."

Allie watched Nikki throw her head back and laugh.

"Just fun with friends."

Allie sighed. "I know. You don't have to lecture me."

"Someone should."

"Shut up, Des." Allie smiled in spite of herself. "You know, when we're in California, she's with her father all week and I only have her with me on the weekends. I'm used to it just being her and me."

"And now you're having to share her attention with other people. Me, Barney, Cara—and now Mark and a new group of friends. I get it," Des assured her. "The older she gets, the more people she'll let into her life."

"Oh, I get it, too," Allie admitted. "I just don't like it."

"She's going to keep on growing up, Al. It's her job to grow up."

"I know that, too. It's just that . . . she's all I have, understand?"

"I do." Des put her arm around her sister and turned her toward the side of the field where Seth, Cara, and Joe waited.

"Come on. We'll get the others and then go get ice cream."

They'd almost made it to the edge of the field when Allie stopped. "There's that man again."

"That man . . . ?" Des frowned, then laughed. "You mean Ben."

"Keep moving." Allie gave her a light shove in the middle of her back.

"So did you save your kid from my cousin's son?" Seth asked when they caught up.

"No. And God knows who all those other kids are. Could be a bunch of budding felons." Allie sounded as if she was only half kidding.

"Hey, want me to run some background checks?" Ben said.

"Would you?" Allie's eyes lit up.

"No." Ben shook his head.

"What good is having the sheriff around if he won't come through in a pinch?" Allie complained.

"What good is a sheriff who spies on the local kids at the whim of an overprotective mother?" he replied.

"Spoken like a man who has . . ." Allie's words died in her mouth. A moment later, she finished the sentence. "Like a man who has a sheriff's badge."

Ben stared long and hard at her. He looked at Seth and said simply, "See you around."

"See you around two, you mean," Seth said.

"Yeah, maybe." Ben backed away from the group, his eyes on Allie.

"No maybe, man. I'm counting on you for second base."

Ben walked away, his back stiff.

"Oh my God." Allie's hand covered her mouth. "I can't believe how stupid I am."

"What just happened here?" Des asked.

"I almost said the worst possible thing in the world. Oh God, I hate myself right now." Allie's eyes filled with tears.

"What are you talking about?" Des wasn't sure what she'd missed.

"I almost said . . . when he said I was an overprotective mother, I started to say . . ." Allie was having trouble getting the words out. "I wasn't thinking, I swear it. And it was so obvious. I tried to cover up but . . ."

"What did you almost say that was so terrible?"

"I started to say—" Again she stopped, as if she couldn't repeat the words.

"She was going to say, *said the man who has no children*," Seth finished for her. "Am I right?"

Allie nodded. "I swear I would never . . . knowing what happened to his little boy. Oh God, I am so sorry."

"God probably knows that," Seth told her. "It's Ben you're going to have to convince."

CHAPTER TWELVE

The First Annual MacLeod Farm Fourth of July Bash was everything Seth had promised—loud, crowded, friendly, with lots of food and chatter and competition. Des's head was spinning the entire time. She helped Seth with whatever needed to be done: watching the grill when he had to step away, chatting with people he introduced her to, gathering abandoned paper plates and cups and soda cans and tossing them into the appropriate containers. The day had almost ended when it occurred to her that she had in fact, as Seth predicted, fallen into the role of hostess without even realizing it.

The thought had come unbidden, but there it was. She'd never had a better time, never felt more comfortable in her own skin, never felt more a part of something bigger than herself, other than with her shelter staff back in Montana. Thinking of them gave her a pang—she missed them, even chatty Fran, who never met a story she couldn't drag out. This was different, though. It was as if Hidden Falls was part of her. When had that happened?

She wondered how her father had been able to leave it behind, then reminded herself that in time, she would be doing the same.

She'd watched Seth walk up the hill from the grapevines with his arm around a tall, pretty woman in a linen dress that buttoned down the front and looked so much cooler than the shorts Des wore. The resemblance between them was so strong that Des was certain the woman could only be his sister, Amy.

When Seth sought her out to introduce her, Des said, "I'd know you anywhere. You must be Amy."

"And you must be the girl my little brother can't stop talking about."

Des looked up at Seth, who was one of the tallest men she'd ever known. "It's tough thinking of you as anyone's little brother."

"There was a time when I was taller, if you can imagine that." Amy's eyes were dark and warm like Seth's, her dark curly hair tucked behind her ears. For the first time, Des wondered what color hair Seth had been born with. Maybe sometime she'd ask.

"This is some bash, isn't it?" Amy glanced around at the crowd. "I understand you had a hand in organizing all this. Nice job."

"Thanks." Des grinned. "I wasn't so sure he was going to be able to pull it off, but he did. There must be over a hundred people here."

"Oh, easily. And before too much longer, there

will be even more. The folks who clean up at the park will be finishing up real soon, and I heard they're all heading over."

Des must have looked horrified, because Amy patted her on the arm.

"Not to panic. They're bringing more burgers."

She'd have liked to have spent some time talking with Seth's sister, but Amy was on call and her beeper went off. She excused herself, took a call, then came back with apologies.

"I'm so sorry. I have to go. Could we have lunch one day, just you and me? I'd like to get to know you. I know my brother is very fond of you. He's never really talked about anyone he's dated, but he talks about you all the time. And you got him to take in not one but two dogs. Seth, who never expressed any interest in having a pet, has two dogs." Amy shook her head. "You must have put a spell on him."

"She has." Seth put an arm around Des. "Wait up, Amy. I'll walk you out."

"No need. I'll call you this week. Des, it's been a pleasure. I'll get your number from Seth and I'll call you to see about that lunch." Amy disappeared around the corner of the house.

"Having lunch with my sister, eh? Think you're going to find out all my secrets?"

"Of course. That's what sisters do." Des looked around the backyard. Cara and Joe were sitting with a group under the maple tree, Joe apparently entertaining everyone with a story. Allie, however, was nowhere to be seen. "Have you seen Allie?" she asked.

Seth shook his head. "Barney's over there by the picnic table, and I saw Nikki with a bunch of kids down near the pond, but I haven't seen Allie. She must be here somewhere. Everyone else in town is."

"Is Ben here yet?"

"I haven't seen him, either. He'd better show up soon. The baseball game starts in ten minutes, and he's covering second." He gave her shoulder a squeeze. "How are you in the outfield?"

As it turned out, she was terrible, even with Nikki backing her up. Cara played a mean third base, Mark pitched, Seth played third, and Joe was the catcher. Ben never did show for the game, so one of Mark's friends filled in. Des hadn't ever really been part of a sports team, so all the hooting, hollering, and trash-talking was a bit disconcerting at first. She struck out every time she came up to bat, to the point where the opposing team applauded when she walked to the plate with the bat over her shoulder. She found it liberating to laugh at herself, as if celebrating her shortcomings with a group of friends was a good time.

Of course, they were all Seth's friends—most were Barney's friends as well—but everyone offered that same friendship to Des. She held babies while their mothers pitched horseshoes or served cake, tied shoelaces for toddlers, flipped burgers, and complimented everyone on the dishes they'd brought to share. As for the food itself, she'd never seen so much in the same place. Seth had borrowed folding tables from several of his friends to hold all the dishes that had been brought, and even at that, there were bowls waiting in the refrigerator for space on the tables. She'd never have imagined there were so many ways to make potato salad, from the classic mayo and celery to salads made with purple and gold potatoes, salads with bacon or hard-cooked eggs— several with both. There were mountains of macaroni salad, platters of roasted vegetables sprinkled with balsamic vinaigrette (which Des had noticed Cara went back to several times), salads with mixed greens, plates piled with sliced tomatoes, and several green bean salads. Des had been tempted to sample a little of this and a little of that, and at the end of the day, she had to admit she'd never tasted better food.

"I told you it would all work out just fine," Seth told her after most of the guests had left to head into town for the fireworks display, leaving behind a small cleanup crew consisting of Joe and Cara, Mark, his sister, a few of their friends, and Nikki.

"You did. I have to admit having had a few minutes of panic now and then. It just seemed like such an overwhelming number of people."

"Yeah, we had quite a crowd."

"I was surprised by how many people I actually knew," she said. "People I've seen around town and people I've met in passing with Barney. Everyone knew about the theater and asked when it would be open again."

"Think that'll ever happen?" He was tying off a large plastic bag filled with discarded paper plates.

"I don't know. I'd like to think that someday, someone will take it over. Buy it from us, maybe." Des hadn't really wanted to think about what would happen to the Sugarhouse once they'd done their part.

"Could you do that?" He paused. "Sell it to a stranger and just walk away?"

She had no answer, so she simply shrugged and went inside on the pretext of cleaning up in the kitchen, which she and Cara had already done.

Most of the cleanup completed, the crew took off. Seth brought in the dogs—exhausted after endless games of Frisbee and fetch—and locked up the house. They rode the bike into town, and once at the field, Des sat on a blanket on the lawn between Seth and Joe, leaning against Seth's strong chest, and watched spectacular fireworks overhead. They ooh'd and ahh'd as each display lit up the night sky, and flinched every time a rocket went off with a bang.

"Just like Devlin's Light," Cara said. "Except the fireworks are going over the field instead of the Delaware Bay."

"Best display yet," Joe proclaimed once the show was over.

"We say that every year, bro," Seth reminded him.

"Every year it's true," Joe said.

Des and Seth returned to Hudson Street and settled into a lounge in the backyard together.

"So. Your first Hidden Falls Fourth of July. Your thoughts?" Seth asked.

"Best day ever." Des relaxed back in his arms.

"I'm exhausted. It was like living three or four days in one."

"We'll have to do it again next year."

"Right. This having been the First Annual MacLeod Farm Fourth of July Bash."

"You'll be there?" he asked tentatively.

"Wouldn't miss it for the world. Ever." The thought that in time, another woman might be playing hostess crossed her mind, and she shooed it away. She couldn't think about that now, not when Seth's arms were around her, his breath soft against her forehead, the many moments of their shared day yet to be relived.

"I can't even tell you how much you being there meant to me," he was saying.

"I'm a good second in command."

"It wasn't just that, and you know it. It felt right, you being with me. This is my life, Des. My farm, my family, my community. It meant a lot to me that you shared it with me."

She wanted to say how much sharing it meant to her, too, but she couldn't find the words that wouldn't sound like a promise she wasn't sure she'd be able to keep.

Instead, she said, "Hey, I had a great time. Best birthday party I ever had."

"You didn't tell me your birthday was today." He sat up, his forehead creasing as he frowned. "Why didn't you tell me?"

"Well, it's not really until Saturday, but close enough. And this was like the biggest party anyone ever had. It was almost overwhelming. My head was spinning like that girl in *The Exorcist*."

"Why'd you have to put that movie in my head?" Seth covered his eyes. "I had nightmares for years after I saw that. Didn't even stay till the end. Ran out of the theater screaming like a two-year-old throwing a tantrum."

"You did not." She laughed softly at the visual image that flashed through her mind.

"Ask Joe. Or Ben." Seth paused. "I'm still wondering what happened to Ben today. He never did show up at the farm. I tried to call him a couple of times but he didn't pick up, didn't respond to any of my texts, either."

"Maybe there was some kind of police emergency. Maybe an accident or something," she suggested.

"That would make sense. He probably worked at least one shift today since it was a holiday and I know he likes to give his guys days off when he can. He didn't mention it this morning when I asked him if he'd be at the farm, though."

"I thought I saw him at one point at the field when one of those big rockets went off, but it was just for a second, and he was gone. If it was him." Des glanced at the house, where the only lights were in the kitchen and Barney's room upstairs. "Come to think of it, I didn't see Allie, either."

"That's a really strange coincidence," he noted.

"I'm sure there's an explanation. In the meantime, want to come in?"

"I'll take a rain check. I want to get home, let

the dogs out one last time, then fall face-first into bed. I've got chickens to feed in the morning and a bunch of stuff to pick to take into Clarks Summit to a friend's restaurant first thing. And I know you're tired. You worked your tail off today."

"I did, but it was totally worth it. Your first party was a huge success."

"I don't know that I can wait till next year for another one. Maybe we should start thinking about Octoberfest. Or Halloween. Or—"

"Stop." She laughed. "Let me recover from this one first."

She stood on her tiptoes to kiss him, and she smiled when she felt what she'd come to think of as a little zing in the pit of her stomach.

"Are you smiling?" He leaned back and observed. "You are smiling. I never heard of anyone smiling and kissing at the same time."

"I'm smiling because kissing you makes me happy. If it bothers you, I'll try to stop."

"Are you kidding? That's the cutest thing I ever saw. Let's see if I can make you smile again."

"Betcha can."

"Bet I can."

He did.

"Keep the weekend open for me," he told her as he was leaving. "We'll celebrate your birthday."

Des lay upon the quilt that covered her bed, images from the day running through her brain like a film on fast-forward she was unable to slow down. She hadn't been exaggerating when she told Seth she'd been overwhelmed. Every one of her senses had seemed to be hyperaware. Everything had seemed more vivid, every sensation more intense. The people, the chatter, the laughter. The food. The music. The games. The scents wafting from the grill and from the clover field near the orchard and the various bouquets of flowers guests brought for the tables.

More than once during the day she'd stopped to look around, wondering if the mysterious J was in the crowd, if she'd been part of the crowd that had stood on the sidewalk as Barney drove Lucille through the town, or if she was at Seth's that afternoon, maybe one of the many women she'd met and shared idle chatter with. She couldn't help but wonder who the woman was. It shouldn't have mattered—she knew that—but it was in her head and she couldn't seem to shake it out.

On a whim, Des got up and turned on the light, then opened her laptop. Assuming J would be around Fritz's age, she might have been born between, say, 1948 and 1952. She went to a search engine and typed. Within seconds she had a list of popular baby girl names for the late 1940s through the early 1950s. She glanced over the list and found little variations for those four years: Judith and Judy, Joann and Joanne, Jean and Jeanne, Joyce, Janice, Janet, Jane, Jo, and Jacqueline, the popularity of which she attributed to so many Americans having made the trip to France after the Second World War and becoming enamored of all things

French. But nothing stood out as a name she'd heard that day.

She turned off the laptop just as she heard giggling from the room across the hall. Praying that it wasn't a drunk Allie giggling to herself, she went across the hall and peered in through the open door. Allie and Nikki sat on the bed, Nikki relating a story Mark had told that afternoon.

"I'm sorry you weren't feeling well enough to come out to the farm. It was the best party I ever went to," Nikki was saying. "I have never had so much fun in my life."

"What did you do that was so much fun?" Allie asked quietly.

"Everything. We played baseball. I got to play in the outfield with Aunt Des. Mom, I love her, but she was terrible. She couldn't catch the ball and she couldn't hit it."

"Sad but true." Des was smiling when she came into the room. "Is this a private party?"

"Aunt Des, I'm sorry, I didn't mean to insult you." Nikki looked totally chagrined.

"Not to worry, pumpkin. Every word was true. I suck at team sports." Without waiting for Allie's invitation, Des sat at the end of the bed. "Cara, on the other hand . . ."

"Aunt Cara was awesome. She hit a home run."

"She hit two home runs," Des corrected her. "And she was awesome."

"So what else was so much fun that it was the best party you ever went to?" Allie prodded.

"I learned how to throw horseshoes—that's sort of a game—and I learned how to row a boat. There's a little pond out by the woods and I swung on a rope over the water, but I didn't jump in. Some of the other kids did, though."

Allie toyed with Nikki's hair while they chatted, and while Allie appeared to be totally present, there was something almost foreign in her expression.

"Oh, and I ate like—I hate to say this about myself, but I ate like a little piggy. I ate all day long." Nikki began to run down the list on her fingers. "I had a burger. I had a piece of chicken. I had roasted carrots and potato salad that had green beans cut up in it, and I had regular salad, for like, fiber. Then I had strawberry shortcake. Oh, and a cupcake. I gained five pounds today, I just know it."

"I'm amazed you didn't throw up, all that eating and rope swinging and tossing horseshoes."

"I know, Mom, right?" Nikki yawned.

"Nik," Des said, "could it be you're actually running out of energy?"

She nodded. "I'm going to bed. Besides, Mom was sick and she should be sleeping." Nikki kissed first her mother, then her aunt, then stumbled on her way to her room.

"She'll be asleep by the time her head hits the pillow."

"I'm sure. Isn't that your cue to follow suit?" Allie leaned back against her pillow.

"Not until you tell me why you didn't come to Seth's."

"Since when do I answer to you?"

"Since you were visibly upset after that thing with Ben in the park. Since I'm still your sister and I love you."

"How could you? I'm not a nice person, Des."

"Sometimes that's true, but not always." Des moved closer to Allie and put her arms around her. "You're my sister, and I love you. I always will, Al."

"I've been so mean to you," Allie reminded her.

"True. You have—and I love you in spite of it."

"You heard what I said to Ben today." Allie began to cry. "Talk about being insensitive."

"You didn't say it, Allie. You caught yourself before the words came out."

"But he knew what I'd been going to say. He knew, and it hurt him. Of course it hurt him, his only son—his only child—died." Fat tears ran down her face. "Oh, Des, that little boy was so adorable. And he had this beautiful tiny little smile and the biggest eyes. It's wrong that he died."

Des sat back and stared at Allie. "Wait. How would you know what he looked like? That accident happened long before we moved to Hidden Falls."

"I saw his picture." She sniffed and reached for another tissue from the box on the bedside table.

"Where?"

"On Ben's mantel."

"Okay. Do I have to ask, or are you going to tell me why you were in Ben's house?"

"Apartment. And I went there to apologize."

"Allie, that was very big of you. I'm sure he appreciated—"

Allie's laugh was harsh. "Yeah, right, after he ripped me a new one, he showed his appreciation by showing me the door. He called me several names, which I would not repeat in front of my daughter, and when I told him how terrible I felt, he accused me of making it all about me. About how bad I felt, about how sorry I was." She brushed away the tears. "Well, of course I felt terrible, and of course I was sorry. I couldn't even find the words to tell him how sorry I was."

"So I'm guessing he didn't accept your apology."

"Showed me the door. After he showed me the picture of his son. It was one of the worst moments of my life."

"So you shut yourself in and drank all afternoon?"

"What?" Allie sat up straight. "No. I didn't drink at all. I just couldn't face anyone. I felt like everyone could tell just by looking at me that I'm an insensitive bitch." She drew an imaginary B on her forehead. "I know everyone hates me now. I hate me now."

"Al, no one hates you. Sweetie, I'm so sorry. God knows you have your moments, but I know you would never deliberately hurt anyone because of something like that. So I guess you left it—"

"With me leaving and Ben slamming the door behind me." Allie covered her face with her hands. "If you could have seen the look on his face when he opened the door and saw it was me. Like I was the most loathsome creature. You're right, I have had my moments, but I've never felt as ashamed of myself as I felt standing in that man's living room looking at a photo of his beautiful dead son." She started to cry again. "God, what that man went through, losing his wife and his baby boy. I can't even imagine how you live with something like that. And there I was, reminding him . . ."

"Look, maybe in time, he'll come to realize you didn't mean to hurt him, that you didn't think. Maybe in time he'll get over it."

"I doubt it. I wouldn't." She blew her nose. "And I wouldn't forgive me, either. Here's the thing about Ben. There's always been this sort of weird vibe—I know you've noticed it, everyone has. I don't know why, but we set each other off. He thinks I did this because, hey, just one more way to tweak his nose."

"No way would he think that."

"He does. He said so." She blew her nose again. "'Nice, princess. Guess you told me, right? Way to get in the last word.'"

"He did not say that."

"He did. Those were his words. That's how low he thinks I am." The tears began to fall again. "And maybe I am."

"You're not, Al."

Allie pulled the sheet up around her abruptly. "I want to go to sleep. Could you hit the overhead light on your way out?"

Des hesitated before pushing off the bed. "I know it seems like it now, but this will pass."

"I know you're trying to be a good sister, and you

are. I may not always act like it, but I do love you, Des. Even when I was a bitch to you, I still loved you." Allie turned her back to the wall. "Now good night."

Des opened her mouth, but realizing there was nothing more to be said, turned off the light and went back to her room.

As exhausted as she was, sleep wouldn't come. The day had been too full. At two in the morning, she got up and turned on the shower, hoping a steady stream of hot water would help. When it hadn't, she dried her hair, slipped into a nightshirt and her robe, and went downstairs into Barney's sitting room, where she curled up on the love seat. Buttons followed, jumped up next to her, and they both finally fell asleep.

CHAPTER THIRTEEN

Des had expected Allie to languish for a few days after her confrontation with Ben, but surprise: First thing the next morning, she was downstairs and dressed before Des.

"You're up bright and early this morning," Des noted.

"Places to go, people to see," Allie replied.

"Are you having breakfast?"

"I already ate."

Des watched as Allie prepared a to-go cup of coffee.

"Where are you off to?"

"Cara said Giovanni was starting the plaster repairs early this morning. I want to watch. I want to see how he does it."

"Planning on a second career once you return to L.A.?"

"Just curious about how it's done. And I want to know when it's done so I can begin on the ceiling."

"So you've come around?"

Allie turned and stared at Des blankly.

"The last time we talked about the ceiling painting, you'd pretty much decided not to try."

"I changed my mind."

"May I ask why?"

"Of course." Allie leaned over the back of a chair that was pulled up to the table. "I did a lot of thinking last night. Not just about Ben—and we're not going there again, okay?—but about being here and why we're here. I thought a lot about Dad, how the theater was where he got his first taste of acting and how it changed his life. Mom, too, but we both know she never had the same talent Dad had. She was a wannabe actress. She did okay in the roles she had, but let's face it, she was never going to be Katharine Hepburn or Meryl Streep. Now, Dad could have been a for-real star, but he put his own ambitions aside to let Mom shine. So I do think he loved her, to answer one of your previous questions, but that's not really what I was thinking about."

"Good, because you've lost me."

"Dad wanted us all here for a reason. And the reason wasn't just to renovate the theater. He wanted us to know each other and to work together. Maybe even to learn something about ourselves and each other. You've done a great job keeping track of the money . . ."

"Yeah, such a great job, we're almost out of it."

"Not your fault. A million dollars doesn't go as far as it used to. And no one could have predicted the roof leak. It's set us back, but it isn't going to ruin us. You will get money from the movie posters, and eventually, the book Barney and Nik are working on will bring in a few bucks. Not a windfall, certainly, but enough to pay a bill or two, and that's what you were looking for for the immediate future, right?"

Des nodded, still not sure where Allie was going, but she was willing to tag along.

"And Cara's done a great job keeping all the mechanicals for the building on track. She's had some help from Joe—okay, a lot of help from Joe—but let's face it, she has no background in construction. She asked a lot of questions and took the time to learn what she had to know so she could make good decisions. Again, yes, with Joe's help, but still, you have to give her a lot of credit. She's kept it all moving.

"Which brings us to me." Allie looked down for a moment, then met her sister's gaze. "I haven't been as engaged as you two have been. I haven't taken this as seriously as you two have. I came here because if I didn't, none of us would inherit a dime from Dad's estate and Uncle Pete would have the honor of choosing which charity would get everything."

"Al, where are you going with this? What's your point?"

"My point is that it's time for me to step up. I didn't think I had anything to contribute. But I can paint those missing sections of the patterns on the ceiling, and I believe I can do just as good a job as anyone else, including the Balfour Group's artist." Allie's chin jutted out with just a touch of defiance.

"When I'm finished with that ceiling, no one is going to be able to come into that theater and tell the newly painted sections from the old."

"Wow. It's the old Allie, full of confidence and fire. Welcome back. After last night, I was afraid that—"

"We're not talking about last night."

"Okay. But can we talk about what brought on this new wave of *yes, I can*?"

"It's like I said, I need to contribute. I need to be a part of the success of this venture, Des. This is what I can do." She paused. "This is a legacy not just for Nikki, but for any kids you or Cara might have. And the legacy is not just the theater, it's the town and the college and the park and everything that Reynolds and everyone else has contributed over the years. I want Nikki to know I was part of that. I don't want to be like Mom. I don't want to be a wannabe. I want Nikki to be proud of me."

"Wait, what? You're nothing like Mom, Allie. And Nikki is proud of you. So am I."

"Don't make me go for the tissues again, Des."

Des laughed, and Allie made a move to leave, picking up her bag from the window seat.

"You know, Cara and I aren't the only ones who might yet have kids. You're still young enough to have another one or two."

Allie snorted. "Gosh, had I mentioned I was considering in vitro via sperm donor? No? I didn't think so." Laughing, she turned for the door. "Sorry, I'm done with that. No hot prospects in my future."

"If you could wait until I find something to put on my feet, I'll go with you."

"You have two minutes. But that means you won't have breakfast."

"I can grab a take-out sandwich from the Goodbye if I get hungry. I want to see what's going on in the theater, too." Des hurried from the kitchen and up to the second floor in search of her sandals. She was back down before the two minutes had expired in Allie's mental clock.

"I left a note for Nikki and Barney, though I suspect Barney is already out walking with her early-morning group."

"Nikki might sleep for a few more hours. She had a big day yesterday."

"It sounds like Seth's party was the place to be. I'm sorry I missed it. It sounds like everyone had a great time."

"You'll join us next year."

"You're planning on next year already?"

"Thinking about the possibilities."

"I think you'd make a great farm girl."

Des laughed. "I would. I love that place of Seth's. I love the fields and the gardens and the orchard and the vineyard."

"And Seth?"

"Could be headed in that direction."

"Wow. Who'da thunk it?"

They crossed the street to the theater once traffic had cleared—the morning rush hour of seven cars— and walked past Joe's truck and one other to the front door, which was unlocked. Once inside, they made their way into the lobby, where the scaffold had been completed and the lights were all ablaze. At the very top of the scaffold, Giovanni stood as confidently as he might stand in his own house. Next to him, on the platform, sat Cara.

"Hey! What's doin' up there?" Des called.

"Watching the master perform surgery on our ceiling." Cara held up a camera. "And taking pictures so we'll have them for the scrapbook."

"What scrapbook?" Allie asked.

"The one I'm making chronicling the transformation of the Sugarhouse from empty and abandoned to *Mama, look at me now*." She turned all the way around and asked, "Want to come up?"

"Ah, no. No, thanks. It might disturb Giovanni," Des said.

"No disturbing me," he told her without taking his eyes from the ceiling. "Unless you shake the platform."

"I'd like to come up," Allie said.

"You're actually going up there again?" Des frowned. That would make two trips up for Allie. "How can you stand it?"

"It's something I really want to do. And it helps if you don't look down."

"I'll come down," Cara said. "You can have my space on the platform."

Des watched Cara descend with all the grace of an acrobat.

"You make that look so easy," she said when Cara had landed on the ground.

"It is easy." Cara turned to Allie. "So have you decided to be our artist in residence?"

Allie nodded. "Crossing my fingers and hoping for the best."

"I think it's a brilliant idea that you had, and I have total confidence in you. It's going to be beautiful." Cara gave Allie an unexpected hug.

"Thanks," Allie said softly. "So how's he doing up there?"

"Amazing. Honestly, the sections he's filled in so far are flawless. Except for the fact that the ceiling is blue and the plaster is white, you'd never be able to tell where it's been repaired. It's that smooth. It's taking a lot of time, it's slow going, but he's just perfection."

"Take that, James Ebersol," Des murmured.

"I've never painted on plaster before." Allie was staring up at the ceiling, where high above, Giovanni appeared oblivious to the conversation going on below, if in fact he could even hear them. "I think I'd like to go up and watch, see what the surface of the ceiling is like now that there's some plaster on it. This is also a good time to get used to being up so high. Here goes . . ."

Allie placed her hands on the bottom rung of the scaffold and took a deep breath, then pulled herself up. A fascinated Des watched her sister climb to the top and lower her body to sit next to where the plaster wizard stood working with his hands over his head.

"I'm just speechless," Des said.

"About what?" Cara's gaze was still focused on the ceiling.

"We've both always been so afraid of heights. I can't believe she was able to just . . ." Des gestured toward the scaffold.

"Mind over matter, Des."

They watched the scene overhead, the short, elderly bowlegged man whose hands worked magic with plaster, and the young woman, blond hair streaming over one shoulder, whose heart may have been pounding in fear, but who was apparently managing to hold a conversation nonetheless.

"Well, I think I'm outta here. I've done my due diligence and watched the man do his thing. I'm so grateful we found him. He's truly a master of his craft." Cara looked around for the bag she'd brought with her earlier and found it near the bottom of the scaffold. "I guess I'll see you back at the house."

Des nodded.

"Hey, by the way, Joe and I had a blast yesterday. Your man really knows how to throw a party."

"Oh, he's not really my . . ." she began to protest, then, when Cara raised an eyebrow, Des laughed. "Well, I guess he sorta is."

"He's the real deal, Desdemona," Cara told her.

"I know."

"And for the record, Barney is over the moon."

"Why?"

"She thinks she's got us right where she wants us."

"Where's that?"

"Looking for a reason to stay in Hidden Falls."

Cara grinned and headed for the door. "And she might be right."

Des passed the better part of a half hour reading and responding to email and taking pictures of the interior of the theater to post on Instagram. Another ten minutes passed, and she decided she probably had better things to do than sit and wait for Allie to come down, so she called up to her sister.

"Al, I'm going back to the house now."

Apparently still in conversation with Giovanni, Allie waved an acknowledgment that she'd heard. Des walked back to the house, pondering the unexpected changes in her sister's behavior. First there was her newly accepted sense of responsibility where the theater was concerned. Then there'd been her determined climb to the top of the scaffold, where she still sat, chatting away with Giovanni. As much as Des had hated to see the pain Allie'd gone through the night before, the experience seemed to have shaken something loose inside her. Whatever the reason, this new Allie was showing a side Des had once suspected might be there but had never seen.

It might be a long shot, but she hoped the new Allie would stick around a little longer.

Early the next morning, Des and Cara set out to run together. Since Cara was already in shape and Des was in catch-up mode, they'd agreed Des would be free to stop anytime she needed to.

"How can you keep on going in this heat?" Des gasped. "I can't stand it."

"I just think about something else. I sing a song inside my head, or play a scene from a movie." Cara had stopped to wait for Des.

"Look at you. I'm gasping and you're barely breathing hard. No fair." They were in the park, Des leaning over the back of a bench.

"What's your favorite romantic movie?" Cara asked.

"*Pride and Prejudice*."

"Which version?"

"I like all of them." Des took several long, deep breaths.

"Well, just think of your favorite scene while you're running. Makes the time go faster."

"Will it make my lungs feel better? Because time isn't really the problem here."

Cara laughed and set out running again, and Des followed her for a few blocks before dropping off. She walked back to the house, her chest heaving the entire way.

Her conversation with Cara came back to her on Saturday night.

No one ever had made much of a fuss over her birthday, and that was okay with Des. Unless, of course, they were on the set of *Des Does It All* on her birthday, when her mother would make a big deal about it, bringing in a very fancy cake and ice cream and decorating the lounge with balloons and crepe paper streamers. Otherwise, nada. Des learned at an early age that her birthday wasn't much of a special day, so her expectations had never been very high.

Seth picked her up at seven, and they drove to Rose Hill and had dinner at the restaurant she'd once passed over in favor of Seth's grilling steak. From there, they drove back to Hidden Falls. As they came through town, Des expected him to make the right onto Hudson Street to take her home, but instead, he made a U-turn in front of the theater.

"Why are we here?"

"I want to show you something." He was at her door by the time she unfastened her seat belt. "Come on."

As he unlocked the theater door, she asked, "Where'd you get a key?"

"Borrowed it from Barney." He swung the door open and they went inside.

"It's really kind of spooky in here at night, in the dark." She ran her hand along the wall, searching for the light switch. She found it and snapped it on. "Oh, so much better. What did you want to show me?"

"Upstairs." He took her hand, and they walked up the steps to the balcony level, then into the projection room.

There, on the table, was the projector he'd taken home to tinker with.

"You fixed it?"

He nodded. "Took me longer than I thought, but it's working." He led her back out to the balcony, and to a seat in the first row. "I thought for your birthday, we'd have a private viewing of your favorite romantic movie."

"Wait, *Pride and Prejudice*?"

"Yup."

"You talked to Cara. You had her ask."

He nodded.

"And she was so clever in the way she did it."

"She's a smart cookie, all right. I thought she was my best bet. Nikki couldn't keep a secret. Allie would forget to call me back. Barney never knows where her phone is, so she'd never have gotten my message."

"That does pretty much sum up my family."

"I'll be right back." Seth disappeared into the projection room, then a moment later, Des heard the soft whine of the projector. Seth turned off the lights, then hurried back to sit next to her.

He put his arm around her, and she snuggled in.

"Ooh, I like this version. This was a TV miniseries in 2005. It's a lovely movie."

"Shhh. I haven't seen it."

"There's a surprise."

"What's that supposed to mean?"

"It's sort of a chick flick."

"Real men are not turned off by chick flicks."

Des giggled, he shushed her again, and they watched the film to the end.

"That was the best birthday present ever."

"It wasn't bad. That was some romantic line he laid on her there when he was proposing."

"Oh, you mean, 'You have bewitched me, body and soul . . .'"

"Yeah, that one. Jane Austen had a seriously romantic way of expressing herself."

She got out of her seat and sat on his lap. "Jane Austen didn't write that line. It never appeared in the book. They wrote it for the movie." She kissed him, thinking tonight she'd have that chance to make out with a hot guy in a movie theater she never had when she was a teenager. "Thank you, thank you, thank you."

"Ah, Des, I think you might want to . . ." He was attempting to sit up when all the lights in the theater came on.

"Surprise!" came the cry from below.

Des peered over the balcony railing. There stood her family and the friends she'd made here. Cara and Joe, Allie, Barney, Nikki and Mark, his sister and two of her niece's friends, Barney's friend Tom, Ben, and Seth's sister, Amy. Was it her imagination, or were Allie and Ben deliberately not looking in the other's direction?

"Oh! Look at you all down there!" She turned back to Seth. "You planned this?"

"I did." He looked enormously proud of himself. "Obviously I didn't have a lot of time for planning, but next year, I'll be ready."

"It's perfect. You couldn't possibly top this." She kissed him again. "You are the best guy. Thank you."

"You're welcome. Now let's go downstairs and take a look at your present."

"My present?" She made a face. "I just had my present. The movie . . ."

"That was a private showing. And it was good. Can't say it was my favorite film of all time, but I didn't mind it. But you have to admit, there was something missing."

"What?"

"What's one of the things you most look forward to when you go to see a movie in a theater?"

She thought about it for a moment, was about to give up, when she smelled it.

"Popcorn! I smell popcorn." She jumped up and ran down the steps, hugging people as she joined them on the first floor. "Where is it?"

A laughing Cara directed her toward the lobby.

"OMG, as Nikki would say, you had the machine fixed!"

"Ah, no, Des. You wouldn't have wanted to eat anything that came out of that old machine. Bugs, mouse nests . . . not healthy." Seth walked over and tapped the top of the stainless steel and glass machine where the corn was popping into a white mound. "This is new, commercial grade. I thought I'd kill two birds with one stone. Birthday gift, grand opening night gift."

"I love it." Des all but danced around it.

Seth handed her a box. "Here. Serve your hungry guests so we can get on with the show."

"We already saw the movie."

"That was just for you. The next one has—how shall I put this?—a more universal appeal."

"I can hardly wait." She scooped up popcorn and passed it around until everyone had a box.

"There's water here in a cooler," Barney announced. "No soda—no machine set up yet—but water's better for you anyway. Take a bottle and run up to the balcony and get your seats."

Five minutes later, everyone had a seat, a bottle of water, and a large box of popcorn, and happy chatter surrounded her.

Des sat with her feet up on the balcony railing the way she figured she would have done had she grown up coming to this theater—and she wished with all her heart that she'd been given the chance to have done that. How much more fun would those childhood favorite movies have been if she'd watched them here, with her dad, her sister, a younger Barney.

She realized with a start she hadn't included her mother in that happy scene. In an instant, Des was overcome with sadness. She missed what her mother could have been. She missed her father. He was a scoundrel, she'd no doubt of that, but that was who he was, and she'd loved him. Sitting here, in a seat he might have sat in at one time, in the theater her family had built and where Fritz'd graced the stage so many times in any number of plays, she felt generations of other Hudsons surrounding them. And here in this place where her parents had met, she understood that whether Fritz and Nora had loved each other was not an issue. Allie and Seth had both been right about that. Whatever it was, good or bad, had been between Fritz and Nora.

Of course, she'd thought her father was crazy when Pete Wheeler called her and Allie to his office to discuss the terms of Fritz's will. Little did they know how their lives were about to change after that afternoon. As crazy as she'd thought the idea at the time, coming to Hidden Falls was the best thing that had ever happened to her. She'd discovered a sister she never knew she had, and an aunt who'd become more dear to her than she could say. And she'd found Seth, a man who was not only her best friend, but had turned out to be a whole lot more.

Des knew that she and Allie still had things to work out, but there were times these past few months when they'd been closer than they'd ever been, except maybe the time before Des had been cast in *Des Does It All*. She'd come to love and appreciate her family and their accomplishments, their generosity of both spirit and resources, those who'd come before her, and those she shared a home with. The grand house on Hudson Street was a home, in the truest sense of the word, for all of them. Des was happier than she'd ever been in her life.

She looked around in the dark, waiting for the movie to start. She wasn't sure what it was, but she knew she'd love every minute of it, because it was planned by a truly wonderful guy who had put so much thought into making this a birthday she'd never forget.

Bewitched. The line from the movie played over and over in her head. Right at that moment, Des felt as much bewitched by Seth as Mr. Darcy had been by Elizabeth. She mused over the possibility of that single word as a small tattoo gracing somewhere on her back, or maybe her arm. It could happen.

It was hands down the best birthday of her life.

Seth returned to his seat and put his arm around her, entangled one of her curls with his finger, and Des smiled in the dark.

Definitely bewitched.

The familiar theme song began to play, and she clapped her hands and whooped out loud when she realized what movie he'd selected. Her all-time favorite.

The original *Ghostbusters*.

Best. Birthday. Ever.

Don't miss book three of the Hudson Sisters series

THE GOODBYE CAFÉ

By Mariah Stewart

Available Spring 2019 from Gallery Books!

Allie Hudson Monroe's life—and her daughter's—is in California, and she cannot wait for the day when the renovations on the Sugarhouse Theater are completed so she can collect the inheritance from her father and leave Hidden Falls, Pennsylvania. But fate has a curveball or two to toss in Allie's direction—she just doesn't know it yet.

THE
SUGARHOUSE
BLUES

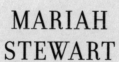

MARIAH
STEWART

This readers group guide for The Sugarhouse Blues *includes an introduction, discussion questions, and ideas for enhancing your book club. The suggested questions are intended to help your reading group find new and interesting angles and topics for your discussion. We hope that these ideas will enrich your conversation and increase your enjoyment of the book.*

INTRODUCTION

In Mariah Stewart's second novel in the Hudson Sisters series, readers find Allie, Des, and Cara back in Hidden Falls as they continue their work restoring the local Sugarhouse Theater. The women reluctantly band together to take on their father's challenge—all with the goal of completing the restoration and gaining their inheritances—but soon it becomes apparent that the work will be more extensive than they originally thought. Des, elected to handle the money, needs to find ways to stretch the remaining savings while searching for new sources of funding, with the aid of the town's local residents.

As the Hudson sisters spend more time in their hometown, they must try to come to terms with the father they only thought they knew and find a way to welcome new friends and embrace the truth of sisterhood.

TOPICS AND QUESTIONS
FOR DISCUSSION

1. Discuss the title *The Sugarhouse Blues*. Why do you think Mariah Stewart selected this title, which follows the first book in the series, *The Last Chance Matinee*? Given that we know the series is about the sisters rebuilding and renovating the Sugarhouse Theater, what do you think the "blues" in the title represent?

2. The book follows the sisters through the next stage of the restoration. Consider where the three women stand in light of the unexpected delays in repairs due to new water damage to the roof and other surprise expenses. Which, if any, of the sisters seems most comfortable with the idea of staying in Hidden Falls longer? Do you expect any of them to remain in the town after the restoration is complete? Why or why not?

3. Allie tries her best to hide her drinking from her family members. By the book's end, do you

feel she or her sisters have properly addressed her drinking habits? What would you do in this situation if she were a friend or family member? Discuss the ways in which your group believes Allie's drinking may factor into the next and final book in the series.

4. Des views the time spent on the restoration in Hidden Falls as an opportunity for her to reconnect with her sisters. Discuss the different distances between Des and her sisters. By the book's end, do you think she has succeeded in reconnecting with Allie? Does she foster a sisterlike relationship with Cara? Discuss your own family relationships. Are there any wounds in your own families that need to be healed?

5. "But I agree that a change might be a good thing. Maybe if we could get her to change her surroundings a little, we could help her to move on in other ways." (page 32) Does Des's comment about her aunt Barney apply to the other characters in the book? Which characters need to move on, physically or mentally, from their pasts? Do you think any of the characters seem to be stuck in old routines or in the past? Why or why not?

6. Cara finally shares with her sisters the box of letters that she found in *The Last Chance Matinee*. How do Allie, Cara, and Des differ in their

reactions to the letters? Discuss Allie's reaction on page 251 and her view of her parents' relationship. Can you relate to one of the sisters more than another in this moment? How would you react to discovering news of one of your parents' infidelities or extramarital affairs?

7. In Chapter 8, Des and Allie have a very tense moment discussing their experiences as actresses on the same television show. Given the recent headlines and current events between men and women in Hollywood, are you surprised Des kept so many secrets from her family for this long? Allie also mentions that she should have known based on Brandon's history. Do you think she should have intervened then? As a group, discuss how you might handle being in a similar position. How do you lend support when a friend or family member has such a traumatic ordeal? In what ways do you react?

8. There are a lot of secrets in the family that resurface in this series. Discuss what sort of secrets you may have found out about later within your own families. Do you have any long-lost family members or interesting family histories, like a great-great-grandfather who built a historic theater, by any chance? What family history has been shared with you, and what will you share with your children?

9. The topic of childhood labor, including that of child actors, is oftentimes a difficult one for people to discuss. How do you think Des's and Allie's time in Hollywood shaped their lives? How is this sort of work different from what some children may experience working in factories? Would you ever consider bringing your child in for a casting call? Were you or any of your family members made to work, either in the family business or otherwise, at a young age? Discuss the differences between work like Des's and Allie's versus your own childhood experience.

10. As a single mother, Allie admits that most of her time spent with Nikki was just the two of them. Do you think she is an overprotective parent? How does Allie finally find a way to let Nikki get comfortable in her life in Hidden Falls?

11. In the book, Des puts up many boundaries around men. Discuss how she comes to terms with her feelings for Seth and how she moves past her early opinions of him. Discuss the issues of judgment between the characters and how this contributes to many of the characters' decisions in the book. Do you think Des rejected the possibility of being with Seth because she, or someone else, judged him?

12. The book closes with Des's birthday and a special movie screening in the theater. As a group, make some predictions about how Mariah Stewart will end the series. Do you think all three sisters will stay in Hidden Falls after the restoration? Who do you think will leave to return home? Of all the couples, which do you think stand a chance to start a serious relationship? Are there any other cliffhangers that you hope to see resolved?